The Dying Hours

ALSO BY MARK BILLINGHAM
FROM CLIPPER LARGE PRINT

Buried
The Burning Girl
Death Message
Lazybones
Lifeless
Sleepy Head
In the Dark
Bloodline
From the Dead
Good as Dead
Rush of Blood

The Dying Hours

Mark Billingham

W F HOWES LTD

This large print edition published in 2013 by
W F Howes Ltd
Unit 4, Rearsby Business Park, Gaddesby Lane,
Rearsby, Leicester LE7 4YH

1 3 5 7 9 10 8 6 4 2

First published in the United Kingdom in 2013
by Little, Brown

A CIP catalogue record for this book is available
from the British Library

ISBN 978 1 47124 112 3

Typeset by Palimpsest Book Production Limited,
Falkirk, Stirlingshire

www.printonden   orough, England

This book is made entirely of chain-of-custody materials

For Katie. I could not be more proud.

Revenge is a kind of grace . . .
Tim Lott, *Under the Same Stars*

PROLOGUE

How much blood?

When he'd finally found the right website, once he'd waded through all the mealy-mouthed crap about having something to live for and trying to seek some kind of professional help, once he'd found a site that really told him what he needed to know, that was the one question they hadn't answered. All the other stuff was there: how and where to cut, the bathwater helping when it came to raising the body temperature and engorging the veins or whatever it was. Keeping the flow going . . .

It was irritating, because once he'd decided what he was going to do he was keen to get everything right. To have all the information at his fingertips. So, how much blood did the body have to lose before . . . the end? Pints of the stuff, presumably. It certainly looks to have lost a fair amount already. He watches the clouds of claret swirl in the water, sees it sink and spin until finally there isn't an inch of water that isn't red. Until he can't see the knife on the bottom of the bath any more.

1

Shocking, just how much of it there is.

He thinks about this for a few minutes more and finally decides that in the end, it doesn't really matter. He might not know exactly how much blood will need to be lost, how many pints or litres or whatever it is now, but there is one obvious answer and it'll certainly do.

Enough.

Not painful either, at least not after the initial cuts which had definitely stung a bit. He'd read that it was a pretty peaceful way to go, certainly compared to some and they weren't an option anyway. This was perfect. Messy, but perfect.

There's another question he's been wrestling with on and off since he'd made his mind up and as far as he knows there isn't any website that can give him so much as a clue with this one.

What comes afterwards?

He's never been remotely religious, never had any truck with God-botherers, but right now he can't help wondering. Now, sitting where he is. Christ on a bike, had the water level actually *risen*? Was there really *that* much blood?

So . . . the afterwards, the whatever-ever-after, the afterlife.

Nothing, probably. That was what he'd always thought, just darkness, like when you're asleep and not dreaming about anything. No bad thing, he reckons, not considering the shit most people wade through their whole lives, but even so, it might be nice if there was a bit more going on than that. Not clouds and harps, choirs and all that carry-on, but, you know . . . peace or whatever.

Yeah, peace would be all right. Quiet.

He looks up when the man in the bath, the man who is actually doing all the bleeding, starts to moan again.

'Shush. I've told you, haven't I?'

The man in the bath moves, his pale body squeaking against the bottom of the tub. He begins to thrash and cry out, blubbing and blowing snot bubbles, spraying blood across the tiles and sending waves of bright red water sloshing out on to the bathmat.

The man watching him adjusts his position on the toilet seat and moves his feet to avoid the water. 'Take it easy,' he says. He gently lays his magazine to one side and leans towards the figure in the bath. 'Why don't you calm down, old son, and have another mouthful of that Scotch?' He nods towards the blood-smeared bottle at the end of the bath. 'It'll help, I read that. Just have another drink and close your eyes and let yourself drift off, eh?' He reaches for his magazine.

'Soon be over, I promise . . .'

PART I

CROSSING THE BRIDGE

CHAPTER 1

Tom Thorne leaned down and gently picked up the small glass bottle from the bedside table. It was already open, the white cap lying next to the syringe, a few drops of cloudy liquid pooled beneath the tip of the needle. He lifted the bottle and took a sniff. The faint smell was unfamiliar; something like sticking plasters or disinfectant. He offered it up to the woman waiting behind him, raised it towards her face.

'What do you reckon?'

He had spent the last half an hour taking a good look around the house. In the bathroom he had found plenty of medication, but that was not particularly surprising given the ages of those involved. Nothing seemed to have been disturbed and there were no signs of forced entry, save for the broken window in the back door. That was down to the woman now taking a good long sniff at the bottle, a young PC named Nina Woodley. She and her partner had been the first officers at the scene after the dispatch had been sent out.

'That's insulin,' Woodley said, finally. 'My brother's a diabetic, so . . .'

Thorne put the bottle back. He pulled off the thin plastic gloves and stuffed them back into the pocket of his Met vest.

'Thing is,' Woodley said, 'it's normally prescribed.'

'So?'

'There's no label on the bottle.'

They both turned as the bedroom door opened and one of the PCs who had been stationed downstairs stuck his head around it. Before the officer could speak, the on-call doctor pushed past him into the room; young, rosy-cheeked and rugger-bugger-ish. He spent no more than a few minutes examining the bodies, while Thorne watched from the corner of the room. Downstairs, Woodley hammered a small piece of MDF in place across the broken window while another PC made tea for everyone.

'Right then,' the doctor said. He closed his bag and checked his watch to get an accurate time for the pronouncement. 'Life extinct.' He sounded rather more cheerful than anyone had a right to be at quarter to four on a drizzly October morning.

Thorne nodded, the formalities out of the way.

'Nice easy one for you.'

'How long?' Thorne asked.

The doctor glanced back at the bodies, as though one final look might make the difference. 'At least twenty-four hours, probably a bit more.'

'Sounds about right,' Thorne said. The emergency call had come in just after 1.00 a.m. One of the children – a man, now living in Edinburgh

– was concerned that he had not been able to get either of his parents on the phone since teatime the previous day. Neither of his parents was reliable when it came to answering their mobile phones, he had told the operator, but there was no reason why they should not be picking up at home.

Searching the house an hour before, Thorne had found both mobiles, side by side in the living room. Half a dozen missed calls on each.

'Assuming they go to bed nine, ten o'clock,' the doctor said, 'dead pretty soon after that, I would have thought. Obviously it depends on what they did, how long they waited before . . . you know, but insulin's a good way to do it. The right dosage and it's all over in about an hour.'

'Right.'

'Very popular with doctors, as a matter of fact. As a way to go, I mean. If you're that way inclined.'

Thorne nodded, thinking that coppers were more likely to be 'that way inclined' than almost anybody else he could think of. Wondering how most of them would choose to do it.

How *he* would choose to do it.

The door opened again and Woodley appeared. 'CID's here.'

'Here we go,' Thorne said. 'Fun and games.'

'I'll leave you to it then,' the doctor said.

Thorne said, 'Right, thanks,' and watched the doctor gather up his jacket from the corner of the bed and leave the room without bothering to close the door. Pills, most probably, Thorne decided, but he guessed that if he were feeling desperate enough, then he might have other ideas.

Just a shame that the quickest ways were also the messiest.

He turned back to look at the bodies on the bed.

They look tired, Thorne thought. Like they'd had enough. Paper-thin skin on the woman's face. The man: spider webs of cracked veins on his cheeks . . .

He could already hear the voices from the hall below; a bored-sounding, mockney twang: 'Up here, is it?' Heavy footsteps on the stairs, before the man appeared in the doorway and stood, taking a cursory look around the room.

Detective Inspector Paul Binns was based at Lewisham police station, as Thorne was, though CID worked on a different floor, so their paths had crossed no more than a few times in the three months Thorne had been working there. Binns was several years younger than Thorne, somewhere in his mid-forties, and he was carrying a lot less weight. He had shaved what little hair he had left to the scalp and over-compensated for the appearance and demeanour of a cartoon undertaker with a grey suit and a tie that might have been a test for colour blindness. He gave Thorne a nod and walked over to the bed as though he were browsing in the furniture department of John Lewis.

'So?' he asked after a minute. 'What am I doing here?'

Before Thorne could answer, a message came through from one of his team's patrol cars. Things were kicking off at a house party on the Kidbourne estate and it was suggested that Thorne might want to get down there. He said that he was still tied up, ordered two more units to head across, then turned the volume on his radio down. 'I told one of my constables to call you,' he said.

'Yeah, I know *why* I'm here.' The nod from the doorway had clearly been as polite as the detective intended to get. He pointed towards the bodies, straightened his cuffs. 'Seems fairly straight-forward, doesn't it?'

What the doctor had said.

Thorne moved to join Binns at the end of the bed. 'There's something off.'

Binns folded his arms, barely suppressed a long-suffering sigh. 'Go on then, let's hear it.'

'The old woman took her teeth out,' Thorne said.

'*What?*'

'False teeth. Top set. They're in a plastic case in the bathroom, probably the same place she leaves them every night.'

'So?'

'You take your teeth out when you're going to bed. When you're going to sleep, right? That's what you do on an ordinary night, isn't it? It's not what you'd do if you were planning to do . . . this. It's not what you'd do if you and your old man were going to take an overdose of insulin and drift off

11

to sleep in each other's arms. Not if you knew you weren't ever going to wake up.'

Binns stared at him.

'It's not how she would have wanted to be *found*,' Thorne said.

'You knew her, did you?' Binns shook his head, sniffed, snapped his fingers. 'Next!'

Thorne took a breath, took care to keep his voice nice and even. 'Where did they get the insulin from? There's no label on the bottle, so it obviously wasn't prescribed. Nothing anywhere else in the house to suggest either of them was diabetic.'

'They could have got it anywhere.'

'So could a third party.'

'I'm not exactly getting excited here.'

'Where did it come from?'

'How should I know?' Binns said. 'Internet? I saw there was a computer downstairs.'

'I don't think so.'

'Come on, you can find anything on there, you look hard enough.'

'Maybe.'

'You decide to top yourself, you find a way, don't you?'

Thorne said nothing.

'That it, then?' Binns asked. 'The false choppers and the insulin? Seriously?'

Thorne stared down again at the bodies of John and Margaret Cooper, aged seventy-five and seventy-three respectively. The duvet had been pulled up high, but it was obvious that Margaret

Cooper's arm was wrapped around her husband's chest, her face pressed against his shoulder. Spoons, he thought. Couples 'spooned' in some of the old songs his mother had listened to, crooning love's tune or whatever it was; the same songs this pair might have heard on the radio when they were teenagers. The old woman's mouth hung slightly open. The cheeks, hollowed. The top lip sucked in towards the gap where the plate would otherwise have been. Her husband's lips were curled back, yellowing teeth showing, a sliver of greyish tongue just visible. His eyes were screwed tightly shut.

They had died pressed close to one another, but Thorne could not pretend that they looked remotely peaceful.

'Anything else?' Binns asked. 'I've got paperwork I could be getting on with.'

There *was* something. Thorne *knew* there was.

His eye had taken something in within those few seconds of entering the room for the first time: a piece of visual information that had not quite made sense, but which his brain had so far failed to process fully. A shape or a shadow, a *something* that was wrong. It stubbornly refused to come to him, like a tune he recognised but could not place.

Without making it too obvious, he looked around the room again.

The wardrobe, closed. The curtains, drawn. Cosmetics and other bits and pieces on the dressing table: hairbrush, wallet, wet-wipes. A few coins in a small china bowl. A woman's dressing gown draped across one chair, a man's clothes neatly folded on another. Shoes and slippers underneath. A biro, book and glasses case on the wife's bedside table, a paperback book of crossword puzzles on the floor by the side of the bed, a large black handbag hung on the bedstead. The bottle and syringe on the husband's side. A half-empty water glass. A tube of ointment, a can of Deep Heat . . .

What was wrong with the picture?

'There isn't a note,' Thorne said.

Binns turned round, leaned back against the bedstead. 'You know that means nothing,' he said.

Thorne knew very well, but it had been the best he could come up with while he tried and failed to identify what was really bothering him. His friend Phil Hendricks had told him a great deal about suicide during the last investigation they had worked on together . . . the last case Thorne had worked as a detective. The pathologist had recently attended a seminar on the subject and delighted in giving Thorne chapter and verse. The fact was that in the majority of cases, people who killed themselves did not leave notes. One of the many myths.

'I know what you're doing, by the way,' Binns said.

'Oh, you do?' Thorne ignored the burst of twitter from his radio. Reports of a suspected burglary in Brockley. The violence escalating at the house party on the Kidbourne. 'I'm all ears.'

14

Binns smiled. 'Yeah, I mean considering where you were before and where you are *now* . . . it makes perfect sense that you're going a bit stir crazy, or whatever. Only natural that you might want to make something ordinary like this into . . . something else.' He casually checked the mobile phone that had not left his hand. 'I understand, mate. I sympathise, honest.'

Patronise, Thorne thought.

'If I was in your position, *Christ* knows what I'd be doing.'

'You'd be getting pissed off with smartarse detectives who think they know it all.'

'Really?' Binns feigned a shocked expression. 'What type did *you* used to be then?'

Thorne wrapped his hand around the old-fashioned metal bedstead and squeezed. 'I want to get the HAT car round,' he said.

It was the job of detectives on the Homicide Assessment Team to evaluate any possible crime scene and to collect vital evidence where necessary before handing the case over. It was solely their decision as to whether or not a 'sudden' death had occurred. A *suspicious* death.

'Well, you know how *that* works.' Binns walked across and leaned back against a wall next to an old-fashioned dressing table. 'Different system these days. Between your lot and my lot, I mean. Different to your day anyway, I would have thought.'

'You'd have thought right,' Thorne said.

15

Your day. Nearly twenty-five years since Tom Thorne had pulled on the 'Queen's Cloth' every day to go to work. Since he'd worn a uniform.

Crisp white shirt with his two shiny inspector's pips on the epaulettes.

Black, clip-on tie.

The fucking cap . . .

'It's my decision,' Binns said. 'Whether or not to bring the HAT team in.'

'I know how it works,' Thorne said.

Binns told him anyway. 'Only a *detective* inspector can make that call.'

'Got it,' Thorne said. 'So, on you go.' Binns had been right to suggest that the procedure had been somewhat different two decades earlier. The protocol a little more flexible. The chain of command not followed quite so religiously. There might have been a few less backsides covered, but it was certainly quicker.

'Frankly, I can't really see the point.'

'Can't you?' Thorne said.

'That stuff about the false teeth is near enough laughable and I don't think anyone's going to give a toss where the insulin came from.' Binns cast an eye around the room and shrugged. 'I pull Homicide in here and they're only going to say the same thing, aren't they? You know, we both end up looking like idiots.'

'All the same,' Thorne said, 'I'd be happier if you made the call.'

Binns shook his head. 'Not going to happen.'

16

'Right,' Thorne said. He could feel the blood rising to his face. 'Because of where *you* are and where *I* am. Prick . . .'

Binns reddened too, just a little, but otherwise gave a good impression of being impervious to an insult he'd clearly been on the receiving end of before. 'You think whatever you like, pal, but I'm not going to waste anybody else's time just because you're seeing murders where there aren't any.' He walked towards the door, then turned. 'Maybe you should have taken a bit more time off after what happened. Maybe you should have chucked it in altogether. King of all cock-ups, that one.'

Thorne could not really argue, so did not bother trying.

'Take this up with the MIT boys if you want,' Binns said, gesturing back towards the bed. 'We've got a Murder Investigation Team at Lewisham, haven't we? A nice big one.'

A team just like the one Thorne used to be part of. 'Yeah, well, I might just do that.'

'I mean it's up to you, if you want even more people taking the piss.'

Thorne was suddenly more aware than usual of the various *pro-active* items attached to his Met vest.

Cuffs, baton, CS gas . . .

'I'll be off then,' Binns said, straightening his cuffs one final time. 'Leave you to wind this up.' The detective turned away and was checking his BlackBerry again as he walked out of the bedroom.

Thorne took half a minute, let his breathing return to normal, then bellowed for Woodley. He told her to contact Lothian and Borders police and get someone to deliver the death message to the Coopers' son in Edinburgh. He told her to find out if the dead couple had any other children, and, if so, to make sure the message was delivered to them wherever they were. He told her to stay put until the on-call Coroner's officer arrived.

'Try not to disturb anything in this room though,' he said. 'Not just yet.'

Woodley raised an eyebrow. 'Guv.'

Thorne took one last look round, grabbed his raincoat and cap then hurried downstairs and out to the car. No more than a few minutes with the blues and twos to the Kidbourne and if things were still lively he really felt like wading in. There was every chance he would find himself on the end of a smack or two, but it could not make him feel any worse.

CHAPTER 2

It was almost eight o'clock in the morning by the time Thorne got back to the flat in Tulse Hill and, as was usually the case if he didn't miss seeing her altogether, he walked in to find Helen just about to leave. She was in the kitchen, which opened out into an L-shaped living area: a sofa, armchair, stereo system and TV; the floor littered as usual with toys and children's books. She finished buttoning her son's coat and removed an uneaten piece of toast from her mouth. 'God, you all right?'

Thorne tossed his raincoat on to a kitchen chair, yanked off the clip-on tie and unbuttoned his shirt. He touched a fingertip to the lump beneath his right eye and winced a little. 'I'll live.'

'Did you wind up that bolshy skipper again?' Helen asked. 'I said she'd deck you one day.'

Thorne smiled and walked across to flick on the kettle. 'Some idiot fancied a party and thought it would be a good idea to put the address on Facebook. Three hundred people trying to crash one of the flats on the Kidbourne.'

'Sounds like fun.'

'It was once we sent a couple of dogs in.' Thorne reached up to grab a mug. 'Cleared the place faster than a Phil Collins single.'

Helen laughed and tore into her toast.

'Nicked half a dozen for affray.' He touched his face again as he poured the hot water. 'Plus the lad that did this.'

'Nice.' Helen chewed. 'Other headlines?'

Thorne shrugged. 'A few break-ins.' He mashed the teabag against the side of the mug and thought through some of the reports he'd signed off on at the end of the shift. 'A three-way knife fight come chucking-out time at the White Lion. Two kids trying to smash up the KFC with baseball bats, because *apparently* they got beans when they asked for coleslaw . . .'

'Fair enough,' Helen said, stepping out into the hall.

'A bus driver assaulted with a machete after he told a woman to stop pissing on his bus—'

'What, the *woman* had the machete?' Helen reappeared in the doorway, one arm inside a long down coat.

'Obviously,' Thorne said. 'A shiny new Volvo driven straight into the front of a house on the High Road when someone tried to nick it. The normal quota of pissheads, the usual domestic argy-bargy. Oh, and a bit of dogging in the car park behind Comet.'

'Well, no harm treating yourself after a long night, is there?'

He dropped the used teabag into the bin. 'I was only looking, honestly!'

'Nice easy shift, then?'

Thorne turned. He cradled the mug as he watched Helen check that everything she needed for work was in her bag, then hang the bag with everything Alfie would need over the handles of the pushchair. 'There were a couple of bodies as well,' he said. 'An old couple, dead in bed.'

Helen looked up. 'A couple? What, they killed themselves?'

Alfie wandered across to the cupboards next to Thorne, began opening and shutting one of them, enjoying the noise.

'Probably,' Thorne said.

'*Probably?*'

Thorne could not quite read her expression. Concern? Suspicion? They still did not know one another quite well enough yet. 'It's fine,' he said.

'Sure?'

'I had a bit of a run-in with some DI about it, that's all.'

'Doesn't sound like you.'

Thorne smiled. He knew when she was being sarcastic well enough. 'Tosser wouldn't give the necessary *authorisation*.' He took a mouthful of tea to wash away the taste of the word. The memory of his altercation with Binns.

'Listen, I need to get going . . .' Helen moved over to collect her son. She lifted him up and

21

plonked him down in the pushchair, began fastening the straps.

'Why don't I take him?' Thorne asked. He stepped across, took the small woollen hat from Helen's hand and put it on the boy's head. Once or twice, when Helen had been running very late, Thorne had walked her eighteen-month-old son down to the childminder's. He enjoyed the time he and Alfie spent together, but the shift patterns meant there was precious little of it. Precious little with his mother, come to that.

Ships in the night, especially when Thorne was on the graveyard shift.

'It's fine,' Helen said. She kissed him and straightened her son's hat. 'You get to bed.'

'It's no trouble.'

''Nana,' Alfie shouted.

Helen said, 'When we get to Janine's,' and pushed her son out towards the front door. 'I'll call you . . .'

'Have a good one,' Thorne said.

After a few seconds she reappeared, buttoning her coat, while from the hallway Alfie continued to demand a second breakfast. 'We can talk about this later if you want,' she said. 'OK?'

'Nothing to talk about,' Thorne said. He turned around to occupy himself, wiping away the ring his mug had left on the worktop, then putting the milk back in the fridge, until he heard the front door close.

He carried his tea across to the kitchen table.

He spent a minute or two turning the pages of the previous day's *Evening Standard*. He moved across and switched on the TV in the corner, watched the news without taking any of it in.

Three months, since he and Helen Weeks had begun more or less living together. 'More or less', because they had never really talked about it as a formal arrangement, the understanding being that as long as he was based at Lewisham, it was far more convenient for Thorne to stay in Tulse Hill than it was for him to travel all the way down from his own place in Kentish Town. They had talked once or twice about renting Thorne's flat out, but Thorne was reluctant, despite the fact that the extra income would have come in useful. He didn't particularly want strangers in his place and could not be bothered with the legal hassles of being a landlord, but if he were being really honest, it was more to do with the hope that he might find himself back in north London sooner rather than later.

The truth was, Thorne would always be a north Londoner and anywhere south of the South Bank still felt alien to him. Sprawling and soulless; dun-coloured. The air just that little bit harder to breathe. Estate agents and arty types in the south-east doing their best to make 'edgy' and 'gritty' sound like selling points. The better-off in the greener bits talking about the tennis or the rugby or the deer in Richmond Park and all of them looking enviously across the water towards Camden,

23

Islington and Hackney. The abysmal transport links and the terrible football teams . . .

Thorne knew very well that a good many south Londoners would view north London with the same horror, but he didn't care. North London was the city he knew, that he loved.

Not that he had said any of that to Helen.

He still crossed the river as often as he could. He went back to meet up with Phil Hendricks at the Grafton Arms or the Bengal Lancer, and occasionally with Dave Holland, a DS in the Murder Squad at Becke House in Colindale. Thorne's old squad . . .

'How you finding it?' Holland had said, the last time. Then he'd seen the look on Thorne's face and gone back to studying his pint, knowing he could not have asked a more stupid question if he'd tried.

Three months, since the case that had brought Thorne and Helen together, the case that had seen him demoted to uniform.

'Not a demotion strictly speaking, of course,' the chief superintendent had told him. 'You're still an inspector at the end of the day.' The man had barely been able to conceal his glee at finally being shot of Thorne, having tried on many previous occasions. 'Who knows? You might end up feeling that this was a very good move.'

Slapped down, that was how Thorne *felt*. Though bearing in mind how he had earned it, he supposed that he'd got off relatively lightly.

24

He knew that what he had done – what he had *needed* to do – to ensure a young mother's survival during an armed siege in a local newsagent's was never going to play well with the powers that be. Ultimately though – as he told himself often, pulling on that crisp white shirt with the epaulettes, straightening that cap – he had saved Detective Sergeant Helen Weeks and, much to the surprise of both of them, ended up in bed with her.

'*Another* one?' Hendricks had said when Thorne had told him. 'After the last one turned out so well?'

Thorne's previous girlfriend, another copper. They had split up only a few months before he and Helen had got together.

'You want to knock this business with women on the head, mate. Come to the dark side.'

'I don't think so.'

'You know it's always been a matter of time.'

'Actually, it's not even the sex that bothers me,' Thorne had said. 'It's having to like small dogs and musicals.' It was the kind of crack Thorne could get away with, as Hendricks was the least stereotypical gay man anyone could imagine. Heavily tattooed with multiple piercings and likely to break someone's arm if they so much as mentioned Judy Garland.

'I give it three months,' Hendricks had said. 'Tops.'

Thorne took his tea and walked into the hall

25

and across to the small bathroom. He laid the mug on the toilet cistern while he pissed.

Detective Helen Weeks.

Thorne flushed and told himself he was being an idiot for even thinking that Helen was the sort to play those games. Not in a million years. He took a packet of painkillers from the mirrored cabinet above the sink and shut the door hard.

Said, 'Twat.'

He stared at the face looking back at him. Duller, *deader* than it was the last time he looked. Grey hair that was still more pronounced on one side than the other, but was now more pronounced everywhere. The small, straight scar on what had once been the only chin he had.

Thorne's mobile rang in the kitchen and he hurried back through to answer it. Helen sounded out of breath. She had just dropped Alfie off and was on her way to the station, she told him.

'So we'll talk when I get home, then. About last night.'

'I told you, I'm fine,' Thorne said.

'You didn't look fine.'

'I'm just tired. Feeling sorry for myself.'

'Well don't,' Helen said. 'Now go to bed, for God's sake . . .'

He walked slowly through to the bedroom that still smelled of sleep and mango body-butter. Helen had not bothered to open the curtains. He sat down on the edge of the bed and began to get undressed, looking forward more than anything to

26

slipping beneath a duvet that he knew would still be warm.

One of the few perks of incompatible shifts.

Presuming that Helen got back before he had to leave, he would play it down, the business with the Coopers. He told himself it was because the last thing Helen needed was any of his shit to deal with. Because her own job was stressful enough. Because there was really nothing he could do about it now and he was almost certainly being ridiculous anyway.

He swallowed three painkillers with the last of his tea.

Not because he was worried that she might agree with Paul Binns.

CHAPTER 3

He eats in cafés, most days. Always breakfast and lunch, then maybe an Indian or a Chinese come dinner time. He's way past worrying about his weight or the state of his arteries and he's spent far too long eating meals cooked by somebody else to start doing any of that for himself.

Not that he was ever up to much in the kitchen.

Or anywhere else, come to that.

He lays down his knife and fork. He can imagine her saying it . . .

Tossing aside the tattered copy of the *Sun* that was lying on the table when he came in, he signals to the teenage girl behind the counter – what is she, Russian? – and indicates that he wants another mug of tea.

'One pound fifty,' she says.

'A bit stronger this time,' he says.

It's certainly pricey, eating out three times a day, a damn sight pricier than it used to be, but there's enough money sloshing around so he's not too bothered on that score. It's good to get out and about now he's got the chance and besides, the last thing he wants to do is impose more than he already has on the people putting him up by demanding to be fed. A bed for a few nights is enough of an ask as it is.

Not that they wouldn't be happy enough to do it. Whatever else has happened, he's always been able to count on his friends. Or the people who might not think of themselves as his friends, but owe him a favour or two anyway. No sell-by date on that kind of thing and he doesn't need to tell them to keep the fact they've got a houseguest to themselves.

'Stay as long as you like,' that's what most of them say. Old times, all that. They're trying to look like they mean it, but he doesn't mind the fact that they really don't. For obvious reasons he doesn't want to stay anywhere for more than a day or two, plus he's given himself a fair amount of running around to do if he wants to get things done properly.

Work through his list.

Funny, he thinks, the way people seem to drift and spread out. Families and friends. Going where the work is, most likely, or getting away from the stupid prices. *Forced* out, probably, some of them.

London feels like a dozen different cities.

The girl brings his tea across and lays it down without a word. The old bloke doing the cooking shouts something to her, in Russian or Polish or whatever it is, and she shouts back at him as she

29

clears empty plates from an adjoining table. The tea's still not strong enough, but he can't be bothered to say anything.

A lesson he's learned. A fuss is what gets remembered.

He stares down at what's left of an obscenely large full English breakfast (£12.99 or free if you can finish it). He moves the tip of a finger through the bright smear of ketchup and thinks about the man in the bath. It's odd, he thinks, how it's that one he keeps coming back to, but it's probably because that was the one where he really saw it. The life leaking out.

He's been thinking about that question ever since – the *BIG* one – and how strange it was that when he was sitting there watching it happen, it was pearly gates and angels and all that carry-on going round and round in his head. Bloody ridiculous really, when, given the circumstances . . . given everything that's happened . . . he should probably have been thinking about the other place. The fiery furnace, whatever.

Nonsense, all of it, he knows that . . . but still it's odd that when he was thinking about what might come after, just wondering if there *could* be something, 'heaven' should even have come into it! He's not an idiot. He knows that he's never been 'good'. Not even close. Even his nearest and dearest – back when he'd had any – would never have claimed that.

He stands up and turns to let the girl behind

30

the counter know he's finished. He picks up his jacket and reaches for his wallet.

He stares out of the steamed-up window at the blur of traffic moving past and thinks: Right, but what if not believing in it doesn't rule you out? What if by any chance you turn out to be wrong and there's more of an open-door policy than you thought there was? Forgive and forget, kind of thing. If that's the case, then all this stuff he's been thinking about isn't so odd after all. Because maybe there's a small part of him hoping that, when the time comes, he might . . . get away with it.

He takes a twenty-pound note from his wallet.

He remembers the list in the same pocket and decides that getting away with it is going to be a seriously tall order.

He waves the note at the girl, shows her that he's leaving it on the table and tells her she can keep the change.

She mumbles something that doesn't sound like a thank you.

He calmly picks up his mug, still half-filled with piss-weak tea, and drops it on to the floor. The other customers turn at the noise of the mug smashing and he walks towards the door, deciding that if heaven and hell did exist, and if there were things that could determine whether you ended up going upstairs or downstairs, fucking politeness would be one of them.

CHAPTER 4

There were perhaps thirty officers gathered in the briefing room for the 10.00 p.m. parade. Conversation died down quickly as the senior officers came in and took their seats. The start of the final night shift before a four-day break, and for Thorne it could not come quickly enough.

Friday nights, though, were usually the worst of all.

The PCs were sitting on plastic chairs that had small writing tables built into them, notebooks at the ready. The sergeants sat off to one side, save for one – the briefing officer – who worked at a computer in the corner, running the PowerPoint presentation that displayed on a large screen at the far end of the room. Ken 'Two-Cats' Pearson; balding with bad skin, harder than he looked and so-named after an occasion a few months earlier when he'd run over a cat in a patrol car. He'd dutifully driven back to check that the animal was dead and, on finding the poor creature still breathing by the side of the road, had put it out of its misery with his truncheon. Unfortunately, the moggy Pearson had run over was already dead, this one being another cat altogether who had been innocently napping in the sunshine.

Everyone had a nickname – except Thorne, as far as he was aware – but this one had generated more mileage than most.

Pearson got the nod from Thorne to begin the briefing and, within a few seconds, images of half a dozen individuals appeared on the screen. As usual, the miaowing began the moment Pearson opened his mouth to speak.

'Hilarious,' he said.

'Only time he's ever had pussy twice in one day,' somebody shouted.

Thorne let the laughter die down a little before raising his hand to quiet everyone.

'Right,' Pearson said. 'You all done?'

The sergeant ran through details of the various individuals that patrols should be keeping a lookout for. Dates of birth and number plates were read out, along with several addresses where domestic disturbances had been recently reported or drug dealing suspected.

Some officers jotted details down while others doodled. A few just stared at the photographs.

When Pearson had finished, it was Thorne's turn, but there was little he wanted to add. He told his team to be particularly watchful around the town centre and main shopping parade. He knew they would be extra vigilant on a Friday night anyway – when the pubs would be more crowded than usual as wage packets were pissed away – but he had been warned by his opposite number on the late shift that there was trouble brewing between a Tamil outfit operating in the area and one of the local gangs based around the Kidbourne estate. It was a boy from this same gang, the TTFN crew, who Thorne had charged with assault the previous night after getting smacked in the face.

If such a gang was plying its trade in a leafier area of the city, where the hoodies came from John Lewis and the dealers had their car stereos tuned to Radio 4, the initials might have stood for Ta-Ta For Now. In Lewisham, they stood for something different.

Tell The Filth Nothing.

'That's about it,' Thorne said. 'Hope it's Q---- out there.'

Not *quiet*. Nobody ever said that word for fear of tempting fate. A long-held superstition that could make an officer seriously unpopular if it was flouted.

Finally, Thorne nodded towards Sergeant Christine Treasure, who called for hush before announcing the pairings for the shift and allocating the rest times. She glanced over at Thorne. 'Fancy coming out with me in the Fanny Magnet?' There were groans, some whistles from the other officers. There was only one remotely flashy car waiting in the courtyard: a BMW used as the Area Car for high-speed pursuit. Treasure and Thorne were

34

likely to end up in a clapped-out Ford Focus, but such was the sergeant's sexuality and self-confidence that she firmly believed any car she was driving to be a Fanny Magnet.

Thorne walked across to Treasure as the briefing broke up. 'Give me half an hour, OK? I've got a few things to get sorted here.'

Thorne closed the door of his office and took out his mobile.

Ten thirty on a Friday night, he wasn't too concerned that he'd be getting Phil Hendricks out of bed. All being well, his friend's night would barely even have started. A pub or two first, then a club; somewhere to drink and dance and pull. Getting away from the dead for a few hours by celebrating life the best way he knew how. Looking for the next sexual partner, whose conquest he would memorialise with a new tattoo. Secretly hoping – Thorne knew – that each tattoo would be the last he ever needed.

There was a good deal of background noise when Hendricks answered his phone. Raised voices, a song Thorne recognised. Shouting over the racket, Hendricks told Thorne he was in the Duke of Wellington in Hackney, that he would be heading into the West End later on. 'It's a nice pub,' he said, 'but the music's awful. Why does everyone assume all gay men like Lady sodding Gaga?'

Thorne made no comment. Musically, she was

35

not exactly his cup of tea either, but he wouldn't kick her out of bed for Waylon Jennings.

'I need a favour,' he said.

Hendricks told him to hang on while he found somewhere quieter. The music got louder for a few seconds and Thorne heard Hendricks ask someone to get him another beer. Beer to kick things off, then shots later on at Heaven or G-A-Y, and maybe one or two other substances that Thorne preferred not to know about.

'Right,' Hendricks said, eventually. 'Go on . . .'

'Like I said, a favour.'

'Come on, hurry up. I'm freezing my tits off out here.'

'PMs on an elderly couple,' Thorne said. 'Lewisham hospital, I'm guessing. Probably done earlier today, maybe tomorrow if things are backed up. It would be great if you could get a quick look at the reports for me, let me know the headlines.'

'These are homicides, are they?'

'Can you or can't you?'

'Not being funny, mate, but couldn't you do this yourself?' Hendricks asked. 'I mean they haven't taken your warrant card away just yet, have they?'

'Only a matter of time,' Thorne said. He could easily have requested a copy of the PM reports on John and Margaret Cooper, but he knew that coming from an inspector outside CID, especially the one who had already signed the deaths off as suicide, such a request might well be a . . . talking point. As far as Thorne was concerned, the fewer people talking about him, about this, the better. 'Look, I'm *asking* you.'

Hendricks let out a theatrical sigh. Said, 'Yeah, all right. I'll see what I can do.'

Thorne gave him the names. Told him to have a good night.

'That's one you owe me,' Hendricks said. 'Another one.'

There was a knock on the door and Christine Treasure marched in without waiting to be invited. Thorne watched as she dropped into the chair opposite him, tossed her cap on the desk and began casually rummaging around for reading material. She looked up and nodded, as though giving Thorne her blessing to finish his call.

Thorne nodded back, mouthed a sarcastic 'Thank you.'

'Listen, thanks, mate,' Thorne said. His voice was a little lower than it had been before the sergeant had waltzed in. 'Give me a shout when you've had a chance to look through the . . . you know.' He glanced up, saw that Treasure appeared to be paying no attention to what he was saying. 'The paperwork.'

When Thorne had finished the call, he got up and walked across to the grubby mini-fridge in the corner. He pulled out a carton of milk and sniffed it, then checked the kettle for water. 'You want one?'

Treasure shook her head. 'You all right?'

Kettle in hand, Thorne turned and looked at

her. Treasure was the 'bolshy' sergeant whom Helen had mentioned that morning. Thorne knew the famously filthy temper was usually only unleashed upon those who deserved it and suspected that, beneath all the bluster, she was actually rather more delicate than she wanted to let on. She disguised this 'sensitive' side brilliantly, with language that would make Malcolm Tucker blush, genuine enthusiasm when it came to breaking wind, and being what Hendricks would have called a 'full-on' lesbian; never reticent when it came to letting anyone – fellow officers included – know who she would like to sleep with and exactly what she would do with them if she had the chance. While secretly being more than a little frightened of her, Thorne liked Treasure's attitude. At twenty-seven she was a far better copper than many he knew with nearly thirty years on the job and, despite the fact that the patrol car could get a little . . . rank after an hour or two, she was always his first choice when it came to pairing up.

'Yeah, I'm fine,' he said. 'Why?'

Treasure's bleached-blonde hair was cut very short at the sides. She ran fingers through the longer hair on top, teased it into spikes. 'Heard you had a run-in with a couple of suits last night.'

'God's sake,' Thorne said, quietly. Woodley or one of the others mouthing off. Not that he could really blame them. He had guessed that the locker

38

room would be full of it. He put the kettle down and switched it on. 'Just the usual handbags.'

'That's what they *do*,' Treasure said. 'You should know that better than anybody.'

'Why should I?'

'Come on, you saying you were any different when you were one of them?'

'Yeah, I was,' Thorne said. It was the question he had been asking himself on a regular basis since his transfer. Now that the highly polished black boot was on the other foot. He tried to make his answer as convincing as possible. 'I *was*.'

Treasure shrugged. Whether or not she believed him, it clearly didn't matter to her either way. 'You need to get past it though, because it's going to happen again. It's going to happen a lot.'

Thorne turned back to the fridge and picked up a stained teaspoon.

'Come on though, isn't this better?'

'*Better*?' Thorne spooned instant coffee into his mug. Stood over the kettle as it began to grumble.

'Were you really any happier before?' Treasure asked. 'Sitting watching CCTV footage for hours on end? Talking to the wankers at mobile phone companies? I mean, that's what most of the suits do all day, isn't it?' She picked up her cap, spun it round a finger. 'We're getting something different every ten minutes. We're getting a bit of variety. God knows what we'll run into tonight, could be anything, and that's what makes it so bloody exciting. I'm actually buzzing on the way to work, d'you know that? Seriously, I can't bloody wait. It's like when you know you're going to get your end away.'

Thorne poured hot water into his mug then turned around to look at her.

'You really prefer poncing around in a suit? Doing endless paperwork and getting screwed over by the CPS?'

'It's not always like that,' Thorne said.

Blinking away a gallery of killers and their victims.

A girl in a coma, a man running towards a bridge, a brother and sister laughing as they take something out of a bag.

The faces he still woke seeing sometimes.

'You want to swan about, being a dick like those two last night?' It was clear from Thorne's silence, the look on his face, that this was not something he really wanted to talk about, so Treasure shrugged and changed the subject. She pointed to her eye, then to his. Said, 'That's looking good.'

Thorne said, 'Yeah, not bad,' and touched his finger to the bruise below his eye that had swelled up and turned purple while he'd slept. An almost perfect half-moon.

'It's quite sexy, actually.'

'You on the turn, Christine?'

'You wish,' Treasure said. She jumped up and fixed her cap on. 'Come on. Let's get among them, shall we?'

Thorne raised his mug. 'Hang on—'

'Leave it,' she said. 'We'll stop off at the BP, get

40

some decent stuff.' The petrol station was a regular port of call on the night shift as it gave out free Wild Bean coffee to police officers. A small reduction in the profits of British Petroleum in exchange for the presence of uniformed coppers on their forecourt every half an hour or so.

'Yeah, all right.' Thorne put his mug down and gathered up his cap and raincoat. The radio chatter had already begun to get interesting. A group of young Tamils gathering near St Saviour's church. 'Promise me you've not been eating sprouts today.'

'You're perfectly safe, sir,' Treasure said. She waited for Thorne in the doorway and, as he walked past her, she put a hand on his sleeve. 'That suicide last night. Those two idiots playing "whose cock's the biggest?" You really need to let it go.'

CHAPTER 5

As usual, there was half an hour's paper-work to be done at the end of the shift. Thorne had to prepare the handover sheet, and add a line or two before signing off on reports of the more serious incidents. Thankfully, there had been fewer than might have been expected. A stabbing outside a club, a late-night grocer robbed at knifepoint, a fight in the Jolly Farmers between a group of less than jolly scaffolders, several of whom had taken scaff bars into the pub with them just in case. As a result of the heavy police presence in the town centre, the Tamil and TTFN boys had restricted them-selves to no more than serious eyeballing and verbal abuse. Nastier stuff was coming, but merci-fully it had not taken place on Thorne's final night shift of the rotation.

As soon as he was done, Thorne changed out of his uniform and stuffed the bits he was taking home into a plastic bag. He took his leather jacket from his locker and put it on. In the courtyard, dropping the bag into the boot of his car, he exchanged a few words with one or two of the lads as they left. They all agreed how much they were looking forward to four days off.

Thorne said his goodbyes, but he was not going home just yet.

He walked back inside, past his office and straight on until he came out by the stairwell behind the station's front desk. He hung his ID around his neck then climbed two flights to the second floor. He skirted the CID offices, interview rooms and forensic suites, and eventually found himself standing at the entrance to the bridge.

Lewisham station, reputedly the biggest in Europe, was composed of two entirely separate four-storey blocks linked by a covered walkway, thirty feet long and walled in glass. The block in which Thorne worked housed the Borough departments: CID and Uniform, Mounted Unit, Dogs. The other building was home to some of the more specialist squads: Firearms, Serious and Organised Crime and a Murder Investigation Team (MIT) that was the largest in south-east London.

In the three months Thorne had worked as a uniformed inspector at Lewisham station, he had never crossed the bridge.

He hesitated for a second or two, then began to walk across. He kept his head down as people passed him in both directions, angry with himself for feeling jittery, as though he were back at school and creeping nervously towards the headmaster's office. He felt a little better by the time he reached the other side. When he remembered that Treasure called it the 'Wanker's Walkway'.

The smell was different in this block. Or perhaps it was just the absence of those distinctive smells he had become accustomed to in recent months; in the locker room and the custody area. There was carpet rather than painted cement or peeling floor tiles and there was a good deal of polished, blond wood. There was space.

Thorne pushed at the door to the MIT major incident room, but it would not open. He stepped back and noticed the entry panel; its ten shiny, numbered buttons. He tensed and swore under his breath. There was nowhere in his own building to which he could not gain entry by swiping his ID, but it was clear that access to the hallowed territory of the Murder Investigation Team was only granted to the privileged few who knew the code.

Privileged did not always mean bright, however. Thorne pressed 1-2-3-4 and pushed again. This time he swore loudly enough to turn the heads of two women chatting further along the corridor.

He knocked on the door.

Through the small window in the door, he watched the man at the desk only a few feet away look up, stare blankly at him for a few seconds, then turn back to his computer. A woman on the phone at an adjacent desk spared him no more than a glance.

He knocked again, a good deal harder, and

leaned closer to the glass to make sure that anyone who could be bothered got a good look at his expression. Finally, the man at the computer dragged his backside out of his chair. He walked across to the door as though furious at the absence of a butler to do it for him.

'I want to speak to the DCI,' Thorne said. He lifted up his ID, held it nice and close.

The officer studied it for a lot longer than was necessary. He said, 'What do you want him for?'

Was there a hint of a smirk?

'What's your name?' Thorne asked.

The officer told him and though Thorne had forgotten the name almost as soon as he'd heard it, he'd got all the information he needed. He knew the man's rank. Thorne took a second, then walked slowly across until his face was no more than six inches away from the detective sergeant's. He smiled and whispered, '"What do you want him for . . . *sir*?"'

'Sorry?'

'You heard,' Thorne said. 'Now, I couldn't give a toss about your flashy suit, because even though I don't wear one of those any more I've still got a nice white shirt with two shiny pips on the shoulder. Now, last time I checked, an inspector was still one notch above a sergeant. Don't tell me that's changed as well, since my day.'

'No,' the sergeant said, confused.

Thorne waited.

'No, sir.'

The man was clearly not intimidated, the word spoken with as little colour as possible, imbued with the same level of respect he might have for a pimp or a paedophile. Thorne recognised the tone. It was one he'd used often enough himself; carpeted by some bumptious chief superintendent or desperate to twist the arm of an over-cautious DCI. But he was not going to accept it from a tosser like this. Not now; not simply because the tosser was the 'tec and Thorne was the one with the uniform in his locker.

The Woody.

'Well, I'm glad we've got that sorted, *Sergeant,*' Thorne said. 'Cleared the air a bit. Now piss off and fetch your guv'nor, there's a good lad.'

It was not yet eight o'clock in the morning, but the place was already buzzing. Fifteen, twenty officers moving quickly between desks, conferring with colleagues or working alone at screens and on phones. Thorne watched and listened; the noises, the *focus* of it all, painfully familiar to him. He turned and studied the whiteboard that ran the length of one wall: the photographs of suspects, witnesses, victims. The all-important names and dates scribbled in felt pen: closed cases in red, open in green. Thorne had spent so many years in rooms like this, tapping into the same kind of energy, feeding off it. Standing where he was now, as it hummed and crackled around him, he was dry-mouthed suddenly and disoriented. He was slightly dizzy.

He felt like a man on the wagon, with a beer in his hand.

After a couple of minutes, a man appeared at the far end of the room and waved Thorne across. He greeted Thorne by name and introduced himself as Detective Chief Inspector Neil Hackett. Thorne followed him into a large and tidy office, took the chair that was offered and glanced out across Lewisham High Street.

The view across the DCI's desk was not an awful lot prettier. Hackett was at least six-four, but his height was not enough to disguise the extra weight he was carrying and when he undid his jacket, the gut that spilled out threatened to burst the buttons on his expensive shirt.

'Let me guess then, Tom.' Hackett let out a sigh as he sat down and the chair did much the same. 'This is in relation to your double suicide Thursday night.'

Thorne took a couple of seconds. Said, 'Right.' Clearly, the jungle drums were even louder, or just being beaten more furiously, than he'd suspected. He was certain now that he'd done the right thing in asking Phil Hendricks to look at the Coopers' PM reports.

Hackett smiled, as though Thorne's train of thought was blindingly obvious and he was paying him the courtesy of an explanation. 'Paul Binns is a mate of mine.'

'That's nice for you,' Thorne said.

'He's a good officer.'

'I never said he wasn't.'

'Good. Besides, Paul isn't one of mine, so no point coming crying to me with some sort of complaint.'

'Nobody's crying to anyone.'

'Even better,' Hackett said.

'I just think that someone might want to take another look at it,' Thorne said. 'That's all.'

'Someone like me?'

'It can't hurt, can it?'

Hackett sat back and reached to pat down sandy-coloured hair that was swept back from a widow's peak. Fat-faced as he was, his head still appeared small by comparison with the rest of him. 'I might be missing something here, but haven't you already signed off on this?'

'I didn't have a lot of choice,' Thorne said.

'But you're not happy.'

Thorne paused, wanting to choose his words carefully. 'I didn't get the impression that it was being taken seriously.' *That* I *was being taken seriously*.

'This would be the insulin bottle without a label,' Hackett said. 'And the fact that the old lady took her teeth out.'

'Sir,' Thorne said. That, and something else. A part of the picture that did not make sense, but which stubbornly refused to dislodge itself from the silt in Thorne's mind and bob to the surface. 'Look, I know it sounds a bit . . . thin.'

'Thin? It's bloody anorexic.' Hackett shook his

head. 'You do know that the old man was a retired doctor, don't you? I mean, there's your insulin mystery solved.'

'No,' Thorne said. 'I didn't know that.'

Hackett leaned forward. 'Listen, if I'd been there, I would have done exactly the same as DI Binns and I wouldn't have been nearly as reasonable about it. It's not like we haven't got enough genuine murders on the books right this minute.'

'It didn't feel right,' Thorne said.

Hackett laughed. 'Oh Christ, are you talking about a "hunch"?'

'No, sir—'

'I've heard all sorts about you, mate, but nobody ever said you were one of those idiots.'

'I'm not,' Thorne said. Simple, measured. The truth.

'So what, then?' Hackett had stopped laughing. His face darkened and he suddenly looked in the mood for a scrap. 'What does "right" mean, exactly, Inspector? Right, like the shit you pulled a few months back? Right, like forcing a civilian into the middle of an armed siege?'

Thorne felt the blood move fast to his face. The case with Helen. When everything had fallen apart.

'Oh, I know all about it,' Hackett said. 'I know that you messed up big time and that you cut one or two other corners that we won't bother bringing up now, and that's why you got bumped off the Murder Squad. It's why you're working downstairs on the other side of that bridge and hating every bloody minute of it.' He leaned forward. 'Tell me I'm wrong.'

'I'm hating every minute of *this*,' Thorne said.

Hackett smiled. 'I know you're hating it, because I know damn well that I'd hate it too. So, it strikes me you've only got two options.'

'I'm guessing you're going to tell me what they are.'

The DCI pointed a fat pink finger. 'You're the one taking up *my* time, remember. So, stop being a smartarse and listen. You can get out. Nice and simple . . . chuck it in and open a pub, get yourself a hobby, whatever. Or, you can suck it up and do your job. Your choice. If you decide to stay on, you can start by remembering that when somebody kills themselves it's not *actually* a murder, OK? You can stop playing detective.'

Thorne stood up and said, 'Thanks for your time.'

Walking out through the incident room, he returned the stare of the man who had opened the door, but Thorne looked away first.

He stopped halfway back across the bridge. He pressed his hands and then his head against the glass.

Two options.

CHAPTER 6

'He made me feel like such a twat,' Thorne said. He smacked his palm against the fridge door, then turned to Helen who was sitting at the kitchen table, feeding Alfie his lunch. When she looked up at him, Thorne recognised the expression. 'OK, like even more of a twat.'

'What did you expect?'

'God knows.'

'Seriously.'

'I know,' Thorne said. 'It was stupid.' He traipsed across and dropped into the seat opposite her. At the end of the table, Alfie was spitting out more than he was eating and happily smearing orange mush across the plastic tray of his high chair. 'Really . . . stupid.'

'Yeah, well it's easy with hindsight, isn't it?' Helen leaned across to scoop a spoonful of orange mush – carrot? Sweet potato? – back into Alfie's mouth. 'So, there's no need to beat yourself up about it.'

Thorne said, 'Yeah, I know,' thinking: Since when did 'need' have anything to do with it. Of course, in hindsight, he *should* probably have thought things through a little more before marching across that bridge and trying to tell someone like Hackett what he should be doing. Not that any amount of thinking would have made too much difference in the end. Because Thorne had known from the moment Christine Treasure had told him to let it go, that he could not.

'Come on, let's get you sorted out.'

Thorne had been staring down at the table and looked up, but he saw that Helen was talking to her son. He passed her a few feet of kitchen towel from the roll on the table and watched as she cleaned Alfie's face and wiped away the mess on his chair. Thorne moved to stand up.

'Stay there,' she said. 'I'll do it.'

Thorne nodded, grateful, and sat back down. He had not got to bed until just before nine and had barely managed four hours' sleep before waking and finding himself unable to get off again; trudging into the kitchen like a zombie in pyjama bottoms and a Hank Williams T-shirt.

'One thing you might want to ask yourself though,' Helen said. She put the dishes into the sink and tossed the dirty bib on to the worktop.

'What?'

'Well . . . going in there like that, stirring things up—'

'I wasn't stirring anything up.'

'OK.' She smiled. 'Whatever you call it.' She walked back to the table and lifted Alfie out of the high chair. 'Was it because you honestly still believe there was something iffy about that suicide the other night? Or was it really just because you were pissed off at being ignored?'

Thorne shook his head.

'Tom . . .?'

He had told Helen some of what Hackett had said to him. The lecture about making choices, the gleefully sarcastic comments about what had happened in that newsagent's five months before. He hadn't bothered to pass on Hackett's final words of wisdom.

The line that had stung more than anything else.

Stop playing detective.

'Look, it would be perfectly understandable.'

'Understandable or not,' Thorne said, 'that isn't what's going on.'

'You sure about that?'

'Yes.' He looked at her. 'I'm sure about that.'

'Juice,' Alfie said. 'Juice.'

Thorne watched Helen put Alfie down and walk across to the fridge. 'Is that what you really think?' he asked.

'I'm just saying you need to ask yourself that question, that's all.' She reached into the fridge, her back to him. 'Look, I'm not saying I blame you.'

Thorne pushed his chair back hard. 'Oh, good.' He stood up. 'And yes, I *still* think it's bloody iffy, OK?'

Helen turned, shaking the small carton of juice

in her hand. She was still smiling, but suddenly her voice had a little less colour in it. 'Maybe you should go back to bed. I'm taking Alfie down to the playgroup, so we won't disturb you. With any luck you'll get up in a better mood.'

Thorne was already on his way.

He waited until he heard Helen go out, then sat up and propped a pillow behind his head. He had made a note of all the numbers he thought he might need before leaving the station. Now, he unfolded the piece of paper on which he'd scribbled everything down, set his open laptop on the bed next to him and reached for his phone.

As offices went, this was certainly the cosiest Thorne had ever worked in.

Assuming that the deaths of John and Margaret Cooper were not the suicides they appeared to be – and whatever had told Thorne that was the case still refused to make itself known to him – it was safe to say that their two children were not serious suspects. Both were in their fifties, with children of their own. The son, Andrew, had been in Edinburgh at the time of his parents' deaths and his sister, Paula, lived in Leicester. Both were now staying at a hotel in London while making the funeral arrangements, and when Thorne called Andrew Cooper's mobile he was able to speak to each of them in turn.

He passed on his sympathies and assured them that having spoken to the pathologist, their parents would not have suffered. That it would have been over quickly. Each of them told him how shocked they were. Stunned, they both said. Their parents had both been in relatively good health, had seemed well and happy, and nobody in the family would ever have expected something like this.

'The *last* thing . . .'

The more Thorne heard, the more certain he became and the less bothered by his own subterfuge; the fact that he was not calling them for altogether benign reasons.

'I'm sure you've got a lot on your plate,' he said to Paula. 'But have you managed to talk to everybody that needs to be informed? I mean, it's probably the last thing you want to think about, but presuming there was a will . . . I just wondered if you'd spoken to your parents' solicitor?'

It *was* the last thing either of them was thinking about, she told him and when Thorne offered to do it for them, she said there was really no need. She said she did not know this was the sort of thing the police did for bereaved families. 'It's not going to be complicated anyway,' she said. 'It's only me and Andrew and it's not like it's a fortune or anything.'

Thorne felt no more than a twinge of guilt when she thanked him for calling.

'We just have no idea *why*,' she said, before she hung up.

Paula had been talking about why her parents

would have wanted to take their own lives, but lying there, studying the pattern of cracks on the bedroom ceiling, Thorne was equally lost when it came to why anyone would want to murder them and make it appear that way.

It was certainly not about money. It was not a burglary gone wrong and it was not done in a hurry, or in a rage.

The bedroom was tidy.

Nothing had been disturbed.

So what was wrong with the picture?

The last thing – always the last thing – to be considered was that there simply *was* no clear motive of any sort; nothing that Thorne had come across before, at any rate. Margaret and John Cooper might have died for no other reason than that specific to the individual who had killed them. If this was the case – and more than anything, Thorne hoped that it was not – then another possibility would need to be considered that was altogether more disturbing.

That whoever killed them had done so simply because it was enjoyable.

Thorne looked up another number and dialled.

'It's Tom,' he said, when the call was answered. When the woman at the other end of the phone did not respond immediately, he added, 'Thorne,' then said, 'Are you busy?'

Elly Kennedy was a civilian intelligence analyst based at the Peel Centre in Colindale, in an office just along the corridor from the one Thorne had worked in. The two of them had flirted on and off for a while and there had once been some drunken fumbling at a party. Thorne had not spoken to her for over a year.

She laughed. 'Well, I might have known it wasn't a social call.'

'Can you speak?'

'Meaning, can anyone hear me? No, go on, you're fine . . .'

Thorne told her what he needed her to look for and gave her some hastily thought out parameters.

'Bloody hell, you don't want much, do you?'

'I know, and I'm sorry to be asking, but I really couldn't think of anyone better.' This was true, but only because her job gave her access to a wide range of both police and civil databases. All the same, Thorne was hoping that shameless flattery would do the trick.

'You're lucky,' she said. 'I'm on a break, so I *might* be able to get something to you soonish.'

'That would be great.'

'Once I've finished this Kit Kat, obviously.'

'Thanks, Elly,' Thorne said.

'So, how are you?'

Thorne guessed that she was really asking if he was seeing anyone, but he did not think it would help his cause to give a straight answer. 'I'm fine,' he said. 'Getting on with it.'

'Not going mental, stuck down there with the Woodies?'

'It's not too bad,' he lied.

'Well, if I come up with anything, maybe you can buy me a drink to say thank you.'

Thorne promised that he would and asked Elly to write down his private email address. The significance of Thorne not wanting her to use his @met. police address was clearly not lost on her.

'Better make that dinner,' she said.

CHAPTER 7

Thorne opened his eyes, and for several seconds was uncertain where he was. What manner of policeman he was. Later, he would feel more than a little guilty at the disappointment of realising he was not in his own bed. But those few precious moments before the cold wash of remembrance – what had happened to him, what he had lost – were something he would cling on to until it was all over.

It was nearly five o'clock and Saturday was darkening beyond the bedroom window. He sat up and turned on the bedside lamp. He could not hear anyone in the flat, so he reached for his phone and called Helen.

'I went out for coffee with some of the other mums,' she said.

'Oh, OK.'

'Did you get some sleep?'

'Yeah . . . only just woke up.' He wasn't sure if Helen had stayed out to leave him undisturbed or to get away from his bad mood. Either way, he realised that he should probably be saying sorry.

'I won't be too long,' she said. 'Alfie's tired.'

Thorne could hear the boy grizzling in the background. 'Listen, I'd better go . . .'

When he tossed his mobile down, Thorne noticed the laptop on the other side of the bed. He got up, pulled on a dressing gown and carried the computer through to the kitchen, remembering that it had been the noise of email arriving in his inbox that had woken him.

He made himself some tea and went to work.

Picking what had sounded like a reasonable time frame, he had asked Elly Kennedy to go back three months and to search for any cases in the Greater London area. He had told her to concentrate on suicide victims aged seventy and above and to look out most especially for any instances involving couples. Though she had found none that directly mirrored the Coopers, she had been able to access enough key sources to gather information on a dozen or so cases she thought Thorne might be interested in. He was looking for the relevant information in police and coroner's reports, transcripts from the inquest where there had been one and, most importantly, statements from family members. She had sent the files across relatively quickly and it became clear that there had not been enough time to weed out every case that did not quite fit the bill.

The attachment took almost five minutes to download.

Thorne read carefully through all the material Elly had sent, discarding any instances where there was clear evidence of serious physical illness or depression. He also discounted those where the victim had recently lost loved ones or was living in isolation. He knew there would always be occasions where family, friends and social services had simply not paid close enough attention to suicide indicators, but he still believed that the totally unforeseen and inexplicable cases would stand out.

After more than an hour, he was left with two.

A seventy-one-year-old man from Hounslow had slit his wrists in the bath a fortnight before. The week before that, a seventy-year-old woman from Hendon had left her house in the middle of the night and walked into the Brent reservoir.

In both cases, the deceased had appeared happy and healthy before their deaths, and the families had said much the same things Thorne had heard from Andrew Cooper and his sister.

He would never have done anything like that.
She'd just booked a holiday, for heaven's sake.
It doesn't make any sense . . .

Thorne read through all the documentation one more time and nothing that he saw could convince him that these grieving sons and daughters were wrong.

By the time Thorne was putting his recently acquired reading glasses back in their case, it was after six. He turned on the TV to check the football scores and was happy to see that Spurs had turned Sunderland over at the Stadium of Light. Better yet, Arsenal had only scraped a draw. It was more than an hour since he'd spoken to Helen and, as they were still not back, he could only assume that Alfie had perked up. Thorne was ravenous, and wondered if she might fancy a take-away when she eventually got back. He was midway through sending her a text suggesting exactly that when his phone rang.

'Did you get everything?' Elly Kennedy asked.

Thorne told her that he had just finished reading it and thanked her again.

'Listen, bearing in mind what you're after, I thought you might be interested in an odd one that came in earlier today. I only just saw it, so—'

'What?'

'Hang on.'

Thorne could hear the keyboard clicks as she called up the appropriate screen.

'Seventy-three-year-old male. Suspected suicide by overdose and exit bag . . . nice and thorough . . . and there are Murder Squad detectives already on the scene. So, something sounds dodgy, doesn't it?'

Thorne reached up to scratch at the back of his neck; a strange yet familiar tickle. 'Where?'

'Stanmore,' Elly said. 'Some of your old lot, I think.'

Thorne wrote down the address and hurried through to the bedroom to get dressed. As he scrambled back into the same clothes he'd come home in that morning, he tried to formulate what would be the perfect opening line for DCI Neil Hackett when he called him.

'*Looks like I won't be opening that pub just yet,*' or '*Fancy coming out to play detective with me?*'

Perhaps not, but he would think of something.

Hackett was there before him. Thorne watched the man ease himself slowly out of a BMW that was considerably newer than his own as he pulled up. The DCI had been at Lewisham station when Thorne had called, so could not have got to Stanmore that much ahead of him. Nevertheless, an apology seemed like a good idea.

'Traffic was bad,' Thorne said.

Hackett grunted and shoved his hands down into the pockets of a long black overcoat; *de rigueur* for the stylish DCI about town, though Thorne had never seen one in quite this size before. 'Still not sure what I'm doing here,' he said. He did not give Thorne the chance to answer and instead nodded past the two patrol cars towards the pair of uniformed officers standing outside the house. 'Whatever the hell's going on in there, it's the wrong side of the river for us anyway.' There was the first hint of a cold smile. 'Your old stamping ground.'

'I'm not convinced what happened to the Coopers was a one-off,' Thorne said.

'No?'

'I think there might be at least two more.'

'Two more suicides that aren't really suicides?'

'Two more cases that should be looked at again at the very least.'

'All this based on what, exactly?' Hackett asked. 'Nothing even a moron would call evidence, I know that much.' He snapped his fingers. 'Oh, yes of course . . . sorry, I forgot . . . we should all just go ahead and allocate money and manpower and waste every bugger's time based on you thinking that something isn't "right". He turned his face away from the wind. 'Good luck with that.'

Thorne looked at the house. The officers on duty outside looked bored to death. He pointed. 'This is nothing to do with me, is it?'

'Sod all to do with me either, far as I can work out.'

'Look, somebody in there thought it was worth calling the 'tecs in, didn't they? So there's obviously something dodgy gone on.' Thorne was struggling to sound assertive while keeping his temper. 'If it *isn't* a suicide, then it might well have *everything* to do with you, because there's every chance it's connected to our case the other night.'

'Your case,' Hackett said. 'Uniform's case.'

'Not if I'm right.'

Hackett nodded, the hint of that smile again. 'And if that turns out to be the case, Inspector, I shall of course be very grateful that you called me.'

Thorne stared at him, waiting for the smile to become a smirk; some sign that Hackett was taking the piss. He didn't see one.

The DCI gestured towards the house. Said, 'On we go, then.' He walked straight across the small garden to the open front door, ignoring the officers outside it and stopping on the threshold; inviting Thorne to enter the house ahead of him.

Thorne muttered a 'Thanks.'

There were more uniforms inside. Thorne produced his warrant card and was pointed upstairs. Walking up, he became aware of a smell he recognised, something sweet and similar to one he'd encountered at the Coopers'. He had not been the only one. Back at the station that night, someone had said, 'Cats, I bet. Crinklies always have loads of cats, don't they?' Somebody else had laughed and said, 'Bloody hell, don't tell Two-Cats. He'll be round the nearest old people's home with his truncheon . . .'

It wasn't cats. Thorne had owned one for many years and knew only too well what cat piss smelled like. This was not unpleasant, like old furniture and soap. Lavender, maybe.

Wasn't that what his mother had worn? That or Parma Violet . . .

Thorne could see the body through the open bedroom door and when he stepped inside he saw two detectives standing by the window, drinking tea and laughing. One of them turned, saw Thorne and said, 'Bloody hell.' Thorne was aware that Hackett had entered the room and was leaning against the wall behind him.

'Hello, Dave,' Thorne said.

DS Dave Holland was someone with whom Thorne had worked closely for almost ten years.

65

Thorne had watched as the shine was taken off him day by day; seen him graduate from floppy-haired, wide-eyed new boy to an officer whose approach to the realities of the Job was now every bit as practical as his haircut.

Holland was understandably surprised to see Thorne and said as much.

'It's complicated,' Thorne said. He could picture the smile forming on the face of the man behind him. 'This might tie in with something at my place, that's all.'

Holland seemed happy enough not to ask any more and introduced Thorne to the DC he was working with. The woman nodded a greeting.

'What's the story?' Thorne asked. He took a few steps towards the bed.

Holland moved to join him, nodded towards the body. 'Topped himself, guv . . .' He stopped, a little embarrassed at the slip of the tongue, and Thorne saw him glance towards Hackett. 'But same as you said . . . it's complicated.'

The old man was sitting up, a pale-blue pillow propped vertically behind him. His face was some-what obscured by the plastic bag over his head; the 'exit bag' that Elly Kennedy had mentioned. The bag was partially steamed up and pasted to one side of his face. Vomit had spattered the inside of it and was gathered at the bottom, leaking in thin trails where the bag was tied around the man's neck with what looked like the cord from a dressing gown.

There was an open bottle of tablets on the bedside table.

'Who called it in?' Thorne asked.

'The wife,' Holland said. He nodded back towards the door. 'She's in the spare room with DI Kitson.'

'Yvonne's here?' Another close colleague until a few months before.

Holland nodded. 'It's the wife that's the problem.'

On cue, Thorne heard a door close along the corridor and a few moments later, Yvonne Kitson appeared in the doorway. She stopped and took in the scene. 'Tom? Are you . . .?'

Hackett spoke without looking at her. 'It's complicated.'

'What's the problem with the wife?' Thorne asked.

Clearly a little thrown by Thorne's presence, Kitson stepped into the room, picking up the mug of tea or coffee that she had left on top of a cupboard. 'Well, she's not saying she helped him do it, but she admits being here when it happened. So, not assisted suicide as such, but you never know, the CPS might see things differently. The law's all over the bloody place with stuff like this, but I think we'll just have to arrest her and see what happens.'

'Waste of bloody time,' Holland said.

Now Thorne knew why detectives had been called in. He felt as though he'd just driven fast over a hump-backed bridge.

'I know,' Kitson said. 'But we're here because

we have to be.' She cradled her mug and stared down at the old man. 'Stomach cancer, apparently. She said they'd been talking about doing it for ages. Said that he'd begged her.'

'The things we do for love,' Hackett said. 'Fantastic song, that.'

When Thorne turned and saw the look on the man's face, he suddenly understood that Hackett had known exactly what to expect; that he had come into the house before Thorne had arrived. It explained why Holland and the others had not bothered to acknowledge him, why Hackett had been content to stand back and watch as Thorne was made to look and feel like an idiot.

Thorne could see just how much Hackett had enjoyed it.

'We'll be off then,' Hackett said. He looked at Thorne then turned towards the door. 'Maybe you'd like to walk me to my car . . .'

Thorne walked a few steps behind Hackett, who took more time on the stairs than even a man his size might need and stopped to exchange a few pleasantries with the officers outside the front door. Nobody spoke until they were almost at Hackett's car. He pressed the remote to unlock the door, then said, 'Happy?'

'Look, I wasn't the one who called Homicide in,' Thorne said. 'I was only going on what I'd been told and it seemed to fit. Obviously, I'm sorry it didn't turn out like that.'

Hackett waved the apology away. 'Don't be sorry,

Inspector. I honestly can't remember the last time I had that much fun.'

Thorne nodded, noticing how bad the man's teeth were when he smiled, and wondering whether a punch or a kick in the bollocks would put him down first.

'More to this job than having fun though.' Hackett's smile vanished. 'So, let's make sure that's the last time I hear so much as a whisper about dodgy suicides, all right? Stick to burglaries and arresting drunks, and next time you come across that bridge, it better be because you've got lost. Fair enough?'

Thorne swallowed and said that it was.

'Seriously, the wrong side of me is not where you want to be.' Hackett opened the car door and heaved himself inside. 'I might be a fat bastard, but I am far from fucking jolly.'

CHAPTER 8

After a late breakfast, Thorne fetched the Sunday papers and they walked across to Brockwell Park. It was not exactly warm, but the day was bright enough and Alfie got more excited the closer they got to the children's playground.

'Eh-owd,' he said. 'Eh-owd . . .'

There were plenty of other people at the play area and they needed to wait a few minutes before Alfie could get a turn on the swings. Thorne stood with Helen while she pushed.

'You OK?' she asked.

He had not told Helen about his trip to Stanmore the night before, telling her when he finally got home that he'd been out for a drink with one of the boys from the station. Last-minute thing. He had stopped off on his way back to pick up a couple of cans and drunk them in the car. It helped with the breath, with the lie, but he had needed them anyway.

'Still tired, I think,' Thorne said. He was doing his best to appear cheerful, but wasn't sure that he was making too good a job of it. He had that kind of face and he knew it, a default expression that often made others wary. Thorne could be pig-in-shit happy and people would still ask him what the matter was.

They sat for a while watching as Alfie jumped on and off a series of raised, plastic stepping stones, letting out a loud yelp of excitement each time he did it. When he landed awkwardly and fell, Helen was off the bench in an instant. Thorne had not been watching but jumped up as soon as he saw Helen do it. Alfie got to his feet, his face screwed up tight as though he had not decided whether to laugh or cry and when he opted for the former and climbed back on to the stepping stone, Thorne and Helen sat down again. They pulled the papers out of a plastic bag and Thorne began looking for a report on the Spurs game.

'Sometimes I think I worry about him too much,' Helen said. 'That I'm being overprotective.'

'You're bound to be,' Thorne said.

She looked at him, a hint of suspicion. 'Why?'

He put the paper down. 'Well, your job for a kick-off.' Helen was a DS on a Child Abuse Investigation Team. She had told Thorne stories that had been hard to listen to. 'You've seen what happens when parents don't give a shit.'

She shook her head. 'Kids aren't abused just because their parents don't give a shit.'

'You know what I mean.'

Helen stared at her son, waved when he looked briefly in her direction before toddling away again.

'Maybe it's because it's just me and him. Well, it *was* . . .' She hesitated, a little flustered.

'I know.'

'I mean, for quite a while.'

Though he and Helen had come together following the siege in which she had become involved months earlier, he had actually met her briefly more than a year before that. Her partner, Paul, had been killed in unusual circumstances and Helen – heavily pregnant – had taken it upon herself to try and find out why. Thorne knew that Paul had not necessarily been Alfie's father, that there had been an affair before Paul had died. Thanks to listening equipment installed by a surveillance team during the siege, a *lot* of people knew, though he and Helen had never talked about it.

'Louise lost a baby,' Thorne said. 'Not long before we split up.'

Helen reached for his hand.

Thorne had not spoken too much about his previous relationship. Louise was just his 'ex'. 'Actually, it's probably why we split up, you know, looking back on it.'

'It's hard,' Helen said.

'I didn't react very well.'

'That's understandable.'

'I think the problem was I didn't react *enough*,' Thorne said. 'Something like that happens and it's no good if you both . . . go to pieces, so I was the one that just got on with things. Work, whatever.

72

I think it came across like I didn't care enough. I know that's how it came across.' He turned, saw that Helen was staring at him. 'I did though . . .'

Helen was about to speak when Thorne's mobile rang. When he answered and recognised the voice on the other end, he stood up and walked away from the bench.

'Thorne? We need a quick chat.'

There was a roving uniformed chief superintendent on call at all times on either side of the river. They were there to give the necessary authority when required: to extend custody from twenty-four to thirty-six hours, to 'ping' a suspect's mobile phone. What Christine Treasure called the 'sneaky-beaky' stuff. They were also there, of course, to dish out the slaps when they were deemed to be called for. One of the few crumbs of comfort Thorne had gained from his move to uniform was that he would no longer have to deal with the one senior officer he had come closest to thumping during his years on the Murder Squad. The unctuous weasel who had taken sitting on the fence to Olympic heights and who returned Thorne's evident antipathy with interest. Thorne had been horrified to discover, within a day or two of taking up his new post, that the chief super working south of the river was that very same weasel.

Trevor bloody Jesmond.

'I understand you've been rather overstepping your boundaries,' Jesmond said. His tone was that unique mixture of emotions that Thorne knew only too well. Disgust at the behaviour and unbridled delight at being able to stamp on whoever was responsible. 'Some things never change, do they?'

'Been talking to Neil Hackett then,' Thorne said.

'It doesn't matter.'

'That's a yes then.'

'It doesn't matter who I've been talking to, because now I'm talking to you.'

'I thought we could be looking at a murder.'

'Yes, I know.'

'That it might be part of a pattern.'

'You thought wrong, didn't you?'

Thorne swallowed. 'Looks like it.'

'Besides which, that's not your job,' Jesmond said. 'Much as you might wish it still were.'

The man was strictly a by-the-book merchant, so Thorne had asked himself what on earth *Jesmond* could have done to find himself working on Borough. Had he been caught with the Commander's wife? Mother? Dog? It was far more likely that he had requested the transfer purely out of a desire to make Thorne's life as miserable as possible.

He was extremely good at it.

'I get that,' Thorne said. He turned and saw that Helen was watching him. If he appeared less than delirious a few minutes ago, he wondered what his face was showing now.

'Good. You've been warned.' Jesmond let that sink in, then chuckled. Fingernails on a black-board. 'Just like old times.'

Thorne grunted.

'Best not make a habit of it though, eh? You might not relish what you're doing at the moment, but trust me, you'd enjoy being a sergeant a damn sight less.'

When Jesmond had hung up, Thorne walked back to the bench and sat down. He picked up a paper, did nothing with it.

'All right?'

Helen had clearly heard enough to get the gist. 'Jesmond,' Thorne said.

'Ah . . .'

'Yeah, well, that's me told.' Thorne opened his paper. 'Hackett clearly had a major problem with me going across that bridge, so MIT is now strictly off-limits.'

'This still about that double suicide?'

Thorne continued to turn the pages.

'You never finished telling me about what happened with you and Louise,' Helen said. 'What we were talking about before.'

Thorne shook his head. 'I think the moment's gone, don't you?'

They sat in silence for a few minutes. Helen read her paper while Thorne stared towards the playground, every shout and squeal cutting right through him. His phone chimed in his pocket and he took his time reaching for it, guessing that Jesmond had not finished with him.

The text was from Hendricks.

Cooper paperwork done.

A few minutes later, Thorne said, 'I think I might go out for a drink with Phil a bit later.'

'Yeah, OK.'

'I'll probably stay at the flat.'

'Makes sense,' Helen said. 'You don't need to drive.'

Thorne nodded. 'I wouldn't be very good company anyway.'

Helen looked up as Alfie came running across. He wrapped himself around Thorne's leg and wiped a runny nose against his jacket.

She said, 'Whatever you think.'

CHAPTER 9

He's heading west for this one.

The travelling doesn't bother him a great deal. He'd always known he'd need to do a fair amount of running around and, besides, it gives him a chance to see a bit more of the city. He'd missed London. Missed it more than some of his family in the end, but that wasn't much of a contest. He'd given what was left of them up as a bad lot the same time they'd turned their backs on him. If they couldn't be bothered, then he sure as hell wasn't going to try too hard.

You got back what you put in, that was the way he saw it.

He drives out through Shepherd's Bush towards the Westway, first time he's seen the place in thirty-odd years. He knocked around here a fair bit as a younger man, back when you could still see speedway or greyhound racing at White City Stadium and the BBC made shows at the Empire and Lime Grove studios, where the Beatles recorded their first-ever broadcast. He recalls some of the scrapes in the Springbok or the Crown and Sceptre, the odd spot of argy-bargy with the QPR boys on match days, and he remembers plenty of more serious business done later on. Here and in Chiswick. In the West End too, of course. Not better days, necessarily, he's not soft about it, not sentimental. Different, though, no arguing with that.

He was sentimental, he'd hardly have that bag sitting on the back seat, would he? He wouldn't be bowling along the A40 on his way to use what was in it.

Thinking about how this one's likely to play out, he can't even remember why he chose to do things this way, why he wanted to make each one different. It was probably just because he'd had so much time to sit on his backside and think about it. He'd made a plan, so he was going to stick to it, simple as that. It wasn't even as if one method was any more or less enjoyable than another, because enjoyment didn't enter into it, not really. No question it made things a bit more interesting though, added a bit of mustard to the proceedings. Variety might well be the spice of life, but it definitely made death a bit more interesting too.

He pulls across into the inside lane, in no great hurry. Singing that Beatles song about lonely people and funerals nobody goes to, and thinking that the music definitely *was* a damn sight better back then.

Thinking that variety is something he hasn't had in a long time.

CHAPTER 10

'I'd only have thrashed you anyway,' Hendricks said.

'Yeah, course you would.'

'And it really upsets me when you cry like a girl.'

Thorne was bemoaning the fact that they could no longer play pool in the Grafton Arms. The room upstairs where they had spent many evenings playing for beer was now a multi-purpose 'function suite'. Salsa classes, birthday parties and a comedy night once a month, to which Hendricks had insisted on dragging Thorne a few weeks earlier. Thorne had made the mistake of sitting near the front and been mercilessly picked on by a hectoring compère. He was still not sure how the comic had found out he was Old Bill – the smart money was on Hendricks, of course – but the ribbing had carried on for most of the evening, the man milking as many cheap laughs as possible from asking, 'Can I smell bacon?' every time he came on stage.

After the show, Thorne had sought the comic out at the bar and congratulated him on doing a good job. The comic had shrugged and said, 'No hard feelings, mate.' Thorne said what he thought he should say, that he didn't know how anyone could get up there in front of all those people, hardest job in the world. The comic had grinned and said, 'Money for jam, mate. Hundred and twenty quid, cash in hand.'

'I hope you're declaring that,' Thorne had said. As the comedian's mouth fell open, Thorne had leaned closer and said, 'Oink!' before sauntering away.

'So, curry back at yours, is it?' Hendricks asked. He raised a bottle of Czech lager and put a third of it away.

Thorne swallowed a mouthful of Guinness. 'Sounds good,' he said. 'At least you can walk home now, instead of stinking up the sheets on my sofa bed.'

'We'll see what kind of state I'm in, shall we?'

Hendricks had recently moved into a flat in Camden, which was no more than a ten-minute walk from Thorne's in Kentish Town. The pub was spitting distance away from Thorne's place and he had dropped the car off before walking back to meet Hendricks.

'All settled in?'

'Still in boxes, mate.'

'Well it's not too late to change your mind,' Thorne said. 'Admit you've paid way over the odds for what's basically a tin shed.'

Hendricks had bought one of the futuristic-looking, aluminium-clad flats on the banks of the Regent's Canal. The flats – the work of the same designer responsible for the Sainsbury's directly opposite – were highly prized, but Thorne thought they looked like space-age toilets and said as much.

'I like it,' Hendricks said. 'Besides, it's dead handy for the supermarket, or if I ever fancy throwing myself in the canal.' He raised his beer. 'Talking of which . . .'

'Yeah,' Thorne said. 'I suppose we should get it over with.'

'Hang on, I thought this was why you were so desperate to meet up.'

It had been. Thorne had spent the day clinging to the hope that Hendricks might have found something to explain why the Cooper suicides had felt so wrong. That the bodies themselves might have provided the answer. Driving north though, the notion that double-checking the post-mortems could possibly vindicate him or somehow justify the unholy amounts of crap that had rained down in the last few days had begun to appear ridiculous. Worse than childish. By the time he was pulling up outside his flat, he was resigned to being there for no other reason than a simple and overwhelming need to see his friend. To get some sympathy and to get wasted.

Now, twenty minutes and a pint and a half into it, he said, 'Go on then.'

'Your bog-standard insulin overdose,' Hendricks said. 'Nice easy one.'

'Suicide, yeah?'

'Nothing else going on that I could see.'

81

Thorne nodded, drank.

'I mean the old man had a touch of liver disease and some of his wife's arteries were none too clever, but that's what happens at their age. Well, you'll find out yourself soon enough.'

Thorne put his beer down. 'What if someone gave them those injections?'

'No signs of struggle,' Hendricks said. 'No tissue under fingernails.'

Thorne grunted. That much had been obvious at the crime scene. 'There's something else.'

'What?'

'Buggered if I know,' Thorne said. He stared down at the table. 'It's doing my head in.'

'This? Or the whole thing? The uniform, I mean.'

'I don't know. Bit of both.'

Hendricks sat back, sighed. 'Come on then, let's hear it.'

Thorne told him. The apparent suicide of an elderly couple for which there seemed no reason and the similarity to at least two other cases. The nagging doubt that had become a fixation. His clash with Neil Hackett and how it had all fallen apart the previous evening at that house in Stanmore. When he'd felt like an over-enthusiastic novice.

'Jesus . . .'

'"Jesus, that's a really interesting theory" or "Jesus, how could you be such a knob"?'

'Define "interesting",' Hendricks said.

'There was no reason for the Coopers to do

that,' Thorne said. 'No reason at all. There was something wrong in that bedroom.'

'Yeah, but look at it from their point of view, Hackett and his lot. You're not exactly giving them much to get worked up about, are you?'

Thorne reached down and pulled out a sheaf of papers from his bag. He slapped a file down on the table and pushed it across. 'No reason for it,' he said. 'No reason for Brian Gibbs to slash his wrists in the bath.' Another file. 'No reason for Fiona Daniels to drown herself in the reservoir. Look at the statements from the families for God's sake.'

Hendricks moved his beer as the paperwork piled up in front of him.

'Look at it, Phil.'

Hendricks picked up a file and flicked through the pages. 'Yeah, but what does "no reason" actually mean, though? Most of the time we've got no idea why people do *anything*. You know that better than anyone.'

Thorne shook his head, but he knew that his friend had a point. How often had he really known what was going on inside the head of a killer? Whenever some mild-mannered quantity surveyor butchered his wife and kids there were always friends and neighbours queuing up to tell people what a 'perfect' family they were. How it was the last thing anyone had expected. Was it really any different with loved ones? Had Thorne ever known what was going on inside his own parents' heads? He'd certainly made a right royal balls-up of trying to figure Louise out and she would probably say the same thing about herself.

'Sorry, mate, but it's not enough,' Hendricks said. 'Thinking they "weren't the type" to kill themselves counts for sod all.'

'OK, but you can't argue with the facts and figures.' Thorne reached down, produced more papers. 'I've looked into this and the numbers just don't stack up. There's only four hundred and something suicides in London every year and the majority of those are a lot younger than the people we're talking about here. Agreed?'

Hendricks shrugged a 'maybe'.

'Now . . . you get into the over seventy-fives and it's more like two hundred a year, *nationwide*. Women, it's less than half that.' He stabbed at the files on the table. 'There's two women in *there*, for God's sake.'

Hendricks thought about it. 'Sorry, but I don't think those figures are quite as impressive as you think they are.'

'*What?*'

'Look, I do know about this stuff.'

'Come on, Phil.'

Hendricks held his hands up. 'All right, let's be generous and call this a "cluster". I don't think it is for one minute, but even if it was, sometimes there's just no explanation for these things. Remember a few years back? Twenty people killed themselves in one year, all under twenty-five, all in the same small town in south Wales. Now, *that*

84

was a cluster, but nobody's any the wiser about why it happened.' He gathered up the files, squared them off. 'There's nothing . . . sinister about it. Or about this.' He handed the files over. 'There's no bogeyman, mate.'

Thorne took the papers and shoved them hard back into his bag. He picked up his glass and sat back.

Hendricks grinned. 'Look at you though.'

'What?' Thorne said.

'With your "theories" and your actual "research". You're more of a detective now than when you *were* one.' He picked up his beer bottle, prepared to empty it. 'Sodding Inspector Morse! Have you started listening to opera and doing crosswords an' all?'

Thorne looked at him; blinked slowly then swallowed fast.

'Mind you, opera would definitely be preferable to your bloody cowboy music. Lonesome bloody whippoorwills or whatever.' Hendricks saw Thorne's expression. 'What?'

'What you said before.'

'What, about opera?'

'No . . .' Thorne was already reaching for his phone. Hendricks shook his head. 'You've lost me, mate.'

'Drink up,' Thorne said.

'It's a bit early to eat, isn't it?'

Thorne ignored him. He was looking through his list of recently dialled calls. Searching for a grieving son's number.

CHAPTER 11

A hundred yards or so from his front door – walking as quickly as he was able in an effort to prevent his dinner going cold – Alan Herbert decided that when a trip to the fish and chip shop was the highlight of your day, things could definitely be better.

Sundays were always, well . . . *Sundays*, but even so.

The day had not panned out quite the way it was supposed to. He hadn't planned on dozing away most of his afternoon for a kick-off. Waking up with a crick in his neck and drool on the front of his sweater, surprised to see that it was already dark outside. He had never intended to spend the majority of his waking hours slumped in front of the television, eking out the Sunday paper and using what little energy he could summon up to heave himself out of his chair every hour or so to go and put the kettle on again.

Drowning in bloody Tetley's.

By rights, he should have been seeing them off about now. 'Take care' and 'See you soon' and the kids waving out of the Hyundai's back window.

He should be sorting out the leftovers from their lunch; a chicken sandwich for supper, maybe.

His son had called bright and early to let him know they wouldn't be able to make it after all. His youngest coming down with something, so he said. Really sorry, he said, because they were all looking forward *so* much to visiting. One of the kids was always coming down with something. Almost as often as his daughter-in-law had to change her plans for the weekend at the last minute because of work, or there was a problem with the car.

Always something.

There were lights on in many of the front windows as he passed. Curtains were drawn or blinds were down. He walked on, wondering how many of the people behind them had spent their Sunday unconscious, drooling, drinking tea.

Killing time.

It might help of course if he didn't get up so ridiculously early. There would be fewer hours to get through. He'd always thought it was stupid, the way old people did that, when the fact was that most of them had bugger all to do. All the same, there he was, dragging himself out of bed before seven most days; wide awake and dressing in the dark so as to be good and ready for a day doing nothing.

A collar and tie, for pity's sake.

Down to a life wearing one sort of uniform or another, he supposed, but still . . .

'You should see someone,' his son had said to him on the phone a few months before.

'Doctor, you mean?'

'Well . . . or some of your old mates. Get out and about a bit more.'

'I can't be arsed.'

Some days I can't bring myself to turn the lights on and those trips to the kitchen feel like an assault course . . .

He had been to see the doctor.

'It's not unusual to be depressed,' the GP had told him. 'Given your age and circumstances.'

'Depressed? Both my knees are buggered and I can't hear for shit. I'm bloody *livid*!'

Easier to make a joke of it, same as always.

The hinges screamed when he pushed open his front gate and he remembered that there was oil in the garage, somewhere. It had been a long while since he'd ventured inside. He hurried up the path, stopping only to kick aside a fast-food container that some passing drunk had thrown into the garden. The smell of his haddock and chips increased his hunger, the bag warm under his arm. He'd taken the vinegar out of the cupboard before he'd left, buttered some bread.

He had just turned the key in the lock when he heard the voice behind him.

'Hello, stranger.'

He turned, saw an old man walking up the path towards him. A cap and a long, dark coat. The face was familiar, as much as he could make out in the half-light, but Herbert couldn't place it.

'Sorry,' he said. 'Do I . . .?'

'Yeah, been a while, mate. Definitely been a while.' The man was walking faster, only a few feet away.

'Christ,' Herbert said, dropping his dinner as the name came to him, just a second too late.

CHAPTER 12

Andrew Cooper stood on the doorstep of his parents' house and studied his visitors for a few seconds before inviting them in. He was short and stocky, a rugby player's build, with a full head of almost entirely grey hair and blue eyes that were watery behind his glasses. He might well have resembled his father, but based on what Thorne had seen of John Cooper, it was impossible to tell.

The son looked exhausted.

'Thanks for letting us come round,' Thorne said. 'I know it's a bit late.'

'Glad of the break,' Cooper said. 'I've spent all day putting stuff into boxes and bin-bags.' He nodded at nothing in particular. 'Paula's back at the hotel. She couldn't face this, so . . .'

'It's understandable.'

'I got the short straw,' Cooper said.

Thorne and Hendricks followed him into the living room. The furniture had been pushed back against the wall and the centre of the room was now taken up by those boxes and bin-bags

90

Cooper had mentioned. Thorne saw him staring at Hendricks and made the introductions.

'Doctor Hendricks is helping me out,' Thorne said.

'I'm a pathologist,' Hendricks said, at a loss for anything else to say.

Cooper said, 'You're not the one who . . .?'

'No,' Thorne said.

'No,' Hendricks repeated, shaking his head. 'I'm just a consultant.'

The three of them stood a little awkwardly and looked around the room. Thorne and Hendricks were both still chewing the gum they had stopped off to buy on the drive down. It wasn't lost on Thorne that he was doing exactly the opposite of what he'd done the night before, when he'd *wanted* the beer on his breath.

Thorne nodded towards the upright piano against the far wall. 'Which one of them played?'

'They both did a bit,' Cooper said. He perched on the arm of an old leather sofa. There were patches of sweat under the arms and at the neck of his baggy grey T-shirt. 'Still did. The old songs, you know?'

Thorne nodded, remembering something he'd been thinking about in the room upstairs a few nights earlier.

Spoon, croon, honeymoon.

'So what, like Cole Porter or whatever?'

Cooper laughed. 'More like Gene Vincent or Eddie Cochran,' he said. 'Dad was a Teddy boy.'

'Oh, right,' Thorne said. It was easy to forget that those who seemed so old – even to him – had once been every bit as rebellious in their day as those who came after them. That bondage trousers and Mohicans were no more shocking than drain-pipes and DAs. He tried to picture the old man in all the gear, dressed to the nines in velvet drape coat and winkle-pickers, but the picture would not come.

The yellowing teeth, the sliver of greyish tongue . . .

Cooper stood up. 'You said something about the bedroom?'

They followed him upstairs, waited behind him as he hesitated on the threshold for just a second or two, then stepped inside. There were more bags and boxes. The dressing table and the window ledge, on which Thorne remembered seeing arrangements of family photos, were bare. The bed had been stripped.

'You haven't thrown anything away, have you?' Thorne asked.

Cooper turned to look at him. 'No.'

'No, of course not. I didn't mean . . .'

'Just haven't had the chance yet,' Cooper said. 'That's all. There'll certainly be a few trips to the charity shop once I'm finished, mind you. I mean obviously there's loads of stuff that means a lot, but Paula and I both agreed that there's no point hanging on to clothes or what have you. The knick-knacks, you know?'

Thorne nodded, thinking about his father.

Thinking that there had been no need to choose what to wrap carefully in brown paper and what to bag up for Oxfam. That there had been nothing much of anything left after the fire.

'All the stuff's still in here,' Cooper said. 'So, help yourself.'

'Thanks,' Thorne said. 'Shouldn't take long.'

'I'm still not exactly clear what it's all about, mind you.'

Thorne exchanged a look with Hendricks. 'Well, there's still the possibility of an inquest and, if that happens, I want to be sure my memory of exactly what was in this room that night is as clear as possible.' Cooper considered this for a few seconds and shrugged. 'Just belt and braces, really,' Thorne said. In fact, now that the suicide had been signed off on and the cause of death established beyond doubt, an inquest was extremely unlikely, but Thorne's explanation had obviously sounded reasonable enough. It would have been just his luck had Andrew Cooper turned out to be a lawyer or a coroner's officer.

Thorne felt uncomfortable lying, but it was certainly an easier reason to give for his presence than the real one, and not just because of the distress that might have caused.

'So what if we *do* find it?' Hendricks had asked him in the car. 'What the hell use d'you think it's going to be anyway?'

'Not a clue,' Thorne had said.

Hendricks had groaned, but Thorne had not intended the pun.

Despite Cooper's invitation to help themselves, he remained in the doorway as Thorne and Hendricks began to search.

It only took a few minutes.

They began with the bin-bags, as they seemed more likely to be destined for the charity shop than the boxes and Thorne guessed that what he was after would not be among the items of sentimental value. It was easy enough to assess the contents of each black bag quickly and it was Hendricks who found what they had come looking for in only the third bag he had rummaged through.

He said, 'Here you go,' and handed it to Thorne.

'What?' Cooper said, from the doorway.

The book of crossword puzzles. The tatty paperback that Thorne had seen lying on the floor on Margaret Cooper's side of the bed. On the floor below the bedside table on which book and glasses had been so neatly arranged.

What was wrong with the picture?

'Why was it on the floor?' Thorne had asked as they were driving down.

'I don't know,' Hendricks had said. 'Because she dropped it?'

'When though? It's not like you inject insulin and then bang, you're spark out a second later and the book you're reading falls from your hand, anything like that. And more to the point, I don't

94

think you spend a few minutes knocking off a crossword just before you and your old man top yourselves, do you? You do something like that because it's the same thing you do every night before you go to sleep. That's her routine, right? Same as taking her teeth out in the bathroom. That's what she does on a normal night.'

'It might have been lying there from the night before.'

'No way.' Thorne had shaken his head, adamant. 'Everything else on her side of the bed was neat. Methodical. Just that book on the floor, because maybe she *meant* to drop it . . .'

On his knees, Thorne opened the book and flicked through the pages, past dozens of completed crosswords. He stopped at the first one that was incomplete; the one he believed Margaret Cooper had been busy with on the night she and her husband had died.

The words were easy enough to spot.

The blue biro pressed heavily against the paper, the letters that little bit thicker than the others in the grid.

In seven squares towards the bottom.

HELP US

CHAPTER 13

There's actually a rhythm to it, like what do you call it, like a woodpecker or something. A rat-tat-tat.

The noise that the gun barrel makes against the old man's teeth.

He was trembling enough before – probably had that shaky thing in his hands same as lots of old people have – so it's hardly surprising that it's going like billy-o, now he's got the barrel rattling around in there.

Herbert pulls the gun from his mouth. He fights for breath. He's dribbling and gasping like they might not even need the bloody gun and he says, 'Please . . .'

He's sitting in a chair, probably the same one he sits in to watch TV which is currently tuned to one of those cable channels that show endless repeats. An episode of *The Sweeney*, which is quite funny, all things considered. The TV is turned up nice and loud.

'Come on now. We've been through this.'

'I can't,' Herbert splutters.

There are *two* guns, of course: the one he pressed

into the old man's shaky hand and the one he's currently pointing at the old man's head. Months before, putting all this together, he'd realised he'd need an extra incentive for this one. Something that would stop Herbert simply turning the gun round and pointing it at him. A threat over and above the big one.

'Do you want me to show you again?'

'No,' Herbert says.

'One more look? Might help you feel a bit braver.'

'No!' The old man shakes his head and it's hard to tell if it's tears or sweat that's spattering the collar of his shirt.

'Right. Lovely. So, shut up and get on with it.' He steps back, the gun still pointed, just far enough away to avoid the mess, though he's fairly sure which way that will all be going. He waves a finger. 'You need to angle it up a bit as well.'

Herbert puts the gun back into his mouth. Pushing it past lips that don't want to open, teeth that refuse to stop chattering. He gags and withdraws the barrel an inch or two.

'Probably tastes a bit . . . oily, doesn't it?'

Fear was all he'd seen last thing from the others. Piss-yourself terror, but this one's a game old bird, had to give him that much. Naked bloody hatred in this one's eyes for those few seconds before they close and his finger jerks against the trigger.

Done and dusted.

Not quite so much noise as he was expecting, no more than a banger going off, but he was right about the mess. He puts his gun back in the bag and steps forward to have a good look.

There's stuff stuck to the wall, like bits of mince and eggshell and it gives it a . . . texture. Same as, what was it called? Flock wallpaper.

Like an Indian restaurant.

PART II

YOUR BLOODY JOB

CHAPTER 14

'OK?'

Helen looked up to see DC Gill Bellinger leaning against her desk, papers in hand; just passing. Helen nodded and smiled, but Bellinger did not seem in any hurry to go anywhere. Keen for a little more than a smile and a nod.

'Yeah, fine,' Helen said.

If not quite on a daily basis, Helen certainly heard it every few days. She heard it at the coffee machine, in the cafeteria, during stilted and unnecessary 'catch-ups' with her DCI. She heard it from good friends and distant colleagues, auxiliary staff she barely knew. The same question or some variation on it.

'How's tricks, Helen?'

'So, what's up?'

'Good day?'

Wherever, whenever, whoever; she knew very well what they meant.

Are you all right?

And she knew what they were really asking.

Are you sure you didn't come back to work a little

too soon? Should you not have had a few more of those counselling sessions?

She did her best to answer the questions as casually as they had been asked, but it wasn't easy, because she had begun to grow tired of the concern. Now, even the lamest of jokes or most gentle of enquiries could cause her to snap at someone. This was stupid, because it would only confirm what some of them thought they already knew. She was on edge at best, unstable at worst, and this was anything but ideal when it came to working with abused children.

So she told herself she was being paranoid and tried to curb her temper.

'Fine,' she said again.

Bellinger laid down her paperwork on Helen's desk. She leaned closer and lowered her voice. 'So, how's things with Tom?'

Gill Bellinger was the member of the team Helen trusted most, a solid drinking partner when one was needed and a good friend who had done all she could to take care of Helen's family during the siege three months before. She was also the only person Helen had told about Thorne; a slip, during one of those much-needed drinking sessions. She and Thorne had decided it might not be a sensible idea to go public about their relationship just yet, both well aware that the circumstances in which they had got together – that first tender moment, an honour guard of armed police and Thorne awash with another

102

man's blood – were likely to set too many tongues wagging.

'All good,' Helen said.

'He coping, then?'

Helen looked at her friend. Thought: What, coping better than I am, you mean? Coping with *me*? Then she saw Bellinger's expression change and understood that she had been talking about Thorne's reassignment to uniform. She told herself to calm down.

'Yeah, I think so.'

'Better than we would, I bet,' Bellinger said, laughing. 'God, can you imagine?' She straightened her nicely cut grey jacket and gave a mock shudder. 'Back into those bloody black skirts and old lady tights. Or even worse, the *trousers*!'

Helen nodded towards her computer. 'Sorry, Gill, I'm up to my eyeballs.'

'No probs.' Bellinger gathered up her files and stepped away. 'We'll catch up later . . .'

Helen raised a hand and smiled again and wondered how best to avoid her friend for the rest of the day.

'Lunchtime, maybe,' Bellinger said.

Helen went back to the document on her screen. A statement from the neighbour of a two-year-old discovered at home alone with multiple fractures. A woman who claimed to have been 'worried about that poor child' for months, but not quite worried enough to have picked up the phone and let anyone know.

Thorne was coping pretty well, Helen decided. Certainly a damn sight better than she would be in the same circumstances, Gill Bellinger had been right about that much. Some days were a little more difficult than others, of course. There were . . . silences. There were times when it was best for them to avoid one another and when she couldn't wait for him to bugger off back to Kentish Town and sulk on his own. Tom Thorne was nobody's ray of sunshine 24/7, but she'd heard enough about him to know that he was a moody bugger long before he'd been bumped off the Murder Squad. It didn't bother her too much, because she knew it was something they had in common. Any copper who didn't know what a black mood felt like wasn't doing their job properly. It was just a question of how you chose to handle it, that was all. The people, the things you turned to.

The music, now that *was* an issue, the dead dogs and the lost loves, but it was a minor irritation, all things considered.

Helen tried to focus. The neighbour of the injured child who demanded to know why it had taken this long for the police to do anything. 'We could all hear the poor little beggar crying,' she'd said.

Things had certainly been tense between the two of them over the last few days, since that Friday night shift. Thorne had got a bee in his bonnet about those suicides, about being so firmly put in his place and it was clear that he had been expecting a little more support from her. They had not spoken since the afternoon before, when he'd driven off to meet up with Phil Hendricks. She looked at her watch. He was probably still sleeping off a hangover; the last day's rest before he was back at work.

A little more support . . .

Helen glanced across and saw that Gill Bellinger was watching her from the other side of the office. She turned back to her screen and reminded herself that were it not for the bee in Thorne's bonnet three months before, she might not be sitting where she was.

He would still be doing a job he loved.

She would call him at lunchtime, she decided. See what he was up to. She could see if her sister would take Alfie for a few hours, then offer to drive up to Kentish Town and they could have dinner in that Indian place he was always banging on about.

A young DC stopped at her desk on his way back from the Gents. She looked up at him and smiled.

'Everything all right, Helen?' he asked.

CHAPTER 15

'A couple of hours, Dave. That's all.'

'So, what?' Holland said. 'I just stroll out, do I?'

'Why not?'

'Nip down there on my lunch break and pretend I got lost on my way to the canteen?'

'You'll think of something,' Thorne said.

'Right.'

'Maybe you can say you were visiting a source.'

Thorne waited, listened to Holland breathing on the other end of the phone. He pictured the space Holland was in, one he knew well. He imagined him at his desk in the Incident Room, head down, keen to avoid eye contact with anyone during a conversation he almost certainly should not be having. Holland had known as soon as he'd answered the phone. Thorne had heard it in his tentative greeting, the nervousness as his voice had dropped to a whisper, the pause before the inevitable question.

What can I do for you?

'What about afterwards?' Holland asked.

'I don't know,' Thorne said.

'Good to know you're thinking ahead.'

'We'll cross that bridge when we come to it.'

'It's the *we* that's worrying me.'

'Come on, Dave . . .'

Thorne waited again. Blinked away the faces of Andrew Cooper, Neil Hackett, Trevor Jesmond. Wasn't crossing the bridge what had got him into this situation to begin with? He drummed his fingers against the edge of the table, reached for his mug and took a slurp of lukewarm tea. The low rumble of a train heading from Kentish Town to Gospel Oak rose up through the floorboards and was swiftly followed by the gentle tinkling of glasses in the kitchen cabinet. One of the reasons he'd been able to buy the flat so cheaply.

'Dave . . .?'

He had not slept much the night before. The rush after finding Margaret Cooper's message had only intensified as he and Hendricks had driven north again, as they had talked, argued about what to do next. Now, he could still taste the adrenalin, its metallic tang like a reminder of a heavy night's boozing on that first morning belch. Eight o'clock on a shitty Monday and, notwithstanding the lack of sleep, he felt fresher, more awake than he had in a long time. He wanted to crack on. He wanted to be out of the door and away before any of those second thoughts Hendricks had been so insistent upon.

'Let's talk about *career* suicide,' Hendricks had said when Thorne had dropped him off. Standing on the pavement, the thump of a bass and the shouts of late-night revellers drifting down from Camden High Street. Leaning down to stare back at Thorne through the open car door. 'You know that's what this is, don't you?'

'You a shrink now, as well?'

'Just a mate,' Hendricks had said.

'This about the other night?' Holland asked now. 'You showing up at that suicide in Stanmore?'

'It's . . . connected, yeah.'

'I think I might need a bit more than that.'

Thorne could hear phones ringing in the background, the buzz of voices in the Murder Room. The same seductive hubbub that had made his blood pump a little quicker for so many years, that had left him feeling dizzy when he'd walked into the MIT at Lewisham.

He glanced around his living room. He could do it from here if he had to, from one room, with one phone. Push came to shove, he could do it from his *car*.

He gave Holland the highlights, swallowed the last of his tea.

'So . . . say I go down there,' Holland said. 'I talk to whoever and it *is* part of the same thing—'

'The same series of murders.'

'Yeah, say it is. Then you hand this over, right? You make sure there's a proper investigation.'

'I'll do whatever needs to be done.'

'I've known you too long,' Holland said.

'For what?'

'For that to fill me with any confidence. To be thinking anything except I should run a mile.'

Thorne pressed the phone against his ear. Rubbed the side of his face. 'Listen, maybe I should ask somebody else.'

'Who?' Holland asked. Spat on a whisper, the anger clear enough. 'Who else are you going to ask?' Now, it was Holland's turn to wait. 'Give me one good reason,' he said, eventually. The anger was gone and now there was only resignation. 'Just one.'

Because you're a friend? Thorne thought. No. Because you're a good copper, because once, at least, you wanted nothing more than to be one. Maybe. Thorne remembered what Christine Treasure had said to him, the excitement she felt coming into work, and he remembered the way she had disparaged the desk-jockey detective.

'What else are you going to be doing, Dave?' he asked. 'Watching CCTV footage for hours on end? Talking to the wankers at mobile phone companies?'

When the call was finished and Holland had folded the piece of paper on which he'd scribbled the relevant information into his pocket, he looked up to see Yvonne Kitson on the other side of his desk.

'All very secret squirrel,' she said.

'What?'

'All that whispering.' She smiled and nodded, sipped from a plastic cup of coffee. 'Now, you're blushing. Something I shouldn't know about? Something *Sophie* shouldn't know about?'

Holland tried to manufacture a story and quickly decided that some truth would make the lie more convincing than none at all.

'Thorne,' he said.

Kitson raised an eyebrow. 'He tell you what the hell he was up to the other night? Aside from getting a bollocking, that is.'

'He's got a spare ticket for the Spurs game, Wednesday night.'

'You don't like football.'

'I don't think there's anyone else he could ask,' Holland had said.

They talked for a few minutes about a case they had caught the day before: a fatal stabbing at a christening in Tufnell Park. When Kitson had gone, Holland went back to the report he had been working on when Thorne called. He thought about those few seconds spent staring at the caller ID and wondering whether to let the call go through to his answerphone. He wondered whether choosing to answer it would rank as one of the stupidest decisions he'd made in a while. He wondered how well Yvonne Kitson's bullshit detector was working that morning, and how long he could reasonably get away with taking for lunch.

Twenty minutes or so before his destination, Thorne pulled into a service station on the M4. He filled up the car with petrol, bought a coffee and took one bite of a croissant that tasted as though it had been baked several days earlier. Then, he called Helen.

'Heavy night, was it?' she asked.

'Not particularly.' He pulled off the forecourt and eased the BMW on to the slip road back to the motorway. He glanced at the clock on the dash. It was just after nine thirty. 'It's not that late.'

'No, I just thought you might have called last night.'

'Sorry.' Thorne waited for a lorry to go by in the inside lane, then pulled out and accelerated past it. 'Just putting the world to rights with Phil, you know how it is. By the time I got home it was after eleven and I didn't want to wake you up.'

'It's fine,' Helen said. 'I don't know why you didn't have a lie-in this morning though. Make the most of your days off.'

'I know,' Thorne said. Two more days until he was back at work on the early shift. 'I've got a fair bit of running around to do, so . . .'

'Are you driving?'

'Yeah, I'm just going up to the garage in Highgate,' Thorne said. He pulled into the outside lane and pushed the car up to eighty. 'The brakes felt a bit spongy yesterday, so I'm going to try and get the pads changed.'

'You've still not got that hands-free kit sorted, have you?'

'I'll get round to it.'

'Last thing you need is to get nicked.'

'Yeah, I know,' Thorne said.

'Why don't you talk to the garage about it while you're there? See if they can fit one while you wait?'

Thorne grunted, thinking that getting pulled over for using his mobile while driving would not be too much of a blot in a copybook that was already full of them. More blot than copybook, if truth be told.

Not that there was much of that going on.

'Listen, I was thinking about tonight,' Helen said.

'Actually, I might be seeing Phil again,' Thorne said quickly.

'Really?'

'Boyfriend problems.' He glanced at the sign for the next turnoff; three more to go. 'I mean God knows why I'm the only one he can talk to about this stuff, but there you go.' Helen said nothing. All Thorne could hear was crackle on the line and the soft *shush* of his tyres on a motorway still wet after early-morning rain. 'Obviously I'm going to try and get back, but I don't know how late it'll be, so . . .'

'Not if you've had a drink,' Helen said.

'Well, if I can't, I'll make sure I'm there for when you get in tomorrow night, yeah?'

'OK, whatever.' There was another pause. 'I'd better get back anyway, so—'

'Yeah, I'll let you go.'

'Don't forget about that hands-free thing.'

'Have a good day,' Thorne said.

112

Helen said, 'You too,' and hung up.

Thorne tossed his phone on to the passenger seat and slowed a little as he drew close to a van that showed no inclination to pull over. He reached to reload the CD that had been playing when he'd stopped. Listening to George Jones and Tammy Wynette, loved-up and singing, 'We're Gonna Hold On', he tried not to think about the concern in Helen's voice and how many lies he had told her in a two-minute phone conversation.

George and Tammy had divorced two years after recording that song.

Ten minutes later he was drifting on to the slip road at Junction 10 and trying to imagine how the conversation he was about to have might go. How to play it. Along with the coffee and the sugary cardboard of that croissant, he could still taste the metal in his mouth.

A dozen, he had told her. A dozen lies at least. And all to cover up the biggest lie of all.

CHAPTER 16

'I've got a spare key,' she said. 'Just to be on the safe side, you know? I suppose I could always have called a neighbour or the police or whatever, asked them to pop round, but I just had this feeling when he wasn't answering the phone, so I drove down there and let myself in.' The woman's face tightened. 'I could smell it the second I walked through the door.'

'How long had it been?' Thorne asked.

It was not in the information he had been sent by Elly Kennedy, so Thorne did not know how many days the body of Brian Gibbs had lain undiscovered in the bath before his daughter had found it. How advanced the decomposition had been.

She shook her head. 'It wasn't much more than a few hours, I don't think, but it wasn't . . . that. It was the blood. I could smell the blood.'

'Right,' Thorne said.

'Like meat, when it's on the turn.'

They were sitting in the front room of a three-bedroom semi, in a quiet cul-de-sac that backed on to a golf course a mile or so from the centre of Wokingham. Looking around as Thorne had entered, it was apparent that the woman he had come to see was fond of crime novels, Impressionist prints and scatter cushions, while the sweat that began to bead on his forehead almost immediately told him that she liked to keep the temperature in her home ridiculously high. He was happy enough to take his jacket off, though he still felt far from relaxed. Perched on the edge of the armchair opposite him, fingers interlaced on her knees, Jacqui Gibbs was clearly no more relaxed than he was.

'Like meat,' she said again, a little more quietly this time.

During the silence that followed, a small, fat terrier wandered into the room. It was not the prettiest of dogs, with rheumy eyes and a pronounced underbite, but Jacqui clearly found it adorable. She rubbed its ears for half a minute and talked softly to it, before ordering the dog back to its basket in the kitchen. As it waddled away, Thorne said, 'I don't mind dogs.'

'He's old,' Jacqui said. 'Starting to do his business all over the place, bumping into things. I know I should really take him to the vets, but I can't bring myself.'

'It's not easy,' Thorne said.

She looked around the room as though seeing it for the first time. 'I mean, it's just me, isn't it, rattling around in here? Be even worse once he goes and I don't think I could get another one. Not for a while, anyway.'

The room was immaculate; it smelled of polish and some kind of plug-in freshener. People often tidied up before the police paid a visit, but Thorne guessed that this woman had not made a special effort. He looked down at the plate of perfectly arranged digestives and chocolate fingers that she had brought in with the tea.

'Have one,' she said.

Thorne said, 'Thank you,' and took a digestive. The chocolate fingers were already starting to melt.

'My husband and I got divorced as soon as our youngest went to college,' she said. Chewing, Thorne looked across at her and she smiled. 'Stupid really. You stay together because of the kids and then just when they're all set to head out into the big bad world you make it clear that you've actually been unhappy for however many years and they feel terrible. Why do people do that?'

Thorne shrugged. 'I've not got any kids, so . . .'

'So, that's why I'm a Gibbs,' she said. 'Went back to my maiden name as soon as we'd separated. In case you were wondering.'

Thorne had already worked it out, but said, 'OK,' anyway.

'I'm Gibbs on the internet,' she said.

Thorne waited.

'Internet dating, you know?' She waved away any comment that he might be about to make, though Thorne had no intention of saying anything. 'And yes, you do have to watch out for the odd perv or whatever, but there's hundreds of thousands of people doing it these days, especially if you're my age and there's not much chance of meeting anyone at work. I do all the IT at an estate agent's in town and they're all about twelve!'

Thorne laughed and she laughed too, and he could feel a trickle of sweat moving behind his ear. Jacqui Gibbs was somewhere in her mid-to-late forties. She was the kind of woman Christine Treasure would have described as 'milftastic' and slowed the Fanny Magnet down to get a good look at. If there was any grey in her dark hair she had dyed it out and her jeans and well-cut white shirt accentuated a figure that a woman twenty years younger would have been happy with. Thorne guessed that she would attract rather more 'pervs' than she had bargained for.

'I mean, I'm looking for someone who's at *least* eighteen!'

Nerves or loneliness? Whatever the reason, it was evident that Jacqui Gibbs wanted to talk. Thorne was happy enough to let her, relieved to see her relaxing a little, though he was keen to get back to the subject of her father and the manner in which he had died. As it was, she did not make him wait very long.

'He was doing so well, that's the stupid thing.' She spoke casually, as if they had been talking about her father's death the whole time, as though she had not yanked the conversational wheel and veered away on to her search for love, the way her divorce had messed up her kids or the health of her terrier. 'He was in a right state after Mum went, but that was five years ago now and he'd sorted himself out. There were a few bits and pieces health-wise, course there were . . . he couldn't get around as well as he had done and his hearing was definitely getting a lot worse . . . but he was happy enough.'

'That's good,' Thorne said.

'No, not happy *enough*. He was happy.'

'What did you think when you found him like that?'

'I thought it was . . . ridiculous,' she said. 'It sounds a bit mad, I know, what with the knife and all that, but looking at him lying there, and all that blood . . . I thought it must have been an accident or something. I mean, all sorts of stupid things go through your head, don't they?'

'Course they do,' Thorne said.

She looked at him. They listened as a car drove slowly past, the low growl and frantic thump of oversized speakers turned up way too loud. Some drum 'n' bass fanatic on his way to play golf.

'You said something about "looking at Dad's death again".' Once more she moved her hands on to her knees, the fingers locked around one another. 'On the phone, that's what you said. What does that mean exactly?'

This was why Thorne was there and there was no easy way to get into it.

'Can you think of any reason why someone might want to hurt your father?'

'Hurt him?'

'I don't think it was suicide,' he said.

'But I saw him.'

'I think it was made to look like suicide.'

Jacqui said, 'What?' and then thought for a few moments. She took a deep breath and set down her tea, and said, 'I suppose it's still too early for something a bit stronger.'

A quick look at Google Maps told Holland that Graham Daniels lived no more than a few minutes from the reservoir in which his mother had drowned five weeks earlier. It also confirmed that his work address was only a mile and a half from where Holland was based at the Peel Centre. There and back in an hour, tops. By mid-morning, Kitson was deep into a meeting, so Holland decided to go while he had the chance. The lunch hour would have been marginally less risky, but it made sense to try and get away before the man he was going to see had the chance to disappear in search of his own lunch.

Made sense. Like doing it made any bloody sense at all.

It was a small printing business on a busy stretch of West Hendon Broadway, in a parade of shops between St Patrick's Roman Catholic Church and Hendon Mosque. There were no customers waiting. A man and a woman were at work behind the counter, so Holland was fairly sure that the man in the *Pleased-2-Print* T-shirt stepping forward to greet him was Graham Daniels. He was tall and balding and his smile revealed teeth that had yellowed near the gums.

Holland showed his warrant card and asked if he could have a chat. The man stopped smiling and stared at him, and Holland said, 'About your mother.'

Daniels thought about it for a few seconds, then told the young woman, who was busy at a guillotine at the back of the shop, that he would not be gone long.

'My daughter,' he said, following Holland out on to the pavement and reaching for cigarettes. 'Only supposed to be helping out, earning a few quid before she goes to college, but now she reckons she's enjoying herself so much she might not bother with college at all.'

They walked towards a small café a few doors along. It was dry but windy, and while Daniels struggled to light his cigarette, Holland fastened his jacket to prevent his tie flapping.

'What do you think?' he asked.

'I'm torn, if I'm honest,' Daniels said. 'Obviously I want her to go, but it's great having her around, you know? Her mother certainly wants her to go, mind you, so I probably won't have a lot of say in it.'

'Right,' Holland said, like he knew what Daniels meant.

Once Daniels had finished his cigarette, they found a seat in a quiet-ish corner and Holland bought them both a cup of coffee. As soon as it was laid in front of him, Daniels said, 'So, what about my mother?'

'Can you tell me what happened?' Holland asked.

Daniels looked shocked, then annoyed. 'Don't you *know*?'

'Broadly,' Holland said. 'This is a . . . separate investigation.'

Daniels considered this for a few seconds. He sighed heavily. 'She walked out of her front door in the middle of the night in her slippers and dressing gown. She walked across a main road and across the field to the Welsh Harp. That's the Brent reservoir . . .'

Holland nodded.

'She took off her slippers and her dressing gown and she . . . walked into the water.' He swallowed. 'They found the dressing gown neatly folded in the mud the next morning. Her slippers were side by side. Then they found her. OK?'

'How do you know all this?'

'There was CCTV,' Daniels said. 'Bloody everything's on CCTV these days, isn't it? Only as far as the field, and they were able to piece the rest together.' He stared down into his coffee. 'It wasn't the easiest thing to watch.'

'No, I'm sure it wasn't,' Holland said.

'So?' Daniels picked up his cup, studied Holland

across the top of it. 'Listen, I really don't want to be away from the shop too long.'

'Was there anyone else on that footage?'

Daniels blinked. 'Why would there be?'

'I just need to make sure.'

'It was the middle of the night.'

'Nobody walking the same way she was? Just ahead of her or behind her, maybe?'

'I've got no idea,' Daniels said. 'I only watched the bits that my mother was in.' He raised a hand, let it drop to the tabletop again. 'Look, obviously I'm missing something here, because you seem to be suggesting . . . well, I don't know what you're suggesting, but—'

'At the time, you said you were shocked that your mother had taken her own life.'

'Christ, of course I was shocked. Wouldn't you be?'

'No, more than that,' Holland said. 'You talked about how she'd booked a holiday. How she was the last person in the world who would do anything like that.'

'Yes, she'd booked a holiday.' Daniels drew a nicotine-stained finger slowly back and forth along the edge of the table. 'She was a member of a gardening club and she drove to the cinema once a week. She read books and had friends and she loved her grandchildren. She had a life . . . she had a good life and deciding to end it like that was something I never dreamed she might do, not in a million years. None of us did. That doesn't mean that I thought there might be any other explanation. I mean, bloody hell . . . it doesn't mean I thought for one second that somebody else might have . . . been responsible.'

Holland leaned forward a little and lowered his voice. 'Look, I know this is out of the blue,' he said. 'But I need to tell you we're looking at exactly that possibility.'

'*Possibility?*' Daniels opened his mouth and closed it again. 'Based on what? Have you got evidence?'

'I can't really go into details,' Holland said. 'Look, I know this is a lot to take in.'

Daniels appeared to take it in quickly enough. 'Who?' he asked. Then, 'Why, for God's sake?'

'That's something you might like to give some thought to. Maybe talk to some of her friends.'

'Me?'

Holland nodded. *Yes, because this 'investigation' I'm banging on about does not exactly have the biggest of teams working on it.* 'They might be a bit more comfortable talking to you,' he said.

'This is stupid.' Daniels shook his head. 'She was a seventy-year-old woman, there's no reason anyone would want to hurt her. She got on with everyone.'

'We need to make sure,' Holland said.

'So, how . . .?' Daniels' voice cracked. He lowered his head. 'Do you think someone took her into the reservoir? Pushed her . . .?'

'Was your mum a strong swimmer?'

'She was *seventy*, I told you. It was freezing that night. Just the shock of the water must have . . .'

Daniels' voice was raised now and he pushed away tears with the heel of his hand. There were people looking across at them from other tables.

'I'm sorry,' Holland said.

'Are your parents still alive?'

The affectionate father was long gone now and Holland could only sit staring at the bereaved son, whose grief was still all too real and raw. Holland had been confronted with more than his fair share of anguish over the years. He had delivered death messages, stood at hospital bedsides, watched fathers, mothers, husbands and wives break down and demand to be told what to do; told how they were ever supposed to get up in the morning again. That was work. That was what he was paid to deal with.

But this was not his job.

He did not have to do this, should not have let himself get talked into doing it, and at that moment he could happily have punched Tom Thorne.

Thorne pulled on his jacket and watched Jacqui Gibbs pour herself a second small measure of Glenlivet.

'I won't tell anyone,' he said.

She shrugged. 'Who's going to care?' She took a sip, then stood as she saw Thorne move towards the living-room door.

'It's fine,' Thorne said. 'Stay there.'

She walked over to him anyway and they stood together, a little awkwardly, in the open doorway.

'It's funny,' she said. 'Everything you've told me, I mean it's not exactly good news . . . I still can't take it in if I'm honest, but I feel better. Does that make any sense?'

'I think so,' Thorne said.

'If somebody did this, at least it means that Dad hadn't been miserable. He wasn't so unhappy that he'd do that to himself.'

Thorne told her that he understood, though in clinging to that meagre crumb of comfort, he knew that she was somehow ignoring the pain that her father must have suffered. The terror Brian Gibbs must surely have felt at the end. Perhaps the full implications of what she'd been told had not sunk in yet, or maybe that small measure of Glenlivet had been one too many.

Thorne stepped out into the hall.

Jacqui followed him and at the front door he took a card from his wallet and gave it to her. It was an old one, with his mobile number only and with the word *Detective* coming before the word *Inspector*. If he were ever called upon to answer for it, he would say that he had simply handed over an old card by mistake. He doubted that a single misleading word on a business card would be the worst of his problems by that point.

He tried not to think about it too much.

'Call me on that number if there's anything you want to talk about,' he said. 'Or if anything occurs to you.'

Thorne doubted that anything would. He was

almost certain that no run-of-the-mill motive would emerge for the murder of Brian Gibbs or for any of the others. Not that he'd told Jacqui Gibbs there were any others.

'I'll do my best,' she said.

He had not gone there expecting the woman to reel off a list of her father's mortal enemies or to name the individual who had borne a terrible grudge against him after a falling-out over dominoes in the local pub. 'I mean it,' he said. 'You can call me any time you like, about anything.'

'Thank you,' she said. 'It's really nice that you're taking such a personal interest in whatever happened to my dad. You don't expect that kind of thing these days. Everything's call centres, isn't it?'

Thorne nodded and turned away in case the guilt washed blood to his face. Because he was keeping the truth from her. Because, in the interests of self-preservation, he needed her to call him and nobody else. And because he knew that taking such a 'personal' interest rather than handing it over to others who would do the job properly might be the very thing that enabled her father's killer to escape justice.

As he reached for the door, he cast an eye across the framed photographs on a shelf above the radiator.

'What's this?' he asked. He picked up a tarnished frame and studied its contents. He had seen many such pictures before. On a manicured lawn in the sunshine or occasionally outside Scotland Yard, with that iconic sign spinning slowly behind them. The same formation of smartly dressed men and women, senior police officers in dress uniform on either side.

The same ceremony.

Jacqui Gibbs stepped close to him and looked down at the picture. 'Oh, Dad got some kind of medal or a commendation or whatever. Donkey's years ago, this was.' She placed a fingertip to the glass. 'Doesn't he look lovely in that suit?'

'A commendation for what?'

'God, I'm trying to remember it all,' she said. 'He never talked about it that much afterwards. I mean, I can remember us all getting dolled up the day he got it. The dress I was wearing, all that. I'd've been about fourteen, something like that, so that tells you how far back we're talking.'

Thorne waited, tried hard to keep the impatience from his face. 'It would be good if you could really have a think about this.'

'There was a trial,' she said. 'He was a witness at a trial. I'm sure he must have kept all the newspaper cuttings . . .'

A few minutes later, when Jacqui had finished telling him as much as she could remember, she said, 'Do you think this might have something to do with what happened? I saw the look on your face.'

127

'I've no idea,' Thorne said. It was a fact, but so was the tickle at the nape of his neck, his desire to get out of the house as quickly as possible and make a call.

'Do you want to hang on to it?' she asked. 'The picture?'

Thorne looked at it again.

'No, really,' she said. 'It's fine. I mean, I want it back, obviously.'

Thorne guessed that the photograph would not be of any further use. He knew the way the commendation system worked – that there were only a small number of such ceremonies each year and that the members of the public honoured had been of assistance in any number of different investigations – but he thanked her anyway and promised that the photograph would be taken care of.

'I need to clean it up a bit. It got so filthy up in Dad's loft.'

As Thorne walked away from the front door, she was still clutching his card and saying, 'I'll call if I can think of anything else.'

The second he was out of sight and walking quickly towards the car, Thorne reached for his phone. Holland was rather short with him when he answered.

'Listen, I'll be quick,' Thorne said. 'When you talk to Graham Daniels—'

'I'm with him now,' Holland said.

'OK, that's great,' Thorne said. He pressed the

remote on his key fob to unlock the BMW. 'Call me when you've finished. Just make sure you ask him what his mother was doing thirty years ago.'

CHAPTER 17

Monday was a quiet night in the Grafton Arms. No laughter or salsa music from the room upstairs to disturb those in search of a little something to take the edge off before they got home or others quietly drinking away the evening. The mechanised soundtrack of till and fruit machine was lively enough for all concerned. There was certainly nothing close to exuberance from the three men at a table in the corner. This, despite the progress they had made that morning and had continued to make, thanks to the one sitting nearest the toilets; the one who looked the least happy of any of them to be there in the first place.

Thorne handed him his pint and sat down. Said, 'Listen, Dave, I know you've still got concerns, all right?'

Holland swallowed and grunted into his glass.

'I just want you to know I'm taking them on board.'

'How, exactly?'

Thorne's turn to drink.

'I still don't know why you're not handing this

across.' Holland looked to the third man at the table for some support. 'Especially now, I mean, Christ . . .'

'You're wasting your time,' Hendricks said. 'You have worked with him before, haven't you?'

Thorne flashed a sneer at his friend, then looked back to Holland. 'I tried,' he said. He remembered the look on Hackett's face when he'd walked across the bridge to the MIT, and that night in Stanmore. 'I tried on several occasions and I was politely told where to go. Only not very politely. I promise you, Dave, they think it's a joke.'

They think *I'm* a joke.

'Maybe they don't,' Hendricks said. 'Maybe it just suits them to sit on their hands.' He took a drink as Thorne and Holland turned to him and waited. 'Well, let's face it, suicides look a damn sight better on the balance sheet than unsolved murders, don't they?'

Thorne nodded, considering it. Hendricks had almost certainly been half joking himself, but what he had said was horribly plausible.

'Well if this goes tits up, we'll be the only ones who aren't laughing. The ones looking for jobs.'

'I really appreciate what you're doing, Dave. This morning, and the stuff you got for us this afternoon. That was over and above.'

Hendricks raised his glass in salute.

Holland's face softened, but only a little. He said, 'I must need my head looking at, seriously,' then pulled out a few folded sheets of paper from his pocket. He flattened them against the tabletop and handed the other two a copy each.

'It won't go tits up, Dave,' Thorne said.

'Why won't it?'

'Because we're going to catch him.'

Hendricks and Thorne looked at their printed sheets, pints in hand, as if casually perusing a menu of bar snacks. At the top of each sheet was a name.

Terence Mercer.

'He ran a very well-connected firm in south London from the mid-seventies onwards,' Holland said. 'Banks, building societies, security vans, all the usual.'

Thorne nodded. 'Back when the Flying Squad were top dogs, charging about in Cortinas and wearing sheepskin coats like they were on the telly.'

'That retro look's coming back in,' Hendricks said. 'Did you know that?'

'Anyway,' Holland said. 'Then in eighty-three a job went bad at this bank in Croydon and some of his firm got pinched. He only just made it away himself, but the Flying Squad got a tip-off that he was hiding out at an address in Crystal Palace. Bit of a disaster all round from that point on by the looks of things . . . left hand, right hand, all that . . . and the long and the short of it is that some poor DC goes in there without back-up and Mercer shoots him in the face in the back garden.'

'Bet that made a mess of his sheepskin,' Hendricks said.

'So, loads of press coverage, major trial at the Bailey blah blah, and Mercer gets life with a twenty-five-year minimum.' Holland glanced back down to his notes. 'The tariff's increased a few years later when Terence loses his rag in Maidstone and shanks a prison officer and from then on he gets shunted around, basically because one place after another gets sick of keeping him. Regular parole requests, all denied obviously, usual scenario . . . he does thirty years in the end and was finally released from Gartree prison seven weeks ago.'

'Three weeks before Brian Gibbs died,' Thorne said. 'And only a fortnight before Fiona Daniels.'

They laid their sheets of paper on the table.

'So Gibbs was a witness to the shooting,' Hendricks said.

'Saw it from his upstairs window.' Thorne put his drink down. 'Gave evidence, even though he was being threatened by some of Mercer's mates. That's why he got the medal. And Fiona Daniels worked in the bank.' He looked to Holland. 'Right?'

Holland nodded. 'She gave evidence too. I spoke to Andrew Cooper this afternoon and his dad was the doctor who provided the expert testimony about the gunshot injury. That's what proved conclusively that the police officer had been shot at point-blank range, that Mercer hadn't been where he said he was when the gun was fired. Proved it was an execution, pure and simple.'

Hendricks tore at a large bag of crisps, opened it lengthways and put it in the middle of the table.

Thorne and Holland dug in. 'So, basically, Terry's getting his afters on the people he thinks were responsible for having him put away. That's what connects the victims.'

'Basically,' Thorne said. He looked anything but delighted that the connection had been made. 'Piece of piss, this job.'

'Bloody hell!' Hendricks froze, about to put a handful of crisps into his mouth. 'How old must Mercer be?'

'He's seventy-three,' Holland said.

'There's going to be others.' Thorne leaned forward, reached for more crisps. 'Other witnesses, his legal team. God knows how many coppers. We'll need to make a list.' He glanced up at Holland, all three of them well aware that he was the one who would be able to put such a list together, the one with instant access to the computer systems. When the offer was not immediately forthcoming, Thorne stabbed a finger at the sheet of paper in front of him. 'Listen, thanks again for this, Dave. Seriously.'

Holland shrugged. 'Didn't need to do a lot of digging, if I'm honest. Most of that was straight off the internet.'

Thorne did not know if Holland was being modest or if he was simply trying to convince himself that he had not done too much that might get him into trouble later on. Looking at the notes, it was clear that plenty of material had been taken off files that would have demanded access to several Met databases. Access that would certainly have been fully logged and monitored.

'God bless Google,' Hendricks said. 'I reckon you'll be making good use of it.'

'Maybe we need to bring somebody else on board,' Thorne said. 'Spread the load a bit.' He looked at Holland. 'Make it a bit harder for them to join the dots later on, if it comes to that.'

'Such as?' Holland asked.

'What about Yvonne Kitson?'

Holland looked unsure. 'I reckon she's got more reason than most to say no.'

'I can only ask,' Thorne said. 'If she doesn't want to get involved, I think she'd just pass and forget I ever asked her. Got to be worth a try, though.'

'Maybe,' Holland said.

Hendricks began humming a tune and held up four fingers.

'What?' Thorne looked confused.

The tune became suddenly recognisable: Elmer Bernstein's iconic theme from *The Magnificent Seven*. Hendricks said, 'I'm Steve McQueen, obviously.'

Even Holland smiled. 'I reckon a Mexican bandit would be a damn sight easier to deal with than Terry Mercer. They had the villagers to help them, remember.'

'There'd have to be an address on file,' Thorne said, thinking out loud. 'Probation arrangements or whatever. Must be some way to get that without ruffling too many feathers.'

'What about the prison?' Hendricks asked.

Thorne nodded. 'I've got a contact up there. On top of which, I reckon it might be useful to find out who was visiting Mercer before he was released.' Looking at Holland and Hendricks, Thorne could see that they'd already reached the same conclusion he had. What Terry Mercer was doing would have taken a good deal of planning. For the killing to have begun so soon after he was released, there had to have been someone helping him.

'So, what about this list then?' Hendricks asked. Thorne had been fighting shy of coming straight out and asking Holland, but Hendricks clearly had no compunction.

Seeing Holland's hesitation, Thorne stood up, guessing that the time might not be right to push. 'Who wants another drink?'

When he returned and handed out the beers, Holland said, 'It's going to mean pulling another file.'

Thorne waited, sipped his beer like he was in no hurry.

'At least one other file.'

'You've done more than enough, Dave,' Thorne said. 'We're up and running, so if you'd prefer to call it quits now, that's not a problem. And however this pans out, it won't come back on you, I swear.'

Holland looked at Hendricks, then Thorne, then his beer. 'What the hell,' he said. 'In for a penny.'

Hendricks helped himself to the last of the crisps. Said, 'In for a P45 . . .'

CHAPTER 18

Some of them are dead already, obviously.

The ones who'd been knocking on a bit even back then – that hatchet-faced old bastard on the bench, who'd droned on about his duty to protect the public, the clear and present danger to society, all that – had happily turned up their toes while he was still inside. Saved him the trouble.

It's not a very long list, as it happens.

He holds it pressed against his chest as he lies on the bed and stares at the small TV in the corner, flicking through the stations, searching for something decent. Some bunch of Geordie kids shouting the odds, getting hammered and trying to sleep with one another. Another lot from Essex doing much the same thing. Gypsies, estate agents, bottle-blonde housewives who've been under the sunbed too long . . .

The phones that do everything but make the bloody toast, the computers you can hold in your hand, he couldn't really argue with any of that stuff, but Jesus H, the TV had gone to pot in the last thirty years.

He can hear the family moving about downstairs. The nephew of an old mate: some jumpy, tattooed coke dealer and his lovely wife; his three lovely kids. He'd heard the whispered argument earlier on, had a good laugh listening to the wife hissing and spitting and demanding to know how long the 'old man' was planning on staying. The man of the house begging her to keep it down, promising it wouldn't be for long and asking her to tell him what the hell else he was supposed to do?

It wouldn't be for long, of course. Maybe one more night in their youngest's bedroom and he'd be on his way. Leave them a nice bottle of Scotch for their trouble, perfume or something for the wife, and a good long look at the front door, just to make sure they'd forget he was ever there.

He lifts up the creased and tattered piece of paper and looks at his list, the names crossed off and the names of those he's yet to visit. The one he's saving until last.

It's personal, he wouldn't deny that, but how could it not be?

He never had time for busybodies, the ones who stuck their beaks in. They got what they deserved, simple as that, a long-overdue lesson about minding their own business. Them, and the ones who gave their so-called 'expert' opinions. People who saw nothing, who weren't even there, but decided because they'd got letters after their names that they were fully entitled to stand up in court – for a decent fee, let's not forget that – say their piece and help a jury decide how he was going to be spending the rest of his life.

Well, it might have taken a while, it might have been years since they'd forgotten his name, but eventually they learned that sometimes it's best to keep your opinions to yourself.

They finally found out what *he* was an expert in.

He hears the wife coming upstairs to get the kids into bed. She whispers, urging them to be quiet as they pass his door. She raises her voice just a little when the youngest starts whining and demands to know why he can't sleep in his own room.

'Who *is* he, anyway?'

It's a fair question. One he'd have to think about himself for a minute or two, if he was ever asked.

It's strange, but he can't remember what his ex-wife looks like any more, not clearly, and even when he dreams about his kids – wherever the hell they are – it's like he's seeing their faces through bubbly, coloured glass. But the faces of the men and women on his list, the way they *were* anyway, have never blurred, never so much as gone fuzzy around the edges.

Funny, he thinks, how love fades so much quicker than hate.

He smiles as he folds the list up and lays it down on the bedside table. He turns off the television and closes his eyes, listens to the sounds of the kids in the bathroom next door.

Anyone who said 'time heals' had clearly not done any.

CHAPTER 19

'He was grizzly all morning,' Helen said on the other end of the phone. 'Took me ages to get him ready and get out of the house and he was still crying when I left the childminder's.'

'Maybe he's coming down with something.'

'He didn't have a temperature.'

'I'm sure she'll call if she's worried.'

'I made sure there was Calpol in his bag anyway.'

'He'll be fine,' Thorne said. 'He just got out of the wrong side of the cot, that's all.'

'He is a bit funny sometimes, you know. If you're not there in the mornings.'

'Really?'

'Yeah, I've noticed. I mean, kids like routine, don't they?'

Thorne said, 'I suppose,' and watched a woman light a fresh cigarette from her nub-end. She closed her eyes as she flicked away the butt and the smoke escaped on a single breath. Thorne hadn't smoked for a long time, but had found himself thinking about it a lot in recent weeks. Perhaps it was because the last time he had smoked heavily was when he had been in uniform first time round. The association, the stress, whatever.

He wondered if the woman would give him one if he asked.

'What have you got on today, then?'

'I'm going to catch up on some paperwork,' Thorne said. 'Get it all out of the way before tomorrow.'

'Makes sense.'

'And there's a record fair in Camden, so I might wander down there if I get time.'

'Have fun,' Helen said. 'How was Phil, by the way?'

'Sorry?'

'Last night.'

'Oh, he was fine,' Thorne said.

'What about this boyfriend stuff?'

Thorne remembered the specifics of his lie. 'He's just being a drama queen,' he said. 'Just wanted to whinge, really.' He glanced across and saw that the smoker had moved away. 'Listen, I thought I might cook tonight.'

'Sounds good.'

'A chilli or something.'

'You want me to get the stuff?'

'No, I can do it,' Thorne said. 'I should be home by the time you get back—'

'Oh listen, I told Jenny she could come round for dinner tomorrow night, is that OK? I haven't seen her for a while, so . . .'

Helen's sister. Thorne had only met her once and he was not sure that she altogether approved of him and Helen living together. Being together. 'Yeah, course.'

'Not a big deal and she won't stay late. We'll probably just get a Chinese or whatever.'

'It's fine.'

'Great,' Helen said. 'Thanks. Oh, and I don't suppose you fancy picking Alfie up later, do you?'

Thorne hesitated; his day, for the most part, dependent on others. 'Yeah, that's probably all right.'

'You sure?'

'I'll call you if anything comes up.'

'Thanks.'

'Shouldn't be a problem though . . .'

When Helen had hung up, Thorne turned and walked back into St Pancras. The station had certainly been given one hell of an impressive makeover – the sculptures, the statues of lovers and poets, the longest champagne bar in Europe – though Thorne wondered, sumptuous as it undoubtedly was, why it seemed easier to buy a glass of Moët & Chandon or a designer suit than it was to find the platforms or the timetable. Annoyed, after walking around the concourse for ten minutes, he finally found the information board.

There was a train to Market Harborough in twenty minutes.

He wasn't sure if errant senior members of the Prison Service ever got slapped back down to the role of humble 'screw', but they certainly seemed to move around every bit as much as police officers. Thorne had known Caroline Dunn for the best part of ten years, during which time she had served on the management teams at Chelmsford, Wakefield and Long Lartin. She had been a deputy governor at HMP Gartree for the last eighteen months. The prison held more murderers than any other in the country, with lifers accounting for 85 per cent of its seven hundred inmates.

Sitting in Dunn's office, Thorne thanked her for making time to see him at such short notice.

'It sounded interesting,' she said. 'It's usually interesting when it's you.'

'You need to get out more,' he said.

Dunn laughed, loud and dirty. She was some-where in her mid-fifties, with dyed blonde hair and a fraction too much make-up. Sitting across from her, Thorne realised that she reminded him a little of Jacqui Gibbs.

More than once in recent days, Thorne had been happy to let those he was speaking to believe he was a detective and make no real effort to convince them otherwise. It was a risk, but one he had decided was worth taking. He would take no such chances with a deputy governor, who, for all he knew, might well be aware of the fact anyway.

She certainly did not seem overly surprised when he told her.

'So, come on then,' Dunn said. 'What did you do?'

Thorne shrugged, the tease deliberate.

'I could turn Her Majesty to the wall, if you like?'

143

Thorne looked at the picture high on a wall to his left. Built in the mid-sixties, Gartree was a relatively modern institution and was certainly run in accordance with a progressive penal policy, but like many prisons in the system it nevertheless had a thriving drug trade, a racism problem and a portrait of the Queen on the wall of the governor's office.

'I was stupid,' Thorne said. 'That's all.'

Dunn leaned back in her chair and grinned. 'You know, I've got a list of coppers, more than you'd think actually, who I always thought might mess up somewhere along the line and wind up inside one day.'

'I'm on the list, am I?'

'You're top,' Dunn said.

Now it was Thorne's turn to laugh, or at least to give a decent impression of someone who was laughing. 'It was nothing that bad, Caroline. I promise.'

'If you *were* to end up in here, I couldn't guarantee any special treatment, you know that.' She was still smiling. 'An extra pillow maybe, and that's about it.'

The mild flirtation done with – Dunn was a happily married mother of four – they got down to business. She opened the bulging manila folder on her desk and began leafing through the documents inside. She glanced up at Thorne, said, 'So what's our lovely Terence been up to?'

'Nothing serious,' Thorne said. Then he took a

leap. He was fairly confident that, on his release, Mercer would not have given the authorities any address he was intending to spend any time at and would certainly not have been staying in regular contact with the probation services as he should have. 'It seems that he's violated the terms of his licence.' He was fairly sure that he was on safe ground, but still he felt another small crack appear in the limb he was out on.

Dunn sighed, having clearly heard the same story many times, and scanned the document in front of her. 'Right, so you've spoken to Alison Macken?'

Thorne nodded. Without having had to ask, he had been given the name of Terry Mercer's probation officer.

One job done.

'It's come through to us,' Thorne said, 'and we're trying to trace him, but there's been some high-level discussion about just how much we should prioritise this. The usual bullshit. Does he still represent a danger to society, all that.'

Dunn closed her folder and leaned back. 'Look, I know what he was in for,' she said. 'But I wouldn't be overly concerned.'

'That's good to hear.'

'You're not to quote me on that, obviously. I don't want a knock on the door in six months when he runs into McDonald's with a machine gun.' She shrugged. 'He had a reputation early on and I think he played up to it. There was that business with a prison officer a few years after he went inside, but actually I got on with him perfectly well. People change, you know? They get old.'

Though she had obviously been joking at the time, Thorne felt a little better about what Dunn had said earlier. That stuff about the list. She was clearly not quite the judge of character he had thought she was.

'Happens to us all,' he said.

'Since I took this job we've actually been doing a lot that's geared towards the older prisoners. We had quite a few in their late sixties and seventies and it was felt . . . well, *I* felt that we should try and do a bit more for them.'

'What, like bingo?' Thorne asked.

Dunn flashed him a sarcastic smile. 'We work with them to promote access to rights and services for the elderly. Most of them are going to need a lot more looking after when they get outside.'

'Makes sense,' Thorne said, thinking that Terry Mercer had adopted a rather different approach when it came to taking care of the elderly. 'Can you let me have a list of his visitors in the last year or so? Might give us a lead in terms of trying to find him.'

'I don't think so,' Dunn said.

'Why not?'

'Because that is a very short list. Not a soul on it.'

'No visitors at all?'

'None.'

'What about family?'

She shook her head. 'Mercer hasn't had a visitor in years. As far as I know there's been no contact at all with his family, not for a very long time. I got the impression he didn't really mind, or at the very least that he was used to it.'

Thorne thought for a few moments. 'Was there anybody he was particularly matey with in here? Anybody he hung around with, who he might still be in touch with?'

Dunn said that there had been. 'A prisoner named George Jeffers,' she said. 'More or less the same age. But if they are still in touch it's probably down the pub.'

Thorne waited, though he could guess what was coming.

'Jeffers was released about eight weeks before Mercer was.'

Thorne scribbled the name down while Dunn gave him a few more details. Jeffers had been serving the latest in a long string of sentences for a variety of offences, though none that was anything like as serious as Mercer's. Jeffers had looked up to Mercer, had done him plenty of favours.

It seemed logical to Thorne that, whether or not he knew exactly why he was being asked, George Jeffers might continue to do his mucker a favour or two as soon as he was on the outside.

Do a little of the groundwork.

Somebody else they would need to trace.

'I don't suppose you could give me the name of Jeffers' probation officer, could you . . .?'

147

A few minutes later, when Thorne thanked her for all her help, Caroline Dunn slipped briefly back into mild-flirtation mode. 'It's always a pleasure, Tom,' she said. She showed him to the door and as he opened it to leave, she said, 'All right . . . an extra pillow and a pair of monogrammed pyjamas. I can't say fairer than that.'

Standing in the car park, waiting for his taxi back to the station, Thorne pictured Terry Mercer sitting meekly at a desk in one of the prison class-rooms. He imagined an old man in a faded blue prison shirt listening politely and taking notes as he was told all he needed to know about pensions and winter fuel allowances. Sharing a joke with his classmates while a well-meaning social worker talked far too slowly about healthcare, sheltered housing and the difficulties of readjustment to the outside world.

Smiling and nodding, taking the literature when it was offered.

Thinking only about fatal dosages and the silky opening of veins.

A man who could fool an old hand like Caroline Dunn.

Thorne felt for the phone in his pocket, pulling his jacket tighter across his chest as the wind picked up. He called Yvonne Kitson and was still choosing his words when the call went to answerphone.

He left a message, waving as he saw his taxi come round the corner.

CHAPTER 20

The chilli was a big hit.

Helen had developed an aversion to anything too spicy while she was pregnant, so Thorne had gone easy on the chilli powder then spiced his own up with Tabasco once it was served up. Alfie ate with them, burbling cheerfully at the end of the kitchen table as he smeared macaroni cheese across everything within reach.

Thorne said, 'I don't know if he's a messy eater or some sort of performance artist.'

He tuned the radio in to *Bob Harris Country* and cleared up while Helen put Alfie to bed.

'So, how was the record fair?' Helen asked when she came back in.

'Good.' Thorne took a San Miguel from the fridge and held up an open bottle of white wine. 'Got a couple of things.'

Helen nodded an enthusiastic yes to the wine. 'Let me guess. Both by someone called Hank or Lefty or whatever.'

'That kind of area.'

'You left them at your place, right?'

'We're talking about a couple of Merle Haggard albums,' Thorne said. 'It's not torture porn.'

She nodded towards the radio. 'Actually, this is all right.'

Thorne told her that *this* was Rosanne Cash and that there might be hope for her yet.

They carried their drinks through to the small living room and slumped down in front of the television. Thorne flicked half-heartedly through the channels while Helen talked about her day. The child found injured at home was thankfully recovering, but his mother was still refusing to admit that her boyfriend had anything to do with it.

'Maybe he didn't,' Thorne said. 'Maybe it was her.'

'It was him,' Helen said. 'I watched his eyes when we read him a list of the child's injuries. Fucker didn't even blink.'

Thorne took a swig of beer. 'So, maybe she just loves him.'

Helen turned and stared at him as though he were mad.

'What would you think?' Thorne said. 'If you came home one day and I was the only person here and something had happened to Alfie?'

'Don't be stupid.'

'Seriously, what would you do?'

'I don't want to talk about this.'

'I'm just saying. Would your first thought be that it was me?'

150

Helen shook her head. '*I'm* not a hopeless junkie,' she said. 'And neither are you.' They stared at the television for a few minutes, some quiz show or other. Then Helen said, 'Her child should have come first. The child *always* comes first.'

Thorne considered suggesting that perhaps the truth should be the thing that comes first and, not for the first time, he wondered if the parents of young children were necessarily those best equipped to work on Child Abuse Investigation Teams. However detached they felt able to remain, was there not at least the possibility of tunnel vision? He knew that Helen would point out somewhat icily that for every mistake that was made, every mother or father who was falsely accused, a hundred children were saved. She would quite reasonably ask where *he* stood exactly, when it came to taking killers off the streets? What was a fair price to pay? She also knew him well enough to point out that, as far as tunnel vision was concerned, they were firmly in pot and kettle territory.

Thorne kept his mouth shut, and his eyes on the quiz show.

Yes, children came first . . . while those so old that it was hard to imagine they were ever *anyone's* children were often ignored. Marginalised at best. Violent death was violent death and Thorne would never quantify it in terms of a victim's age. Certainly not when it came to considering the steps he had already taken in pursuit of Terry Mercer.

That cracked and creaking limb.

On television, a young couple gambled all they had won so far on one final question and lost the lot.

They made love without a great deal in the way of preliminaries, each with an ear out for crying from the next room.

Afterwards, Thorne said, 'I want to point out that the only reason that didn't last longer was because I'm aware we don't always have a lot of time, all right? I'm learning to make the most of any opportunity I get.'

'It's fine,' Helen said. 'At least you're enthusiastic.'

He nudged her.

'I'm kidding.' She nudged him back. 'It was nice.'

Their timing was spot on. Alfie began crying before Thorne's breathing had returned to normal and Helen brought him into bed, laid him down between them. Thorne enjoyed the feeling of the small, warm body against his own, Helen quietly shushing her son from the far side of the bed.

Despite the thoughts clattering about in his head – the war being waged between excitement and blind panic – Thorne was asleep before either of them.

CHAPTER 21

'Four days off or not,' Treasure said, 'the first morning back's still a major arse-ache.' She took the Fanny Magnet past a white van with its hazards flashing and, for want of anything more interesting to do, turned off the High Street towards Ladywell Fields.

'You've changed your tune,' Thorne said.

'Have I?'

'What happened to that buzz you were telling me about?'

'Yeah, well.'

'Like getting your leg over, you said.'

Treasure's half-smile became a full-on yawn. 'Fat chance of anything that exciting this time of the morning, is there?' She groaned and hit the brake hard as the green light up ahead changed to red. 'Earlies are shit.'

Treasure had a point. The 7.00 a.m. briefing had not thrown up anything that was likely to get her or anyone else's pulse racing. The usual follow-ups on the burglaries and minor assaults that had come in overnight. Half a dozen stolen cars to watch out for. The faces of a few local drug dealers who would probably not be dragging their sorry arses out of bed much before teatime.

Thorne was not complaining, of course. With everything else that was going on – his off-the-books investigation gathering momentum, a collection of stories he needed to get straight – he had more than enough juggling to do.

A shift that was nice and . . . Q---- suited him down to the ground.

He had clocked the email's arrival while Two-Cats was busy with his PowerPoint; his phone on silent, the single pulse of it against his chest, and once the patrol pairings had been organised and the first few vehicles had pulled out of the station yard, he had hurried back to his office to get a good look at it.

From Holland's personal email account to Thorne's.

Mercer Trial: List

It was as Thorne had expected: the judge; the key members of the legal teams on both sides; the witnesses and prosecution experts; the senior investigating police officers. Holland had indicated which of the police officers was now retired and had put D for deceased next to the names of those on the list they would no longer have to worry about. Those who had died while Mercer was in prison – senior investigating officer, judge and QC included – and those he had taken care of himself since his release.

Dr John Cooper. Fiona Daniels. Brian Gibbs.

Thorne knew that it would be problematic to say the least to talk about what was happening to a serving copper, so he was pleased to see that the senior Flying Squad officer on the case thirty years before was one of those no longer on the force.

He underlined the name.

It would be hugely useful to get the insights of somebody who knew their suspect well, who Thorne could confide in and who would . . . *should* have more to worry about than procedure or chain of command.

Somebody who might well be the next person on Terry Mercer's list.

'That's more like it,' Treasure said. She switched on the blues and twos and put her foot down. 'Tom?'

'Right,' Thorne said.

Thorne had not really been listening. Jolted back in his seat as Treasure pushed the car up to seventy-five, he leaned forward to read the Computer Aided Dispatch details on the screen. A suspected sexual assault in Brockley Cemetery.

They were only minutes away.

In his time, Thorne had done some fairly dangerous driving of his own. He remembered tearing through rainy streets only months earlier; a man, white-faced and swearing threats in the passenger seat, the night his career had come so spectacularly off the rails. Even so, it was those moments when the sirens were blaring and the blue light danced across the cars ahead, doing motorway speeds down quiet suburban streets, that terrified him more than almost anything else the job entailed.

A dog running out in front of the car. A child.

In the time it took for Thorne's heart rate to return to normal, he and Treasure were able to establish that the 'sexual assault' was no more than a hysterical woman laying flowers on her sister's grave and a teenage boy bunking off from Forest Hill School and caught short in the trees fifty feet away. Nina Woodley had arrived at about the same time, so Thorne was happy to leave her comforting the woman and telling the boy to be a bit more careful about where he chose to piss and to piss off back to school. Fifteen minutes after the dispatch had come through, Thorne and Treasure were back on the main road, driving slowly south towards Catford.

'Tell you what,' Treasure said. 'If she could see his cock from that far away, he's going to be beating the girls off with a shitty stick.' She looked in her mirror. 'Hello, who's that?'

Thorne looked over his shoulder and saw that the car behind them was flashing its lights.

'Is she mental?' Treasure said, raising her hand.

'It's fine,' Thorne said, having recognised the car and its driver. He asked Treasure to pull over and told her that he would be no more than a few minutes. Before the sergeant could ask him any questions, he got out and walked back to the blue Mondeo that had now drawn up behind them.

'Did she give me the finger?' Yvonne Kitson said, when Thorne had shut the door. She nodded towards Christine Treasure who had turned round in her seat to stare at them.

'Probably,' Thorne said. 'Trust me, you really don't want to upset her.'

The car radio was tuned to LBC; somebody saying that having a mayor who spoke Latin didn't mean that the bus service was any better. Kitson leaned forward and turned it off. Said, 'So, come on then.'

'Not sure where to start,' Thorne said.

'You weren't offering Holland any football tickets, were you?'

'Sorry?'

'When you called him the other day. He gave me some crap about spare football tickets.' She turned and stared at him. 'I haven't got all day, Tom.'

So, Thorne told her. Then, he asked her.

Kitson thought for a minute or so, then let out a long slow breath. 'You can understand why I might be a little reluctant to do anything stupid. Job-wise.'

'Course I can.'

'And this would be a damn sight more stupid than last time . . .'

This was what Holland had been alluding to in the pub on Monday night, the reason Yvonne Kitson might be more than a little 'risk averse'. A few years before, her own career had hit a brick wall almost as hard as Thorne's, after an ill-judged affair with a senior officer. While her lover had walked away still smelling of roses and Paco Rabanne, Kitson's own career prospects – once considered extremely bright – had been all but wiped out. She had worked her arse off to get back to where she presently was and Thorne knew perfectly well how reluctant she would be to jeopardise that.

'You don't ask, you don't get,' Thorne said.

Kitson shook her head as if to clear it, then asked Thorne the same questions Holland had, the same reasonable questions. He gave her the same unreasonable answers and told her what he had learned about Mercer during his trip to Gartree the day before. 'This bloke Jeffers would be a good place to start, I reckon.'

Kitson held up a hand. Thorne was getting way ahead of himself.

'Assuming that Mercer *is* in breach of his licence, there's already going to be officers out looking for him, surely.'

'They won't be in any great hurry,' Thorne said. 'He's just an old bloke who's gone missing.'

'An old bloke who shot a copper.'

'A long time ago. Come on, you know as well as I do that finding someone who hasn't spoken to a probation officer for a few weeks isn't going to be top of anyone's list of priorities.'

'Besides which,' Kitson said, 'you want to find him first.'

'I *need* to find him first,' Thorne said. He let that hang, knowing that Kitson would understand there was more than just the obvious reason why.

Thorne turned and stared ahead. Treasure was still watching from the Fanny Magnet. He turned down the chatter from his radio; a dangerous dog on the loose in Deptford.

'You're asking a hell of a lot,' Kitson said. 'Too much.'

'Look, Yvonne . . . if I thought I could do this on my own, don't you think I would?' Thorne tried to keep the desperation from his voice, but it wasn't easy. 'It's not even about finding the time. I could always throw a few sickies, do whatever I needed to at night. Even then . . .'

'You don't have the access any more.'

'Right,' Thorne said. 'And yes, I know I'm asking too much.'

'What if you don't find him?' Kitson said.

'I can't afford to think about it.'

'Come to that, what if you do?'

'If we do, nobody's going to give a toss how we did it.'

'Really? You think?'

'I don't know what else to tell you,' Thorne said.

'Either way, if all this comes out, the unauthorised use of time and resources . . . the lying, where does that leave Holland?' Kitson cocked her head, asked nice and simply, 'Where does that leave me?'

Thorne turned to look at her again. Took a deep breath. 'OK, listen. I didn't really want to tell you this, but I don't think I've got a lot of choice.'

'Oh.' Kitson angled her rear-view mirror, checked herself in it. 'This sounds like it's going to be good.'

'I'm not really back in uniform,' Thorne said. 'That's what everyone's supposed to think. That I got my wrist slapped.'

Kitson waited, a small shake of the head.

'Truth is, I've been put in undercover by the DPS.'

'*The Rubberheelers?*'

Thorne nodded.

'*You?*'

'They think there's something iffy going on in the MIT at Lewisham, have done for a year or more. Somehow what's going wrong on the other side of that bridge is connected to this Mercer business and that's why I've got to come at it like this.' He shrugged. 'Under the radar.'

Kitson let her head drop back, said nothing for half a minute. 'You're joking, right?'

Thorne held the pause for a few seconds, then blinked. 'Of course I am. Bloody hell, Yvonne, you seriously think the Directorate of Professional Standards would trust me to do *anything*?' There was a hint of a smile, but it quickly vanished. 'But if you're ever asked to explain yourself, to justify anything you've done, you tell them that's what I told you. You tell them I lied through my

160

teeth, that I conned you, that I've lost it. I don't care . . .'

Kitson nodded slowly, taking it in. 'I don't think that last bit would be much of a stretch,' she said. 'You losing it, I mean.'

'I haven't even started,' Thorne said.

Kitson sat back again and laughed; relief or genuine amusement it was hard to tell. She said, 'You needn't worry about being bumped down to constable. They'll throw you off the force. You'll probably go to sodding prison.'

Now, Thorne let the smile spread just a little. 'Why do people keep telling me that?'

'Take a guess,' Kitson said.

A minute or so later, Thorne got out of the car. As soon as he'd closed the door he gestured to Kitson and, as the window slid down, he put his hands on the roof and leaned in. 'Whatever you decide is fine, Yvonne,' he said. 'I mean it. Thanks, for giving me a chance to explain.' Then, without giving Kitson time to reply, he winked and said, 'George Jeffers,' and walked quickly back towards the patrol car.

'Girlfriend?' Treasure asked, as they pulled away.

Thorne told her to head for Deptford. 'Let's go see how dangerous this dog is, shall we? With any luck, it'll have bitten the moron that owns it.'

'Come on, is she or isn't she?'

'Maybe,' Thorne said, the lies coming easier and easier.

'She's a bit pushy if you ask me.'

'I didn't.'

'Fit though,' Treasure said. 'Too good for you anyway. If she ever decides she's had enough of you huffing and puffing on top of her, point her in my direction, would you?'

'I'll try and remember.'

Passing Brockley station, Thorne's mobile rang and, after a glance at the caller ID, he answered, pressing the phone hard to his left ear and turning slightly towards the window. He said, 'Thorne,' hoping that Holland would understand it was tricky to talk and would keep his voice down.

'I think we might have another one.' Holland said it nice and quietly.

Something turned over in Thorne's stomach. 'Go ahead.'

'Bloke called Alan Herbert,' Holland said. 'Sixty-five-year-old from Uxbridge, put a gun in his mouth last Sunday night. Or had it put in his mouth for him. Sergeant I spoke to over there says they're still looking at it just because there was a firearm involved, but reckons it's going down as self-inflicted.'

'OK, so how does that fit in as far as the list goes?' Thorne could not recall the name. He was aware of Treasure turning to look, but he did not acknowledge it.

'He's not on the list,' Holland said. 'He was a retired security guard, so I can't really see how he fits in. I mean, I suppose he could have had some-thing to do with the bank that Mercer was trying to rob, but each of the victims so far has had some

162

connection with his trial.' Thorne said nothing, trying to think back. 'I mean maybe this bloke isn't part of it at all. Maybe he did top himself.' The line went quiet for a few seconds. Thorne watched the brightly coloured shop fronts on Lewisham Way drift past the window. Then Holland said, 'Any thoughts?'

Thorne certainly had one, but it was nothing he could give voice to with Treasure listening in. He thought back to his first few cases at the Old Bailey. Not quite thirty years ago, but he thought he was remembering it right. He tried to recall the men in the dock, the uniforms they were wearing.

He told Holland he would call him back later and hung up.

When he turned back towards Christine Treasure, she showed no sign whatsoever of having paid attention to his conversation. She turned sharply on to Creek Road, undid her seat belt a few minutes later as they approached the entrance to Deptford Park.

'A fiver says this dog's called Tyson, or Asbo,' she said.

CHAPTER 22

Mercer jogs in the park – nice and easy, nothing ridiculous – and he looks at the faces of the kids and the young couples as they pass him. Some smile, there is the occasional nod and a muttered greeting, but he knows what they're thinking, give or take.

Silly old sod.

Game old bird.

Stupid old bugger's going to kill himself.

They see him, but they don't have the first idea what they're looking at.

He slows to a brisk walk, hands on hips, puffing a bit, and thinks how odd it is that expressions don't ever change. Not really. Faces aged, course they did. Lines etched themselves and bags took up residence. Things puckered, yellowed, dropped; he'd watched it happening in that shitty excuse for a mirror, year after blasted year.

Not the expressions though.

Were they lifelong, he wonders. Was a baby's look of confusion that first time it sees a dog or a cloud or a garden covered in snow the same as when it grows old and frail and stares death in the face? The same as when a gun barrel gets jammed against its gums?

The hate in that old bastard's eyes, the movement around the mouth, he certainly recognised *that* from thirty years before. The same look Herbert had worn on his fat face every morning when he'd collected him from that cell beneath the Bailey. Standing there and scowling, like he'd been sent to fetch a scabby dog or pick up a turd.

And it was such a simple thing he'd asked him to do. A simple, stupid thing that cost him dear in the end. Cost all of them, if you want to look at it like that.

He sits on a bench and watches a few lads messing about with a ball, shouting the odds. He's bloody sure he never swore quite so much when he was their age. He takes a swig from a plastic bottle of water, lets his head drop back, listens to a blackbird singing her little heart out.

Hard to tell it apart from a song thrush, but he knows the difference.

He'd been amazed, the first time he'd seen the photograph; wondered how much the reporter had paid to get into the house, to take the picture in the first place. Plastered all over the front of the previous day's *News of the Screws*, it was. That stupid headline in the biggest typeface they'd got, his own ugly mug underneath it.

The Murder Garden.

Sitting there in his cell and staring at the photograph, it had been clear as bloody day. It was obvious. It was taken from the same window Gibbs said he'd been standing at, showed exactly what he would have seen from there, which was precisely sweet F.A. and that picture proved it.

He'd almost shat himself with excitement.

Brian Gibbs would not have seen a thing . . . couldn't have, certainly not what he claimed to have seen, not clearly anyway, not unless he had some kind of X-ray vision and was able to see through a dirty great tree. One of those huge things neighbours got stroppy about, right there between the gardens. Smack in the nosy sod's line of vision.

That Monday morning he'd barely been able to contain himself, standing at the cell door, lively as anything when Herbert opened it, bang on nine o'clock as usual. He'd waved the newspaper at him. He'd told him exactly what it meant, asked him if he'd mind doing him this one favour, passing it on to his brief, they'd be able to take it from there.

The usual expression. Lack of interest, *distaste* . . .

He'd begged him . . . come on, mate, just give it to my brief, not like I'm asking a lot, and eventually . . . *eventually*, the miserable toe-rag had mumbled something and taken it. Taken it and kept it. Done the crossword or looked at the football pages or wanked himself silly staring at the dolly-birds, then chucked it away.

Too late, of course, by the time his brief had finally found out about it. Too late to be accepted into evidence, and when the judge had said *that*,

Herbert was standing right there in the dock next to him, eyes front doing his job and smirking like an idiot.

He'd actually shrugged.

Not so anyone else could see, just a little shift of those shoulders he was so proud of, meant for no one else but the poor mug whose chances he'd just flushed down the toilet.

Like, 'Sorry, mate, forgot . . .'

Mercer makes a fuss of a small dog that's sniffing around his ankles. He talks to its owner about the good weather that's set to change, then stands up and starts to jog again.

He didn't forget.

One bit of selfishness, a couldn't-give-a-toss attitude that cost Alan Herbert his life. Herbert knew it too, it was there in his eyes right at the end. That was what was going through his head, a second before most of it ended up plastered across the wallpaper.

Another ten minutes, he decides, and he'll knock it on the head. Knees aged every bit as much as faces. Once more around the park should do it, then home for a bit of lunch and a kip . . . and he can still hear that blackbird, going like billy-o, as he turns right at the far end of the pond.

Thinking about the next one.

CHAPTER 23

As it turned out, the dog was by far the most dangerous criminal that Thorne and his team encountered for the rest of the shift. Things got a little hairy at one point when the dog – actually called Geezer, though Thorne had not taken Treasure's bet – threatened to chew Nina Woodley's leg off and armed officers were summoned. In the end, the beast showed the good judgement to let go and was taken away to meet a rather more prosaic fate at the hands of a local vet.

Twenty-eight stitches for Woodley, and the needle for Geezer.

The presence of a firearms unit, together with the injury to an officer and a request to have the animal destroyed, resulted in more paperwork than would usually have been the case. It meant that Thorne got to spend the best part of the afternoon in his office, and he wasn't complaining. He was certainly having a better day than his stitched-up constable or the soon-to-be-dead dog.

He was able to get the paperwork out of the way fairly sharpish and concentrate on other things, fired up by the text message from Yvonne Kitson that he received just after lunch.

Don't know whether to call the dps or the funny farm. Because it's you, I'll wait a while. Maybe it's me that needs to go to the funny farm. Y x

He called Holland back and told him it was his guess that Alan Herbert had been one of the security guards on duty during Mercer's trial. These days, the City of London police were responsible for running security at the Old Bailey – ferrying the accused to and from the holding cell, standing guard over them in the dock – but Thorne was almost certain that back then the job had been done by a private company.

Holland told him he would check.

Having explained that his was one of the teams charged with trying to locate Terence Mercer for breaching the terms of his licence, Thorne was not surprised to learn from his probation officer that the address provided by Mercer on his release had turned out to be entirely bogus. In a brief conversation, Alison Macken went on to explain how Mercer had failed to show up for a single one of his monthly meetings and that his mobile phone appeared to have been disconnected.

'Say hello from me when you find him,' she said. 'Actually, make that hello and goodbye. Can't say I'm too upset that he'll be going back inside.'

Thorne was ticking off jobs.

He'd been thinking about the trickiest one of all since he'd spoken to Holland. They'd talked about their list, about those men and women without a D next to their name, and Holland had said, 'Aren't we going to warn them?'

It had been in Thorne's mind since Holland had first put the list together, something he'd unconsciously been putting off for reasons he did not wish to examine too closely. This latest killing, though, had tipped the balance. It was just a question of how best to do it without revealing the details or letting anyone know what was going on who didn't have to.

The chat with Alison Macken provided the obvious solution.

'*We're looking for a recently released prisoner who's breached the terms of his licence and it struck me that you might not even be aware he* has *been released. Terence Mercer? I understand you were involved in the case thirty years ago, so I thought I'd call just to give you a heads-up. Nothing to worry about, I'm sure, but it can't hurt to be aware of these things, can it . . .?*'

Mercer's QC was long dead and the junior barrister – now a senior judge – was away on holiday. Thorne left a message, asking him to call when he returned. There were four detectives on Holland's list who had been part of the murder or armed robbery investigations and were still serving either in the Met or elsewhere. By the end of the afternoon, Thorne had managed to get hold of two.

Both officers had thanked him for getting in

170

touch and for the heads-up. 'Not everybody's quite so bloody thoughtful,' one of them had said.

Two was better than none at all and Thorne certainly felt a lot better about things, about himself, by the time he made the call to the one person on the list he was intending to warn face to face.

With fifteen minutes until the end of his shift at four o'clock, Thorne rattled through the sign-offs and the handover sheet. He asked a limping Nina Woodley how she was feeling, turned off his radio and tossed his uniform into his locker.

He was in his car by five past.

The owner of the eclectically stocked twenty-four-hour grocer in Finsbury Park was a young and garrulous Turkish man called Yilmaz. Within moments of Yvonne Kitson introducing herself, he had explained in heavily accented English that working all hours God sent, along with two shift-less brothers who did not pull their weight and getting crap from his wholesalers, meant that the last thing he needed was problems with the small flat he rented out above the shop.

'The flat is cheap,' he said. 'It's a bit of extra money, that's all, but definitely not worth all this trouble.'

'I won't keep you long,' Kitson said.

'This man, Jeffers, he pays me a month's rent and then he vanishes. No notice, nothing like that. So then I have to find another tenant, put an advert in the paper, all that. Three weeks to find someone else. Three weeks without any rent.'

Yilmaz was at the till, waiting for someone to come from the stockroom and take over so that he could show Kitson the flat. She stood off to one side as he talked and continued to serve customers, grabbing packets of cigarettes from behind him, ringing up baskets of groceries, taking the money and handing back change without a word.

'When was the last time you saw him?' Kitson asked.

Yilmaz thought about it, holding out his hand to a woman who had laid a magazine and a bottle of milk on the counter. 'He took the flat around the end of June and he was here for about a month.' The woman slapped a five-pound note into his palm. He put it into the till, dug out the change and held it towards her, still looking at Kitson. 'So, nine, ten weeks, maybe.'

'No, thank *you*,' the woman snapped angrily.

Yilmaz nodded towards Kitson. 'She's from the police,' he said, as though talking to a five-year-old; as though that explained what Kitson guessed was his usual attitude to customers.

The woman was already on her way out.

Yilmaz shrugged and slammed the till shut. 'At last,' he said, nodding towards a woman plodding up to the counter from the other end of the shop. 'Now, I can show you the flat.' He muttered something to the young woman in Turkish, then came

172

round the counter and showed Kitson out of the shop and along to a small door that separated it from a dry-cleaner's.

He reached into his pocket and took out a bunch of keys.

'I thought you said you had a new tenant,' Kitson said.

'A nice girl.' Yilmaz nodded. 'Turkish. *Quiet . . .*'

'Won't she mind you just waltzing in?'

Yilmaz slid the key into the lock. Said, 'She's at work.'

After giving Kitson the address, George Jeffers' probation officer had explained that her client had shown up for their first meeting shortly after his release, but that there had been no contact since, so Kitson was not surprised at what Yilmaz had been telling her. It made sense. Jeffers would not have wanted to stay in one place any more than his friend Terry Mercer, not if he was working for him in some way. Still, Kitson had decided that it might be an idea to take a look at where he'd been holed up for that first month, especially once the landlord had told her on the phone that Jeffers had left some of his belongings behind.

'It's a small flat, but it's nice,' Yilmaz said, as he pushed the door open.

They stepped into a narrow hallway leading to a steep flight of stairs. Kitson could feel particles of grit and other things crunching beneath her feet as she walked across the thin carpet, wondering exactly how Yilmaz defined 'nice'.

173

At the top of the stairs was a landing, with a small kitchen, bedroom and bathroom running off it. Yilmaz showed Kitson into each of the rooms, opening the doors one by one, as though revealing hidden treasure. The bedroom was very tidy, the bed nicely made and the cosmetics neatly lined up on a table in the corner. Yilmaz nodded, pleased. He seemed perfectly at home in the place and Kitson could not help wondering if he ever came into the flat on his own to poke around in his tenant's underwear drawer.

Kitson could see quickly that there was nothing to be gained by spending any more time here. 'Where are these things that Jeffers left?' she asked.

Yilmaz pointed to a small cupboard built into the wall on the landing. 'This is another thing,' he said. 'He leaves this for me to deal with.' He reached inside and yanked out a dusty red sports bag, explaining that the girl in the flat did not mind it being here. The flat was cheap, after all, so she had not objected to the bag, or to the card-board boxes of toilet tissue, tinned goods and shampoo Yilmaz was storing in the kitchen.

'Nice of her,' Kitson said.

Yilmaz dropped the bag on to the floor. 'It is a good job I am a nice person,' he said. 'Most land-lords would have thrown this into a skip.' He watched as Kitson knelt down and unzipped the bag. 'When he disappeared, I thought maybe he had just forgotten where he lived, something

174

like that. He was an old man and sometimes they forget things, you know?'

Kitson pulled out a pair of shoes, some socks and underpants, brown trousers and a dark jacket. There were a couple of tatty paperback thrillers at the bottom, some empty crisp packets and beer cans, a small radio. She held up the empty cans. 'I think you could have thrown these away.'

Yilmaz shrugged and she understood that he had not been generously holding on to Jeffers' belongings in case he ever came back. It had simply been the quickest and easiest way to tidy the place up, to prepare the flat for the new tenant. He'd simply grabbed everything he could see that had not been there when Jeffers had moved in, stuffed it into the bag and shoved the bag into a cupboard.

'How much longer?' Yilmaz asked.

Had she not been pushed for time, Kitson would have found something to arrest him for, just for the hell of it.

'Only, that girl on the till is an idiot.'

Kitson lifted up the jacket and began to look through the pockets.

CHAPTER 24

Retired Detective Chief Inspector Ian Tully had asked Thorne to meet him in a car park behind Bromley Museum, a mile or so from where he lived. When Thorne arrived, ten minutes after the allotted time, Tully was leaning against a car and holding on to a boisterous golden retriever, straining at the end of a leash.

'Sorry,' Thorne said. 'Traffic.'

Tully nodded and said, 'Stupid one-way system,' though he looked far from happy at having been made to wait. 'Right, come on then.' He marched off across the car park towards some trees, heading for a gap between them that opened out on to Priory Gardens.

'Thanks for making the time.' Thorne quickened his pace a little to catch Tully up.

'Sod all else to do.' The dog strained even harder as they moved through the trees and Tully pulled him back. 'Got to walk him anyway.' He leaned down to unfasten the leash from the dog's collar. 'We can talk while I'm picking up dog-shit.'

'Lovely,' Thorne said.

Tully was somewhere in his mid-to-late fifties,

176

round-faced with a full head of grey hair. He looked like someone who might once have been very fit – 'useful' even, in the way that a lot of the Flying Squad boys were back then – but the muscle had turned to fat in the years since his retirement. A zip-up grey fleece was his only concession to a temperature which had dropped several degrees in the last hour or so, while Thorne shivered beneath his leather jacket.

They watched the dog tear off across the grass, slow down and circle for a minute or two, then squat. They walked towards it, Tully pulling a plastic bag from the pocket of his fleece. 'Terry Mercer isn't a name I've heard in a while,' he said.

'Not one I'd ever heard,' Thorne said. 'Now he's on my to-do list every bloody day.'

'Didn't know he was out.'

'Yep, out and about.' Thorne watched Tully bend to bag the dog's waste while the retriever ran off to mooch in the long grass at the edge of the treeline. 'Not sure where, though, that's the problem.'

Thorne spun him the same line he'd given Alison Macken and the two officers he'd spoken to earlier. Breach of licence, no contact, urgent need to trace, etc., etc.

Tully started walking again. 'Weird thing is I can remember that investigation really clearly,' he said. 'I mean, it was a pretty big one, obviously. Fairly straightforward too. Hardest bit was the Flying Squad working with the Murder boys, you know? Flying egos, more like, cocks being measured.'

'I don't think much has changed,' Thorne said.

'Trial was a piece of piss, though. We had eye-witnesses, ballistics, the lot. Never in any doubt, really.'

'Nice easy one, then.'

'Easy as they come, but Mercer didn't see it that way. He thought he was going to get off all along. Never believed it would go against him, always cocky. He was not at all happy when the verdict came in, but how many of them ever are? He did a prison guard later on, didn't he?'

'I gather he calmed down a bit after that,' Thorne said.

They walked in silence for a while, past fenced-off ornamental gardens, a lake with ducks and geese; Tully calling the dog back every time it threatened to harass a passer-by or roll in something unmentionable.

'Calm or not, you're obviously very keen to find him. A bit keener than I might have expected, to be honest.'

'Well, bearing in mind what he did,' Thorne said.

'Thirty years ago.'

'We've still got to be sure he isn't dangerous.'

Tully turned and studied him. It was clear that Thorne's words had failed to convince him of something.

'*I* think he's dangerous,' Thorne said.

A few yards further on, Tully said, 'I think.'

'Sorry?'

'I think he's dangerous. That's what you said.'

178

Tully nodded and whistled for the dog. He smiled to himself, like he'd worked something out and had the evidence to prove it. 'Usually *we*, isn't it? *We*, the members of this team, *we*, the people running this investigation. Am I right?'

They had reached the treeline at the far end, but rather than turn and head back the way they had come, Tully waited. It was clear to Thorne that the man was still a pretty decent detective, one who had quickly seen through Thorne's half-truths and, watching him calmly feeding his dog a couple of chews, he decided there was no harm in telling the truth. Tully was no longer a copper after all, no longer playing by the rules, presuming that he ever had. On top of which, something in his attitude told Thorne that this was not someone with any great love for the powers that be; someone who might have at least some sympathy for the way Thorne was doing things.

Tully tossed a chew in the air and the dog jumped for it.

'I know that Terry Mercer's dangerous,' Thorne said. 'Because he's killed at least five people since he was released. All people involved in that nice easy trial you were telling me about.'

The dog ran off into the trees, and Tully let him go.

Walking back towards the car, Tully told Thorne all about his retirement six years earlier. Even then, it had no longer been compulsory for those with thirty years' service. For some though, getting out still made sense. The pension would not get any bigger and those who had joined the force at eighteen or nineteen were still young enough to start new careers. The fact was, however, that the brass wanted them to go; the ones who went willingly *and* those who would have preferred to stay on. This, together with a policy of taking on fewer new recruits, got them some way towards reaching their targets as far as making the necessary cuts went.

Whether they were still 'working together for a safer London' was a different matter entirely.

'So they encouraged you to leave?' Thorne asked.

'Pushed me out,' Tully said. 'Simple as that. All they had to do was take away anything resembling the job I was used to doing to the point where I wouldn't have a lot of choice.'

Thorne said nothing. It sounded very familiar.

'I was working on Serious and Organised by then and I ended up being the mug who did the organising. Writing up the operations they'd given to detectives twenty years younger than me. I might as well have been making the bloody tea, so I told them to stick it. I felt like a hero . . . for about five minutes, because I'd done exactly what they wanted.'

'They're good at that,' Thorne said.

'I was an idiot.' Tully sounded bitter, and evidently believed he had reason to be. He was clearly a good copper, but Thorne could tell that he was also one of those unfortunate ones who were lost without a warrant card.

Job-pissed, job or not.

'So what are you up to now?' Thorne asked.

Tully looked as if he had something foul-tasting in his mouth. He swallowed. 'I walk, I try and read, watch far too much television. I listen to the sound of my brain cells dying off. It's non-stop excitement.'

'You married? Kids?'

'Never got round to it.' He looked at his feet as he trudged across the damp grass. 'Come on, you know what the Job can be like.'

Thorne said that he did, but in his experience, those whose every relationship foundered on the rocks of police work were actually few and far between. Those who *blamed* an inability to settle on the pressures of the Job were common enough of course. Thorne's own marriage had failed, but that was a long time ago and he'd had plenty of relationships since.

Some better than others, but still.

'Yeah, it's difficult,' he said.

As they arrived back at the car park, Tully stopped. 'Listen, if you need any help . . .'

'Oh,' Thorne said. The dog was jumping up at him, pawing mud across his jeans. 'Right.'

'I'm serious.'

'I can see that.'

'I might be out of the loop officially, but I've still got plenty of contacts, you know what I mean?

Plenty of favours I can call in.' Tully pressed a button on his remote and the boot of his car opened slowly. The dog ran across and jumped in without being told. 'From what you've told me, it sounds like you could do with all the help you can get.'

'It's not the reason I wanted to meet up.'

'All the same, it's a genuine offer.' Tully stared at his foot moving back and forth across the gravel. 'Tell you the truth, you'd be the one doing me a favour.'

'I actually came to warn you,' Thorne said. 'Bearing in mind what Mercer's doing, you know, it might be a good idea to watch out for yourself.'

Tully laughed. 'I'm not going to lose any sleep over Terry Mercer.' He patted his chest. 'Anyway, these days I'm grateful for anything that gets this beating a bit faster.' He walked round his car towards the driver's-side door, shouted over the roof. 'Think about what I said.'

Thorne was already thinking about it.

Having an ex-cop with plenty of friends on board might not be a bad idea and at the very least it would take a bit of the pressure off Holland and Kitson. As far as needing all the help he could get went, Thorne wasn't going to argue, and the offer of providing some was obviously sincere, desperate, even.

As things stood, bagging dog-shit was clearly the most useful thing ex-DCI Ian Tully did all day.

CHAPTER 25

As soon as Thorne walked through the door, he heard voices from the kitchen, and the first person he saw on entering was Helen's sister Jenny, who looked up at him from her place at the kitchen table. She smiled and said hello without a great deal of enthusiasm.

'I'm really sorry,' Thorne said.

He had completely forgotten she was coming over and dinner was already well under way.

The man sitting opposite Jenny turned to look at him, at the same moment that Helen walked over from the fridge with more wine and beer. She introduced Jenny's husband, Tim, then went back to the fridge and got a beer for Thorne. Tim stood up and walked across to shake hands as Thorne threw his jacket on to a chair.

'All right, mate?' he said.

Helen sat down and poured herself some wine. 'I just got you some Singapore fried rice and that squid thing you like.'

'That's perfect.'

'It's in the oven.'

Thorne said, 'Thanks,' and went to get his

dinner, stooping to kiss Helen as he passed, hoping that she could not taste the burger he'd stopped off for on his way home from Bromley.

'Sorry,' he said again. He scooped the food from its cartons on to a plate that had been warming alongside them in the oven. 'It's just been a pig today and I didn't get a chance to call.' He looked over towards Jenny and Tim. 'An officer was seriously injured on duty and I had a ton of paperwork to do just for that, so . . .'

'It's fine,' Helen said. 'We've not long started, have we?'

Tim shook his head and Jenny neatly forked in a mouthful of whatever she was eating.

Thorne walked back over to the table and sat down. He caught Helen's eye and she smiled, seemingly unconcerned that he was late. He wondered if she realised that he'd forgotten completely. If she did, she was hiding her annoyance very well. 'This looks good,' he said.

Tim washed down a handful of prawn crackers with a mouthful of beer and said, 'What kind of injury?'

Thorne looked at him.

'This officer.'

'Oh . . . an American pit bull terrier took a very decent chunk out of one of my constable's legs.' He looked at Helen. 'Nina Woodley.'

'She OK?' Helen asked.

'She's not going to be playing table tennis for a while.'

184

'I don't know why anyone would want to keep a dangerous dog,' Tim said. 'Is it like a status thing?'

'No such thing as a dangerous dog,' Jenny said. 'Only dangerous owners.'

'Fair point,' Tim said.

Helen reached across for more food. 'That's what the gun lobby always come out with whenever some child gets shot accidentally.'

'Oh, come on!'

'Like it's not the guns that are the problem.'

'It's not the same thing at all,' Jenny said.

Thorne knew that the relationship between Helen and her sister could occasionally be fractious. She resented Jenny's repeated interference, the unwanted advice, especially about childcare. He could sense an argument brewing. 'Anyway, loads of forms to fill in,' he said. 'So that's why I couldn't get away.'

'Goes with the job though, doesn't it?' Jenny said.

'I suppose so.'

'Stupid hours, not knowing what you'll be doing from one day to the next. It was the same thing when Helen was with Paul.' She looked at Helen. 'Wasn't it?'

Helen grunted, glanced over at Thorne.

He said, 'It's certainly not nine to five.'

Jenny was still looking at Helen; somewhere between pity and condescension. 'Hardly saw each other a lot of the time.'

'Who wants nine to five anyway?' Helen said.

Thorne could see that Helen was irritated. She

had told him on several occasions that her sister had not had a good word to say about her former partner while they were together, but that her attitude had miraculously changed since his death.

'Well some people just aren't cut out for it, are they?' Jenny said.

'No, they're not.'

'Paul certainly wasn't.'

Another look from Helen, the smallest roll of the eyes. Now Thorne understood what she had been talking about. Jenny had actually bowed her head just a fraction and spoken the name with something like reverence; as though Paul's death had sanctified him.

'You a fishing man?' Tim asked, from nowhere.

Thorne looked at him. 'No,' he said. 'Can't say that I am.'

'You should give it a try. A couple of hours in the fresh air, nice and relaxing, just you and the water. Best thing in the world for dealing with stress.'

'Maybe I'll give it a go,' Thorne said, hoping he'd faked a sufficient degree of interest.

'Yeah, definitely. I mean there can't be too many things more stressful than your job, can there? We know all about being a detective from Helen.'

'Tom's not a detective,' Jenny said.

Thorne looked at her.

She widened her eyes, a picture of innocence. 'Sorry, have I got that wrong?'

'Well, even so,' Tim said, spearing a pork ball.

'Still a stressful business, isn't it? I mean look at today, that business with the dog.'

When Thorne's mobile rang, he almost shouted with relief. Right then, he would have happily excused himself for someone trying to sell him insurance, but seeing the name on the caller ID he had to control the urge to rush from the room.

'Sorry, I need to take this,' he said.

He answered his phone on the way to the bedroom and once the door was closed behind him, he quickly told Yvonne Kitson he was free to talk.

Kitson said, 'Got the chief superintendent round for dinner then?'

'Worse,' Thorne said.

She told Thorne about her visit to the flat where George Jeffers had been staying and what she had found in the pockets of the jacket he had left behind. 'A few receipts . . . nothing to get excited about. His free bus pass and a business card I think you might be interested in.'

'Tell me.'

Thorne was certainly interested, struggling to control his excitement as he walked back into the kitchen to rejoin the others. It did not look as though he had been missed.

Helen asked if everything was all right and he told her that it was.

'He's definitely a sparky little so-and-so,' Tim said.

They were talking about kids; about Jenny's two

and about Alfie. Jenny said how well both her boys were doing at school, how bright each of them was in very different ways. Helen did not bother trying to compete in the parenting stakes. Instead, she took care to mention that Thorne had picked Alfie up from school the day before and that he was starting to get upset if Thorne was not there when he woke up in the morning.

'Really?' Jenny said, sounding less than thrilled.

Thorne smiled at Helen as he spoke. 'Apparently.'

Fifteen minutes later, when Helen began clearing the plates away, Thorne still had half his food left. Helen asked if he wanted her to put the leftovers in the fridge. Thorne pushed his fork half-heartedly through what was left of his rice and said, 'I'm not feeling too clever, actually.'

'That squid looked a bit iffy to me,' Tim said.

'Don't be ridiculous.' Jenny was helping to clear the table. 'It wouldn't happen that quickly.'

'No, I suppose not,' Tim said.

'Maybe it was the sandwich I had at lunch.' Thorne stood up and rubbed his stomach. 'But I definitely don't feel too good.'

'Do you want me to get you something?' Helen asked. 'I could nip to the late-night chemist.'

Jenny dumped the plates on to the worktop. 'It's probably just an overnight thing.'

'I might just call it a night,' Thorne said. 'Sorry.'

'Don't be daft,' Tim said, turning as Thorne moved past him. 'Listen, we should go and get a beer some time and don't forget about the fishing, yeah?'

Thorne said that he wouldn't forget and, after apologising to Helen for leaving her with all the clearing away to do, he headed towards the bedroom.

He lay in the dark, listening to the muted conversation, the only laughter coming from Tim, almost certainly at one of his own jokes. Half an hour after he had got into bed, Thorne heard the good-nights being said and the front door finally closing. A few moments later, Helen put her head round the door.

'How you feeling?'

'Not too bad,' Thorne said. 'I mean I'd really rather not phone in sick tomorrow.'

'See how you feel in the morning.'

'Thanks for being so good about me being late, by the way.'

Helen moved into the room and sat on the edge of the bed. She turned on the bedside light. 'The last thing I was going to do was have any sort of row in front of Jenny,' she said. 'She doesn't need any more ammunition.'

'Against me, you mean?'

'Against the whole thing. She wasn't very keen on me living with another copper the first time round, with Paul.'

'So you think we would have had a row?' Thorne asked. 'If your sister hadn't been here.'

Helen grinned. 'You forgot she was coming, didn't you?'

'Completely,' Thorne said.

They looked at one another for a few seconds until Alfie began to cry softly in the next room. It usually started this way, small and weak like a new-born's whimper. They both knew he'd be ramping up the volume fairly quickly.

'Great,' Helen said, getting up. 'Well, you'll probably be spark out by the time I'm done with him, so I'll try not to wake you in the morning.'

'I'm sure I'll be fine,' Thorne said.

As Thorne reached for the light, Helen stopped at the door.

'I think you should definitely take the day off,' she said. 'You do look seriously rough.'

CHAPTER 26

Thorne had seen the business card Kitson had described once before. Thin and flimsy, with a basic font and simple layout; one of those you could get printed up in batches of fifty from machines at railway stations.

FA Investigations.

The year before, Thorne had become professionally involved with a young private investigator named Anna Carpenter. She had dropped out of university and gone to work for FA Investigations with high hopes of an exciting new career, only to find herself acting as bait in seedy honeytrap operations, when she wasn't working as a glorified bookkeeper or fetching her boss's booze.

Thorne, and the case they worked on together, had been her escape.

He had not wanted anything to do with her at first, had been forced into it for the sake of the investigation. By the end, they had become close; a new lease of life for Thorne every bit as much as it was for her. Though Anna's boss was not directly at fault for the way things had turned out, Thorne had seen and heard enough of the man she had worked for to wish that he could have blamed Frank Anderson for what happened.

Blamed him and done something about it.

Now, at ten fifteen on a drizzly Thursday morning, while Helen and his chief inspector thought he was laid up in bed, Thorne stood on a pavement in Victoria, outside a narrow brown door with cracked glass, and dragged his thoughts back to the present. The five dead and the dog-eared card found in George Jeffers' pocket.

He rang the bell.

Half a minute later, Frank Anderson answered the door. Perhaps he was having trouble finding a new 'secretary' on the pittance he was paying, or else he was not making enough money to afford anyone at all. Either way, it was good news.

'What do *you* want?' Anderson said. It had taken him a long few seconds to remember where he recognised Thorne from and he did not look very pleased when it finally came to him. Thorne enjoyed the man's discomfort and confusion, the way he shrank back just a little in the doorway.

They had last seen one another at Anna Carpenter's funeral.

'Well, I certainly don't want to stand about chatting on your fucking doorstep.' Thorne had not meant to sound quite so aggressive. He was hoping for a degree of co-operation after all, but something about Anderson's face – vulpine, florid – had triggered a momentary desire to knock the man on his bony arse rather than waste any time being polite.

He bit back the urge and glanced skywards, as if it was just the rain that was making him tetchy.

Anderson said, 'Yeah, all right, calm down,' and turned inside, inviting Thorne to follow him upstairs. The office was much as Thorne remembered it: a drab collection of chairs and filing cabinets in brown and gunmetal grey. A job lot acquired on the cheap when some fifties council building was upgraded.

'You want some tea?'

Thorne said no, as politely as he could.

Anderson dropped into a swivel chair behind a scarred wooden desk. He was wearing a tired suit that near enough matched the decor, a striped tie hanging from an undone collar. He was probably early fifties, but drink had put ten years on him. He looked like the schoolteacher you might think twice about before letting him take a PE class.

'I'm interested in one of your clients,' Thorne said. 'A man named George Jeffers.' He waited. 'He *was* one of your clients, right?'

Anderson's hands were clasped together. He unclasped them then moved them back together. Admitting nothing, but making no denial. A tacit invitation for Thorne to carry on.

'I believe that Jeffers asked you to trace a number of individuals for him, is that correct? A number of elderly individuals?'

Anderson thought for a few seconds. 'Look, you know I can't talk about my clients.'

'I'm asking nicely.'

'I'm saying no nicely.'

'You really think I'd be here if it wasn't important?' Thorne said.

Anderson's expression changed, *softened*. Perhaps as someone who spent his working life spying on unfaithful husbands or benefit cheats, he relished his input being important for a change. Or perhaps he decided that talking to Thorne about this was preferable to talking about the past. 'OK, let's say that George Jeffers was a client.'

'Did you know that he'd just come out of prison?'

Anderson nodded. 'He never said anything, but you can smell it on them, can't you? He had that . . . pallor, whatever you call it. Like he was see-through.'

'So you traced these people for him.'

'Not unheard of, is it?' Anderson shrugged. 'You come out of prison after a long stretch, only natural you might want to get back together with a few people you've lost touch with.'

Thorne nodded. Thinking: It wasn't Jeffers who had lost touch with anyone, and there was nothing natural about what the man who wanted these people found was planning to do. 'How did he pay you?'

'Now you're pushing it.'

'Come on, I'm not going to tell the taxman. Cash?'

Anderson said nothing.

'Scotch?'

Anderson scowled at him. 'My business.'

'I need a list of the people he asked you to find.'

Anderson leaned back in his chair, swivelled back and forth. 'No chance.'

'You've already admitted Jeffers was a client, so what's the big deal?'

'That's as much as you're going to get,' Anderson said. 'Besides which, I've admitted nothing of the sort. I start handing on the details of particular cases, all the ins and outs, I'm betraying my clients' confidence and completely compromising the integrity of my business.'

It was a struggle not to laugh. 'Right. They might throw you out of the Association of British Investigators. Still using their logo, I see.'

Instinctively, Anderson reached for the stack of notepaper Thorne was eyeing up. He gathered up the pile and thrust it into a drawer, then began straightening up other objects on his desk: a calendar, a mug filled with pens, a telephone attached by a cable to a digital recorder.

'That's naughty,' Thorne said. 'I wonder what would happen to the integrity of the business if your clients discovered that you'd never been a member of the ABI? That you were using that logo illegally.'

'So, I forgot to send in the membership fee,' Anderson said. 'I can sort that in five minutes, so don't think that's any sort of threat.'

'What about the fact that you spend half your time calling up your competitors, posing as a prospective client and arranging non-existent meetings?'

'Firstly, it's what everyone does and secondly . . . you're starting to sound a bit desperate.' He stood up. 'Right, I think we're about finished, aren't we?'

'I really need that list.'

'Well, come back with a warrant and we can talk about it.' Anderson must have sensed Thorne's hesitation, seen something in his face. 'Oh, I see.' He sat down casually on the edge of the desk. 'This one's off the clock, is it?'

'That doesn't matter.'

'It bloody well does to me,' Anderson said. 'Even more reason for me to tell you to piss off. Like I *needed* another reason.'

Thorne looked at him. If he was struggling to control his desire to slam Anderson's smug face hard on to his desk, then Anderson was fighting a similar – if rather more foolish – urge to do much the same to him. A year before, in this very office, Thorne had made Frank Anderson look like an idiot, and clearly that still rankled. Thorne looked, making no effort to hide what he was thinking, but saying nothing, because he had nothing else to say.

'So?' Anderson smiled. 'Piss off.'

Ten minutes later, Frank Anderson was enjoying his second whisky of the day, thinking that although there weren't too many things that could brighten his life up at the moment, sending that prick

196

Thorne away with his tail between his legs was definitely one of them.

He raised his glass in a toast to his own brilliance; muttered, 'One each, I reckon.'

Anderson's interest in the whole George Jeffers thing had been sufficiently piqued by Thorne's visit, by his obvious desperation for the details, that he spent the next few minutes trying to figure out what might be in it for him. Was there any way he could make some money out of it? Were there any angles he could exploit to his own advantage? Bar actually selling the information to Thorne he couldn't think of any offhand, but he was still wrestling with the conundrum when the phone went.

A new client. The day was looking better and better.

The man suspected that his wife was having an affair with a work colleague. A stylist at the hairdressing salon where she worked, who had conned everyone into thinking he was gay, when that was obviously just a cover story. Anderson had heard similar stories a thousand times and he listened patiently, before making the man fully aware of his rates, including the charges for the conversation they were now having.

'I just need proof,' the man said. 'Proof of what she's doing to me and to our kids.'

'I'll get you proof one way or the other,' Anderson said.

'If we get divorced, she'll try and turn me over. I mean, that's what always happens, isn't it?

But if I can prove that she was the one playing away, it might not be so bad. I might even get a chance to keep my kids.'

'Sounds like money well spent then,' Anderson said.

He told the man that he would need to come into the office to make formal arrangements and they agreed a time the following week. The man thanked him, said he was a lot less worried about things now he'd spoken to a professional.

'Glad I can help,' Anderson said.

When the call had ended, Anderson sat back in his chair and raised his glass a second time. 'Professional,' he whispered, before draining it. He was still clutching the glass containing his third whisky of the day when he went down to answer the door a few minutes later.

Tom Thorne, looking rather more cocky than when he'd left.

'It's always the stupid laws that prove to be the handiest,' Thorne said. 'The really boring ones.'

'What?'

But Thorne was already pushing past him on his way up the stairs, talking as he went while Anderson trotted after him. 'I mean they got Al Capone for tax evasion in the end, didn't they? And they only caught the Yorkshire Ripper because there was an irregularity with his tax disc. This one, though . . . this one's my absolute favourite from now on.'

Anderson shouted, 'What the hell d'you think

you're doing?' as Thorne marched into his office and around his desk. He could only stand and stare as Thorne reached for the digital voice recorder and pressed play.

'*I just need proof,*' the tinny voice said. '*Proof of what she's doing to me and to our kids . . .*'

Anderson's shoulders slumped when he saw the expression on Thorne's face and realised.

'Not bad,' Thorne said, 'even if I say so myself. I just poshed my voice up a bit . . . reckon I sound like Hugh Grant. I think the stuff about the kids was a nice touch, don't you? And you sounded ever so sympathetic.'

'You're an arsehole,' Anderson said.

'I might well be, but because you failed to inform me that our conversation was being recorded, you're the arsehole who's in breach of the Telecommunications Act of 2003.' Thorne sat down in Anderson's chair, opened a drawer and took out a sheet of the headed notepaper he had seen Anderson put away earlier. He waved it towards him. 'So, do I arrest you now, or do you save us both a lot of trouble by writing those names down for me?'

'Arsehole,' Anderson said again.

'I mean, I don't think we're talking about prison or anything, but it's probably a hefty fine and it's not going to look good on the CV, is it?'

Anderson stepped forward and snatched the paper, muttering curses as he leaned across to take a pen from the mug on his desk. He nodded towards the computer, the muscles flexing in his jaw. 'I'll need to . . .'

'Oh, of course.' Thorne vacated the chair and watched Anderson come around and call up the file he needed, stabbing furiously at the keys of the grimy PC. He picked up the half-empty bottle of Bell's from the top of the filing cabinet. 'Times must be hard,' he said. 'I had you down as a single malt man.'

'Here.'

Thorne felt more pumped up than he had in a long time as he took the piece of paper Anderson was brandishing and looked down at the names.

'So, we finished then?'

But Thorne wasn't listening. However ingenious he had been, however big a fool he had made of Frank Anderson, he could feel the rush evaporate, the ticking in his blood slow to a dull, monotonous throb.

He was the arsehole, after all.

Four names he recognised, four names he already knew.

He had wasted his time.

CHAPTER 27

'I reckon I could get used to this,' Hendricks said.

Holland looked at him. 'What?'

'Working from here.' Hendricks looked around. 'I mean, in terms of my own speciality, yes, it's definitely a bit limited. There's probably a freezer in the back somewhere and I could always improvise as far as a slab goes, but otherwise the facilities do leave something to be desired. That said though, you can't argue with fancy Italian lager on tap and all the crisps and nuts you can eat.' He turned, nodded across to where Thorne was waiting to be served at the bar. 'Mind you, bearing in mind that we're doing this out of the goodness of our hearts, I do think he should be buying all the drinks.'

'That why you're doing this then?' Holland asked. 'The "goodness of your heart".'

'Something like that. Someone needs to keep an eye on him.'

'Not sure why I'm doing it.' Holland loosened his tie. 'Buggered if I can see the funny side, though.'

'I spent all afternoon cutting up a thirteen-year-old

boy,' Hendricks said, quietly. 'So pretty much everything else has got a funny side.'

When Thorne arrived back at the table and laid the drinks down, Hendricks said, 'Here we are again then,' and began whistling a recognisable refrain.

'Wrong movie,' Thorne said. 'That's *The Good, the Bad and the Ugly*.'

Hendricks reached for his drink. Said, 'I'm well aware of that.'

'Yvonne told me to say sorry she couldn't make it,' Holland said.

'It's fine,' Thorne said. 'She texted me.'

'She's got a lot on with the kids, you know? But she's still . . . on board.'

Thorne nodded, said, 'Right then,' and laid down the list he had extracted from Frank Anderson. He had already explained to the others that it contained only the names of the victims they had already identified. 'Fiona Daniels, Brian Gibbs, John Cooper, Alan Herbert.' He counted them off on his fingers. 'Margaret Cooper killed just because she was there and he couldn't leave her alive. Four people Mercer had a grudge against, so he gets George Jeffers to find them. Jeffers uses Frank Anderson to do it for him and all the information Mercer needs is waiting for him when he gets out.'

'Tidy,' Hendricks said.

Thorne stabbed at the scrap of paper, now damp with beer from the bottom of glasses. 'So, where the hell does this leave us?'

'Maybe it's finished,' Hendricks said. He swirled the beer around in his glass. 'Maybe this *was* Mercer's list and he's crossed them all off and now he's done.'

Thorne shook his head.

'Maybe he's looking forward to a nice cosy retirement. Putting his feet up in Eastbourne or somewhere and watching *Antiques Roadshow.* Doing a spot of gardening or whatever.'

'He's not done,' Thorne said.

'You *want* there to be some more?'

'Don't be stupid,' Thorne snapped.

Hendricks looked at Holland.

Thorne held a hand up. Sorry. 'Just one more name on that list and we might have at least had a chance. We might have known who he was going after and got there before he did.'

'But there's no way of knowing what order he was doing it in, is there?' Holland said. 'I can't see how it would really have helped.' He sat back and folded his arms. 'I mean, I hope Phil's right, I hope there aren't any more.'

'So do I, obviously,' Thorne said. 'But look at Alan Herbert. If Mercer's going to all this trouble to murder the poor sod who just happened to be standing next to him in the dock, you've got to believe there are going to be others. Jury members, officers of the court . . . somebody who looked at him the wrong way, whoever. This has been festering for thirty years, for God's sake.' He raised his glass, then stopped and stared down into it as if something that should not be there was floating in his beer. 'Who knows who else he's nursing grudges against?'

'So why aren't they on this list then?' Hendricks asked.

They sat and drank for a minute or two. The place was busier than the last time they were here and they had been having to lean closer to one another to make themselves heard, while still keeping their conversation private. There were a couple of Grafton regulars at the next table with no such concerns, arguing loudly about the new striker West Ham had bought. For a few moments, Thorne wished that he could join them; arguing the toss and getting fiercely worked up about something that would not keep him awake at night. Then he glanced down at the damp scrap of paper on the table and remembered the famous Bill Shankly quote about football being more important than life and death.

Shankly was a great manager, but he was talking out of his arse.

'There is another possibility,' Holland said. 'There could be others that Mercer didn't need to trace, because he'd already done it from inside.'

'He had no visitors, remember.'

'Phone calls then, letters. Easy enough, I would have thought.'

'I'll check with Caroline Dunn,' Thorne said.

'He'll have had access to a computer too,' Hendricks said. He rubbed a palm across his closely shaved scalp. 'And a bloody long time to figure out the best way to use it.'

Holland said, 'That might explain why there's no police officers on the list. No lawyers.'

Thorne nodded, getting it.

'Almost anyone with any sort of professional profile has some kind of internet presence, if you look hard enough.' Holland looked at Hendricks. 'Right? The world and his wife has a sodding blog.'

'Thinking I might start one myself,' Hendricks said. '*Gab from the Slab*. Sounds all right, doesn't it?'

'Maybe the names on Anderson's list were the only people he *hadn't* been able to trace.'

'Christ.' Thorne downed what was left of his pint. 'So, what do we do?'

'How's he funding all this?' Hendricks asked, after they had all taken a drink. 'I'm not sure the old age pension covers it.'

'I was thinking about that,' Thorne said. 'Did they recover everything that was taken in the original robbery?'

Holland said he didn't know, that he'd try and find out.

'Even if they did, you can bet he had something stashed away. Long-term villains like Mercer have always got a nest egg.'

'So, we're not going to find him through credit cards, anything like that.'

'No chance.'

'What about DVLA? How's he getting around?'

'Worth thinking about,' Thorne said. 'We could try and get a look at CCTV at all the locations where the victims were found. See if any vehicle comes up more than once.'

'Not sure how the hell I'm supposed to get the authority for that,' Holland said. 'There's a shedload of forms to fill in. Well, you know.' He thought about it for a few seconds, the other two staring at him. 'I'll have a word with Yvonne,' he said. 'See if she's got any bright ideas.'

'Any ideas at all would be good,' Thorne said. After the disappointment of his meeting with Frank Anderson, he had been hoping that getting together with Holland and Hendricks might at least help point the investigation in the right direction. So far, it felt as though the brick wall they were in danger of running into was just going up three times faster.

'It might help if we talked about the big question,' Holland said.

'Which one?' Hendricks leaned forward and stared, mock-serious. 'Is life ultimately meaningless? Does God exist? Chocolate HobNobs or plain? They're all equally tricky.'

'Ignore him,' Thorne said.

'There's never any sign of force,' Holland said. 'No defence wounds, nothing, so how's he doing it?' He looked at Hendricks, who was no longer seeing the funny side, and then at Thorne. 'How the hell is he making these people kill themselves?'

*　　*　　*

Holland left before the other two and, after a quick half for the road and fifteen minutes spent arguing about whether Liam Brady had been a better midfielder than Paul Gascoigne, Thorne and Hendricks wandered out into the car park. Thorne grimaced into the drizzle as he rooted in his pockets for car keys.

'You're over the limit,' Hendricks said.

'Hardly.'

'Why don't you leave the car here and stay at your place?'

'Can't,' Thorne said. 'I need to get back to Helen's. I'm in enough trouble as it is because she knows I've not been ill in bed all day.' He held out his mobile phone. 'Four missed calls.'

'So, just tell her you were meeting me and Dave. She knows it's important, so what's the big deal?'

Thorne took half a step away and grunted something non-committal.

'You *have* told her what you're doing, haven't you?' Hendricks said. The look on Thorne's face was answer enough. 'Oh, bloody hell.'

'What?'

Hendricks shook his head and raised his arms, exasperated, then began waving to flag down a black cab that was heading towards Chalk Farm Road. The cab slowed, did a U-turn and pulled over. Hendricks ushered Thorne towards it. 'Here . . .'

Thorne yanked open the cab door. Said, 'Tulse Hill.'

'No, sorry, mate.' the driver said, without turning round.

'What?'

'Not going south of the river this time of night.' He began to ease away, the door still open.

'You've got to.' Holding on to the taxi's door, Thorne stepped into the road. 'It's the law.'

'Yeah, and it's my cab.'

'You've got to take me.' Thorne's voice was raised. 'I'm a police officer.' He thrust his hand inside his jacket, one pocket then another, scrabbling for his wallet.

Hendricks moved in front of him, said, 'Leave it,' and slammed the door. The cab pulled quickly away from the kerb.

'Twat!' Thorne shouted after it. He aimed a kick at a plastic bottle in the gutter. '*Fucking* south London.' He dug for his car keys a second time and turned to look for his friend.

Hendricks had already begun walking towards the main road, but stopped after a few yards to turn and shout back. 'You need to tell her, you stupid sod.'

Maybe it was the fact that he hadn't really eaten properly that day, that he'd put away three and a half pints of Guinness on top of two bags of crisps and a dodgy-looking Scotch egg, but suddenly Thorne felt every bit as sick as he'd been pretending to be.

CHAPTER 28

Holland had no intention of telling his girl-friend where he had been and certainly not with whom. Her animosity towards Tom Thorne was of long standing, dating back to when he and Thorne had first begun working together. What Thorne had brought upon himself three months earlier had only confirmed her belief that he was not the sort of copper anyone – least of all the father of her child – should be modelling himself upon, and while she had not exactly crowed about what had happened, she did say that nobody should have been particularly surprised.

That Thorne's fall from grace was long overdue.

Holland did not agree, but had said nothing and he could certainly say nothing now.

'Your dinner's in the dog!' Sophie had been half asleep in front of the TV and grinned as she reached up to him from the sofa. Holland leaned down to kiss her and she smelled the beer. 'Don't tell me, another leaving do.' She sat up and the smile became a yawn.

'One of the other teams had a result, that's all. The DCI was getting them in, so . . .'

'So, why not?'

Holland was angrier with himself than he was with Thorne for being in this position, for putting his career on the line, but he really resented having to lie. 'How's the Teeny Tyrant?'

Chloë, their five-year-old daughter; angel-faced and ruthless.

'Oh, plenty of big decisions today,' Sophie said. 'She doesn't like cheese, she thinks Iggle Piggle is stupid and that joke about the dog? She wants one.'

'We haven't got the space,' Holland said.

'I told her we'd think about a hamster.'

Holland crept into his daughter's bedroom and watched her sleep for a minute or two, then crept into his own and called Yvonne Kitson.

'I was just going to bed,' she said.

'Sorry.' Going to bed with the new man in her life about whom she said very little. He was not a copper though, Holland knew that much. He told her what had been discussed in the Grafton.

'The CCTV sounds like a good idea.'

'I'm not sure I can do it,' Holland said. 'Any of it.' He had perhaps been exaggerating a little to imagine that his entire career was in jeopardy, but he knew that if what he had been doing for Tom Thorne ever came out, he would not be making DI any time soon. 'Think about what we've got to lose, compared to him.'

'So, tell him,' Kitson said. 'He's not going to hold it against you.'

'It's not just that, though, is it?' Holland lay back on the bed, stared at the cracks that spider-webbed out from the central light fitting. 'This is a major investigation, or at least it should be. Don't you think it deserves to be done . . . properly?'

'Meaning by other people.'

'What if there are more killings and we didn't do everything we could to try and stop it?'

'You want to go behind his back?'

Holland closed his eyes. He heard the television being switched off in the other room. 'I'm just saying.'

'I'm tired, Dave,' Kitson said. 'And you've been in the pub.'

CHAPTER 29

For Richard Jacobson, the evening every four weeks when his wife went out to attend the monthly meeting of her book club was the one he looked forward to the most. Not that she and her friends actually talked about books a great deal. From everything he had heard, there was a cursory five minutes spent saying, 'Yes, I liked it,' or 'No, it was pretentious twaddle,' and the rest of the conversation revolved around hairdressers, house prices and the daily agonies of dealing with teenage children.

He didn't really care what they talked about – nominally, this evening's 'title' was something about Chinese girls with pushy mothers – as long as she was out of the house for a few hours. Once every few months of course there was the nightmare scenario of his wife being the hostess for the evening; when the gaggle of big-haired women would descend on his house and he would be desperate to get out, but when he had the place to himself, as he did tonight, he could really kick back and enjoy it.

He could pull on a scruffy old jumper, open a bottle of something decent and enjoy his collection.

It wasn't the only time he spent pottering with his machines of course, but it was never the same when Susan was about. He could sense her disapproval seeping through the walls; from the pristine kitchen or the Sitting Room of a Thousand Cushions into the cold, dusty garage where, to a soothing soundtrack of fifties and sixties jazz, he would happily fill hours restoring rollers and oiling chains.

His Royal Blades, his Ambassadors, his cherished Eclipse Rocket.

Stepping into the garage and waiting for the strip lights to flicker into life, he breathed in the glorious smell of them all. The oil and the polished wood and still the heady whiff of grass from fifty, sixty, a hundred years ago. He moved eagerly towards his workbench, having already decided that tonight would be Sonny Rollins and some more restoration work on the 1965 Ransome Marquis he'd bought the week before.

He switched on the CD player and, once the music had begun, he moved, snapping his fingers to the beat, towards the metal shelving unit stacked with oil cans, paint tins and neatly labelled jars filled with antique screws, nuts and bolts. He jumped back and cried out in alarm when the old man stepped from behind it.

A noise more than a word.

Sonny Rollins' sax kicked in at that moment, as if Jacobson's yelp had been a cue, but he was unaware of it, and after those few seconds it took for his breathing to even out just enough for him to speak, he had to shout above the frantic drumming in his chest.

'Who the hell are you?'

The old man stared casually around the garage, nodding his head gently in time to the music. 'Yeah, well. Sixty-four-thousand-dollar question, that one.'

Jacobson took a step towards him, energised by a welcome surge of anger and adrenalin. Some tramp sleeping off the booze, it had to be; a shock of white hair and a plastic bag dangling from his fingers. The clothes looked too new though, and something about the smile, the enjoyment in it, was becoming familiar.

'You can bugger off now, or I can call the police,' he said. 'Simple as that.'

The old man didn't move, content to let his plastic bag swing a little.

'The police know me,' Jacobson said, his voice breaking slightly.

The old man nodded. 'Well of course they bloody do. Important bloke like you.'

Jacobson felt his breath catch. If the intruder knew who he was, it had to be bad. It must mean he had been targeted for some reason. He felt a wave of relief as he remembered that he was alone in the house; that whatever was going to happen, his wife was safe.

'Your problem is, they know me as well. I haven't seen them for a while, that's all.' The old man smiled when he saw Jacobson's eyes widen with recognition; when the penny dropped. '*There* you go,' he said.

'What do you want?'

The old man began to walk slowly towards him – no great urgency to the sway and swagger, moving to the music – and Jacobson was simply unable to step away. Rooted to the spot, too terrified to move a muscle. God, how many times had he heard that story at work?

'There's money in the house.'

'I'm sure there is.'

'Isn't that what you want?'

'Unfortunately not.'

'Then what—?'

The old man was quick; faster and fitter than he had any right to be, than Jacobson had ever been, lifting up the plastic bag suddenly and rushing forward when Jacobson's eyes moved with it.

Richard Jacobson sucked in a last gasp of grass and motor oil, half a second before the old man punched him in the face.

CHAPTER 30

Alfie was wide awake, and crying, which certainly didn't help.

Wailing, he threw himself around on the bed, as if his little world were coming to an end. Helen kept leaning across to grab him, pulling him towards her, but he writhed in her arms, unwilling to be cuddled, until she let him go again.

'I feel like such a bloody idiot.' Helen was sitting up in bed, Thorne standing at the door, a reversal of their positions the night before. The expression of concern Helen had been wearing then was nowhere to be seen.

'I'm sorry,' Thorne said. 'I can only say it so many times.'

'When I called you this morning I thought you might be asleep. So I waited a bit and when you still weren't answering I kept trying your mobile, then eventually I gave up.'

'I *was* asleep, and when I woke up I was feeling better, so—'

'Bollocks, Tom.' She held a hand out towards Alfie, but he swatted it away. 'That's bollocks and I don't want to hear it.'

216

Thorne let out a slow, beery breath and closed the door. He sat down near the bottom of the bed, just outside slapping distance. 'I wanted the day off, OK?'

'So, why not just say "I fancy throwing a sickie" or whatever? Why bother lying to *me*?' Before Thorne could answer, she said, 'It feels like there's been a lot of lying lately and I'm fed up with it.'

Thorne said, 'What's that supposed to mean?' because it felt as though he should, though he knew he was only prolonging the agony.

'Oh, come on.'

'No, tell me.'

'All that crap about catching up on paperwork and going to non-existent record fairs. The other night, when you said you went to see Phil.'

'I was with Phil,' Thorne said. 'I was with him again tonight.'

'More "boyfriend trouble", was it?'

Thorne shook his head, took a few seconds to think about the best way into it. Alfie crawled across, softly butted his head against Thorne's arm a few times, then moved away again. 'I made that up because it was easier,' Thorne said. 'And all that other stuff.' A deep breath. 'Phil's been helping me out with this suicide thing, all right? Dave Holland as well.'

Helen sat up a little higher. 'Suicide thing? You're talking about that couple a week ago, right?' She shook her head. 'I thought you were told to leave that alone. I mean, Jesmond called.'

'It wasn't suicide and it's not just them.' He moved a little closer to Helen. 'Five murders so far, all made to look like suicide. I found out exactly what links them together and I know who's doing it.' He saw the look on her face. 'Helen, *really*. Listen . . .'

'No.'

'I'll call Phil.' He fumbled for his phone. 'You can ask him!'

'Bloody hell.' She was still shaking her head, more in exasperation than shock at what was she was hearing.

He told her the rest of it.

When Thorne had finished, Helen drew her son to her again. She held him tightly to her chest and stroked his head, shushing him gently while she thought about everything Thorne had said. Alfie had calmed down a little, though he was still crying, still not ready to settle.

'You said Phil's helping you? And Holland?'

Thorne nodded, relieved that he had finally got through to her, that she could see the scale of the case he had stumbled across. 'And Kitson as well. A bit of the legwork.'

She nodded, still shushing, still thinking. 'But Phil's a pathologist, and Kitson and Holland are *north* London MIT.'

Thorne did not need to ask what she was thinking. 'Look, you know I went to MIT at Lewisham. I tried to tell Hackett what was going on and he wouldn't have any of it.'

'That was before,' Helen said.

'Before what?'

'Listen to yourself! That was before you put all this together. Before you had five murders. Go to him with exactly what you've just told me and hand it over so it can be investigated properly. I think he might listen now.'

'They had their chance.'

'God, how old are you?' She tried to hang on to Alfie, but he wriggled away on to the bed. 'Do your bloody *job*.'

'I have been doing my job,' Thorne said. 'How d'you think I put this thing together? *Me*, OK?'

'Good, well done.' She spat the sarcasm out. 'Give yourself a pat on the back, Inspector. Then get your head out of your arse and do the right thing for everybody.'

The child crawled across to Thorne. He reached out a hand and Alfie used it to haul himself to his feet. Thorne held on to him. 'Do you want me to move back to my place?'

Helen shrugged. 'Do what you want.'

'Obviously it's handier for me to stay here, but if you'd rather I was out of your way . . .'

'It's done now, isn't it?' Helen sounded sad and sullen, her eyes on Alfie as he bounced on the bed, still whimpering as he clutched Thorne's sleeve. 'So I can't really see what difference it makes. You've told me, so I can't pretend I don't know what you're up to.'

'I didn't want to keep on lying.'

'Oh yes, well done for being honest.' The anger flashed back into her voice. 'Now we just have to deal with the huge mess you've made.'

'You don't have to deal with anything,' Thorne said.

'Really?' She pushed the duvet away, as if she were suddenly hot. 'Have you any idea of the position you've put me in? Do you honestly believe that when this all comes out, and it *is* going to come out . . . they won't think that I knew what you were doing? How many careers are you trying to ruin, exactly?'

Thorne had nothing to say, certainly nothing that would help things. He was grateful when Alfie came into the crook of his arm and instinctively he raised his free hand and laid it against the boy's forehead. 'He feels a bit hot,' Thorne said. 'Maybe he's got an ear infection or something.'

'Oh, really?'

'Do you want me to go and fetch the Calpol?'

'No.' Helen was already half out of bed and she quickly snatched Alfie up from Thorne's arms without a word. She looked less than happy when he began to cry even louder.

'Listen, it wasn't even my idea to tell you.'

'Oh, great,' Helen said.

'Christ, I can't win, can I?'

Helen stopped at the doorway, hoisting Alfie a little higher on to her shoulder. 'No, Tom,' she said. 'I really don't think you can.'

CHAPTER 31

Mercer is a little startled when Jacobson comes round suddenly, coughing and spluttering. He'd been looking around the garage while he was waiting, killing time and struggling to take in all the old rubbish Jacobson has amassed.

Unbelievable . . .

He's sitting a few feet away on a metal stool he's dragged from behind the workbench. He has the plastic bag on his lap and now he's wearing the thin, plastic gloves that had been stuffed in his pocket. He's turned the music off.

'Who the hell collects old lawnmowers?' he asks.

Jacobson says nothing. He just moans, his hand moving to his shattered nose, and he shuffles back until he's sitting against the wall. He spends a few seconds trying to work out why he's wet, what's dripping from his hair.

He says, 'Oh, God,' when he smells the petrol.

'Handy for me though,' Mercer says, 'because I didn't have to bring any with me in the end. All the petrol anyone could want sloshing about in this load of old junk, isn't there?' He sticks a foot

221

out, nudges one of the mowers. 'I mean, I know everyone needs a hobby and all that. Stamps or trainspotting maybe, but this is just stupid. What's the point of it?' He doesn't wait for an answer. He knows he isn't going to get one, that Jacobson has better things to think about. 'As it happens a lot of lads take up hobbies inside, but, you know, at least they've got an excuse with all that time on their hands. Spending weeks making models, ships in bottles, all that carry-on. Endless boxes of Swan Vestas, just so they can make a scale model of some cathedral or what have you out of match-sticks. Months and months it takes them . . . years, sometimes. Lovely to look at, I'm not denying it . . . or at least they are until some nutcase smashes it to bits just because they got a smaller portion of steak and kidney pie in the canteen.'

He shrugs. 'Waste of bloody time in the end.'

He reaches into his jacket. Says, 'Talking of matches,' and takes out a box from his pocket.

He shakes it.

Jacobson says, 'Oh no . . . oh, Jesus.'

'It was such a simple thing I asked you to do, Richard, and now look where we are.' Mercer smiles. 'You haven't got the first idea what I'm on about, have you? You can't even remember it.'

Jacobson tries to speak, but his words are lost in a fit of spluttering and he reaches up to wipe away the petrol that is running into his eyes.

'I know you were only a pupil barrister back then, doing all the menial stuff, but that was supposed to include carrying messages backwards and forwards, wasn't it?' He opens the matchbox slowly, then quickly shuts it again. 'Remember a woman called Fiona Daniels? No, course you don't . . . well, she was the silly cow behind the counter at the bank in Croydon, the one standing on the other side of a *very* filthy bit of glass, I should add. Coming back now, is it?'

He waits, and Jacobson manages a small nod.

'Right, well I should probably kick off by letting you know that Mrs Daniels got what was coming to her a couple of weeks ago. All got a bit much for her by all accounts, so out of the blue she just gets up and walks into a reservoir, poor old soul.' He sits back, his hands together on top of the plastic bag that is still sitting on his lap. 'Not a bad way to go, I suppose. Compared to some, at any rate.'

Jacobson cries out and throws his head back into the brick wall behind him.

'Now, all you had to do was make sure they asked Fiona Daniels about that screen. The one she stood behind all day long doling out readies or whatever. Pointed out that it was dirty . . . cracked as well, let everyone know that she couldn't possibly have been as certain as she said she was, that her positive identification was hardly positive at all. That was all. Just make sure your boss pulled her up on that, but you never passed it on.'

'Couldn't,' Jacobson croaks.

'Come again?'

'It would have . . . incriminated you.' The shouting makes Jacobson cough loudly and he turns his head to spit out the blood and the petrol that has leaked into his mouth. 'Shown you'd been in the bank.'

'Yeah well, that's crap for a start. I could have gone in there any time to cash a cheque or something, same as anybody else.'

'I couldn't . . .''

'You *didn't*,' Mercer says. 'So, thirty years later, here we are.' He shakes the matchbox again and now Jacobson struggles to stand up. Mercer comes off the stool fast and moves towards him and Jacobson quickly drops to the floor and begins to cry.

Mercer sits down again and holds up the matchbox.

'Now, let's get one thing straight. This *is* going to happen one way or another. There's no way out of it, so no point whatsoever begging or struggling or generally messing about. Fair enough? But . . . you do have a choice.'

He takes a battered green folder from the plastic bag, opens it, then leans down to lay the contents out on the floor. He spreads them out carefully in front of Jacobson. 'You see where I'm going with this?'

Jacobson says, 'No!' Screams it.

'So, you need to have a quick think and make a decision, old son.' He watches Jacobson move on to his hands and knees, moaning as he reaches towards the things that Mercer has laid out on the floor. 'That's right, have a good look at that lot. It's obvious what they mean, isn't it? Then have a think about what's going to happen if you *don't* do the noble thing and let me know.'

'Please,' Jacobson says. 'Please, please . . .'

Mercer leans forward and takes a match out of the box. 'Are you going to strike this thing, or am I?'

PART III

THE STATE OF THE REMAINS

CHAPTER 32

When Mercer steps out of the van in the rear courtyard, he sees that tosser Herbert in the doorway, jabbering to one of the other gorillas from the security firm. They're sharing a cigarette and some joke that clearly they both think is hilarious. They keep nodding towards him and pissing themselves; him standing there like a prize plum in his polished shoes and his best blue suit, handcuffs locked that extra bit tightly so it takes the skin off his wrists.

Shivering his tits off and waiting for them to finish, keen to get inside.

'Bit of a pickle this morning,' Herbert says. 'Seems like the world and his wife's on trial for something or other today so all the holding cells are full.'

Suddenly the other security guard is next to him and he and Herbert take Mercer's arms and lead him towards the doors. 'Not a problem though,' Herbert says and cheerfully tells him that they're taking him to the old holding cells instead. The ones down in the basement, the ones the tourists go to look at.

Everywhere you look in the basement there are museum pieces: a door from Newgate, inches thick; some medieval stocks; an ancient set of shackles streaked brown with rust or old blood. The holding cell that has not been used for more than a century is the last one on a damp, musty-smelling corridor.

The special cell.

'Won't keep you long,' Herbert says, as he slams the door.

So, he paces for a while, avoids leaning against the wall for fear of dirtying his suit, knowing that he needs to look his very best up there in the dock. When Herbert does not come back, he sits and wraps his arms around himself and tries to block out the whispers that come up from the floor, the voices repeating the messages gouged long ago into the crumbling, blackened brickwork.

Bastads.

No justiss for the lykes of us.

Only God can be my judge.

It might be hours later when the door eventually opens again and he screams at Herbert. He tells him that they're going to be late, that the trial will have started already. Herbert tells him to calm down. 'The trial's already finished,' he says. 'Job done. Bish, bash, bosh.'

He tries to protest, to force his way past the guards, but they push him back, laughing, towards the small black door at the other end of the cell and out into the light.

Dead Man's Walk.

He is shoved along the narrow passageway. It's tiled with grubby cream bricks and water runs down the high walls on either side and he knows he is tramping across the dead, the ones who have taken this walk before him. He can hear them below him. They are laughing too, the rhythm of it rising up through the soles of his good shoes and, for the life of him, he can't think what they've got to laugh at; stuck down there, godless and gaping, their mouths filled with black mud and quicklime.

He walks on, passing beneath a series of low arches that seem to get narrower the further he goes. It's like Alice in Wonderland or something, like an Alfred Hitchcock film, and by the time he reaches the final arch he can barely squeeze through. It's not an illusion, he realises, it's deliberate; designed that way to prevent the condemned man turning and trying to run, and he has to hand it to the vicious so-and-so who built it, even as his legs start to give way and he's shoved through and round the corner and he gets his first sight of the rope.

'Might as well,' Herbert says. 'Seeing as we're here.'

Guards step forward then with the thick leather belts for his wrists and ankles, and the hangman's lips are moving as he makes his calculations, and for some reason they're still hammering the crossbeam into place when Mercer opens his eyes . . .

There's banging outside – workmen in the road below his window – and for a few seconds he cannot be certain where he is.

He knows he's no longer dreaming, knows it's a bed and not cold earth, but still it takes him a few moments to get his bearings. To remember that he's not staying with the coke dealer and his family any more. That he's woken in the umpteenth different room since he left Her Majesty's facilities behind.

He stretches and farts; he needs to piss.

He knows he'll be dreaming about prison for the rest of his life and even when he was inside he dreamed about the trial; those last few weeks when he was technically innocent, when he still had some hope. But he's been dreaming about little else since he came out. He's decided it's because of what he's doing. His subconscious or whatever it is, giving him a nudge; reassuring him that he's doing the right thing. Taking away the twinges of doubt and reminding him of what they did.

What he's lost.

When he can't hold on any longer he gets up. He pulls on underpants and a T-shirt and pads out on to the landing then along to the bathroom. He can hear voices downstairs, hushed so as not to wake him or be overheard if he's already awake.

The toilet's been cleaned very recently and, as he's pissing the bleach up into a froth, he thinks about those bits of his dream that remain vivid;

yet to fragment and scatter. Maybe this one was rather more than a nudge and he's always been able to take a hint when he's given one. Gift horses and all that.

He flushes, and as the cistern slowly fills he can still see the water running down those grubby cream tiles on either side of him. He moves to the sink and washes his hands, enjoying the smell of the expensive soap as he thinks about the one he still blames the most. The one who's already on Dead Man's Walk, even if he doesn't know it yet.

The one who's been hiding.

CHAPTER 33

The days following Thorne's meeting with Frank Anderson and the confrontation with Helen seemed endless. Hectic and stressful, packed with major headaches and minor incidents. They were also hugely frustrating as Thorne made the decisions he was paid to make, filed reports and stared at clocks in overheated meeting rooms while he waited for something to break in the Mercer investigation, well aware that Holland and Kitson were busy on the jobs they were *supposed* to be doing. Waiting for Mercer himself to make his next move; terrified that if and when that happened, he would wonder if it was a death he could have prevented, if he'd only done what Helen was telling him to do.

What they were all telling him to do.

Two days on late turns – 2.00 p.m. until midnight – then the worst day of the rotation. The 'day off' between late turn and night shift, when you fell into bed at one in the morning – if you were lucky – got up around 10.00 a.m. and started your night shift at 10.00 p.m. the same day. Twelve hours down time, then twenty-four without sleep.

It was the day they all hated, but falling on a Sunday, when Helen was at home, had made it potentially more unpleasant than usual.

They had not seen much of each other since the argument, Thorne eager to please whenever they had been in the flat together and Helen seemingly happy enough to let him try. They slept in the same bed, but no more than that. Their exchanges had been pleasant enough, workman-like. Sunday, though, would mean an effort to avoid one another and Thorne's plans to do just that by sleeping as late as possible then offering to take Alfie out for a few hours had been scuppered when he'd woken at nine to find it pissing down outside.

'I know,' Helen had said. She had moved to join him at the window, the rain like tin-tacks thrown against the glass. She sounded every bit as unhappy about the day ahead as Thorne did, but her half-smile made him feel a little better. She said, 'We are going to be watching a *lot* of *Peppa Pig*,' then made them both bacon, egg and beans.

As it was, they only ended up having to watch a couple of hours of a programme that had clearly been thought up by someone who was as high as a kite. When Alfie went for his nap in the afternoon, Thorne was able to watch the football, while Helen sat at her computer and lobbed the occasional sarcastic comment across. Later, she cooked them all pasta and, by the time Thorne was thinking about heading in to work, he had decided

235

that the day had gone a whole lot better than it might have done.

That things were pretty much back to normal, in fact.

Just before he had left, though, Helen had said something about hoping he had a good shift, said it in such a way that it was clear she had forgotten and forgiven nothing. That she was pleased to see him going to do the job he was getting paid for and that the shitty weather had at least kept him at home; kept him from getting himself and others into even more trouble than they were in already.

Now, three hours into his shift and one hour into a no less shitty Monday morning, trouble of a very different kind was brewing. The TTFN crew were gathering in numbers outside a fast food place in the shopping precinct and the units in attendance were calling for back-up.

'Doesn't look like they're queuing for kebabs,' Woodley had said, when she'd radioed in.

Thorne had been sitting in his office, staring at the photograph of Terry Mercer that Holland had dug out, copied and emailed to him. It was the photo taken on Mercer's arrest more than thirty years ago and, though he would obviously look very different now, it was the only one they had. Thorne had seen countless such pictures over the years, but not too many of the men and women in them had been smiling. Cocky, that's what Tully had said. Always thought he would walk away. Thorne had every reason to believe that Terry

Mercer would be thinking the very same thing three decades down the line.

Another burst of radio chatter. The TTFN soldiers were now openly taunting the officers in attendance.

Thorne folded up the picture and slipped it inside his Met vest as he walked out to meet Christine Treasure. On their way towards the car, a message came through that a unit was on its way in with a young male arrested on suspicion of rape. Thorne and Treasure went through to the custody suite to wait, while the details filtered through.

A woman attacked walking home across Ladywell Fields. The description of a suspect quickly circulated. A young man arrested within twenty minutes, still carrying a kitchen knife and making no attempt to hide the scratches on his face.

When the suspect was brought in, Thorne recognised the boy from the cemetery; the harmless truant who had been 'caught short' four days earlier. The waste of time. The boy saw Thorne staring at him, nodded a casual greeting as the handcuffs were removed.

As the boy was being booked in, Treasure took Thorne to one side. 'Come on, there's no way we could have known, is there?'

Thorne was still looking across at the boy with the ragged wound beneath one eye and blood on his collar, watching as he turned out his pockets and handed their contents across to be logged by the custody sergeant. A few feet away, the arresting officer was on the radio to a colleague who had accompanied the victim to Lewisham Hospital. He said, 'Run the rape kit as soon as she's been patched up.'

'It was a judgement call.' Treasure hitched up her vest and straightened her hat. 'Nobody's fault.'

As much to himself as to anyone else, Thorne said, 'I keep getting them wrong though, don't I?'

It had always been in Thorne's mind to avoid going straight back to the flat when his shift had ended and wait until Helen had left for work. Even though things on the domestic front seemed to be moving in the right direction, he decided that he would stick to his original plan and stop off somewhere for breakfast.

No point pushing his luck at home as well.

So, half an hour after signing off reports on the rape, what turned out to be a minor fracas in the shopping precinct and a dozen other incidents, Thorne stared down at his second fry-up in less than twenty-four hours. The tinned tomatoes spilling from the plate, what might have been an egg, sausages like fat, pale fingers. If the Job was messing with his head, it wasn't doing the rest of him a lot of good either.

'Yes? What you wanted?'

Thorne looked up at the teenage girl behind the counter – what was she, Russian? – and nodded. Said, 'Great, thanks.'

He took out the photo of Terry Mercer and propped it up against the plastic, tomato-shaped ketchup dispenser. If the food itself didn't do the job, he guessed it might curb his appetite a little.

He studied it as he ate.

Mercer had been a good-looking man thirty years ago. A Mediterranean face, fine-featured with thick black hair and dark eyes. A charmer, Thorne guessed, when he wasn't wearing a balaclava and pointing a sawn-off shotgun at you.

What had Caroline Dunn said to him at Gartree? *People change. They get old . . .*

He became aware of the teenage girl hovering at his shoulder, waiting for the chance to lean over and take his plate away. He turned and looked up at her.

'Finished?' she asked.

Thorne said that he was.

'No good?'

'I wasn't as hungry as I thought,' Thorne said.

The girl reached across to pick up the dirty plate and he saw her looking at the photograph. She stood still for a moment or two, one hand on the plate, her mouth creased in concentration as if she was trying to work something out.

'OK?' Thorne asked.

She shrugged and said, 'It's nothing,' and was moving back towards the counter as Thorne's phone began to ring.

'This is Alastair Howard . . .'

It took Thorne a few seconds to place the name.

'You left a message, asking me to call?'

'Yes, of course,' Thorne said. 'Thanks for getting back to me.' The junior barrister on Terry Mercer's defence team, now a senior judge. Thorne was hugely relieved to be hearing from him, having been unable to make contact four days earlier when he'd rung around to put the word out that Mercer had been released from prison.

'I'd have returned your call sooner,' Howard said, 'but I've been away and then I came home to discover that an old colleague of mine had died. So, all been a bit hectic.'

'I'm sorry,' Thorne said.

'I'd known him over thirty years, so it was something of a shock.'

Thirty years. Thorne swallowed and looked at the picture of Terry Mercer. Those big dark eyes, a smile like it was a holiday snap. He said, 'God.'

'I know, and it was extremely unpleasant.'

'Oh?' Thorne looked across, saw that the teenage girl was watching him.

'I hope you're not eating,' Howard said. 'I really don't want to put you off your breakfast.'

Helen had evidently left for work in a hurry, as the breakfast things had not been cleared away. There was a half-drunk mug of tea on the table near the front door and gobbets of Alfie's porridge clung to every available surface in the kitchen. Thorne knew there were Brownie points available for cleaning up, but, much as he needed them, they would have to remain unearned.

240

He desperately needed to sleep – at least for a few hours – before he left the flat again. He trudged through to the bedroom and called Holland as he undressed. He told him about his conversation with Alastair Howard, about Richard Jacobson's death.

'I heard about that,' Holland said. 'I was going to call you.'

Thorne said, 'Right,' but could not shake the suspicion that Holland was lying. He dropped down on to the edge of the bed and, with a groan, reached down to take his socks off.

'Good news is there's a Murder Squad looking at this one.'

Thorne grunted. Howard had mentioned it.

'Understandable, though.'

'Should have looked at the Coopers,' Thorne said. 'Should have looked at all of them.'

'Not too many suicides like this though, are there?' Holland was talking quickly, he sounded nervous. 'Immolation, or whatever you call it. Kind of thing people usually do when they want to make a point about something . . . you know, in public. Plus, I think the judge might have had a quiet word. Put some pressure on.'

'Why is it *good news*, Dave?'

'Sorry?'

Thorne said nothing. He lay down and pushed his feet beneath the duvet, reached for the edge of the cover and dragged it slowly back towards his throat.

'Come on, it's got to be a good thing, surely? Whichever way you look at it.' Holland paused, waiting for Thorne to cut in, then pressed on a little more tentatively. 'If they do put it down as suspicious . . . you know, if they can get some sort of decent lead and they follow it up, this can get done properly.'

'And you're off the hook.'

'Well, yeah,' Holland said. 'With any luck. We all are.'

Thorne reached to turn the bedside lamp off. Holland was still talking, winding up, saying something about keeping an ear to the ground. A blade of grey light cut into the room through a gap in the curtains, but Thorne was too tired to get up and do anything about it.

CHAPTER 34

There were jokes, of course, there had to be. All part and parcel of the Job; the defence mechanism, the pressure valve, whatever you chose to call it. The Kidnap Unit had their fair share of comedians as did the Counter-Terrorist lot. The Homicide Command – naturally – and Serious and Organised, and there were probably even a few chuckles to be had every now and again in Wildlife Crime and Dog Support. On a Child Abuse Investigation Team though, for all the obvious reasons, there were more than most.

Laugh a bloody minute on a CAIT.

'It's the way we cope, isn't it?' One of Helen's colleagues had been philosophising one night, after a few drinks too many. 'You have a laugh and a bit of a giggle and it stops the really terrible stuff getting through, doesn't it? Not all of it, I mean we're only bloody human, right? But we try and see the funny side, so we only get the damage in small doses, so hopefully we don't get damaged ourselves. It's a bit like homeopathy, I reckon . . .'

It had sounded a bit like bollocks to Helen, though she'd said nothing.

Yes, you did whatever you could to keep certain things at arm's length and that famous black humour helped some people deal with what they saw and heard every day. For others though, it was no more than a justification for filthy jokes; for remarks that would be wholly unacceptable in any other context.

Her own strategy was rather more straight-forward.

Some days, she just went home and held on to Alfie that little bit tighter.

Still, she joined in, she laughed along when it was expected. Even more so since she'd come back to work. The last thing she wanted was to give those she worked with any more reason to believe that she had been affected by what had happened three months before.

It was a little harder than usual at the moment.

This morning, it was nothing she hadn't heard before; just Gill Bellinger and a few of the others, sharing a joke at the drinks machine after the briefing. The one about the stingy paedophile asking kids to pay for the sweets. Last time Helen had heard it, the comedy paedophile had been Jewish, but Bellinger had clearly not wanted to offend DC Susan Cohen.

Helen watched Cohen laughing loudest of the lot and thought how strange it was, where people drew the line when it came to causing offence, or taking it. Clearly, her own laughter had not been quite convincing enough, because as soon as everyone had begun drifting back towards their desks, Bellinger wandered over and asked how she was.

'Heard the joke before, that's all,' Helen said.

Bellinger grunted. 'I need some new material.'

'What about this two-year-old with half his bones broken?' Helen nodded towards her computer screen. 'Should be something in there.'

Bellinger blinked. Said, 'Everything OK at home? Alfie all right?'

'He's fine.'

'So, Tom then?'

'I don't want to talk about it, Gill.'

But Helen did. The problem was finding someone to whom she could talk. She had already arranged to go and see her father at the end of her shift, but she knew how that would turn out. She would bitch about Jenny for a while and he would be sympathetic and then they would end up talking about Paul. The two of them had always got on and her father had been something of an ally when everything had fallen apart and her younger sister had begun to stir things. With Paul gone though, Jenny had miraculously appeared to forget she had ever disliked him and cast her beady eyes around for another target, aside from Helen herself, obviously. Tom had been the natural choice. Helen guessed, even though her father had yet to meet Tom, that he would take her side, as he did on most things. Comforting as that would be, she would not be able to talk to him about the situation Tom had got himself into professionally.

*Un*professionally . . .

There was probably only one person who would understand, who knew Tom well enough to talk frankly about what was happening. Helen had been considering it ever since the argument with Tom, but guessed that it would not prove to be the easiest of conversations. She might well be opening a can of worms, but with nowhere else to turn she just kept telling herself that Tom had already opened a far larger and more dangerous one.

She did not have the number on her phone.

As soon as Bellinger had gone, Helen went into her database and looked up the contact details for Hornsey Mortuary.

CHAPTER 35

The Jacobson house was a detached Georgian property on one of the most exclusive roads in Blackheath; the 'London village' that had become an enclave of professionals and well-heeled media types and was one of the priciest areas in the south-east of the city. It was certainly a world away from Catford or Lewisham, just three miles up the road.

Eliot Place skirted the 'black' heath itself. It was thought by some to have been so-called in memory of the plague victims buried there, though the name was probably and somewhat more prosaically derived from the colour of the soil. There *were* bodies beneath it of course, as there were beneath most of London's green spaces, but Thorne knew they were more likely those of the many killed in the battles and duels fought here or the highwaymen who had once roamed the heath and were sent to the gallows by the legal antecedents of Richard Jacobson QC.

Jacobson, who had once been a fresh-faced pupil barrister.

Thirty years before, when he was only twenty-two years old, when he'd been a lowly part of Terry Mercer's defence team and done something for which he had never been forgiven.

Thorne parked around the corner. The early-morning rain had long since cleared and it was unseasonably warm enough for him to leave his jacket in the car. He walked half the length of Eliot Place and stood looking at the house from the other side of the road.

I really don't want to put you off your breakfast . . .

The door to the double garage was closed, giving no hint of what had gone on behind it. A silver Audi was parked on the drive but there was little sign of life behind the mullioned windows upstairs or down. As Thorne crossed the road, a black and white cat jumped up from a flower bed on to the low wall that ran around the front lawn. It stretched, front paws then back, and sat watching his approach.

Thorne stifled a yawn and wiped his fingers across eyes that were scratchy and raw. In the end, he had only managed three hours' sleep and the buzz he might otherwise have expected at the scene of the latest murder was only dimly felt in heavy limbs and a head filled with cotton wool. He reached out to stroke the cat. It mewed and lifted its chin.

'Can I help you?'

Thorne looked across to see a woman standing near the Audi. She was in her mid-fifties, possibly

248

a little older; full-figured, with dark hair cut just short of her shoulders. She was wearing jeans and what looked like a man's striped shirt. She had definitely not emerged through the front door, so Thorne guessed that she had come from the back of the house; from the passageway that ran alongside the garage and probably led to a garden at the rear.

Thorne raised a hand and walked towards her. He reached into his pocket for his warrant card as he got closer.

'You're a bit early,' she said.

Thorne had no idea what she was talking about. He said, 'Sorry, I don't think I'm who you're expecting.'

'You're not here about Richard?'

'Well, yes, but I just stopped by.' Thorne introduced himself, told her he was with Uniform. She wiped her hands on the back of her jeans before she shook hands and Thorne wondered if she'd been gardening.

'Susan Jacobson,' she said.

'I was just wondering if you'd like us to arrange for a patrol car to come by once or twice every evening,' Thorne said. 'Keep an eye on things.'

'Really?'

'It wouldn't be a problem.'

'What things?'

He could well understand that she might be perplexed at his offer, even a little annoyed. Stable doors, horses that had already bolted, all that. 'Just to check that you're OK, that's all.'

The irritation that had been apparent behind the woman's fixed smile washed itself from her face as the compulsion towards simple politeness kicked in. She nodded and said, 'Yes, why not. Thanks.'

Thorne told her that he would arrange it.

They looked at each other for a few seconds, the cat trotting over to rub itself against the woman's legs. 'Would you like something to drink?' she asked. 'Water or something, I mean.' She smiled. 'Don't want you to think I've got a bottle of wine open before lunchtime.'

'Water would be great,' Thorne said.

Susan Jacobson led Thorne around the car and into the passageway that ran down the side of the garage. There was a large plastic water butt, black and green rubbish bins and recycling boxes; the utilitarian nature of the space balanced by the plants in a collection of old chimney pots and the hanging baskets attached to the wall every few feet.

There was a door into the garage halfway along. Susan Jacobson walked quickly past it, but Thorne stopped.

'Would you mind if I had a look?' he asked.

She hesitated, then shrugged. 'I'll be in the garden,' she said. She nodded at the door. 'It's open . . .'

There was a light switch just inside the door. Thorne waited for the strip lights to splutter and fizz into life, then stepped inside and closed the door behind him.

Began breathing through his mouth.

The garage was huge. Cupboards lined one wall and freestanding metal shelving units were arranged almost ceiling high along another. The collection of mowers and old engines had been pushed back towards the edges and covered, but wooden handles protruded through the array of tarpaulins and slivers of rusty blade could be glimpsed through gashes in black bin-bags.

The smell was everywhere: fuel and cooked meat.

Beyond a light dusting of fingerprint powder on the metal shelves and around the door-frame, the Scenes of Crime team had left little evidence that they were ever there. No chalk lines, no fluttering remnants of crime-scene tape so beloved of TV shows. The only physical sign that anything had merited a police presence in the first place was the large scorch mark on the garage floor.

There was no clearly recognisable shape. It was ragged and uneven, some areas darker against the grey cement than others. Still, looking down as if he had been confronted with some oversized ink-blot test, Thorne could not help seeing the patterns of hopelessly flailing arms and of legs that kicked against the agony.

A black snow-angel.

Thorne took a deep breath – the taste of what lingered in the air no more pleasant than the smell – and looked around. The large boxes, the tarpaulins, those dark spaces between the rows of shelving. There were plenty of places to hide.

Ever since that first night in the Coopers' bedroom, Thorne had been asking himself how Mercer got so close to his victims. How he got inside their houses and flats. The open door to the garage had confirmed his suspicion that these killings had been carefully planned, with plenty of time built in to watch and wait. To look for the times when his targets were at their most careless, to study the patterns of behaviour that made them vulnerable.

Fiona Daniels (70), Brian Gibbs (71) and the others.

Mercer had known that the elderly were that little bit more likely to be careless when it came to matters of security; that an opportunity would eventually present itself. Thorne guessed that one or two had simply opened their front door to him.

The side door to the Jacobsons' garage was almost certainly locked at night, but Thorne was betting that Mercer had been well aware it was often left open during the day. That he had crept in many hours before the murder would be carried out, then settled down to wait. Such a possibility would not have been lost on the Murder Investigation Team of course, but they would need more than that. Knowing that someone else *could* have been in that garage when Richard Jacobson had set fire to himself was never going to be enough.

Thorne doubted that Terry Mercer had left them anything.

⋆   ⋆   ⋆

Susan Jacobson was sitting on a raised terrace with the promised glass of water. When Thorne joined her at the table she passed the glass to him and said, 'I'll redecorate in there, obviously. Haven't had much time to think about it the last few days. Well, you know.'

'All that stuff can wait,' Thorne said.

'God knows what I'm going to do with all those bloody machines of his. I don't know which ones are valuable.'

'What about a museum?'

She took a sip of water, thought about it. 'Yes, I think he would have liked that.' She stared out at the garden for a few seconds. 'I think his brother should have all his old jazz records. I mean *I* certainly don't want them and it'll be nice to have a bit more room.'

Thorne nodded, drank. He'd seen this many times before; the need to plan, to think ahead, to stay busy. It was understandable, but he was not convinced it was altogether healthy in the long term. It was only putting off something that needed facing up to and getting through. He had done much the same thing when his father had died . . . when his father had *been killed* . . . and he had come to regret it. He had thrown himself back into work far too quickly, taken on more than he could manage, when he should have allowed himself the time to take it in. He'd heard a counsellor talk once about 'owning' your grief. Thorne had certainly never owned his.

'Sod all wrong with wallowing,' Hendricks had said, and as usual he had been right.

'I can't stand all that parping and noodling,' Susan Jacobson said.

'Sorry?'

She looked at Thorne. 'Jazz . . .'

'Oh, me neither,' Thorne said.

He could not recall having seen a bigger garden in London. It sloped away from them, probably more than a hundred feet long and almost as wide, with tall trees – oaks, sycamores, a huge copper beech – shielding it on two sides and an old stone wall running along the third. The beds were wide and filled with flowers and the terrace was dotted with bay trees and box balls. 'This is lovely,' Thorne said. The lawn was neatly mown into stripes and he wondered how recently Richard Jacobson had used one of his precious machines on it. How long it would take for the stripes to fade.

'Should probably get rid of that thing too.' Susan Jacobson nodded towards the large trampoline, standing next to a rickety-looking shed in one of the corners. 'While I'm sorting things out. I mean, the kids are too old to want to use it again and I spend my life clearing away the leaves and fox poo. The fox *certainly* enjoys bouncing on it.' She smiled. 'I had a go myself last year after we had a party out here and put my back out for a month. Silly old mare . . .'

Her face crumpled suddenly and she looked down into her glass.

Thorne looked back towards the trampoline. Two squirrels were chattering and chasing each other through the tangle of branches above and there was music coming from a couple of gardens away.

'Have you heard anything?' she asked. 'I know you're not CID or whatever it is, but . . .'

'Sorry,' Thorne said. 'I don't know any more than you.'

'They took loads of stuff away.'

'All routine.'

'They were in there for ages, scraping and putting things in bags. They must know something.'

'What is it you're hoping to hear?' Thorne asked.

She looked at him.

'Which would you rather it was?' He inched his chair a little closer to her. 'Would knowing one way or the other really make all this any less painful?'

Jacqui Gibbs had told him that knowing her father had not taken his own life had made her feel a little better. The difference was, he had felt able to tell her the truth. With a Murder Investigation Team already looking into her husband's death, he could not tell Susan Jacobson what he believed. She would immediately pass it on, and then it would just be a question of whether he jumped before he was pushed. If Caroline Dunn would need to sort out that nice, comfy pillow for him at Gartree.

For reasons he knew were wholly selfish, Thorne

wanted, *needed* to hear that knowing whether her husband had been murdered or had committed suicide was not going to make this woman feel any better.

That it would not make any difference.

'I don't know,' she said, eventually. 'How could anyone possibly answer that?' She shook her head, turned to look out at the garden. 'If Richard . . . did that to himself, at least I'll know that's what he wanted. That it was his choice. I'll always wonder why though . . . and why on earth he chose to do it like that.' She took a few seconds, swallowed. 'If someone did that to him . . . all I can think about is how frightened he must have been and how long it . . . lasted.' She turned back to look at Thorne. The colour had gone from her face and her eyes were wide and glassy. 'I can't answer that question,' she said. 'I don't even know why you would ask me that question.'

'I'm sorry,' Thorne said. He finished his drink. He let the silence lengthen, hoping that it might become less awkward, but it didn't. He stood up and said, 'I'll leave you to it.'

He told her he would see himself out and, as he walked down past the garage towards the front of the house, he thought: Leave you to what, exactly?

To *what*?

As he emerged on to the sunlit drive, Thorne saw a car on the other side of the road. A BMW, its engine still running. Leaning against it, he recognised the unmistakable figure of DCI Neil Hackett.

Thorne stopped and stared across the road.

'Come over and get in,' Hackett shouted cheerily and beckoned Thorne towards him, squinting up at the sun and fanning his hand theatrically in front of his face. 'The air-con's running.'

CHAPTER 36

'Been to see the widow, then?' Hackett asked. 'Interesting.'

Thorne settled back into the soft cream leather of the BMW's passenger seat. So, Hackett was the officer Susan Jacobson had been expecting. The man who was leading the team looking into the circumstances of her husband's death. Thorne was not sure if this was good news for her, but he could not see any way in which it would work out well for him.

Like Hackett said.

Interesting.

'Just popped by to see if she wanted a patrol car to look in for the next few evenings,' Thorne said. The same think-on-his-feet bullshit that had seemed to work half an hour earlier with Susan Jacobson. 'Keep an eye on her.'

'That's extremely thoughtful.'

'Community policing,' Thorne said.

Hackett shifted his considerable bulk and leaned forward to adjust the temperature. It was certainly nice and cool in the car, but clearly not cool enough for him. Thorne had no idea how long Hackett had been leaning against his car, but there was a trickle of sweat running from his ear down to the collar of his expensive-looking shirt. He turned the dial a notch further into the blue zone. 'OK for you?'

'Fine,' Thorne said.

'Some music?' Hackett said. Without waiting for an answer he leaned forward again and turned on the sound system.

Thorne braced himself for the inevitable onslaught of soft rock; a nice Bryan Adams power ballad would be the perfect way to make him feel even more uncomfortable than he was already. He was pleasantly surprised to hear the opening chords of a familiar Johnny Cash track. His cover version of a Tom Petty number, 'I Won't Back Down'.

Thorne smiled, unable to shake the suspicion that there was a less than subtle message in Hackett's choice of song. If so, were the words meant to be a dig at Thorne or a description of Hackett himself? An accusation or a warning?

Hackett nodded his head in time with the music. 'This your kind of stuff, isn't it? Country.'

'Is there anything you don't know about me?' Thorne asked. 'My inside leg measurement in some file?'

Hackett smiled, drummed his palm against his thigh.

'You brought this along deliberately, did you?'

Thorne nodded towards the sound system control panel.

Hackett shook his head, laid it back against the headrest, both palms now tapping out the rhythm. 'I didn't even know I was going to be seeing you,' he said. 'Someone's getting paranoid.'

'So, just a coincidence.'

'Well, I know why *I'm* here,' Hackett said. 'I had an appointment. So I think the coincidence is that you're here. That's right, isn't it? I mean, it is a coincidence?'

'Like I said.'

'Right. The caring face of Uniform.' He left a beat. 'Oh, and it's thirty inches.'

'What?'

'Your inside leg measurement.' Another smile. 'Just a guess . . .'

They said nothing for ten, fifteen seconds. 'So, what are you going to tell her?' Thorne asked. 'Suspicious death or not?'

Hackett turned to look at him. Thorne could not be sure if the DCI was deciding whether or not to answer or simply picking his words. Choosing a lie, perhaps. Looking back at Hackett, Thorne suddenly found himself hoping – despite everything – that the man would simply say, 'Yes, it was murder and we know who did it.'

Nice and simple. The choice made for him, the truth out in the open and his own future in the lap of the gods, or at least the Top Brass. Would that not be better for all concerned?

'Waste of bloody time,' Hackett said. It sounded like he meant it.

'How come?'

'Haven't we already had this conversation?' Hackett said. 'What's that little thing we were talking about before? Oh yeah, evidence.' He shook his head. 'Bugger all of that as far as this one's concerned.'

It was more or less what Thorne had been expecting. Mercer had been jailed a year or two before DNA profiling came in, so he would have no worries on that score. His fingerprints would be on record, but Thorne was sure that a man who had planned his killing spree so carefully would not have jeopardised it for want of a pair of rubber gloves. While watching his victims he would have taken careful note of where any CCTV cameras were, along with the movements of any potentially nosy neighbours.

Not that being noticed once or twice would have worried him a great deal.

It was something else Terry Mercer had going for him.

People would always remember the menacing-looking gang of youngsters or the kid in the hoodie, but an old man was as good as invisible.

'Still, I suppose we had to go through the motions,' Hackett said. 'I mean it *was* an unusual one. Plus he was a QC, so there's always the chance someone he put away had a score to settle.'

Not someone he put away, Thorne thought.

'And he had some powerful friends, did our Mr

Jacobson. Some judge ringing up to give us grief every day.'

Thorne took a quick decision. 'Alastair Howard?'

Hackett turned and looked at him.

'I still have friends on the MIT,' Thorne said. 'I hear things.'

If Hackett was bothered by what Thorne was telling him, he didn't show it. It just seemed like a good idea to Thorne that if and when the you-know-what hit the fan, it would appear that he had been fed certain information rather than gone digging for it. He dried a sweaty palm in front of the air vent, wondering suddenly if he might just have inadvertently implicated Dave Holland and Yvonne Kitson.

Too late now.

'Anyway, nothing's panning out,' Hackett said, leaning back again and mouthing a few of Cash's words. 'So His Honour can carry on calling all he bloody well likes. Forensics have got sod all, nothing on CCTV, neighbours didn't see or hear anything. Looks like the poor bastard finally found some use for that collection of useless old crap in his garage.'

'That what you've come to tell her?'

Hackett nodded. 'Make all the right noises, you know. Assure her that we've done everything we can. At least she can have the body back now, get on and sort the funeral out.' He glanced at Thorne. 'Mind you, he's already done the cremation bit.' He waited for the laugh that didn't come, then sat forward. 'So, what the hell is it with you and suicides anyway?'

'No idea,' Thorne said.

'Whenever some nutcase tops himself, up you pop. Not thinking of going that way yourself, are you?'

'Coincidence, like you said.'

'Maybe you should look for a vacancy at the Samaritans.' Hackett did not bother waiting this time and just went ahead and laughed himself. He hauled himself forward and checked his hair in the mirror. 'Listen, maybe we could have a pint later on. Have a natter.'

'You serious?'

'Why not? Now we know we've got the same taste in music.'

'I've got to go to work.'

Hackett was still smoothing down a strand of hair that stubbornly refused to lie flat. 'Right,' he said, nice and slowly. 'So you have.'

It was plain enough that his audience with the DCI was at an end, so Thorne climbed out of the car. Walking away, the afternoon seemed even hotter and he was aware of the driver's door opening slowly behind him. He turned and watched Hackett lock the BMW, then amble across the road towards Susan Jacobson's house, hoisting up his trousers and straightening his tie.

Pasting on his best give-a-shit expression.

Halfway back to his own car, Thorne felt the vibration of an alert from his phone. He pulled it from his back pocket, turned off the silent mode and read a message from Ian Tully.

how's it going?
fancy another walk?
i think my dog liked you!

CHAPTER 37

It's the last one he's most nervous about.

Mostly because it *is* the last one – though he knows there's going to be a spot of clearing up needed as well – and he's not really sure how he's going to feel afterwards. Bound to be an anti-climax, he knows that. How could it be anything else after thirty years, but it's more a question of what he's going to do with himself when it's finished. Find himself a suitable hobby? Evenings at the bingo hall? A spot of fishing or a friendly game of dominoes with the other coffin-dodgers?

Fat fucking chance.

It's also because it's been the trickiest of them all to arrange, because finding the individual in question has not been easy. He never thought it would be, of course. The man has spent the best part of that same thirty years trying very hard not to be found.

Thirty years, though? You get careless eventually, don't you?

Mercer is on his way to meet the man who's going to help him. He's counting on being able to stop worrying and start making plans. He's hoping for good news.

Driving south on the A21, he tries to stay calm and keep his temper, but it isn't easy. When the hell did London traffic get so ridiculous? When did people start driving like idiots? It was like trying to get anywhere in one of those stupid cities you saw on the news like Shanghai or Calcutta. He's half expecting someone to pull up next to him at the traffic lights on a donkey.

When he does have to stop at a pedestrian crossing, he watches, hands clamped tight around the steering wheel, as an old dear with candy-floss hair steps out into the road in front of him. One pavement to the other, twenty feet or whatever it is, and it might as well be a marathon. Shuffling and hunched, slower than a pallbearer, as though the weight of the world is pushing down on her narrow shoulders.

He's tempted to jam his fist down on the horn, give the old girl a fright. Anything to put some bloody life into her. She's probably younger than he is, for heaven's sake, and she looks like she's doing nothing but waiting for death.

What happened to people?

Why did they reach a certain age and promptly give up?

You had to find *something* to make it worth struggling out of bed in the morning. Surely to God. He'd spent almost half his life shitting in a metal bucket – or as good as – and he still managed to stay alert and keep on fighting.

266

He knew people who'd thrown the towel in, course he did, but some people just weren't cut out for a life inside. Even when he was out he'd known a few who'd hit sixty or sixty-five and turned into the walking dead. He can't understand it, never could.

She's still only halfway across. Slippers on, for crying out loud and a coat when it's shirtsleeves weather. Head down, like she'd be happy enough for some lorry to come ploughing into her.

Yes, the bloody government didn't make life easy. Went without saying. Tough for some of them to survive on what passes for a pension and the whole world seems designed for kids these days. You had to adapt, though, you needed to find things to keep the blood pumping if you didn't want to shrivel up. You were just taking up space other-wise and there was no excuse for that.

Finally the old woman reaches the pavement on the other side. She takes a few seconds to catch her breath when she gets there, then totters slowly away.

Mercer puts his foot down.

Maybe staying angry is what keeps him feeling young. Maybe it was losing so much so early on. Either way, he didn't have a lot of choice in the matter and yes, it's done him a few favours. He knows he's luckier than most in having enough stashed away so he doesn't have to dress like a scarecrow or live on dog food and Cup-a-Soup.

Nothing you can do about illness, he knows that.

Nobody's fault if bits and pieces start to pack up, let you down or whatever. But as long as you were fit enough and still had all your marbles, you owed it to yourself to stay useful. Who the hell needs a corpse on legs?

Come the day he's got sweet FA to live for, he won't think twice. Ironic, all things considered, but he'll have the Scotch and the sleeping pills open smartish.

Talking of which.

He looks at his watch. He's going to be a few minutes late for his meeting, which needles him. Can't be doing with that, not when you've spent most of your life doing what bells tell you.

Now he's *really* hoping it's going to be a worthwhile trip, that the man he's meeting will tell him what he wants to hear.

Then he can crack on.

He'll enjoy getting rid of someone who's been taking up space for far too long.

CHAPTER 38

The weather was on the turn yet again by the time Thorne pulled off the small road that ran behind Bromley Museum. Tully was standing with his dog beneath one of the trees at the edge of the car park, peering up at a sky which had been all but cloudless half an hour before and was now darkening by the minute.

He had a suggestion and two observations to make.

'Sod this for a game of soldiers,' he said. 'It's going to piss down and she's already had a walk this morning, so why don't we just go back to the house?' Then he squinted at Thorne and said, 'You look rough as arseholes, mate.'

Thorne followed Tully's car to a house on a quiet street behind the leisure centre. Tully lived in the flat on the ground floor: a kitchen diner, one bedroom and a small bathroom. Tully walked through and opened the back door, let the dog out on to a patio half the size of the Jacobsons' terrace, then came back and put the kettle on.

'Used to have somewhere a lot bigger,' he said. 'Then my mother got taken ill. Police pension's all

269

right, long as something like that doesn't come along. Had to sell the house just to keep her looked after.' He told Thorne to sit down and reached up for mugs, a jar of coffee. 'Fifty grand plus every year for a care home! They're having a laugh if you ask me, and God knows how they're actually treating her. Far as I know they could be feeding her on boiled rice and keeping her locked in her room all day . . . cleaning her up and slapping on a bit of lipstick when they know I'm coming to visit.'

'You'll go mad, thinking like that,' Thorne said.

Tully took milk from the fridge. 'Don't get old, mate.'

Once he'd delivered Thorne's coffee, Tully opened the back door for the dog who was scrabbling to be let back in. The promised rain had now arrived, though it was not particularly heavy. The dog trotted across and lay down at Thorne's feet.

'Fancy a sandwich?' Tully asked. 'I've got a decent bit of cheese.'

'No, thanks.'

'There's a can of tuna somewhere.'

'I'm fine.' If he'd had any appetite to begin with, the smell coming off the dog at his feet would have been enough to kill it stone dead, but even though Thorne had not managed to eat very much of his fry-up six hours earlier, he was too tired to think about eating anything. In truth, he was already dreading the moment when he would have to get out of the chair he had dropped into.

He was hoping the coffee would wake him up a little.

Tully made himself a sandwich anyway. He talked about his dog while he put it together; cheaper than a wife or girlfriend, probably a damn sight more loyal, etc., etc. Thorne chuckled along, wondering when Tully was going to get to the reason he'd called. He was on the point of asking when Tully brought his lunch across and saved him the trouble.

'So, come on then, what's the state of play? I'm guessing you haven't caught our friend Terence yet.' Tully sat down and took a bite and when Thorne did not respond immediately, he swallowed quickly. 'Look, my offer still stands, you know, but when you didn't get back to me wanting any . . . *practical* help, I just thought you might be grateful for the chance to knock some ideas around. Talk it through, bounce stuff off me, whatever.'

'He's killed another one,' Thorne said. 'The pupil barrister on his defence team. Set fire to himself.'

'Jesus.'

'I just came from there.'

'That can't have been easy.'

'His wife's in bits. I mean, she's trying her best *not* to be.'

Tully licked his fingers. 'I meant for you.'

Thorne said nothing. The dog got up, padded

271

over to the other chair and dropped back down at her master's feet.

'You know,' Tully said, 'what with you worrying about whether it might have happened at all if you'd said something. Gone back to the Murder Investigation boys with everything you've found out. I mean, feeling guilty, that's only natural.'

'Is it?'

'I understand, all right?' Tully held out his arms. 'Listen, I'm on your side, mate. I know what they're like.' He took another bite and chewed noisily for a few seconds. 'And I know why you're doing this.'

'I'm all ears,' Thorne said.

'You got knocked back. That hurts.'

'That's not what it's about.'

'Trust me,' Tully said. 'I know how it feels. The number of times I've gone to them, told them I'm available. They've got all these cold case units now, right? I'd be perfect for one of those, but I've never had so much as a sniff. They haven't got the funding or I'm not sufficiently up to speed with the new technology, some crap like that. Like I've never worked a computer or something! I'm not even sixty, for God's sake.' He held tight to what was left of his sandwich, a sliver of cheese sliding from between the slices of white bread. 'So, I do know what it feels like to get ignored.'

'It's not the same thing,' Thorne said.

'Course it is. You were offering them expertise

'. . . your professional opinion. They chose to turn their backs.'

'Like I said. That's not what this is about.'

Tully shrugged and carried his empty plate across to the sink. He tore off a strip of kitchen towel and wiped his hands.

'So, where do you suggest I go from here?' Thorne asked. 'With Terry Mercer.'

'Tricky.' Tully walked back and sat down again. 'You've got no idea who he's targeting next and none of the obvious ways of tracking him. All you could do last time was hope for a bit of luck or wait for him to do something.'

Thorne nodded. It felt good to hear it.

'He's not exactly giving you a lot to work with, is he? Then again, he was always careful, even when he was just turning over banks and building societies. He always thought about the details.'

'How did you catch him?'

'We received intelligence,' Tully said. 'We knew when and where the job was going to be. It just went wrong when we tried to grab him, that's all.'

'You knew the officer that was killed?'

Tully gave a small nod and reached down to rub the dog's head for a few seconds. 'Listen, all I'm saying is that even if you had gone back and said something, the MIT wouldn't have been able to do a lot more than you did yourself. There'd just have been a few more of them sat about waiting, that's all.'

'They're looking into this new one,' Thorne said.

273

'For all the good it's going to do them.' He told
Tully about the investigation into Jacobson's death
that looked like drawing a blank and about his
encounter with Neil Hackett. 'You know him?'

'Big fat bastard?'

'Big fat, scary bastard.'

'I know *of* him,' Tully said. 'Never had the
pleasure though.' He thought for half a minute.
'Well maybe they'll get lucky and you can back
away. As long as they never find out you had any
information to begin with, you'll be all right.'

'Maybe.'

Tully smiled. 'Unless I'm reading this all wrong,
of course, and you're secretly hoping that you *won't*
be all right.'

'What's that mean?'

'You never thought about getting out, doing
something else?'

'Sometimes,' Thorne said. 'Everyone does.'

'Not me.' Tully shook his head firmly. 'Never
had anyone telling me I should either. A wife or
a girlfriend or whatever. The last thing I wanted
to do was stop being a copper, but it wasn't up to
me in the end, was it?'

'I still don't see—'

'Maybe, deep down, you've had enough.' He
nodded to himself. 'Yeah, this would be a good
way of doing it without actually quitting, and you
don't strike me as the type to do that.'

'You're being stupid now,' Thorne said.

Tully raised his eyebrows and smiled again,

warming to his theme. 'I remember having this girlfriend once . . . ages ago, back when I was a teenager. I wanted to finish with her . . . think there was some other girl I had my eye on at the time . . . but I didn't have the bottle to chuck her. So, I just behaved really badly. Treated her rotten, ignored her, until *she* turned round and dumped *me*, which was what I wanted all along, of course.' He sat back, enjoying the memory. 'I'm not even sure I knew I was doing it, you know?'

He looked at Thorne. 'Thinking back though, I can see exactly what I was up to.'

'I should make a move.' Thorne leaned forward and finished what was left of his coffee. 'I think we've probably bounced enough ideas around for now.'

'No rush,' Tully said. 'Listen, if you fancy it we could go out and get something to eat a bit later. Grab a curry or something and talk a bit more.'

Thorne thanked him for the offer, told him he needed to be in for the night shift. Said, 'Another time, maybe.'

'OK, well never mind . . . but listen, there's no need to shoot off. You look like you could use some rest, to be honest. Put your feet up for a bit. I've got stuff to do, anyway.' Tully stood up and the dog followed suit. 'I might shampoo the dog, something important like that.'

Thorne did not really want to stay very much longer, but forcing himself to his feet was proving as difficult as he had thought it would be. It felt as though his jacket was lead-lined, as though the cotton wool in his head had turned to cement.

He closed his eyes. Just for a few seconds . . .

Remembering Hackett's invitation, the first of two inside a couple of hours. Thinking that, despite his best efforts to alienate as many people as possible, he could not remember the last time he'd been this popular.

CHAPTER 39

'Thorne's taking the piss,' Holland said.
Kitson looked at him. 'He's a friend.'
'Which is exactly why he's taking advantage.'

They were sitting at a corner table in the Royal Oak, a watering hole midway between Becke House and Colindale station and hence a pub where lock-ins tended to get ignored, while any civilian unfamiliar with the venue's clientele and foolish enough to cut up rough was likely to be confronted with several dozen unhappy coppers, each trying to avoid having to make the arrest.

It was a table they had shared many times with Tom Thorne, a spot where victories had been celebrated and sorrows drowned. They had bitched about the Brass here and gossiped into the early hours about the arse-lickers and the dead weight. Those on the fast track to promotion and the Woodentops-in-waiting; the ones who couldn't cut it and would be lucky to end up waggling hand-held speed cameras on the A1.

The irony was not lost on either of them.

They had arranged to meet after work during a

snatched and whispered conversation at lunch-time. Now they were here though, neither seemed to be finding it particularly easy to talk. There was a good deal that was going unsaid; a tension at the small table that was not lost on DS Samir Karim when he blithely wandered over – slurping at a pint – and attempted to join them. He got no further than 'Mind if I . . .?' before clocking the looks on their faces and backing awkwardly away.

'Have you done anything else?' Kitson asked. 'Since the last time you saw him.'

Four days before, in the Grafton. When Thorne, Hendricks and Holland had looked at the list Thorne had extracted from Frank Anderson. Holland had said he'd try and find out if any money from Mercer's bank robberies was still unaccounted for and that he'd see about getting a look at CCTV footage from the areas in which the earlier victims had been killed.

He hadn't tried particularly hard.

'That was the same night Jacobson was killed,' Holland said. He picked up his beer bottle, stared at it. 'Remember? Looked like we might not need to do anything else.'

Kitson nodded. The two of them had found out about the 'suicide' in Blackheath the day after it had happened. Without saying as much to one another, it was clear they had both been counting on the Murder Squad team that was looking into it coming up with something that would save them both a lot of trouble.

278

What had Thorne said to Holland on the phone? They would all be 'off the hook'.

That morning, though, word had filtered through that Richard Jacobson's death was now being treated as a suicide; that the investigation was being wound down with immediate effect.

'So now it's just him again,' Holland said. 'Him and us. Soon as Thorne finds out, he'll be back on the phone.'

'So, say no,' Kitson said. 'We've been through this.'

'What will *you* say?'

Kitson shook her head and reached for the small glass of wine in front of her that had so far gone untouched.

'Why do I get the feeling this is all about me?' Holland asked. 'That I'm the one that's being disloyal or ambitious or whatever. It's like you're trying to make out I'm the only one with any doubts about this.'

'I've never said that.'

'I saw your face when we heard about Jacobson.'

Kitson put her glass down, now virtually empty. 'Do you know what you should be asking yourself? What would Thorne be doing if he was in your shoes and you were the one wanting the favour?'

'It's a bit more than a favour now, Yvonne.'

'Would he do it for you?'

Holland shook his head, not needing to think very hard about it. 'Yeah, but we're not as stupid as he is, are we?'

They said nothing for a minute or so after that, their eyes anywhere but on each other. Studying their drinks or their mobile phones, looking round when a burst of laughter erupted from another table.

'What are you thinking, Dave?' Kitson asked, eventually.

Holland emptied his bottle and felt for his wallet, checking it was there before standing up to leave or else getting ready to buy another; to settle in and make a decent night of it.

'Nothing you aren't thinking,' he said.

CHAPTER 40

Helen was not stupid. She knew that in insisting what had happened three months before had left her undamaged, there was at least an element of denial. It was far easier, though, to see how it had affected those closest to her. In the three days she had spent being held hostage by a grief-stricken father, her own seemed to have aged ten years.

'Could you . . .?' Robert Weeks held his grandson at arm's length. 'Could you take him, love?'

Helen stood and collected a wriggling Alfie from her father. Wrapped her arms around him. 'Come here, you,' she said.

'He's full of beans today.'

'He's excited to see you.'

And her father was equally excited, Helen had no doubt about that. He just seemed rather less able to cope with a boisterous eighteen-month-old tearing about his house than he had been before; when the noise and the mess had only broadened his smile and Helen would have had to insist on taking Alfie from her father's arms. He had always been tidy – even more so since he'd been living on his own – but where he had once embraced the happy chaos Alfie wrought, he now seemed far too anxious to relax.

He never said as much, of course. Wouldn't have dreamed. Even when Helen had gone back to work so soon after it had happened and, as per usual, Jenny had not fought shy of making her opinion known.

'*You're being ridiculous. I don't know what you're trying to prove. If you had any sense at all you'd find yourself another job . . .*'

Her father had not added to the concerns being voiced, but Helen knew that, for once, he had agreed with her sister.

'We'll get out of your way in a minute,' Helen said.

'Don't be daft. I'm just a bit tired today, that's all.'

He'd been living alone a long time; more than ten years since Helen's mother had died and five since his second wife had walked out. Neither Helen nor Jenny quite understood what had happened there, and it was never talked about. He had taken up an assortment of hobbies and activities afterwards – baking, book clubs, neighbour-hood watch – and there had even been a brief dalliance with a woman who lived nearby, but those things no longer seemed to interest him. Now, they were simply there to be grabbed at with an ever-waning enthusiasm. Clinging on to life instead of actually living it. Helen glanced down at the paperback books arranged neatly on her father's coffee table. She was pretty sure they were the same ones that had been there last time she had been round.

He was only sixty-four. Helen thought about that stupid, jaunty song and it made her angry. Angrier. *Old* suddenly, and well before his time and it was her fault for making him worry.

I don't know what you're trying to prove . . .

'You should bring him round,' her father said. 'Might be nice to actually meet him.'

It took Helen a second or two. Tom. They had been talking about Tom when Alfie had started making a pest of himself.

'You know what it's like,' Helen said.

'Busy. Yes, I know.'

'I will though, I promise.'

'I'm not Marjorie Proops,' he said. 'But that might be one of the reasons things aren't exactly hunky-dory.'

Helen had not said as much, but she had not needed to. Her father knew her well enough. He had seen her this way umpteen times since she was fourteen and her first boyfriend had got off with one of her friends at the school disco. This was the first time since Paul though.

She did not bother asking who Marjorie Proops was.

'Then there's the whole age difference thing.'

'Oh, come on,' Helen said.

'What is he, ten years older than you?'

283

'Yeah, near enough, but that's nothing.' She laughed, bounced Alfie on her knees. 'Honestly, that's ridiculous, Dad.'

He shrugged. 'OK . . .'

'Has Jenny said something?' Her father shook his head. 'She doesn't seem to like him very much. Banging on about Paul all the time.'

'How is he with Alfie?' He gurned at his grandson; head bobbing as Alfie continued to bounce. 'How is he with my best boy?'

'He's great,' Helen said. 'He's really great with him.'

'Well, that's the main thing.'

Alfie whined to be let down and Helen did so. He tottered across to the collection of soft toys that Helen had brought with her and were now scattered on the rug in front of the fireplace. He picked up a rubber frog and threw it. Helen sucked in a fast breath and reached out to protect the two mugs on the coffee table.

'No!' she said.

Her father said, 'It's fine,' and leaned down with a groan to retrieve the toy. He waved the frog and said, 'Ribbit! Ribbit!' but Alfie had already forgotten all about it.

'Tom's done something stupid at work,' Helen said. 'He's *still* doing something stupid and he knows I don't approve. So, things have been a bit tense, that's all.' She saw the concern on her father's face. 'What?'

'Well, if it's something *you* don't approve of, it must be seriously stupid.'

Helen smiled, but it was not returned.

'I mean you've done your fair share of stupid things.'

'He's not thinking straight,' she said. 'It's not a great time for him.'

'Are we talking stupid enough to get him into trouble?' He looked at her; the same look he'd given her when she'd screwed up at school or when she'd come home later than promised and not been entirely truthful about where she'd been. 'Or stupid enough to get you both into trouble?'

Helen said nothing and so they watched Alfie play for a while, then Helen's father offered to make more tea and defrost a couple of muffins. Helen tried to argue, but she was never going to win.

A minute after leaving the room, her father reappeared in the doorway.

'Look, I've never met the man,' he said. 'So what do I know? I'm a silly old sod, so you know, pinch of salt and all that. I'm just saying that my first loyalty is to you and to Alfie.' He pointed at Alfie, still happily moving his toys around. 'End of the day, that's all I'm concerned about.' He put his hands into his pockets, then took them out again and folded his arms. 'And it's what you should be concerned about too.'

CHAPTER 41

Twelve thirty a.m. and Thorne was on the phone, arguing with Chief Superintendent Trevor Jesmond. He paced around his office, fighting the urge to interrupt, then struggling to keep his tone suitably respectful when he did. There had been the not-so-friendly warning about overstepping his boundaries in the wake of Thorne's visit to the MIT almost a fortnight before but as far as operational matters on his side of the bridge went, this was the first 'frank exchange of views' with a superior that had taken place since Thorne's career had gone south in more ways than one.

He'd missed this.

'I think they're playing us for mugs,' Thorne said.

'You may well be right, but can we really afford to take the risk?'

'We can hedge our bets, surely.'

'We need enough manpower down there so that if it does kick off, we won't be caught with our pants down.'

'With respect, sir—'

'Don't start that, Tom. I know you haven't got any.'

There was no point pretending otherwise.

'I'll ship reinforcements in as and when,' Jesmond said, 'but for now, just get as many units down there as you can. We clear?'

What was abundantly clear was that Jesmond had been relishing the argument every bit as much as Thorne had. More so, as it was one he was always going to win.

Thorne dispatched three more patrol cars to Lewisham shopping centre, then called Christine Treasure. She was on a tea break at Deptford station having been in attendance at a burglary around the corner and sounded excited at the prospect of 'dishing out some slaps'. He told her to calm down, then to come back and pick him up.

Waiting in the car park, Thorne exchanged a few words with one of the civilian staff smoking nearby. The woman said, 'Looks like you lot might be in for a busy night.' Thorne gratefully breathed in her smoke, said, 'Maybe,' then realised it had been an hour or so since he had last thought about the desperate message scrawled into a crossword puzzle. Slippers in the mud by a darkened reservoir or the taste on his tongue in that garage.

As far as the rest of his shift went, Thorne remained convinced that he and his team were wasting their time, but he was grateful that circumstances might – for a while at least – force Terry Mercer into the shadows at the back of his mind.

He walked towards Treasure's car as she turned into the car park, then waited while the officer she was with transferred to another vehicle. When Thorne got in, Treasure was feeling for the can of pepper spray on her stab vest, her cuffs and baton. 'Right,' he said.

'I'm calm, I swear,' she said, grinning. 'I'm calm . . .'

Though the source of the information remained worryingly vague, officers on the late shift had once again received word that the situation was hotting up between the TTFN crew and their Tamil rivals. As per the predictions, known gang members had begun gathering in the shopping centre since midnight. Thorne though was dubious and was not expecting any more serious trouble than there had been the night before.

'It's clever,' he said. 'No getting away from that.'

Treasure accelerated and took the car through a red light. 'Not much else we can do though, is there?'

'We could leave them to it,' Thorne said. 'They'll get bored eventually and go home to their mums.'

Thorne was convinced that the rival gangs had actually started working together in the common interest. The word would go out that trouble was imminent and then a sufficient number of likely lads from either side would gather and look menacing. This was something they had become very good at, but it was no more than a smoke-screen. While an arrest or two might end up being made for minor offences, the manpower required to maintain order would leave other members of both gangs free to go about rather more important business; moving their product around unmolested, while the police officers who should have been trying to stop them were otherwise occupied.

Simple enough, and brilliant. Because even if the plan was rumbled, the Met would still need to show up in numbers to reassure the local community that they would not tolerate public disturbance.

To be fair to Jesmond – galling as that was – there was not a lot else he could do.

'You want to stop at a garage?' Treasure asked.

Thorne turned to look at her.

'Pick up a can of Red Bull?'

'Sorry?'

'You look like you might be asleep by the time we get there.' Treasure spent the next few minutes describing her prodigious sexual adventures of the previous day. She clearly enjoyed doing so – including sufficient detail to keep any gynaecology enthusiast happy – but it also allowed her to turn round at the end of it and say, 'And by the look of it, I still managed to get more shut-eye than you.'

Thorne smiled, said, 'I had stuff to do.' He was aware of Treasure glancing at him more than once; waiting for him to elaborate, before giving up and turning her eyes back to the road.

'Yeah, I know exactly what you were doing,' she said. 'Eyes like piss-holes in the snow, that haunted

289

expression. Too much wanking, mate, that's what that is.'

All things considered, Thorne was pretty pleased that three months earlier he had decided to pair up with Christine Treasure. In spite of the occasional olfactory assault, there were laughs, which were important, but it was more than that. The choice to go with a more experienced, less impressionable officer had been carefully made. Initially, he had thought about teaming up with one of the newer lot, but he'd been down that road with Dave Holland.

A young officer who had once looked up to him, then lost respect.

It was better all round, he had decided, to work with someone who had no illusions to shatter; about the Job or about Thorne himself.

Holland . . .

He had definitely not been himself when Thorne had called him the previous morning.

'Here we go,' Treasure said. 'Slapping time.'

They pulled up at the edge of the pedestrianised precinct, alongside four other patrol vehicles, the Area Car and a pair of Met Police vans. Blue lights had been left flashing. As soon as they were on foot, Treasure radioed their arrival to the other units, then she and Thorne took out their batons and walked towards the noise.

The TTFN boys had gathered once again outside the kebab and burger place. A few were inside but the majority had no interest in eating.

There were twenty or twenty-five of them; young black males with a smattering of white and Asian kids. A similar number of young Tamils was crowded around the entrance to a club called Flash, fifty or so feet away.

There was a good deal of abuse flying around, plenty of hard looks.

Half a dozen officers stood within a few yards of each group with twice that many forming an impromptu cordon midway between them; over half Thorne's team in one place. Manned police vehicles were barring entry at either end, but people were still spilling out of the nightclub and a few of the other bars in the precinct, which made controlling the situation even more difficult.

Thorne and Treasure walked past the entrance to the nightclub and were quickly briefed by one of the sergeants.

Three arrests so far, all for threatening behaviour. None of those arrested had been carrying a weapon.

Smokescreen or not, Thorne felt certain that a few of those currently eyeballing him would be carrying knives, or worse. He made sure everyone knew that the object was to disperse each group with a minimum of fuss, well aware that he was asking the impossible. He looked from one end of the precinct to the other, then across at the two officers – one standing nice and close to each of the groups – who were wielding the most effective weapon the police had in situations such as these.

Thorne understood that these young men were not afraid of the police, but he knew that a snarling German shepherd could put the fear of God into the hardest of Top Boys.

'Anything starts,' Thorne said, 'send the dogs in.'

Then, Thorne glimpsed the distinctive caps and blue and white waterproof jackets of the local Street Pastors; a pair of them talking to members of the TTFN crowd outside the kebab shop. These were inter-denominational volunteers, organised by local churches to patrol the streets in the early hours. To help, wherever they could. They made sure that people got into licensed taxis or found their way to the night bus and, with seemingly endless patience, they did their best to diffuse any threat of violence before the police needed to get involved.

Thorne had no idea why they would want to do what they did, but he was grateful for it.

He wandered across and gently drew one of the pastors aside; a man called Roger, whom he had spoken to several times before. He could not recall seeing Roger without a smile on his face. It tended to disarm most of those he was dealing with, though the fact that he was built like a brick shithouse didn't hurt.

'Anything you can do, Roger,' Thorne said, 'very much appreciated, as always.'

'We're doing our best,' Roger said. As usual, he was carrying a small rucksack, which Thorne knew was stuffed with flip-flops. These would be handed out to young women stumbling out of places like

Flash in the early hours. Those who had lost their shoes or were so drunk that tottering around in high heels would almost certainly result in them being picked up from the gutter with a broken ankle. 'I doubt there will be any real violence. It's just a show.'

'I know, but we still need them to disperse.' Then, over Roger's shoulder, Thorne saw another face he recognised.

Next to him, Treasure said, 'Isn't that the kid who gave you a dig a couple of weeks back? When we were clearing that party?'

Thorne nodded. 'Anthony Dennison.' Nineteen years old, street name 2-Tone. Following his arrest for the assault on Thorne, he had been bailed to return to the station, pending further enquiries; checking witness statements and reviewing available CCTV footage.

'Cheeky little bastard,' Treasure said.

Dennison was standing on the edge of a group of four or five of the TTFN crew. When he saw Thorne looking, he returned the stare with interest, pushing his chest out and turning up his palms as if to ask what the hell Thorne was looking at. Thorne was about to turn back to the pastor, when he watched Dennison take a step or two away from the group and look back at him. The boy nodded, glancing towards an alleyway two doors along from the kebab shop. Then – after checking that none of his friends could see – he turned and hurried into it.

'What's all that about?' Treasure asked.

Thorne was already on his way back to the car. 'One way to find out.'

They drove out on to the main road and then cut right into the maze of side streets that snaked around the main shopping area. After three or four turnings they saw him, sitting on a low wall; headphones on, like he wasn't really expecting to be found.

Treasure wound the window down and Thorne leaned across. 'You got something to say to me, Anthony?'

Dennison stepped to the window and removed his headphones. He peered into the car as if he might be looking to buy it. Said, 'Just you though, yeah?'

Treasure looked at Thorne and shook her head, but he told her it was fine. She sighed, then waited for Dennison to step back before getting slowly out of the car.

'Pat him down, will you, Chris?' Thorne said, leaning across again. 'No point being silly about it.'

'Don't worry, I was going to.'

Dennison assumed a position he was well used to without being asked.

'Anything I should know about?' Treasure asked, as she began to run her hands across the boy's body.

The boy grinned, hands behind his head. 'One or two things you might like.'

'You're not my type, darling,' Treasure said.

Two minutes later, having found nothing but two

mobile phones, wallet and cigarettes, Treasure turned back to the car and gave Thorne the thumbs-up. He nodded, and after Treasure had held the look between them for a little longer than was necessary, she turned and walked away towards the end of the road.

Dennison climbed into the passenger seat.

'Not sure this is the best idea you've ever had,' Thorne said. 'What with me being the reason you were nicked in the first place.'

'Yeah, well that's the thing. Maybe there's things you could do to help me with that. Like for a kick-off, maybe you could say that you was looking to get punched.' Dennison turned in his seat. 'You *was* looking for it, right?'

Thorne said nothing, but the boy had made it very clear that he didn't miss much.

'And maybe there's things I could tell you, so that you would say that.'

'What kind of things?'

'Information.'

'We get all sorts of information about what you lot are up to,' Thorne said. 'And I'm not sure I trust any of it. Like what's going on between you and the Tamils.'

Dennison nodded, impressed, then leaned back and made himself comfortable. 'I'm not talking about any of that nonsense. I'm talking about guns.' He looked to see if the word had had any effect. 'People buying guns.'

'Again, Anthony, I'm not exactly getting a stiffy

here. It's not like you're telling me anything I don't know.'

'Yeah, but you don't know what it is yet, yeah?'

'Go on then.'

The boy sniffed, took a few seconds. This was the chance to make his pitch. 'It's a seriously odd one, which is why I can remember it, you get me? I'm not talking about no black kid or Asian kid or Turkish kid or anything like that. This is a white man . . . a really *old* white man, buying guns. *Two* guns.'

Thorne sat up very straight. He knew that he should probably try and hide his excitement, but he didn't bother. He said, 'When?'

'A few weeks back. A month, maybe.'

'You sold him these guns? This old man?'

'No way,' Dennison said, quickly. 'I don't get into any of that stupidness . . . but I was there.'

'What did he look like?'

Dennison raised his arms, like it was a stupid question. 'I don't know, man . . . like I told you, he was old. White hair and wrinkles and all that.' He turned and looked at Thorne. 'So, you going to help me out, or what?'

'Maybe,' Thorne said. 'I'll need more than that though.'

The boy thought for a few seconds, then said, 'I can tell you about his car.'

CHAPTER 42

In the end, more than a dozen arrests were made in Lewisham shopping precinct, and though several were for possession of an offensive weapon, thankfully no such weapons were actually used on anybody else. There *were* major offences committed elsewhere on Thorne's patch overnight and though he could not help but wonder if some might have been prevented had his officers not been tied up on crowd control, it was not something he was going to feel too guilty about. That was a question he hoped would keep Trevor Jesmond awake for a while.

A night that was far from Q----, but still Thorne managed to get through the write-ups and handover protocols relatively quickly and make it back to Tulse Hill in time to have breakfast with Helen and Alfie.

'Sounds like you had fun,' Helen said.

'You forget how much they hate us.' Thorne was eating cereal – the sugary stuff that actually tasted good – while Helen worked her way through something that was supposed to be good for cholesterol, but looked like it was scooped from the bottom of a budgie cage. 'When you're in plain clothes, you forget that. It's not like anyone's ever pleased to see you, I mean you're always there because something bad's happened . . . but being on the streets in uniform . . .'

'Yeah, but it's the uniform they hate,' Helen said. 'It's not you.' She reached across to push a plastic beaker of orange juice towards Alfie who was happily gnawing a piece of toast.

'I could understand it if it was me.' There was milk left in the bottom of his bowl, so Thorne poured more cereal in. 'A lot of people hate me.'

'It feels like I haven't seen you for days,' Helen said.

'I know.'

'Haven't spoken to you, I mean.'

'We've both had a lot on.'

It had only been thirty-six hours, in fact, since Thorne had left for work after their rain-drenched Sunday stuck indoors. He knew what she meant though. Night shifts could do that, throw your grasp of time off kilter.

'We can catch up tonight,' he said.

'Actually I'll be late tonight—'

'Tom!' Alfie said. Though it might also have been 'dog' or 'toast' or whichever sound he was currently making to announce that his nappy needed changing. 'Tom!'

'I said I'd go for a quick drink with Gill after work,' Helen said. 'Is that OK?'

'Why wouldn't it be?'

'Any chance you could pick Alfie up?'

298

Thorne told her it was fine, that with four days off lying ahead, he could probably pick Alfie up every day if she wanted him to. He didn't mean it of course, he was hoping that he would have other things to occupy him, but whether Helen knew that or not, she thanked him for the offer.

'Well, I'm around,' he said.

'Let's take Alfie to my dad's one of the nights. Go for a meal or something.'

'Sounds good.'

'Actually, he was saying how much he wanted to meet you.'

Thorne nodded, his mouth full, trying to decide if the moment was right.

'OK, I'd better get a shift on,' Helen said, pushing her chair back.

Thorne reached across and laid a hand on her arm. 'Listen, I know how pissed off you were about me lying . . . before. So, I thought I'd better tell you there's been another suicide. Another murder that was made to look like a suicide.'

Helen's mouth tightened. Thorne withdrew his hand.

'But . . . you'll be happy to know that the MIT's looking at this one, so . . . nothing to do with me.' He managed a weak smile. 'Looking at me too, as it happens.'

'What d'you mean, "looking"?'

He told her about running into Hackett and how suspiciously friendly the DCI had been during their chat outside the Jacobson house. 'I don't know what to make of it, to be honest.' He told her what Hackett had said. 'Maybe three hours in that precinct with forty-odd kids looking like they'd happily cut my balls off is making me even more paranoid.'

'Tom!' Alfie shouted, brandishing his toast for extra emphasis.

'Why would it make me happy?' Helen asked.

'Sorry, I didn't mean happy. More like . . . relieved, or whatever.'

'OK.'

'Anyway, I wanted you to know, so you wouldn't think I was doing anything behind your back.'

Helen looked at him for a few seconds, then shrugged as though she really didn't care what he was doing, behind her back or otherwise.

She lifted Alfie out of his chair. Said, 'I'm going to be late.'

While Helen was busy with coats and bags, Thorne talked rather more than anyone who was comfortable had a right to. He asked her to give his best to Gill Bellinger, though he'd only met her once for five minutes. He told her to have a good time and not to worry about Alfie or getting back late. He said that he'd knock something together for dinner and leave some in case she was hungry when she got back. Helen made the appropriate noises; not angry as she had been a few days before, just lacking in enthusiasm, as though she'd flicked a switch off. Thorne found it rather more disconcerting than the anger had been.

He was asking her if she wanted him to get any shopping in when he heard the door slam.

He walked aimlessly into the bedroom, stood there in the semi-dark for a while, then trudged back into the kitchen. He felt irritated, aggrieved, but that didn't last long. He knew very well that he had no right to one single inch of the moral high ground, and not just because he'd told Helen about the MIT investigation but chosen not to tell her it had failed.

For all sorts of other reasons.

He was still hungry, so he made himself toast. He ate it quickly in front of the Breakfast News, then dug out his Met Emergency Contacts list and called the three other inspectors who were his opposite numbers for the various shifts on his days off. He asked each of them if they would mind letting him know – didn't matter what time of the day or night – if any sudden deaths were reported. He gave them all the same story, couched it in language they would understand. Jesmond was on his back and he was making an effort to look like he gave a toss.

The third one he called – a genuinely lazy piece of work called Simon Carlowe – had much the same reaction as the others, but voiced it rather more succinctly.

'Never had you down as an arse-licker, Tom.'

'New leaf and all that,' Thorne said. 'Never too late, is it?'

Then he called Yvonne Kitson.

She sounded vaguely surprised that Thorne had called her and not Dave Holland, but the choice had been carefully made. Thorne still had a nagging sense that Holland was backing away from it all; choosing to take his time doing anything, if not actually coming right out and speaking his mind.

'I know how tricky it would have been getting access to multiple CCTV recordings,' Thorne said.

'Bloody tricky, if you don't want people asking questions.'

'But now we only need to look at one. I've got Mercer's car.' He gave Kitson the make and colour. 'If Dave . . . or you can check out the nearest CCTV to the Jacobson house, get a single shot of that car going in or out—'

'Right,' Kitson said. 'I get it.' She sounded as though talking openly was difficult. 'I'll see.'

'Look, I know it's still asking a lot.'

'I'll talk to Dave.'

'Is he getting cold feet?'

There was a pause. Kitson said she had to go, that she would try and call back later. Then the line went dead.

Thorne sat down in front of the television and began flicking quickly between the channels. *Judge Judy*, *Animal Rescue*, *Homes Under The Hammer*. He managed five minutes of *Jeremy Kyle* before the rage threatened to become murderous, then he turned the TV off and took out the radio he would normally have left in his locker at the end of the shift. Carlowe and the others had promised to call, but Thorne couldn't be certain that they would and this way, if he was lucky, he would find out about any sudden deaths at the same time they did.

He switched on the unit, careful as always to avoid pressing the orange EMER button on the top.

The 'Oh Shit' button.

Use of the button cut across any transmission being made anywhere else and gave twenty seconds' uninterrupted airtime to the user. It was the button you only ever used if you were in real trouble. It usually meant 'officer down'. Thorne cradled the handset in his lap and listened. The Airwave received broadcasts from every officer in every borough in the city, but bearing in mind where Mercer seemed to have been most active, Thorne decided to focus on those in the south-east. He flicked between them every few minutes: Lewisham, Greenwich, Bromley, Southwark.

Papa-Lima, Papa-Delta, Papa . . .

The chatter was almost ceaseless. Hundreds of voices, thousands of incidents. Babble and banter.

A few hours earlier, Thorne had been dead on his feet, but five minutes in the car with a savvy seventeen-year-old had changed everything. Thorne knew it wouldn't last long. The tiredness would catch up with him eventually, but he was determined to stay one step ahead of it for as long as he could.

Right now, the last thing he wanted to do was sleep.

CHAPTER 43

He had almost laughed out loud when he'd finally been given the address.

Now, sitting outside the house, waiting for a glimpse of the man he will soon have the great pleasure to watch suffer and die, he thinks how funny it is, the way that people always come home. They come home to reconnect with their past, he supposes. They come home because it's where they feel safe or because they're desperately trying to hold on to something half remembered that seems precious.

They come home because it's the end.

He's been watching for a while now. The car is parked streets away and he's checked, so he knows that no cameras can see him. He's just standing about, reading the paper; a harmless old codger with nothing better to do. A woman walking her dog on the other side of the road smiles at him.

He smiles back and returns to his paper.

England football team in the doldrums, unemployment through the roof and the economy up the Swanee. Different faces, but still, could have been the same paper he was reading thirty years ago when he went inside.

He glances across at the house again, sees movement behind the net curtains in the downstairs window.

He's trying to read, but he finds himself thinking about the woman who walked into the water, because she was the only one whose face he couldn't see at the end. The nosy cow from the bank. He'd followed her out of the house after they'd talked things over, gone a slightly different route so as to avoid the cameras, but kept her in sight all the way. He'd stopped under some trees and watched her walk up to the edge in the dark; seen her take off her slippers and her nice, toasty dressing gown and pile them up tidy as you like a few feet back from the water itself. Careful that they wouldn't get wet, I mean, how mad was that?

He couldn't see her face, just the side of her lit by a sliver of moon, so God only knows if she *looked* scared, but he remembered how easily she'd gone into the water. There was a moment, course there was, when she took that first step – the shock of the freezing water against her bony white leg – but after that tiny hesitation she just strolled in, good as gold, like she was walking into the pub or something.

I mean, obviously she *had* to, that was the whole point, but at the end it was like she was happy to. OK, he decides, maybe that's putting it a bit strongly, but she was . . . all right about doing it, because in the end, the alternative simply wasn't worth thinking about. Sounds arse-about-face, he's well aware of that, but the truth is she was willing to die because she had so much to live for.

He looks towards the house again, and thinks, that's the irony, isn't it?

Her and the rest of them, the whole sorry shower, have paid the price because they took all that away from him. He made sure they knew it too, while he was opening up his plastic bag and laying everything out. He made sure they knew exactly what he'd lost.

He can still remember the last time he saw her.

What she was wearing, how she smelled, all of it.

His hands tighten around the edges of the newspaper and, for a few seconds, he just wants to march straight up to the front door, force his way in and batter the fucker there and then.

A white blouse and tight jeans. That perfume she got duty free the last time they'd all been on holiday together and big earrings that swung around when she started to shake her head.

'It's not fair on the kids,' she'd said.

It wasn't her he was angry with, never had been. Well, maybe for a while at the time, but in the end she did what she thought was best for her and the kids. He was never one of those nutcases who thought his other half had a sacred duty to stick by him, any of that nonsense. She was still young, they all were, and that kind of sentence was a lifetime.

'What sort of life would it be for them?' Those big silver hoops, swinging. 'Doesn't mean they'll stop loving you though. Doesn't mean *I* will.'

He hasn't seen her or the kids in thirty years and he has no intention of doing so. He's kept feelers out, just enough to know they've all made decent lives for themselves, and he isn't going to throw a spanner in by turning up now like a ghost. A bitter old man, pale and pathetic, trying to claw back all the time he's lost with them.

It was them that put her in that position though. The nosy bastards and the incompetents . . . and *him*, the last one on the list. The ones who got him put away and cost him everything he might have had.

Plenty of anger where they're concerned.

He casually moves a few feet away when he sees the front door open, steps into the cover of a large tree on the corner of the street.

Gets his first look at him.

The years haven't been kind, but fear will do that. Fear and guilt. Whittle away at you, grind you down to skin and bone.

He looks across at the man whose name is as new to him as the face and stance are familiar. He watches him peering out from behind a half-open door and thinks of animals emerging from traps and soft fruit gone rotten.

He thinks: Do you know I'm here? That I'm coming for you?

He remembers his dream; tiles the colour of

cold flesh and the sound of those echoing steps towards the gallows. He'd read once that in the old days, the ones that took the job seriously could calculate the condemned man's weight and work out the necessary drop just by shaking hands with him. No point leaving anyone dangling there and choking to death, but no desire to pull their head off either.

Mercer certainly does not foresee a handshake and besides, he's got no intention of being quite that careful.

Still, looking across at what's left of the man who's now pulling the door shut again – who's almost certainly drawing bolts and dragging chains across – he can't help thinking that a shoebox and a strand of cotton would do the trick.

CHAPTER 44

Thorne was walking Alfie back from the childminder's when Holland called, having done whatever had been required to get access to the CCTV footage nearest the Jacobson house. Thorne thought it was best not to ask how he had done it, but he was pleased that it was Holland calling. That those cold feet appeared to have warmed up a little.

'OK, we've got a red Vauxhall Astra caught on the main road near Blackheath station,' Holland said. 'Heading north towards Eliot Place just before four thirty last Thursday afternoon. We've got the same car on the same cameras, driving south again at quarter to ten that night. Single occupant. Elderly white male.'

Alfie burbled happily as Thorne picked up his pace, urging the pushchair on that little bit faster. The timings fitted with Thorne's theory about how Mercer had been able to get close enough to Jacobson and how he had known enough about the couple's movements to do what was necessary and be out of there before Susan Jacobson returned from her book group. He had taken time and taken care.

Even accounting for however long the killing itself would have taken, Mercer had to have been hiding in that garage for over four hours.

Thorne stopped at the pedestrian crossing and punched the button. 'Have we got a registration?' he asked.

Holland told him that they had, and that he had already run the Astra's licence plate through the system. 'Car was last registered to a dealer in Mile End,' he said. 'Bloke's dodgy as you like, been done half a dozen times already. He'll have sold it to Mercer for cash. No documentation, no questions asked, you know how it works.'

'You spoken to him?'

'Not had a chance.'

'What about Kitson?'

'Same.'

Thorne looked at his watch, tried to work out how long it would take him to get to Mile End. Then Alfie said, 'Tom,' or an approximation of it, and Thorne remembered that he was more than a little tied up for the rest of the day. The lights changed, and Thorne started to cross, quickly weighing his options up. He wanted to get there as soon as he could and put some pressure on whoever had sold that car. If the dealer had decent security cameras installed, they might at the very least get a better picture of Terry Mercer than a CCTV still could provide. Helen had already said she'd be back late, and Thorne wondered how she would react if he tried palming Alfie off on her sister for a couple of hours. He would be back in time to collect him before Helen got home. He wondered if he should just take Alfie with him to Mile End and not tell her.

Halfway across, Alfie dropped his toy frog on to the road and Thorne had to stop and bend to pick it up. He stared at the woman behind the wheel of a Chelsea tractor who was mouthing at him impatiently and said, 'I'll try and get down there tomorrow.'

'Right,' Holland said.

Thorne pushed that little bit harder as they got close to their block, the last hundred yards or so all uphill. 'You know what I'm going to ask you now, don't you?'

'ANPR . . .'

The Automatic Number Plate Recognition system could be used to identify and locate any vehicle of interest to the police. With the national ANPR Centre in Hendon able to store more than 100 million 'reads' per day, of which twenty-five thousand were 'hits' of one kind or another, it was now a hugely important weapon in apprehending criminals ranging from the highly dangerous to the simply uninsured. Thorne knew that if they were able to put Mercer's car into the ANPR database and get lucky, they could locate and track it in more or less real time. He also knew that doing so would leave behind the electronic fingerprints of whoever was inputting the data.

'It's the best chance we've got, Dave.'

'I know.'

Thorne could hear the doubt in Holland's voice, but he had already asked for help in every way he knew how and he was out of ideas. 'Listen, if you and Yvonne are in the shit, that's my fault and I'm sorry . . . but if you're already in it, I really don't see how this is going to make it any worse.'

Holland made a noise that might almost have been a laugh, and said, 'I suppose.'

'So?' Thorne eased the pushchair away from the edge of the pavement as a bus roared past them down the hill.

'I've got a mate in the ANPR office,' Holland said. 'I'll see what I can do.'

'Thanks, Dave.'

'Don't keep saying that.'

Thorne understood. Holland did not want reminding that what he was doing warranted gratitude, that it was so far outside the norm as to be worthy of it. He said, 'Talk to you later, then,' but he was grateful nevertheless; for the help and for the fact that Holland had failed to work out that being up to your neck in shit was actually a damn sight better than being in it over your head.

Half a minute later, he and Alfie arrived at the entrance to their block.

Thorne said, 'Here we go, mate.'

Alfie said, 'Tom,' and jettisoned his frog again.

Thorne made pasta for them both with tomato sauce from a jar in the fridge. Apple juice in a beaker and a can of supermarket lager. Once he had cleaned up, they sat through an hour of *In the Night Garden* on DVD, then Thorne gave Alfie a bath.

He could not say which of them was the wettest at the end.

It was after eight o'clock and fully dark outside by the time Thorne gave the child his final bottle of milk and got him into his cot. Safely wrapped inside his soft, stripy Grobag, Alfie settled quickly. Thorne used a couple of dirty towels to mop up the water on the bathroom floor, then zombie-walked next door and – still wearing shirt, socks and pants – all but fell into bed. Despite that morning's determination to fight the exhaustion, he felt as though he'd been hit by a truck.

He hoped Alfie would sleep through until Helen came home.

There was music leaking from one of the flats a few doors away – a low, urgent pulse of bass – but it could not keep Thorne awake any more than the image of blackened cement or spooning corpses, or the whiff of milky sick on his shoulder.

CHAPTER 45

'I'll try and pop back up next weekend, love.'
'Yeah, well I wish you would,' she said. 'The kids miss you, you know?'

Edward Mallen breathed into the phone, trying to think of something to say to his daughter, deciding eventually that there was nothing he *could* say.

She clearly did not have the same problem. 'I still don't understand why you moved back down there in the first place,' she said, her Geordie accent so different from his own. 'Your friends are all up here. Your family . . .'

'Well, you know.' He shifted in his chair, let a long breath out. 'After your mum and everything.'

'All the more reason to stay put,' she said. 'Times like that you want your family close, I would have thought.'

'Course I did,' he said. 'I *do*.'

'Still, what do *I* know?'

Once again Mallen struggled to find words that would do the trick, but was finding it no easier now than he had a minute or two before. Than he had six months before that, when he'd sat

314

everyone down in the local pub, got a round in and calmly announced that he was moving back down south.

'It's . . . hard to explain,' he said.

'Listen, it's entirely up to you.'

'Don't get stroppy, love.'

'Who's getting stroppy?'

'There's things to sort out, OK? It's complicated.'

'Yeah, you said that.' His daughter sounded tired suddenly. A child was shouting in the background. 'Listen, I need to get your grandchildren to bed.'

'Give them both a big kiss from me, will you? Tell them to behave themselves. And tell them Grandad's got their picture on top of the TV.' He promised to pop a fiver for each of them in the post, assured her he would do his best to get a train up the following weekend.

'You can give them the money yourself, can't you?' she said. 'If you're coming up anyway.'

'Yeah, course. Good idea.'

'Right then,' she said.

'Got *your* picture on the telly too, love,' he said. 'Obviously.'

She said good and that she hoped it was a decent one. She told him to look after himself. She told him that she loved him, then put the phone down before he had the chance to reply.

Mallen put the phone back in its cradle on the hall table, then climbed the stairs to his bedroom. His dinner was repeating on him, acid rising up. There was some milk of magnesia on his bedside table. He sat on his bed and had a healthy swig, sat for a minute or two more then walked through to the bathroom and took some of his other tablets; the ones organised in a plastic container with separate compartments for each day of the week.

Two blues, a pink and a yellow.

Like making them nice and colourful might help you feel a little brighter.

He started to walk back downstairs, feeling as though he was rattling with bloody pills.

It's complicated . . .

Truth was, he couldn't really explain it all convincingly to himself. Once his wife had gone, he couldn't see the sense in putting it off any longer, that was all. The timing was near-perfect too, though she couldn't have known that, poor thing, lying there and wasting away; like she hadn't known so many things.

Time to go home, simple as that.

Time to try and sort things out, clear the rubbish away. A chance to face up to things and be honest, and – probably a long shot – a chance to build bridges, even. Couldn't hurt to try, that was for sure, and however hard it had been for his family to understand, that shot at forgiveness was worth the sacrifice. His faith had taught him that.

Something else he'd found up there by the Tyne.

Along with the sweet, brown beer and a half-decent football team. The woman he'd loved and lied to.

He froze at the sound of the knock, one foot on

the bottom stair, one on the hall carpet. Slowly, he raised his front foot back up, sank down on to the step and stared at the door.

The vague shape beyond the frosted glass.

He told himself that it was probably that nosy care-worker checking up on him. A little later than she would normally call, yes, but maybe she was worried about him. She usually let herself in with the key he'd given her, but there was always a chance she'd forgotten it.

The second knock was louder.

Using the banister, he pulled himself up from the stair and stepped gingerly down. He felt silly, *stupid* for telling himself lies; contriving scenarios that would give no reason for the dry mouth or the twitching fingers. The blood roaring in his one good ear.

Nothing wrong with being afraid, after all.

Mallen knew very well who was at the door.

CHAPTER 46

They had arranged to meet in the Opera Rooms, upstairs at the Chandos pub on St Martin's Lane. The place was fairly busy for a Tuesday night, the pre-theatre crowd colliding with those in need of a few drinks after work, but Hendricks, who had got there first, had managed to snag a corner table in the smaller and quieter of the two rooms. Helen queued at the bar for ten minutes, then carried a large glass of wine across and joined him.

She said, 'Sorry I'm a bit late.'

'I was early,' he said.

Conversation did not progress much beyond the prosaic for the first half a glass. Both had endured working days they were not particularly keen to talk about and there was understandable reticence on both sides about plunging straight into the subject – the person – they were actually there to discuss. Instead, Hendricks chose to engage in a sardonic, whispered commentary as they sat and observed the interactions of their fellow drinkers. The 'slappers on the sniff' and the 'wankers in cheap suits'. He decreed who was likely to get lucky and which of them was barking up the wrong tree and he was more than happy to give Helen a demonstration of what he told her was a foolproof Gaydar. Sizing up a noisy trio of lads standing at the bar and eyeing up the talent, he nodded from one to another and simply said, 'Gay . . . dabbles a bit . . . straight, but eminently turnable.'

On cue, the best-looking of the three turned and smiled nervously at him.

'Bingo,' Hendricks said.

Helen thought Hendricks' observations were hilarious, but could not help wondering what those around them made of him. He was wearing a black, skin-tight Metallica T-shirt; shaven-headed with enough facial adornments to make it look as though he'd had a nasty encounter with a fishing-tackle box. She did not think that too many people would guess what he did for a living.

Then again, she never had any idea what the casual observer would make of her. Did she look like a copper? She'd come straight from work, so made sure she'd left home that morning in a smart skirt and matching jacket; her favourite white blouse. She wasn't sure quite why she'd made such an effort and was now firmly convinced that Hendricks could *see* that she had. That she was nervous.

'I think we got off on the wrong foot,' she said.

'Did we?'

'The first time we met.'

Hendricks took an insouciant sip of Guinness. 'News to me.'

'Probably just me being stupid,' Helen said. 'But I thought perhaps you weren't predisposed to like me, because I'm not Louise, and I know you two were close. Because I've got a kid.'

'And Louise hasn't?'

Helen remembered what Thorne had told her about the miscarriage. She felt herself redden. 'That's not what I meant, but yes, maybe that as well. I just meant . . . listen, I'm not looking for Alfie's new dad, all right? I'm not trying to turn Tom into that, if that's what you were thinking.'

'It wasn't, but thanks for clearing it up.'

'Not that he isn't great with him, because he is.'

Hendricks nodded and when he spoke again, the sharpness was gone from his tone. 'Yeah, he talks about him a lot.'

'Does he?'

'He really wanted to be a dad, you know? He made out like he wasn't that keen at the time . . . just terrified, probably . . . but really he was. He's not the only one as it happens.' Hendricks took another drink, as good as emptied the glass. 'But that's a *very* long story.'

Helen finished her wine and nodded towards what was left of Hendricks' Guinness. 'We're not in any hurry, are we?'

So Helen got more drinks in and Hendricks told her about his own desire to father a child. The moment in a specially designed children's 'suite' at a mortuary in Seattle when he had finally admitted it to himself. He leaned close as he described the thus-far doomed efforts to find a partner who was equally keen; his desperate offers to donate sperm to any woman who so much as mentioned the words 'biological clock'.

'I swear,' he told her, 'I'm just about ready to toss off into a turkey baster and hand it out to strangers at the bus stop.'

There was a longing and sadness in Hendricks' face that the wisecracks couldn't mask completely. Still, by the end they were both laughing and any hint of awkwardness between them had been forgotten. She caught him staring at the lad by the bar and leaned across to poke his arm.

Helen went to the toilet while Hendricks was getting more drinks. At the mirror afterwards, she automatically reached for her bag to freshen her make-up, then decided against it. When she returned to the table, she plonked herself down and reached for her wine.

Said, 'So, what the hell's he up to?'

Hendricks' shoulders sagged and he shook his head. 'Yeah, well . . .'

'I'm guessing it was you that told him to tell me.'

'I couldn't believe he hadn't.'

'Makes two of us.'

'You're not the only one who thinks he's being stupid,' Hendricks said. 'Trust me, there's plenty of us.'

'So, tell him.'

'That why you wanted to meet up? You want me to persuade him to knock all this on the head?'

Helen nodded. 'I think you've probably got a better chance than me.'

'I've tried,' Hendricks said. 'It didn't go down well.'

'If you think he's being stupid, why are you still . . . involved with it?'

'I don't know. Damage limitation, I suppose.' Hendricks picked up his glass, put it down again. 'Making sure he doesn't shaft himself quite as badly as he might.'

'How can you make sure that doesn't happen?'

'Not sure I can,' he said. 'Somebody's got to try though, and I'm the mug that got the short straw. Far as Tom's concerned, I always get the short straw.'

'Because you care about him,' Helen said.

Now it was Hendricks' turn to redden a little. He brought his glass close to his face. Said, 'Yeah, well obviously we both do.'

'So, we're both buggered.'

Hendricks looked at her. 'You worried this is going to come back on you? Job-wise, I mean.'

'Maybe,' Helen said. 'A bit. Does that make me a terrible girlfriend?'

'Makes him a terrible boyfriend,' Hendricks said. 'Like that's something we didn't both know already.'

A group crowded round a table in the adjoining room began singing 'Happy Birthday'. Most of the pub joined in and afterwards the birthday girl stood on the table and took a drunken bow.

'I reckon it's too late, anyway,' Hendricks said, once the hubbub had died down a little. 'I mean at the kick-off, it was a pride thing, wasn't it? He went to those twats in the Murder Squad and they knocked him back. Made him look stupid. He's not awfully good with that.'

Helen rolled her eyes. She didn't need to be told.

'Now though, it's all gone much too far to pull out, because the summit fever's kicked in.'

Helen asked him what he meant.

'It's the reason so many people die on mountains,' Hendricks explained. 'They know they've only got a certain amount of oxygen or whatever and they know that at a certain point, when they don't have enough and the weather's turned to shit, they need to give up and turn back. That's the logical thing to do, right? But a lot of them don't do the logical thing, because the summit's in sight and something gets switched off in their brains and they kid themselves they can make it.' He puffed out his cheeks, reached for his pint. 'Only they don't make it, do they? The stupid sods just curl up and die in the snow.'

'Jesus,' Helen said.

Hendricks shrugged. 'Tom's way past that point already. He's got the summit in sight. He's put a name to it.'

They waited as a police car or an ambulance went past outside, the siren almost deafening for a few seconds, then slowly fading away.

'So what do we do?'

'We've just got to wait and see what happens. Hope he doesn't freeze to death.' Hendricks smiled, the warmth of it belying the armoury of tiny studs and rings he had pressed into his flesh. 'At the very least we can try and make sure the silly bastard's wrapped up nice and warm.'

Helen nodded slowly. Said, 'OK.' She might have hoped, but she hadn't really believed that Tom's best friend would know what they should do about the mess that Tom was in; that he had dragged them all into. But at least now she understood why he had done it. Understood *better*.

'As for what we do tonight . . .' Hendricks sighed heavily.

Helen turned and followed his gaze, saw the three boys who had been standing at the bar on their way out; the best-looking of them throwing a small but resigned nod at Hendricks just before he left.

'Sex is obviously out of the question for either of us,' Hendricks said. He downed the rest of his drink. 'So, I suggest we make the best of it and just get thoroughly hammered.'

CHAPTER 47

S he says, 'It's not fair on the kids.'

'What isn't fair?'

She swallows and says, 'Coming here, every week. Dragging them up here, or to God knows where else, so they don't forget what you look like. I mean they're bound to keep moving you about.'

'It's been all right so far, hasn't it?'

'Every week though.'

'What are you saying?'

'I can't do it . . .'

He stares at her through the square of scratched, greasy Perspex between them. He sees those big hoop earrings sway as she shakes her head and it's like there's someone standing on his chest. Her voice has barely risen above a whisper, but still he can feel the eyes of the cons and visitors at other tables on them. The knowing smiles of the screws watching from each corner.

He leans in close until his lips are almost touching the screen. He says, 'You were happy enough before, when the money was coming in.'

'I was never *happy*—'

'Happy with what it could pay for.'

Those earrings start to move again.

'You always knew this might happen, but that didn't matter long as you had decent holidays and a nice car. Long as you had other women kow towing to you because of who you were married to. Then as soon as the worst happens, soon as it's time for you to do *your* bit, you want to bolt . . . like a fucking child.'

There are tears in her eyes when she raises her head, but she doesn't bother to wipe them away. 'I did my bit,' she says. 'I did it for years, but this is something else. I don't have to worry about you any more, do I? About feeding you and washing your clothes, about what you might be up to. I *can't* worry about you. I've got to think about the kids now, can't you see that? *Our* kids.'

He says, 'Right, our kids, and I want to see them.'

She can't look at him. 'They don't want to see you.'

Those boots on his chest gain a little weight. He swallows and swallows but there's no spit in his mouth and he presses the flat of his hand against the screen for a few seconds until one of the screws tells him to remove it.

'They told me,' she says. 'They can't handle this any more. I've got piss-covered sheets to deal with every morning and they're both getting into trouble at school and they're bright enough to know why that's happening.'

'They'll get used to it.'

'They shouldn't have to.'

'It's normal.'

'It's *not* normal.' She raises her voice for the first and only time and that's when he knows he's lost her, that he's lost all of them. That there's no point clinging on like someone who's forgotten how a man should behave. No point asking his mates on the outside to keep her in line for him. That's when he feels something break. 'It's normal we *want*,' she says. 'Can't you understand that? And if you love us even half as much as you say you do in those letters, you'll give us a chance to try and have it.'

He tells her he loves her *twice* as much, and he leans forward again so he can smell her through the holes at the top of the screen.

The screw in the corner shouts, 'Two minutes.'

And Mercer blinks, back in the present, when the man standing on the chair says, '*Please, Terry . . .*'

Mercer takes a step closer to him. The man on the chair instinctively tries to shy away, but there's nowhere he can go. Not with the staircase at his back and the washing line tight around his neck. 'That's what you did,' Mercer says. 'What you're responsible for. That's why you're going to make me happy and step off that chair.'

Mallen shakes his head, desperate. He tries to speak and manages no more than a mangled croak. He tries again. 'There's no need for this, Terry.'

'What, you just thought we were going to have a quick chat and sort it all out? Thought I'd popped round so we could bury the hatchet?'

'I'm sorry.'

'Thirty years too late, old son.'

'That's what I'm trying to say.' Mallen's eyes are wide and wet. 'Thirty years, for God's sake.'

'Oh, right,' Mercer says. 'Water under the bridge, forgive and forget, all that carry-on.' He nods, like he's thinking about it. 'Only problem is, Mr *Mallen*, I think those thirty years have been a bit kinder to you than they were to me.' He cranes his head forward. 'Now stop whining like an old woman and do it.'

Mallen shakes his head again and his Adam's apple squeezes up and down against the washing line as he swallows. He splutters and coughs a spray of froth, which settles on his collar. 'I can't . . .' There's a tremor in one of his legs, which he is fighting to control. The chair begins to wobble just a little and he lets out a racking gasp. 'Christ . . . oh, Christ.'

Mercer groans, disgusted. When he had arrived, there had been cosy cooking smells lingering in the small hallway between the front door and the kitchen. The sausages the man had eaten for his tea. Now there is only the sharp tang of sweat and urine.

'All the others were only incidental really,' he says. 'None of this would be happening if it wasn't for you.' He gathers up the contents of his plastic bag, which had been laid out in a line at Mallen's feet. 'To be honest, I'm surprised you didn't do this yourself, a long time ago. You had any sort of decency, I could have just pissed on your grave and been done with it.'

He moves even closer. There are three items in his hand. Plenty of leverage with this one.

He holds the first one up, nodding admiringly as he makes a show of looking at it. 'Just imagine,' he says. 'Well, now you know exactly what it feels like.' Then the second. 'I mean, if I have to knock you off there myself, you won't be any less dead, will you?' The final one, pushed hard into his face, sliding against the sweat and the slobber. 'Only if *I* do it, the last thing you'll be thinking, dangling there like a soap-on-a-rope for those final few seconds, is what I'm trotting off to do as soon as I walk out of that door.' He moves his head until he meets his victim's eyes. 'How much I'm going to enjoy it.'

The man on the chair screams in his face; a bellow of rage and of determination.

Mercer steps back to avoid the spittle, but he knows the job's as good as done. He stares, eyes wide as the man sucks in fast, frantic breaths and then begins to mumble.

'You're not serious?' Mercer says. 'Are you *praying*?' He claps a hand to his chest. 'Oh, that's beautiful.'

He is still laughing when Mallen steps off the chair.

CHAPTER 48

There were a dozen or so cars on the lot: low-end models for the most part with high mileage, but polished up to look halfway presentable. The brightly coloured signs inside the windscreens pronounced them all as 'Bargains', 'Star Deals' or 'Good Runners', but Thorne knew enough about the man who was selling them to doubt that many would make it to the top of the Mile End Road. Trading Standards would have had a field day, he decided, weeding out the insurance write-offs and insisting on signs with more truthful descriptions.

'Cut-and-Shut'. 'Clock Turned Back'. 'Riddled with Rust'.

The owner appeared within a few minutes of Thorne's arrival. He materialised like the shopkeeper in *Mr Benn* and sauntered towards the car Thorne was inspecting. He straightened his tie as he passed beneath strips of Union Jack bunting, which were probably bought cheaply a week or two after the Diamond Jubilee.

Keith Fryer wore a light blue suit over a striped business shirt and shoes shaped like Cornish pasties. There was a good deal of jewellery. A strong breeze played havoc with hair that was suspiciously dark for a man who was clearly in his early sixties.

'Best car I've got,' he said. He nodded at the Mini Cooper, which Thorne was slowly circling. 'Done a lot of miles, I'm not going to pretend it hasn't, but there's a full service history.'

Thorne said, 'One lady owner, right?' and bent to peer in through the car's front window.

Fryer laughed, wheezy. 'Are you looking to trade in?' He turned and nodded towards Thorne's BMW, parked on the main road. He had obviously watched it pull up. 'I can give you a decent price for that, if it's in good nick.'

Thorne stood up, stared at Fryer across the car. The man clearly believed in the 'no bullshit' approach to dealing with his customers. The irony would almost certainly have been lost on a second-hand car salesman who made the character of Frank Butcher in *EastEnders* look positively nuanced.

He had more front than Jordan.

'I was actually looking for an Astra,' Thorne said.

Fryer raised a meaty palm to flatten his flyaway hair and looked around, as if there might have been one he'd forgotten about. 'Nah . . . sorry, mate. I can keep an eye out if that's really what you're after, but if you ask me the Golf's a much better bet. Got a nice silver one in yesterday as a matter of fact.'

'No, it needs to be an Astra,' Thorne said. 'A red one, preferably.'

There was no obvious reaction. 'I mean, yeah, we do get them,' he said. 'They're nice motors, so they tend to get snapped up. Reliable, you know?'

'Really?'

'Oh yeah.'

'How reliable was the one you sold Terry Mercer?'

Fryer blinked, sniffed. The wind picked his hair up again, but he was suddenly a little less bothered about it. 'Sorry, who?' he said. 'What was the name again?'

Thorne reached into his jacket for his warrant card.

Fryer was already turning away. 'Yeah, yeah. Obviously . . .'

Thorne watched the man walking towards a rickety, single-storey building that was only a step up from a Portakabin. Hands in pockets and boot-black hair flying, well aware that Thorne was going to follow him.

By the time Thorne stepped into the tiny office, Fryer was wedged in behind a desk in the corner, doing his best to appear busy with a stack of paperwork. Thorne glanced around as he moved to pick up a folded plastic chair from against the wall: a plywood case with rows of car keys on hooks; a tattered Formula One calendar; a signed picture of a dog-faced Millwall player Thorne didn't recognise.

Thorne sat down and Fryer continued to ignore him.

'A lot of red tape, I should imagine,' Thorne said. 'Business like yours.' He waited, got no response. 'Clocking, falsifying service histories . . . lot of shredding as well, I'm guessing. You should get yourself a secretary.'

'You're wasting your breath.' Fryer did not even look up. 'And your time.'

'Don't worry, I've got plenty of time,' Thorne said. 'It's my day off. I might go to the zoo later on.' He dragged his chair closer to the desk, the legs scraping against the cheap industrial carpet. 'Anyway, it's nice to hear the Astra's reliable, because I'm sure Terry Mercer wouldn't want some bag of hammers that's going to keep breaking down on him. He's got places to go, people to see.'

Fryer pushed the stack of papers away and sat back. 'Look, I met Terry Mercer a few times, all right? Thirty-odd years ago, longer than that. I don't know what you're on about, 'cos he's inside anyway.'

Thorne smiled at the attempt and politely told Fryer that now *he* was the one wasting his breath. 'Listen, we know that the red Vauxhall Astra I'm talking about was registered to you. Now, considering you've not clapped eyes on Mercer for so long, it's a hell of a coincidence that it's the same one he's currently getting about in.' He sat back and shook his head at the mystery of it all. 'So, why don't you stop pissing about and tell me about selling him the car?'

'I never sold him any car.'

'So who did you sell the car to? I mean we know you sold it to someone because you haven't got it any more. So why don't you have a look through your sales receipts and remind yourself?'

'I don't remember any red Astra, all right?'

'I've got the registration number if that'll help.'

Fryer shrugged, but for the first time he began to look frightened. Thorne knew that the car dealer had good reason to be afraid and that it was not the police or what they might do that was draining the colour from his face or causing his fingers to flutter against the desktop.

On another day he might almost have felt sorry for him.

'He paid you in cash, right?'

'Who did?'

'Didn't want any records kept.'

'I don't do business like that.'

'Did you owe him a favour? Or did he just put the frighteners on?'

Fryer shook his head, then snatched gratefully at the mobile on his desk when it began to ring. 'Cars' by Gary Numan.

'Nice,' Thorne said.

Fryer listened, grunted once or twice then hung up. 'I've got a business to run, all right? So we'd best call it a day.' He stood and moved towards the door.

Thorne got up and barred his way, a hand on his chest. 'Have you any idea how much shit I can bring down on your head with just one call to Trading Standards? They'll close you down without blinking. I mean clearly you don't want Mercer finding out you said anything, but trust me, I'm going to catch him long before he finds out.'

Fryer stared at him, his face even paler than it was before. He said, 'Do what you have to.'

Thorne stepped aside and invited Fryer to leave. 'Oh . . . I noticed you've got some nice flashy security cameras out there. I'll need to see the tapes from a couple of months ago if that's OK.'

Fryer stopped in the doorway and suddenly he looked a little happier. 'Fill your boots, mate. You're right though, it is pretty flashy. Trouble with these digital things though is the disks get full up so quickly.' There was even a hint of a smile now. 'So every week we just have to wipe them and start again.' He adjusted his tie and his hair, then marched out towards the lot.

Thorne stayed where he was for a few minutes. Waiting until he was more or less certain that he could walk back across the car lot without putting a rock, or a fire extinguisher, or Keith Fryer's head through one of the windscreens. When he did go – a hundred small Union Jacks snapping in the wind above him – he was aware of Fryer clocking his exit; ignoring the customer he was with and watching him every step of the way.

Do what you have to . . .

He pulled the BMW away fast from the kerb and was almost clipped by a van he should really have seen coming. The driver leaned on his horn and, screaming in shock and frustration, Thorne did the same. He accelerated away, but not before he had glimpsed another BMW parked on the opposite side of the road.

One that Keith Fryer would have paid an even better price for.

An uncomfortably familiar figure at the wheel.

CHAPTER 49

Back at the flat, Thorne turned on his radio again to monitor the broadcasts. He ate what was left of the previous night's pasta for lunch, then, faced with the prospect of bouncing off the walls for the rest of the afternoon, he opened up his laptop and set about looking for anything he didn't already know about Terry Mercer.

A Google search produced more than sixty-five thousand hits.

Thinking that a shot in the dark could do no harm, Thorne quickly searched through 'images'. He was rewarded with nothing but the familiar mugshot, a few black and white photos of Mercer as a teenager, a press picture of the garden where the shooting had taken place and, somewhat confusingly, several photos of Ray Winstone and Vinnie Jones.

Mercer even merited his own entry on Wikipedia.

Terence James Mercer (born 1940) is a career criminal responsible for a series of high-profile armed robberies but most notorious for the murder of a police officer, for which he was jailed for a minimum of twenty-five years. He remains imprisoned . . .

Thorne stopped reading and scrolled down, thinking that somebody needed to update the information, then deciding that if things worked out the way he hoped, they should probably not bother.

He glanced at the contents.

1. *Early life.*
2. *Crystal Palace shooting.*
3. *Trial and imprisonment.*
4. *Screen adaptation and legacy.*

The fourth entry pulled him up short. He was amazed and appalled to read that in the late nineties, at the height of the craze for *Lock, Stock*-style gangster chic, repeated efforts had been made to bring Mercer's story to the screen. The failure to raise the finance was clearly no great loss to cinema, but it explained the pictures Thorne had seen before. The go-to screen hard men of the time.

Thorne felt slightly sick, even thinking about it.

However things panned out in the end, and whatever his own part in it turned out to be, it was likely there would be even more film interest in the final chapters of Terry Mercer's story. There were a lot more bodies this time round, after all. Blood usually meant box office.

For Christ's sake, though . . . *legacy*?

Thorne had seen that with his own eyes, had smelled it. The varying state of the remains. Heard it in the voices of John and Margaret Cooper's son and Brian Gibbs' daughter, the dreadful Keep-Calm-And-Carry-On civility of Richard Jacobson's wife.

He closed the laptop and walked quickly to the fridge, needing something to wash the taste of overcooked meat from his mouth.

The bottle of beer became two as Thorne sat and waited for Helen to get home. With the Airwave close enough so that he could still hear the radio chatter, he put on a CD; the same Johnny Cash album Hackett had been playing in his car a couple of days before, one of his favourites. He skipped the song they had listened to together and went straight to the second track. Another cover version.

'Solitary Man'.

Now, Thorne wondered if subconsciously he was sending himself a message.

Hackett . . .

Thorne had been willing to believe that it had been a coincidence, the MIT man turning up like that at the Jacobson house only a few minutes after he had arrived. Hackett had been the one with every right to be there, after all. There was no earthly reason for him to be parked up opposite Keith Fryer's car dealership though.

Thorne was less concerned about what Hackett

wanted than with how he had known where to find him. He must have known what Thorne was doing there and why, and if that was true, there was every reason to believe that he knew everything.

So, why wasn't he doing anything about it?

Why weren't the Rubberheelers banging on Thorne's front door at that very moment?

More importantly, if Hackett did know, then who the hell had told him?

Cash was singing about life alone for the third or perhaps the fourth time, and, lying stretched out on the sofa, Thorne was no nearer coming up with an answer to the Hackett question that was not unthinkable, when he heard Helen's key in the door. He quickly turned off his radio and stuffed it into his pocket.

Alfie was first into the living room, burbling and pulling off his hat, a determined look on his face as he toddled towards the television.

Thorne had not seen Helen that morning and had woken only briefly when she had come to bed the night before after her evening out. Just long enough to smell the drink and mumble something about hoping she'd had a good time; to get the distinct impression that she was feeling horny and to realise that he was still too tired to even think about it. Within moments of Alfie waking up and taking so much as a cuddle off the agenda anyway, Thorne had been asleep again.

Now, Thorne sat up and turned the music off,

and they spent a few minutes catching up while tea was made and Alfie settled down in front of *CBeebies*.

'How did you get on with him last night?' Helen asked.

'Fine,' Thorne said. 'Piece of cake.'

'Really?'

Thorne noticed the half-smile as she turned back to the tea things. He had been hoping she was so smashed the night before that she might have forgotten the carnage in the kitchen or the sopping towels on the bathroom floor. 'Yeah. We had a great time.' He looked across at Alfie, hypnotised in front of the TV. 'Didn't we, mate?'

'I'll have to go out more often,' Helen said, her back to him.

'How was Gill?'

'Oh . . . she was fine,' Helen said. 'Had a bit of a hangover this morning though.'

'Worse than yours?'

'I drank loads of water when I got in.'

'See, I know that's the sensible thing to do,' Thorne said. 'But it becomes a very tough choice when you get to my age.' He mimed the tipping of scales, up and down. 'Lessening the chance of a hangover or pissing the bed.'

Helen turned round. 'So, what have you been up to today?'

There was a moment of tension between them then, a crackle, but no more than that. A hesitation and a glance away.

341

Thorne bent to pick up one of the empty beer bottles from the floor by the side of the sofa. 'Well, it was a relaxing afternoon, I can't pretend it wasn't, but there *were* several hours of meditation first thing this morning. A trip to the gym after that, obviously.'

They carried on laughing as they made Alfie's tea together; Helen boiling the eggs and sorting the juice while Thorne cut toast into soldiers and insisted that it was all a little primitive in comparison to the feast he had prepared the night before. Alfie wolfed down the lot and it was certainly less messy than pasta and tomato sauce.

Half an hour later, Thorne was in the bathroom, his radio sitting on the toilet cistern, when he heard the two words he had been listening out for amid the chatter and hiss. That he had been praying for, and dreading.

Sudden death.

He grabbed the unit and listened for the response. Inspector Simon Carlowe's six-digit ID number came up on the Airwave's screen when he announced that he was on his way to attend. Thorne entered the number and was straight through to him.

'Bloody hell,' Carlowe said. 'I'm not even in the car yet.'

'I need to go out . . .'

Thorne was walking back and forth between kitchen and living room, growing increasingly irritated, unable to remember where he'd left his jacket. He asked Helen if she'd seen it, but she shook her head.

He found the jacket by the side of the sofa and pulled it on.

Helen looked at him, asking the question.

Thorne sighed. Said, 'I don't want an argument.'

CHAPTER 50

The body never quite stopped moving.

That was always the trouble with a hanging. Dead for it didn't matter how long, there was still that hint of a sway, the smallest swing of the feet. A train thundering past somewhere close by might do it, or a lorry on the street outside or, in this case, a hairy-arsed constable coming that bit too quickly down the stairs.

Thorne stood and watched them: the dead man's shoes – black and highly polished – no more than eighteen inches or so from the carpet. Toes down and heels kissing. The constable came charging down the stairs from which the body was hanging and Thorne saw those shoes shift a little.

It was better than looking at the face, though.

The terraced house was on a quiet street off the Woolwich Road, midway between the Dockyard and Charlton Athletic football stadium. The south-east London heartland. The place had been nicely kept, inside and out; magazines piled neatly in the sitting room and washing-up done in the kitchen. Several pairs of shoes were lined up inside the front door, only a few feet away from that nice shiny pair still swaying just a fraction.

The constable turned at the bottom of the stairs, glanced at the body then saw the look on Thorne's face. Thorne was wearing jeans and a leather jacket, so either the officer knew who he was or had him pegged as a casually dressed CID man.

'Sorry,' he said.

'Just go easier,' Thorne said.

As the constable squeezed past the body and tiptoed down the narrow hallway towards the kitchen, Simon Carlowe emerged from the sitting room. The inspector leaned back against the wall, wrinkling his nose at the smell. He took a note-book from his pocket and opened it, then leaned forward to hang his hat on the newel post.

'So . . . Edward Mallen, mid-sixties, but we can't be any more precise just yet.' Chatter erupted suddenly from his radio and he turned the volume down. 'Retired factory manager, machine parts, something like that. Right now we're just going on what the woman who found him can tell us.' He nodded towards the sitting room.

'And who's she?'

'Some kind of care-worker who's been keeping an eye on him. She had her own key, pops in every couple of days.'

'When did she find him?'

'She got here about five thirty, she says.' Carlowe sniffed. 'He probably did it last night or early this morning. Three o'clock, four o'clock, a fiver says it's somewhere around there.'

'Why?'

'That's the most popular time for people to kill themselves.'

'No, it isn't,' Thorne said.

'I'm telling you, I saw it on some website.'

Thorne shook his head.

'So, you're an expert, are you?' Carlowe asked.

It was all stuff he'd got from Hendricks. The statistics and the surprises, like the absence of a note in the majority of cases and the fact that Christmas was actually a period when the suicide rate was lower than normal.

'I swear I'm right.' Carlowe stabbed at his notebook. 'Between three and four in the morning. Those are the peak hours.'

'We're not talking about *buses*,' Thorne said.

'Just saying.'

'You want to die badly enough, one hour's going to be much the same as any other, don't you reckon? Just pick any one of the twenty-four.'

'Come on then, a fiver,' Carlowe said.

Thorne stared past him, said nothing. Most people had no choice as to the hour of their death and Thorne guessed that it was largely arbitrary even for those who chose that death for themselves. He did know that there were twice as many suicides as murder victims and he knew that right now he was looking at the less common of the two.

You want to die badly enough, or kill someone . . .

346

Carlowe shrugged. 'Yeah, well, the doctor should be here in a minute, so he'll give us a rough idea.'

'So, that it?'

Carlowe hesitated, clearly a little riled at being spoken to like a subordinate, but went back to his notes. 'She reckons Mallen had been living up in the north-east for about thirty years, but was from here originally. Still had the accent, by all accounts. He moved back six months ago when his wife died. His kids still live up there.'

Thorne nodded.

For about thirty years . . .

'Obviously, we're trying to get hold of next of kin. The lads are looking around, trying to find contact numbers, whatever.'

'Why did he need a care-worker?' Thorne asked. 'Looks like he was taking care of himself.'

'Well, she's being a bit cagey . . . client confidentiality and all that, but apparently Mr Mallen had been having a few "emotional" problems.' Carlowe looked up at the body, puffed out his cheeks. 'Yeah, right.'

The dead man's lips and the inch of tongue that hung through them were black. His eyes were open, bulging like table-tennis balls cracked with red and a thin streak of blood ran from one nostril down his white shirt. A small swell of hairy belly sagged over the waistband of his trousers.

'Not a nice way to go,' Carlowe said.

Thorne said, 'The worst.'

Over the years, Thorne had been witness to all

manner of damage inflicted on the human body. He had seen how it looked after every kind of assault imaginable; what a machine could do to it, or gravity, or water. The variety of cruel and unusual methods other human beings had confected to make something so familiar practically unrecognisable.

Hanging, though, was unique, in the way that damage was displayed.

Thorne had dealt with perhaps half a dozen in his time and could still remember the first one; standing on a rickety stepladder in Victoria Park as he and a colleague tried to lift down the body of a teenage girl, suspended from the branch of an oak tree.

Rope, wire, dressing-gown cord or washing line, there was always something so unnatural about the way in which the body was still free to move through the air. The dreadful slump and shape of it. That first time *had* been suicide, as had all but one of the others, but every one had spoken more powerfully of loss and desperation than any other body Thorne had encountered. Of brutality.

Though yet to figure out precisely why, Thorne had a good idea who had put this latest body on display.

'Anyway,' Carlowe said, 'it certainly seems kosher enough. Can't find a note, but there's no sign of anything iffy and we've got a first-hand report that he was . . . I don't know . . . depressed or what have you. Bathroom cabinet's chock-a-block with happy pills.' He leaned across to retrieve his

348

hat from the newel post. 'So, I don't think we'll be needing to trouble our friends in suits.' He looked at Thorne. 'What do you reckon?'

Thorne suddenly realised that Carlowe had brought him in, not because he was doing him a favour, but because he was the type that valued back-up when it came to the big decisions. The sort that liked to keep his arse covered.

'It's your call,' Thorne said.

Just then, a female PC put her head round the open front door. 'We've got an old geezer out here who's a bit upset, sir.' She stepped in and straightened her vest, kept her eyes anywhere but on the body. 'Says he's a friend of the deceased. Poor old bugger's been waiting in the pub for him since six o'clock.'

'Get a name and address,' Carlowe said. 'Offer him a cup of tea or something.'

'But what am I supposed to tell him?' She looked nervous. Her face was ruddy, having clearly been on duty outside for the best part of an hour, with the temperature dropping. 'I mean he's seen all the cars and stuff, so he knows something's happened.'

'So, tell him the truth.'

The young woman glanced, horrified, at the body. 'What? You mean about . . .?'

'No need to be specific,' Carlowe said. 'Just tell him his friend's passed away.' He saw the woman shift from one foot to the other. 'Not done a death message before?'

The woman shook her head.

'Well, this shouldn't be too tricky.' Carlowe glanced at Thorne conspiratorially and half smiled, old hand to old hand. 'I mean he's only a friend, isn't he? It's a damn sight tougher when it's family, trust me.'

The PC said, 'Sir,' then turned away, adjusting her hat in the mirror by the front door before heading outside.

'One she'll remember,' Carlowe said.

Thorne ignored him and walked to the door. He opened it a few inches further, in time to see the young officer stepping through the front gate and approaching an old man who was waiting on the pavement.

He wore an old-fashioned flat cap and a heavy coat. He had gloves on but he was wringing his hands all the same. Nervous rather than cold. Perhaps he was hard of hearing, because he leaned closer to the PC as she began to speak, his lips moving as though he were mouthing her words.

Thorne closed the door, having no wish to see the old man's reaction when he was given the news about his friend; the mess it made of his face. It was a night *he* would remember as well.

He turned back into the hall and saw Carlowe leaning close to talk into the radio that was clipped to the top of his vest. The inspector narrowed his eyes and said, 'Say again,' then walked into the kitchen while he listened. Thorne heard one of the other officers already in there say, 'You're kidding.'

A few seconds later, Carlowe came out, shaking his head. Thorne could not read his expression, but it did not look as if there was anything good coming.

'We've got another one.'

'Another what?' Thorne asked.

Carlowe pointed at the hanging man. 'Another one of *these*.' He moved the finger towards Thorne. 'Is there something I should know about?'

CHAPTER 51

Thorne took his own car, staying close behind Carlowe and the young female PC as they pushed through traffic on the Western Way, following the arc of the river until it widened out at Thamesmead. It was a ten-minute drive and they could have made it in even less time, but there was no call for blues and twos; no point risking life and limb when there was only a dead man waiting for them at the other end.

'Not like he's going anywhere,' Carlowe said, when the PC suggested it.

With the grim silhouette of the pumping station up ahead, they came off the main road and half a mile further on, after missing the unmarked turning once, they finally pulled into a narrow, unlit alleyway. It was rutted and pot-holed; the tyres churning up mud and stones as the cars moved slowly past high walls that were crumbling and overgrown. Fifty yards on, the track swung round to the right and broadened out, just as the river had done, into a patch of near-wasteland with a row of four shabby-looking garages at its far end.

Other units had arrived ahead of them. Two officers were leaning against their Fiesta, cradling cups of takeaway coffee, while a third spoke to a civilian a few feet away. The first vehicle on the scene had now been moved and reparked more strategically, its headlights beaming directly into the open garage at one end and lighting up the rear end of the car inside.

Thorne clocked it, and understood everything.

While Carlowe disappeared into the open garage, Thorne took out his warrant card and wandered across to the officers enjoying their coffee. With a number of units still in attendance at the Mallen scene, the two women had clearly been pulled off their break. The elder of them, a sergeant, nodded towards the civilian and explained that he was the one who had made the 999 call.

'Says that nobody really uses these garages at all, just kids smoking weed every now and again. He could hear the engine running inside.'

Thorne looked across at the man. Black, in his late thirties; nodding and gesturing towards the garage while the officer he was talking to scribbled in his notebook. After one final draw, the witness flicked away the remains of a cigarette and immediately reached for another.

'See, it's a damn sight harder with modern cars.' The younger of the two officers took a quick slug of coffee. 'Electrically controlled combustion and catalytic converters, whatever. These days they produce so little carbon monoxide it's almost impossible to do it.'

'So how old you reckon that one is then?' The sergeant nodded towards the garage.

The PC turned to look. 'Fifteen years old, something like that?'

'What is it, a P-reg?' The sergeant began counting back.

'Surprised the engine ran at all, to be honest.'

'You seen the body?' Thorne asked.

The younger woman nodded. 'It was me that went in with a wet hankie over my gob and turned the ignition off.' She sipped her drink. 'You know, in case he hadn't been in there too long.' Her eyes widened above the large plastic cup. 'Very dead, unfortunately.'

The sergeant said, 'P-reg is more like seventeen years old.'

Thorne stepped away when he saw Carlowe emerge from the garage, pulling off plastic gloves with a practised flick of each wrist, sucking in deep breaths and squinting against the glare of the headlights.

He walked to meet him.

'We'll have a proper rummage around when the fumes have cleared a bit more,' Carlowe said. He took another long, slow breath. 'Nothing you wouldn't expect though. There's a note, too . . . sort of. Scrap of paper on the front seat.' Before Thorne could say anything, the inspector leaned down to his radio and casually thumbed the

354

button. 'Listen, anybody at the hanging in Woolwich . . . can you just tell the doctor to get straight over to this one when he's finished?' A voice said, 'Understood,' and Carlowe looked back to Thorne. 'He'll be earning his money tonight.'

'What's the note say?'

'Not a lot.'

'What?'

'A man of few words, obviously,' Carlowe said. 'Or maybe his pen ran out.'

Thorne waited and Carlowe let him. There was the hint of a smile on the man's face, but something decidedly unamused in the narrowing of his eyes, beady slits in the half-light. Suspicious that he was being played for a mug and not happy about it.

'It says, *Job done*.' Carlowe paused. 'The note.' He reached inside his Met vest and scratched. 'Good job too, no question about that. Whoever he is, he was a dab hand with a plastic hose and a roll of gaffer tape.'

'No ID yet then?'

'Nothing in his wallet except cash,' Carlowe said. 'An old photo of a woman and a couple of kids. They're running the car through the system right now, so we'll have the name in a minute.'

Thorne nodded. 'Do you mind if I go and have a look?'

Carlowe thought about it for a second or two, any suspicions seemingly tempered, for the time being at least, by his satisfaction at being deferred to as the senior officer on duty. He said, 'Help yourself,' then turned to greet the female PC who had driven him there and who was now approaching them, open notebook in hand.

'Here we go,' he said. 'We should have that ID now.'

Knowing that they would have no such thing, Thorne walked towards the garage, pausing on the way to tug a pair of plastic gloves from an open box on the bonnet of one of the patrol cars. His hands were clammy as he pulled them on. Moving into the tunnel of yellow light cast by the patrol car's headlamps, he was passed by an officer coming from inside the garage, gulping the fresh air hungrily. Thorne held up his warrant card, but the officer did not bother looking at it. Instead, he pulled a face as though he were stepping from a rank toilet stall and said, 'I should give that a couple of minutes if I were you.'

Against the dark dirt floor, a few fragments of broken glass caught the light. Cobwebs around the door glistened, moving in the breeze, and lingering fumes from the exhaust scratched at the back of Thorne's throat as he approached the Astra. The car was every bit as old and tired as the officers outside had said it was. The patches of rust were far more vivid than the faded red of the paintwork or the dirty streaks of grey filler on both rear wings.

Thorne remembered exactly what the officers had been talking about and wondered if this was precisely the reason Mercer had bought such an old car. If Thorne had been right about him having plenty of money to play with, he could certainly have afforded something a lot better.

Had this been the plan all along?

Job done . . .

He used his phone to take a couple of quick photos, then moved round to the side of the car. His eye followed the line of the white plastic tubing that had been taped to the end of the exhaust and fed in through the top of the rear driver's-side window. That door, like all the others, had been opened to help dispel the fumes, but Thorne could see the remnants of the grey gaffer tape on the glass that had been torn into thick strips and used to seal the opening from the inside.

He moved forward – the fumes even stronger suddenly – and stared through the open driver's door into the darkened interior.

Got his first look at Terry Mercer.

The body was slumped to the left, though not quite touching the passenger seat. Thorne could not be sure if this was how he had been found, or how the sergeant had left him after searching for signs of life. Mercer was wearing a dark jacket and a light blue shirt, training shoes that looked almost brand new in the gloom of the footwell. His white hair looked to have been oiled and swept back, but now a few thick strands hung loose and untidy from the drooping head, as though he'd just woken up. His left hand was a fist in his lap while the other stretched out towards the open door.

Thorne leaned in and touched fingers to Mercer's face. It still felt warm, but, glancing down, he could see that the car's heater had been turned up and guessed it had been running while the engine was on.

No point sitting there freezing for those last few minutes.

Glancing across, he saw the scrap of paper that Carlowe had mentioned and reached for it. Mercer's final statement – simple, triumphant – had been scrawled in slanting capital letters. There was a cheap yellow biro on the floor in front of the passenger seat. Thorne held on to the note for a few seconds longer; it was slippery between his plastic-coated fingers. Then he set it back where he'd found it.

He felt light-headed, uncertain of how to feel.

It was over, his ridiculous phantom investigation, though he and those he had dragged into his doomed orbit might already have spent too much time off the grid to avoid the inevitable fallout. He was happy, or at least relieved, that the killing was at an end. But at the same time he could not help feeling that he had been robbed of something.

That he had been cheated.

He needed air, and not just because of the exhaust fumes.

He stood up and took a step away from the car, but then a glance inside caught the mess of litter on the back seat. An overcoat bundled up on the floor. He wondered if anyone had bothered searching the rest of the vehicle yet or opened the boot.

Had that 'proper rummage' Carlowe had mentioned.

There was only one other officer lurking at the entrance, but she was looking the other way, so Thorne ducked quickly down into the back of the car. He turned over the jumble of discarded cans and fast-food wrappers. He looked through the pockets of the jacket and came up empty. As he was backing out again, he glimpsed the edge of a white plastic bag wedged beneath the driver's chair and reached down to pull it out.

The weight told him it was not empty.

Sitting on the back seat and taking care to keep his head down, Thorne drew a tattered green-cardboard folder from the bag. He opened it and as soon as he had taken out its contents and begun to examine them, he knew *exactly* how to feel. He barely registered the discomfort as he gasped in a lungful of exhaust fumes . . .

A minute later Thorne was walking out of the garage at a nice steady pace; gratefully sucking in the cold air as he moved out of the light, through the low-lying flood of the patrol car's headlights and back into the chill of the semi-dark.

Carlowe turned from a conversation with his sergeant. Said, 'You must be good at holding your breath.'

Thorne managed a sickly smile then pulled an appropriate face and turned away to spit copiously into the dirt. 'I'll get out of your hair then,' he said, wiping his mouth. 'Thanks for letting me tag along.' He began walking towards his car, aware a moment or two later that Carlowe was following a few steps behind and not turning round when he was spoken to.

'No way Jesmond can think you're slacking now, eh, Tom?'

'Sorry?'

'All this, on your night off.'

'Right,' Thorne said.

A car came round the corner – the doctor's possibly – bumping slowly across the ruts towards them. 'Why do I get the feeling you know something the rest of us don't?' Carlowe asked.

Thorne said nothing and reached into his pocket for car keys.

Doing so was a little awkward, with his right arm held rigid at his side; keeping the necessary pressure on the folder tucked away inside his jacket, holding it tight against his ribs.

What he knew, was exactly how Terry Mercer had persuaded seven people to kill themselves.

CHAPTER 52

Helen had a bottle of wine open and was doing her best to stay awake in front of the television, when Hendricks called.

'I thought you should know,' he said, 'Terry Mercer's dead.'

'How?' It took a few seconds for her to get the word out; to shake the conviction that Thorne had managed to track down the man he was after and do something from which there would be no coming back.

Hendricks told her as much as he knew, explained that Thorne had called from his car to ask if he could pull whatever strings were necessary to ensure he did Mercer's post-mortem.

'Can you?'

'This isn't a job where people volunteer too often,' he said. 'I'll make some calls though.'

Helen turned at the sound of a whimper from Alfie's room. She stepped into the hall and listened, but she knew every noise her son made and it didn't sound like he was awake. 'Sorry, Phil . . .'

'Anyway, there you are,' he said. 'It's over.'

'Let's hope so.'

'Come on, I think even Tom might have to let this one go now.'

'Did he sound pleased? When you spoke to him.'

'Yeah, kind of. He sounded . . . enthusiastic.'

Helen grunted, non-committal. In the last few weeks enthusiasm had become something to be afraid of.

'Like I said though, he was in the car and it was only a couple of minutes.'

'Where was he going?'

'Well, I presumed he was on his way home.'

Neither of them spoke for a few seconds, then Helen told him how much she'd enjoyed their night out. Hendricks said that he'd had a good time too, despite having paid for it the following morning.

'Bit of a shaky scalpel hand,' he said.

'Bloody hell.'

'It was fine. I mean, it's not like I'm a brain surgeon, is it?'

Helen laughed, but she was thinking about Thorne searching for his jacket a few hours earlier. The urgency as he prowled between rooms, the adrenalin fizzing in him. It was a drug he had struggled to say goodbye to once and she wondered how easy it would be for him to do it again.

Hendricks said, 'The other night, when I was talking about why he did it.'

'The summit fever stuff?'

'It's like he has this compulsion to do things properly, you know? Like there's only ever one way to come at anything and I know it's a pain in the arse for the rest of us, but it's usually for the right reasons.'

'Yeah, he's a sodding perfectionist when it suits him.'

'Basically, love, you've hooked up with a control freak.'

Helen's voice softened. She wanted Thorne home; wanted to take the piss because secretly he liked it and see his face when Alfie came to him, and trace a finger across the small, straight scar on his chin. 'There are worse things to be,' she said.

'I suppose.'

'It means you give a shit, at least.'

'Did you know more control freaks kill themselves every year than manic-depressives?'

Alfie whimpered again, and this time it sounded as though he wanted attention. 'I didn't, but it's good to know.'

'Sorry,' Hendricks said. 'Bit of a suicide nerd.'

'That must have come in handy the last few weeks . . .'

When Helen had hung up, she called Thorne's mobile, but it went straight to answerphone. There seemed no point in leaving a message, not if he was on his way home anyway. She heated Alfie's bottle, then collected her own on the way to his room, the two of them wide awake suddenly.

CHAPTER 53

Thorne had not expected Frank Anderson to still be in his office at quarter to ten at night, but he'd enjoyed calling on him nonetheless; hammering on the door hard enough to put another small crack in the glass.

Resigned to no more than scant and momentary satisfaction, he suddenly remembered the bar on the other side of the road. The one from which he'd called Anderson on his previous visit and the one – so Anna Carpenter had once told him – in which Anderson drank most days, alone or with prospective clients to whom he did not wish to show the sordid reality of his less than impressive business premises.

Thorne jogged across the road, dodging between cars.

Anderson was at a table just inside the door, sitting close to a woman in her mid-forties. His back was to the door, but the woman saw Thorne approach and immediately stopped laughing.

'New client, Frank?' Thorne waited for Anderson to turn round then pointed at his companion. 'Or is this a lady friend?'

'Oh, for God's sake,' Anderson said.

Thorne stepped closer and looked at the woman. 'Seriously, love, if you're thinking of sleeping with him, you're going to want a really hot shower afterwards.'

The woman opened her mouth but said nothing.

'What do you want?' Anderson asked.

Thorne tossed the folder down on to the table, opened it up and removed the photographs. He held them for a second before dropping them and spreading them out quickly, scattering beermats as Anderson and the woman scrabbled to remove their drinks.

Anderson took a cursory glance. Said, 'And?'

There were more than twenty photographs and though Thorne only recognised two of the subjects – Jacqui Gibbs and Andrew Cooper – he had known straight away who they were. What he was looking at. All of them photographed without their knowledge: coming out of houses, climbing into cars, kicking a football in the park. The families of those Terry Mercer had been targeting.

Men, women and children.

Grandchildren . . .

Mercer had offered his victims a simple choice. Take their own lives or forfeit those of the people they loved. No choice at all.

'You lying piece of shit,' Thorne said.

'Now, hang on—'

Now, people at nearby tables were staring, but Thorne could not have cared less. 'You took these,

365

didn't you?' He stabbed a finger at the picture of Jacqui Gibbs walking away from a supermarket. 'This was all part of the job you did for George Jeffers.'

'You asked me about the old people,' Anderson said. 'Remember? You wanted the names of the old people Jeffers had told me to find and I gave you their names. That was our deal.'

'You found these people too though, didn't you?'

Anderson looked. 'I didn't take all of these.'

'The ones he asked you to find. You took their pictures and handed them over for Jeffers to pass on to his mate.'

'I don't know anything about that.'

'His mate, Terry Mercer.'

'Never heard of him—'

'Have you got any fucking idea what you've done?'

The woman – a blowsy brunette wearing too much make-up – got to her feet a little unsteadily, but Thorne looked at her and she quickly sat back down again. Seeing that one of the staff had moved from behind the bar she leaned across to Anderson and said, 'Shall I call the police?'

Anderson shook his head.

'Already here,' Thorne said.

The woman looked confused. She reached across for Anderson's hand.

'I asked you a question.' Thorne picked up a photo, pushed it into Anderson's face. 'Any idea how many of these people's parents and grandparents are dead now because of these?' He held up the photo of Andrew Cooper. 'This man's mother and father.'

'What's going on, Frank?' the woman asked.

Seeing the fear in his companion's eyes, Anderson seemed compelled suddenly to react as though he had a spine of some sort. 'OK, you've come in here and you've shouted the odds and I'm sure you feel a lot better. Now, we both know full well that I've not done anything illegal, so why don't you take your collection of snaps and leave us to it.' He held out his arms as though all the others in the bar were his friends. 'We're just trying to have a quiet drink, OK?'

Thorne looked at him.

Anderson stood up. 'Right, good. Now, I'm going for a piss.'

He walked around the table, slid past Thorne and disappeared towards the Gents. Thorne stood breathing heavily for half a minute, staring down at the photographs while the woman went back to her drink and those around them returned to their conversations. Then he gathered up the pictures, turned from the table and began pushing through the crowd.

He walked in just as Anderson was turning from the urinal, zipping himself up.

'Oh, this is getting silly,' Anderson said. He moved towards the door, but Thorne barred his way. 'Look, I don't know what your problem is, but unless you've got anything else, I'm on a promise, so . . .'

'You need to wash your hands,' Thorne said.

'So I took some bloody pictures, all right? I was doing my job.' He stared at Thorne, waiting for him to move. 'Come on, that's enough now, I'm trying to be nice about this.'

'*Nice?*' Thorne could not remember the last time he had wanted to hit anyone quite this much. He also knew that whatever else he had done, whether he would get away with it or not, a straightforward physical assault after a confrontation witnessed by a bar full of people would be the end of him. The Job would be gone in a second and there would be plenty of people queuing up to get him put away.

Anderson saw Thorne's hesitation and sensed the weakness. He smiled and said, 'Yeah, I know. You'd love to.'

Thorne punched him hard in the face.

He moved quickly back through the crowded bar, keeping his head down and avoiding the stare of Anderson's girlfriend as he passed the table. He barrelled out through the door, the folder under his arm, his injured hand hanging loosely at his side.

He ran straight into Neil Hackett.

CHAPTER 54

Thorne stepped back and they stared at each other for a few seconds while traffic rumbled by. A couple passed between them, walking towards the bar. The wash of passing headlights showed only mild amusement on Hackett's face, while Thorne knew he looked every bit as horrified as he felt.

'Someone's in a hurry,' Hackett said.

'Need to get home,' Thorne said, dredging up a smile. The rain that had begun to fall was not heavy, but he was aware of each drop landing with an audible *smack* on the folder he was carrying.

'Under the thumb?' Hackett said. 'You need to do something about that.'

'This isn't your neck of the woods, is it?' Thorne still did not know where Hackett lived, but the idea that this bar could possibly be his local would be stretching the notion of coincidence to a ludicrous degree.

'No, it isn't,' Hackett said.

'So why this place?' Thorne nodded towards the bar. As he did so, the door opened and two lads peered out, excited at the sniff of trouble that had drifted from the toilets and keen to follow it outside. Thorne turned away, saw that Hackett was calmly staring them out. He heard the noise from the bar fade quickly as the door closed again.

'I've heard good things,' Hackett said. 'Decent beer, nice crowd. Never any trouble.' He glanced at Thorne's hand. 'Hurt yourself?'

Thorne flexed his fingers, winced. He hoped it wasn't broken. 'Trapped it in a door.'

'Ouch.'

'I'll live.'

'I quite like trying out places I've never been before,' Hackett said. He took a step towards the bar, towards Thorne. 'I'm usually pretty good at making myself at home. Finding interesting people to talk to.' He thrust huge hands into the pockets of his long, dark coat and looked towards the door. 'Any in there?'

'No idea,' Thorne said. 'I just nipped in for a quick one.'

'Right.'

'I'm driving.'

'Because it's not really yours either, is it?'

'What?'

'Neck of the woods.'

'I was visiting a mate.'

'Anything interesting?'

'Not really.'

'In *there*, I mean.' Hackett nodded at the folder in Thorne's left hand.

Thorne lifted the folder up as though he had

forgotten it was there and looked at it. It was clear that Hackett knew *something*, but as yet there was no way of knowing how much. For a second or two, Thorne wondered if he should just casually open the folder up and show Hackett its contents. There was no compulsion to explain them and it would be helpful to see whether or not Hackett recognised the people in the photographs. Thorne thought it might give him some idea of what he was up against. He said, 'No, not particularly.'

Hackett nodded, but there was tension in his face suddenly, a tightening around the mouth, eyes unblinking. 'We should go back in,' he said. 'We could have that drink I was talking about.'

'Better not,' Thorne said, fastening his jacket. 'Driving, remember?'

'Course, and you need to get home.'

'I *want* to get home.'

'Be ironic though, wouldn't it?' Hackett said. 'Getting nicked for drink driving, after everything else.'

Thorne looked at the DCI, not sure what he meant. After everything that had happened to get him bumped off the Murder Squad? Or everything that was happening now? He certainly wasn't going to ask. He started to walk away. 'Enjoy your drink,' he said.

'She's Child Abuse, isn't she?'

Thorne stopped and turned. The message being delivered was simple enough: the futility of trying to keep secrets, the non-existence of privacy. It

371

was not something Thorne needed telling, but Hackett clearly relished doing so anyway.

'Your other half?' Hackett shook his head sadly. 'See, I've always thought it was a dangerous business, shacking up with someone else who was in the Job. A nightmare waiting to happen.' He shrugged. 'What do I know, though?' He turned and walked towards the bar. Said, 'You definitely want to get that hand looked at.'

CHAPTER 55

Holland and Kitson were unable to get away from the office for too long, so Thorne drove over to Colindale. He texted to let them know he'd arrived, and at lunchtime the three of them convened in Thorne's car, five minutes' walk and a few streets away from the Peel Centre.

Kitson asked Thorne what had happened to his hand, but he waved her question away. He wanted to talk about what had happened before he'd paid Frank Anderson a visit the night before.

What he'd found in Terry Mercer's car.

'He might have needed a gun to get them where he wanted them,' Thorne said. He remembered what Anthony Dennison had told him about Mercer buying two guns. 'To get through the door and get everything set up . . . the bath, the pills, whatever. But persuading them to take that final step was easy enough in the end.' Thorne passed the photographs to Yvonne Kitson in the passenger seat. She looked through them and then handed them back to Holland. 'These were all the weapons he needed.'

'Jesus,' Kitson said. 'That's . . .'

'They knew he'd do it, too. Kill them without a

second thought if they didn't do it themselves and then go after their families.'

Nobody spoke for a while. Thorne lowered his window an inch or two to let some air in.

'In the end, you do whatever it takes to protect your kids,' Kitson said.

Thorne nodded.

'Simple as that. Doesn't matter how old you are, or they are.' She turned to look at Holland. 'Right, Dave?'

Thorne felt a sting of irritation seeing the two of them confer; the implication that, as the only one in the car without children of his own, he could not possibly understand.

'I do *get* it, Yvonne,' he said.

Holland picked out a photograph of someone he recognised. 'That's Graham Daniels,' he said. He showed them another, pointed. 'And that's his daughter.' The girl who was helping out in the printer's, earning money to go to college.

There were plenty of other pictures, other faces. Without talking to the relatives of the dead, they could not identify all the people in the photographs. Members of the extended Cooper family, the Gibbs, the Jacobsons . . .

'It's fair to assume that Anderson took most of these,' Thorne said. 'Jeffers probably took the rest, or maybe Mercer himself.'

Holland handed the photographs back to Thorne. 'Well one of them took a trip up to Newcastle,' he said. 'To take the pictures of Edward Mallen's kids.'

Thorne looked at him.

'We did a bit of digging this morning,' Kitson said. 'That's where he was living until recently.'

'We any the wiser about what connects Mallen to the Mercer trial?'

'Yeah, well that's the thing.' Holland looked at Kitson. They had come with news of their own. 'Edward Mallen wasn't his real name. His real name was Barry Mercer.'

Thorne looked at Kitson. 'Brother?'

Kitson nodded. 'Younger brother,' she said. 'He was given a new identity thirty years ago. After he helped the police catch Mercer. They moved him and his family to the north-east under a witness protection scheme. Set them all up with new identities, new lives.'

Thorne nodded, putting it together. It had been Mercer's own brother who had provided the 'intelligence' Ian Tully had mentioned. The information about the armed robbery.

'It's why Mercer left that one until last,' Holland said.

'But why the hell would his brother come back to London, if he knew Mercer had been released from prison?'

'God knows,' Kitson said. 'Guilt, or something? A death wish?'

'Well he got what he wished for,' Holland said.

'More to the point, if he was part of a WP scheme, why did anyone *let* him?' It was a question to which inside experience provided an answer

375

even before Thorne had finished asking it. He knew very well that few programmes of witness protection could be maintained at the highest level of security for thirty years. There simply wasn't the money, or the will. It was perfectly possible that nobody had even bothered to inform 'Edward Mallen' that his brother had been released. Equally, they could have approved Mallen's move back to London and set him up in a WP scheme here, but that begged the question of how Mercer had found the address.

'It does mean we need to draw a line under all this very quickly,' Holland said.

'Well, I think Terry Mercer's already drawn a line under it.'

Kitson said, 'Seriously, Tom.'

'Seriously, what?'

'We're out,' Holland said. 'Me and Yvonne. We can't do anything else, nothing at all.' He looked at Kitson and Thorne could see that they'd spent time talking about this, working out what to say between them.

'That's fine,' Thorne said, holding up his hands. 'Look, you know how grateful I am for what you've done already and I don't see why I'd be asking you to do any more anyway. Now Mercer's dead, I can't see there's a lot more needs doing.'

'I'm sure you would have thought of something,' Holland said. 'So, as long as you understand that I'm done.' He flashed another look to Kitson. 'That we both are.'

Thorne looked at Kitson, but she was facing front. He sat back. 'You've made your point, Dave, but I don't think there's any need to panic. I mean, they haven't put it together so far.'

'I kind of think they might put it together *now* though.' It was clear that Holland was worried and was unhappy about it. 'Even supposing we've got away with it so far, you'd have to be as thick as mince not to work it out now, wouldn't you? Soon as they find out who Edward Mallen really was and who he grassed up. Soon as some genius points out that his brother was released from prison a few months back, I've got a feeling they might have a sneaking suspicion who strung him up.' He slammed a palm against the headrest. 'The whole lot's going to unravel.'

'Dave—'

'I know, you said. "How much more shit can we be in?"'

Seeing the look on Holland's face, Thorne once again found himself wondering how Neil Hackett seemed to know so much more than he had any right to. Where he was getting *his* 'intelligence' from. There was certainly enough anger, enough resentment at what Thorne had asked of him to give Holland cause to go running to the brass.

And if not Holland . . .?

Even *considering* the alternatives was enough to send bile rising into Thorne's throat, but at the same time he had to be realistic. He knew that the number of suspects was limited.

'Look, it's over,' he said. 'One way or another. We should at least be grateful for that.'

'I'm sorry we didn't catch him, Tom,' Kitson said.

'So am I. But that's not always the most important thing, is it?' Thorne looked at Kitson and could see that she didn't believe it any more than he did.

The short silence that followed was broken by the ringing of Thorne's mobile. He saw that it was Hendricks calling, so answered and said, 'Hang on, Phil, I've got Yvonne and Dave here, so I'm going to put you on speaker.'

He pressed the button on the phone then laid it down between the seats.

'Phil . . .?'

'The gang's all here then, is it?' Hendricks' voice was tinny through the handset's small speaker. 'Everyone all right?'

Holland and Kitson muttered their hellos.

'Bloody hell, you lot sound cheery.'

The atmosphere in the car was tense, subdued; a far cry from the raising of glasses privately in the Oak, as they might have been doing had an official investigation ended in the same way.

'We're listening, Phil,' Thorne said.

'OK, so I've just finished the PM on the body in the Astra. Nothing you wouldn't expect. Male of approximately seventy years of age, hypoxia due to the inhalation of carbon monoxide, blah blah. Now, I have got one question.'

'What?'

378

'You're positive that Mercer was responsible for the hanging in Woolwich, yeah?'

'It was his brother,' Thorne said. 'Grassed him up thirty years ago.'

'Ah . . . in which case we *do* have a bit of a problem. Unless Mercer did it from beyond the grave.'

'Sorry?'

'I checked with the pathologist who did the PM on the Woolwich body and we've got a slight issue with time of death. There's not much in it, maybe no more than an hour or two, but the fact is, our man in the car died *before* the man who hung himself.' Hendricks paused. It sounded as though he was eating crisps. 'You see where I'm going with this, boys and girls?'

Holland and Kitson looked at Thorne.

'I'll take that as a yes,' Hendricks said.

Thorne closed his eyes and remembered putting fingers to the dead man's face. Remembered something else that kid Dennison had said: *'I told you, he was old. White hair and wrinkles and all that.'* There could only be two explanations for what Hendricks was telling them and Thorne was in little doubt as to which of them to believe.

Holland leaned forward between the front seats. 'So assuming Mercer *did* kill his brother, it can't have been his body in the car.'

Kitson lowered her head, swore quietly.

'It wasn't Mercer in the car,' Thorne said. 'It was George Jeffers.'

PART IV

NOT SO VERY FAR TO FALL

CHAPTER 56

Mercer walks by the river; taking his time and staying as close as he can to the water, from Rotherhithe on the south side towards Greenwich. He thought about doing this a lot when he was inside. Not that he's ever been one for 'views', as such. The countryside, sunsets, all that picture postcard nonsense. You look at something, you think: Yeah that's nice, whatever, and you move on. He's never seen the point in hanging around. It's the same as looking at paintings. Is it good or is it rubbish? Who wants to stare at anything for ten minutes?

He's always loved the river though, loved the movement of it. Not so much the flow, but the whole tidal thing. The way it rises and falls like it's breathing. The dangerous bits, the way you never quite know where you are with it. Funny that they call it Father Thames, because to him it's always seemed moody, like a woman.

Moody, like *she* was.

He turns off Creek Road then cuts down along the edge of Dreadnought Wharf to the riverbank and thinks, that's not strictly fair. He didn't have to like what his wife had done, but once he'd understood why she'd done it, he'd been able to live with it for the most part. There'd been a moment with Barry too, right at the end. When the begging had started and he'd *almost* been able to see why. He'd always thought there had to have been a good reason for his brother to have done what he did, because he must have known what it would mean. Years spent hiding away like an insect in some shithole, lying every minute of the day and pretending to be somebody you're not, so that even your own kids don't know.

I did it for you, Barry had said; crying like a girl and clawing at the washing line round his neck. Something like that, anyway. What the hell was that supposed to mean? Taking you out of harm's way? Protecting you from yourself?

He's known for a long time that people need to take care of themselves and now that's exactly what he's going to do. That's his new project. As soon as the job was done and that last name was crossed off the list, he knew straight away that would be the way to go.

There had to be *something*, after all.

It was like these idiots who make a bundle and retire too early with sod all to do. Rattling around in big houses. Pots of cash and wives with tit-jobs, but going mental, with nothing to get out of bed for.

He can't just walk away. Fade away . . .

So, now it's all about doing whatever it takes to

stay safe, for however long he's got left. Might be twenty years, might be hit by a bus tomorrow, but there's no way on God's green earth he's going back inside. He knows that much.

He comes to the glazed dome which is the entrance to the Greenwich foot tunnel and walks through. Five minutes across to the Isle of Dogs. It's cool inside; exciting too, knowing that all the weight of that moody old river is right above your head. He watches a woman and two kids coming towards him, the children whooping and shouting, enjoying the echoes. He supposes that some people would find it spooky down here; the dim, amber light and the way the sound bounces off the tiles. Mercer can't understand it. He has dreamed the Dead Man's Walk and has spent far too long hearing the echoes of heavy doors slamming shut and keys turning in locks. Still, he smiles at the woman and her wide-eyed children as they pass.

On the other side of the river he turns east, walks past Island Gardens then stops when he sees the tower of Christ Church. His knees are hurting, so he sits on a bench to take a breather and thinks about going inside. He wonders if there's a vicar or someone in there he can have a chat with. They can't say anything anyway, can they? Can't pass on anything they hear. Not that he's planning to walk in there and confess, nothing like that, but it would be nice to just sit and have a natter.

It was always useful to talk to someone who was actually in the game. Ask them what they thought came after. He's heard that these days there are priests who don't even believe in God, but surely they must all have *some* idea of what's going on.

He'd talked to the chaplains at Gartree a fair bit. There was always a cup of tea in there and a hand on your shoulder, and it was certainly nicer talking to them than the psychologists, because all they ever wanted to hear was how sorry you were. He told them he was of course, told them loads of times, because he isn't stupid. He knew they were the ones the parole board listened to. It wasn't hard, because he *was* sorry, even if it wasn't necessarily about the right things.

Sorry I got caught.

Sorry I've spent thirty years locked up.

Sorry I don't know what my kids look like.

He sits and rubs his aching knees. There's a pub opposite and the church is behind him and he tries to make his mind up.

What he would like to do is talk to someone about the Bible and ask why the God in the new bit is so different to the original one. Later on, it's all forgiveness and cheek-turning, but the first one's always coming down on people like a ton of bricks and getting his afters on anyone he thinks isn't toeing the line.

Mercer knows which one he prefers.

That first God – the *angry* God – has no problem at all getting rid of his enemies.

CHAPTER 57

'It's not broken,' Hendricks said.

'Something, I suppose.'

'Obviously must have been a bit of a pussy-arsed punch.' Hendricks squeezed Thorne's hand once more before releasing it and laughed at the yelp of pain from across the table. 'How's things with Helen?'

'What's that got to do with anything?'

'Just saying, because if you're not getting any action from her, you won't be able to rely on that hand for a while.'

Thorne smiled, rubbing his knuckles. 'A man's best friend.'

'Mrs Fist and her five lovely daughters.'

'Daughters? You?'

'OK, sons in my case. Actually, I've always thought of them as the five members of Take That.'

'Which one's Robbie?'

Hendricks stuck his middle finger up. 'That one . . .'

The staff at the Bengal Lancer on Kentish Town Road knew Thorne and Hendricks well and, as usual, had brought them over a plate of complimentary poppadums to go with the pints of Kingfisher while they were waiting for their food to be cooked. Hendricks applied a delicate karate chop to the pile and they got stuck in.

'I presume your day got better,' Hendricks said, 'after I pissed on everyone's strawberries.'

Thorne grunted. 'Yeah, well finding out our killer wasn't quite as dead as we'd thought didn't exactly go down a storm.' He smeared lime pickle across a fragment of poppadum. 'Dave and Yvonne were out of the car and on their way back to work pretty sharpish, before I could think of anything I might want them to do.'

'Can you?'

'Like Dave said, MIT would have to be pretty stupid not to work it out for themselves now. How long it takes, that's another matter.'

'Mercer didn't really think he was going to get away with it,' Hendricks said. 'Did he? I mean even if the time of death thing hadn't been obvious they'd have run tests, whatever. Jeffers' family would have reported him missing at some point.'

Jeffers' family. Their pictures somewhere among the stack of photographs in that battered green folder. The last faces Jeffers would have seen; the faces he would have focused on as he sealed himself up inside that car and started the engine.

'God knows,' Thorne said. 'He wanted Jeffers out of the way anyway and maybe he thought it might buy him a bit more time.'

'If he's tying up loose ends, you thought about giving Frank Anderson a heads-up?'

'Yeah, thought about it,' Thorne said. He washed the poppadum down with a mouthful of lager. 'Now, seeing as you ask, no . . . the rest of my day wasn't particularly great, as a matter of fact. An hour on the phone buttering up a custody sergeant for a kick-off.'

Thorne explained his decision to have Anthony Dennison's 'bailed-to-return' status cancelled. He had told the custody sergeant that he was cultivating the boy as a source and asked very nicely if the necessary 'amendments' could therefore be made to the files. A couple of mouse-clicks and a courtesy call to the officer who had questioned Dennison on the night and the job was done. Dennison was off the hook.

'I don't get it.' Hendricks reached for the pickles. 'Kid smacked you in the face, for God's sake.' He pointed; the worst of the bruising below Thorne's eye had gone, but there was still a mark. 'A damn sight harder than you punched that private detective as well, not that *that's* saying very much.'

'I made a deal with him,' Thorne said. 'He gave me good information and the simple truth is I provoked the kid.'

'You provoke a lot of people.'

'I went looking for it.'

'Up to you, mate, but you know the kid's going to end up inside anyway, presuming he lasts that long. Better off in prison, you ask me.'

Thorne knew that Hendricks was probably right. He hoped that Anthony Dennison was smart enough to stay out of the sort of trouble that could cost him his life. Still, he could not be certain that he'd done the boy any real favours. 'So, other than that, just sitting around on my arse all day waiting for the axe to fall.'

He told Hendricks about running into Neil Hackett outside the bar where he'd confronted Frank Anderson. How he was more certain than ever that Hackett was on to him, despite the fact that the MIT man seemed to be taking his time doing anything about it.

'I wish he'd just get on with it,' Thorne said.

'Put you out of your misery.'

'Something like that.'

'Maybe you're wrong and he knows bugger all. Maybe he's just digging around.'

'He knows more than enough,' Thorne said. 'Has to.'

'So, he's trying to make you sweat.'

'Well, he's doing a bloody good job of it.' Thorne wiped the sheen of sweat from his forehead, pointed at the bowl of lime pickle. 'Almost as good as this stuff.' He held up his glass, signalled to the waiter for another beer and Hendricks did the same. 'It's not just about him though,' he said. 'It's where he's getting his information from.'

'Yeah . . . that's a worry,' Hendricks said.

'Who he's getting it from. Somebody's telling him what we've found out, what the connections

390

are. He seems to know where I'm going to be every minute of the day.'

'He might just be following you.'

'Yeah, but if he's doing that, it's because somebody's telling him I'm worth following. He knows who I'm talking to and when, and I'm damn sure he knows why.' Despite himself, Thorne's eyes were on Hendricks as he laid out his suspicions.

Looking for a reaction. Not seeing one.

'Something to bear in mind though,' Hendricks said. He spoke slowly, choosing his words, like a doctor delivering unwelcome news. 'Before you get too . . . worked up about all this. If someone *is* telling the powers that be what's happening, they might be doing it for good reasons. For the right reasons, you know?'

Thorne looked at him, but Hendricks had lowered his eyes before he'd finished talking. 'What, to protect me from myself, you mean?'

'Just saying.'

'You got any ideas who that might be?'

'Not the foggiest, mate.'

'Sure?' Hendricks glanced up for just a second and now Thorne saw a reaction. He could tell when his friend was lying.

The beers arrived and they drank for a while without saying much. The place was busy as usual and there was plenty to look at and listen to. A couple who seemed determined not to speak to one another at all, a group of businessmen in shirts and ties complaining about a 'bonding initiative', a loud trio of lads who'd been three parts pissed when they'd arrived.

'So, how *are* things with Helen?' Hendricks asked. 'Really.'

'Yeah, not bad,' Thorne said. 'She was obviously happy to hear about what had happened, that it was all over.'

Hendricks nodded at Thorne's hand. 'What about that?'

'Actually she was pretty relaxed about it.' Thorne lifted his glass up with his good hand. 'She really doesn't like me trying to bullshit her, but she knows where she is when I'm punching someone.'

'I presume she doesn't know about Mercer not being dead.'

'No, and I don't see any point in telling her,' Thorne said. 'Or anyone else telling her.' The night before, he had sensed that Helen was not altogether surprised to hear about Mercer's 'suicide' and guessed that someone had told her already.

Once again, there were not too many candidates.

The waiter appeared at their table with a trolley and picked up the first of half a dozen serving dishes. 'Chicken bhuna?'

'Just put them anywhere you like,' Thorne said. 'We're sharing.'

Hendricks reached for the dish. Said, 'News to me.'

They walked south towards Camden Town, in the direction of Hendricks' new flat and Thorne's old one, where Thorne had left his car. It was after eleven, but there were still plenty of people about, in cars and on foot. Drinking up outside pubs trying to close, coming out of restaurants or hurrying into the chippies and kebab shops that were just starting to enjoy their busiest few hours of the day.

When the beer-goggles lowered all manner of standards.

'So, what's the plan for tomorrow?' Hendricks asked.

'Haven't got one,' Thorne said. 'Last day off, then I'm back on earlies Saturday.'

'Make the most of it, then.'

'I'm open to suggestions.'

'I don't know, go to a sodding museum or something.'

Thorne nodded, like he was considering it. 'Well I was thinking more along the lines of cheese on toast and internet porn, but it's a thought.'

'I'm just saying. Don't . . .'

'Don't *what*, Phil?'

They walked on, falling into step without meaning to, and stopped a minute or so later on the corner of Prince of Wales Road, where they would part company.

'You really think Mercer's gone to ground?'

'If he's sensible,' Thorne said. 'He could be out of the country by now.'

'Yeah?'

'I don't know, do I?' Thorne could see that

Hendricks was unwilling to leave without an assurance of some sort. 'Listen, Phil, I'm out of it, all right? It's done and dusted, one way or another.'

'Good. Because it's time *you* were sensible too.'

Thorne watched his friend walk away, then set off towards his car. As soon as he and Hendricks could no longer see one another, Thorne reached for his phone and made a call. When it was answered, he told the man at the other end of the phone that he was sorry for calling so late. He was assured that it wasn't a problem.

'Just out of interest,' Thorne said. 'You got anything on tomorrow?'

CHAPTER 58

Helen was still up when Thorne got back to Tulse Hill, though as the TV was tuned to a documentary about ice-trucking, he suspected that she'd been asleep on the sofa for some time before he'd come in. He made tea for them both. When she asked, he told her that his hand was feeling a lot better and that Hendricks had been on good form.

'You two should go out,' he said. 'Get to know each other a bit better. See what I've been putting up with all these years.'

He asked her how her day had been. It struck him that, except when he was trying to avoid talking about what he had been doing, it was not something he'd done often enough recently.

She told him she'd had lunch with a social worker, one of those she worked with regularly. 'Not exactly a bundle of laughs,' she said. 'She'd been to see a family she was concerned about in Streatham. Three kids under six, one of them an infant. Found a pit bull terrier chained to the baby's cot.'

'Bloody hell. Was the kid OK?'

'That's the problem,' Helen said. 'Legally they can't touch any of the children they visit, so it's hard to tell. If a child's fully dressed, any injuries from the neck down stay hidden.' She sipped her tea. 'They're all so bloody . . . disheartened, you know? People have them pegged as over-officious lesbians who are trying to take their kids away, but they're the first people that get it in the neck when it all falls apart and a child dies. They're understaffed and under-resourced and the good work they do is completely unrecognised. They've got so much shit to deal with, and *they're* the ones getting their hands dirty and they're doing their best.' She reached down to pick up one of Alfie's toys and casually tossed it into the plastic box next to the sofa. 'Same as we are.'

'I know,' Thorne said.

'The entire system's outdated.'

Thorne sat down next to her. 'I know.'

'Children should not be dying because of neglect in a city like fucking London.'

The ice-truckers had suddenly become a little too noisy, so Thorne reached for the remote and turned the TV off.

'I *mean* it, Tom.'

Thorne had heard other officers refer to Child Abuse Investigation as the 'Cardigan Squad', the perception among some being that those working on a CAIT were no more than glorified social workers. That career-wise it was a dead end and that anyone with an ounce of ambition should be looking at the more glamorous departments with real excitement and decent budgets such as Drug Enforcement or Firearms. He made a promise to himself that the next time he heard the phrase being used, he would do some damage to his other hand.

He said, 'You do an amazing job.'

He looked at her, desperately hoping that his words, which to him now seemed trite and pathetic, had not sounded patronising. God knows, it was the last thing he intended, but he knew there had been a good deal of misunderstanding – all of it his fault – between them in recent weeks.

Helen stood up. She carried her empty mug across to the sink then came back and pulled Thorne to his feet. Together they went to check on Alfie, then carried on through to the bedroom and got undressed.

Helen turned the light out, leaving only the spill from the lamp she always left outside her son's room. Thorne tried to say, 'Sorry,' but she kissed the word off his mouth. The tenderness between them quickly became something more fierce and continued that way until, forgetting his injury, Thorne foolishly tried to take his own weight on his hands and all but collapsed on top of her.

Thorne rolled away, swearing, but Helen gently moved and eased herself on top of him.

'Looks like I'll have to help myself,' she said.

CHAPTER 59

Mercer sits in a branch of a well-known coffee shop, drinking tea and wondering when the hell coffee became so popular. He stares out at the pinched faces of the pedestrians and the necklace of rush-hour traffic crawling past, catching glimpses of the palm trees and sunsets in the window of the travel agent's on the other side of the road.

He remembers a holiday . . .

Margate. Back when he was still working his way up, before the Jags and the conservatories and the family trips to Disneyland or the south of France. A week in Margate: long before the place had galleries filled with modern art that wasn't really art at all and everything was neon and kebab shops. These are the holidays he thinks about most often. When the kids were small and she still bought clothes for them all in Deptford market.

When he wasn't looking over his shoulder quite so much.

He remembers his eldest boy, can't have been much more than seven or eight at the time, in floods of tears on the pavement outside this arcade. He'd been transfixed by the machine with the toy crane inside, had stood there for half an hour and fed it every ten-pence piece Mercer had given him in an effort to grab one of those plastic trolls with the long green hair. He had wanted one of those stupid trolls more than anything in the world and now all his money was gone and he hadn't been able to grab one.

'It's not fair, Daddy,' the boy had wailed. 'It's not fair.'

Mercer had agreed and promptly marched back inside the arcade to have a quiet word with the manager. When he'd emerged a few minutes later bearing aloft one of those trolls as if it were the FA cup, it had been the look on his wife's face he'd clocked first. The suspicion.

'It's all right,' he'd told her. 'I just had a quiet word with him.'

'Yeah, I know what that means,' she had said.

'No, nothing like that.' Obviously the arcade manager hadn't been *thrilled* to see Mercer bearing down on him. Mercer knew he could look a little . . . intimidating, even when he wasn't trying very hard. He leaned close to his wife and whispered, 'I just bunged him a fiver, that's all. Piece of piss.'

He'd turned to his son then and handed the prize across and the boy's smile had made his stomach turn over. A poxy fiver, for that smile. He watched his son clutch the doll to his chest and knew that he would happily have handed over every penny he had, *everything*, just to feel the way he felt at that moment.

'Thanks, Daddy . . .'

'You deserved it,' Mercer had said. 'Must have been something wrong with the machine, that's all.'

His wife was already on her way towards the nearest café, steering the pushchair through the crowd, their youngest already tired and starting to whine. His son took his hand as they followed and held it tight. Mercer squeezed and the boy squeezed back and Mercer knew that his son was thinking the same thing at that moment that he'd felt about his own old man once upon a time.

My dad can do *anything* . . .

Mercer's hands are wrapped tight around his mug.

And I *could*, he thinks.

He's not daft; he knows that every child grows out of that eventually, stops believing that their father is a superhero. The strongest, the fastest, the one who can produce trolls from thin air. The lucky ones though, they get to grow up thinking like that for a while at least and the fathers of those kids are luckier still. Instead, he was left with two kids that pissed the bed and got into fights and forgot that he'd ever done a single thing that made them feel good, or happy, or safe.

He brings the mug to his lips, his gaze still fixed on those posters of palm trees. Happy families on beaches, splashing in pools. The tea's gone cold, so he pushes the mug away.

He starts suddenly when a young woman appears at his shoulder. Well, younger than him, anyway. Late forties, maybe.

She lays a hand gently on his shoulder. Says, 'Are you feeling all right, love?'

Mercer realises that he is crying. He reaches for a serviette and wipes it across his eyes and mouth, then balls it into his fist. He thinks about Herbert, Jacobson, Mallen; their faces at the end.

He thinks about *all* of them, then turns to the woman and smiles.

'Feeling a lot better than I was,' he says.

CHAPTER 60

Keith Fryer was patting the bonnet of a tired-looking Renault Clio as if it were the head of a much-loved dog when he saw Thorne wandering on to his car lot. The young woman on the receiving end of the dealer's practised patter could not have mistaken the look of distaste on his face, or the way in which it became something rather more circumspect when he realised that Thorne had brought someone with him.

'Shit,' Fryer hissed.

His potential customer seemed to lose interest in the car fairly quickly after that and, satisfied that their arrival had had the desired effect, Thorne and his companion watched as Fryer marched away towards his office like a man in sudden need of the toilet, or strong drink.

They gave him a few minutes to compose himself.

'Busy?' Thorne asked, when he stepped into the doorway.

Head down at his desk, Fryer said nothing, opting for the same paper-shuffling routine as last time, so Thorne and the man with him wandered in without being invited. Thorne took the folding chair while the other man stayed standing. He moved slowly around the small space, hands in his pockets; looking at files on shelves, examining sheets pinned on to the noticeboard.

Fryer finally looked up. 'Who's your friend?'

'We'll get to that,' Thorne said. 'I wanted to pick up where we left off the other day, when you were a little unwilling to talk to me about one of your customers. When your memory was playing up a bit. Remember?'

Fryer sat back and folded his arms. 'Vaguely. Like you say, I've got a bad memory.'

'Things have moved on since then, so I'm hoping today might go a little better.'

'How do you mean, moved on?' Fryer kept his eyes on the man he didn't recognise.

'Terry Mercer's dead,' Thorne said.

Fryer sat up. Said, 'Is he fuck!'

'Afraid so. Sorry to spring sad news on you like that.'

'You're full of it.'

'Topped himself.'

'Right. Now I *know* you're full of it.'

Thorne reached into his pocket for his phone, called up the photographs he had taken with it two nights earlier and pushed it across the desk. 'You can use your fingers to blow that up a bit if you want.'

Fryer didn't need to. He picked up the phone and stared at the photo. The back of the car, the pipe taped to its exhaust and running round to the rear window.

'Recognise it?' Thorne asked. 'Honestly, that thing was rustier than Christ's nails, so I hope Terry managed to knock the price down a bit.' He took a few seconds, enjoying the shock on Fryer's face. 'Yeah, I know. Bit of a game-changer, isn't it?'

Fryer put the phone back down on the desk and shrugged. 'Well, there you go.'

'So, now the only person you need to be afraid of is me.'

'Why the hell should I be afraid of you?'

'Well, if not me, then my mate here.' Thorne turned his chair round, drew the man with him into the conversation. 'This is John Williams, from Trading Standards.'

The man took a step forward and waved ID. Said, 'I'm actually based in Barnet, but I've got plenty of mates in Tower Hamlets. I *think* they'd be the ones looking at you.' He glanced at Thorne. 'I can check that.'

'John got himself into a spot of bother a year or so ago.' Thorne closed one nostril with a finger, then sniffed theatrically. 'Stupid really, but I helped him out, so every so often he does me a bit of a favour in return. You see where this is leading, Keith?'

Fryer undid his top shirt button and loosened his tie. 'What's to stop me going to the authorities?' He pointed to the man behind Thorne, then at

404

Thorne himself. 'Telling them he's bent. That you're both bent.'

'Nothing at all,' Thorne said. 'Other than the fact that you're way more bent than either of us.' He leaned forward, the mock-friendliness gone from his voice, keen now to get into it. 'One phone call and John's mates will be round here in a heartbeat to shut you down. You get that, Keith? Shut you down and bang you up.'

'What do you want?' Fryer asked.

'Where was Mercer staying?'

'I've no idea.'

Thorne turned to look at the man behind him. 'What kind of fine are we looking at to start with, John?'

'Five grand for clocking one car,' the man said, quickly. 'Same for falsifying service histories with the likelihood of imprisonment if that's widespread or if the vehicles are unsafe.' He looked at Fryer. 'Pretty likely, I'm guessing.'

Fryer looked as though he was toying with smashing his head down on to the desk. 'I heard . . . Deptford, but he was moving around, so I don't know how long for.'

'Heard where?'

'Some bloke in the pub.'

It rang true on several counts. However careful Mercer thought he was being, however seriously those he had been staying with had been warned to keep his whereabouts to themselves, somebody always said something. A few years before, a major gang of organised criminals had come up with an ingenious way to dispose of a body, burying it in a grave that had already been dug and which was filled in – complete with the body it was intended for – the following day. It was fool-proof and they would certainly have got away with it, had several members of the gang been able to resist telling anyone they went for a drink with just how clever they'd been.

Deptford.

In Thorne's own borough.

It made sense. This was the part of the world Mercer knew best. Where he'd worked, where he'd grown up. Though he'd obviously had to travel outside the area to call on some of his victims, Thorne could well understand why a man released after thirty years into a world he didn't recognise would want to base himself close to home. Or the place that felt most like it.

'Anywhere else?' Thorne asked.

'Deptford was the only thing I heard, I swear.'

'Who was he staying with?'

'How should I know?'

'Thought you might have "heard".'

Fryer's head fell back, then a few moments later he raised it again. 'Look, I heard him on the phone . . . out there.' He nodded towards the lot. 'He mentioned a name, I don't know if it was the bloke he was speaking to, or what.'

'What name?'

'Dean,' Fryer said. 'That's the only name I heard. Dean . . .'

'So, somebody called Dean in Deptford.' Thorne nodded. 'I'm going to need a bit more than that, Keith.'

'I don't know any more.'

Thorne turned as though to confer with the man from Trading Standards again.

'Oh for God's sake . . . look, he might have been a drug dealer.'

'Might have been?'

'He mentioned it,' Fryer said. 'When he bought the car. Saying he didn't want anything flashy, like a drug dealer's car, all that. He kept going on about it. He never liked blokes who did all that.'

'But he wouldn't mind one of them putting him up?'

'No, I don't suppose so.' Fryer was starting to look pale and flustered. He loosened his tie a little more. 'Look, this is just me putting two and two together.'

Thorne turned to the man behind him, who was no more a Trading Standards officer than he was. The man gave a small nod.

It might be nothing. It might be enough.

Seeing there was a chance that he'd finally given his visitors what they wanted, Fryer sat back and sighed. 'Now will you please piss off and leave me alone.' He clamped two hands to his chest. 'I'm on tablets, you know.'

Thorne stood up. 'Just out of interest, what *did* Mercer pay you for that piece-of-shit Astra?'

'Fifteen hundred,' Fryer said.

Thorne shook his head. 'Scared to death of him, but you were still happy to rip him off.' He stepped towards the door. 'You know what, if he wasn't already dead, I'd be suggesting you might want to take a nice, long holiday.'

Walking back across the lot, Thorne's partner stopped to tuck the fake ID he'd knocked up on his computer that morning beneath the Clio's windscreen wiper. 'Think you've got something to work with there,' he said. 'Decent lead.'

Thorne was already thinking hard about it, trying to decide which way to go next. 'There's a lot of drug dealers in Deptford,' he said.

'Can't be too many called Dean, can there?'

'We'll see.'

'Talking of names . . . why "John Williams"?'

'It was that or "Hank Cash",' Thorne said.

The man grinned, and didn't stop talking about what a good team he and Thorne had made until they had reached the car. Thorne looked up and down the road, checking to make sure that Neil Hackett's BMW wasn't parked somewhere close by. Now he was watching out for it everywhere he went, waiting for Hackett to pop up again. He half expected the DCI to be waiting for him whenever he got home.

Thorne opened the doors and thanked the man with him for helping out.

Ian Tully said, 'Any time you want, mate. I haven't enjoyed myself that much in ages.'

CHAPTER 61

Hendricks changed out of his scrubs and walked back to the office he shared with three other pathologists at Hornsey mortuary. He made a quick call and spent a few minutes responding to emails. He put the kettle on for coffee. He looked up at the Arsenal Legends calendar above his desk, then checked his phone to see if there were any messages from the man he'd swapped numbers with in a bar the previous weekend.

He hadn't fancied him that much anyway.

He tried to forget the face of the girl whose body he had just finished so carefully taking apart and crudely stitching up again. The blackened tattoo of track marks on arms, legs, belly, *tongue*. The small, shrivelled heart that had eventually become too diseased to beat.

Half an hour until the next one and a couple more before the end of the day.

'You got a minute, Phil?'

Hendricks had been grateful for the knock on the door and surprised to find Dave Holland on the other side of it. He offered him coffee and

Holland said he was fine, that he hadn't got long. He dragged one of his colleagues' chairs across and told Holland to make himself at home.

'Everything OK?'

'Well, I'm a bit all over the place to tell you the truth.'

'What?'

'Thorne.'

Hendricks laughed, but Holland seemed in no mood to see the funny side of anything.

'I thought it was all over,' he said. 'The Mercer thing.'

'Yeah, I know,' Hendricks said. 'He's alive . . . no, he's dead . . . no, he's alive again.'

Holland picked at a loose thread on his tie. 'I mean once they find out who Mallen really is and they ID the body in the car, hopefully they'll be able to get it sorted, but in the meantime . . . *he's* still going to be chasing about like a one-man Murder Squad. Well, not one man, that's the bloody point, isn't it? One man and his stupid mates.'

'Relax, Dave,' Hendricks said. 'I've been through all this with him and he's done with it.'

Holland looked up. 'You reckon?'

A trolley clattered past outside; two mortuary assistants chatting as they passed the door.

'Why are you talking to me about this?'

Now, there was the thinnest of smiles. 'If I tell Sophie any of it she'll tear me a new one.'

'Kitson?'

'Yeah, well . . . she's sort of in the same place I am.'

'Which is where, exactly?'

'I've still got twenty-five years ahead of me in this job,' Holland said. 'More, maybe. I've got a kid and I want to have another one and . . . I mean, it's all right for *him*, isn't it? What's he got to lose?' He glanced up at Hendricks' calendar. 'He's like some star player who everybody thinks is washed up, and now he's dreaming about coming off the bench and scoring the winner in the last minute.'

'Spurs player though,' Hendricks said. 'Never Arsenal.'

'I'm serious, Phil. There's cases I've neglected because of this, the cases I'm being paid to work on. The ones I'm not going to get chucked off the force for working on.'

Hendricks sighed. 'I don't know what to tell you, mate. It's really him you should be—'

'I spoke to that bloke whose mother drowned herself, didn't I?' Holland waited for a nod of acknowledgement, began counting off on his fingers. 'I found out who Terry Mercer was, went through the files, like he asked me. I looked through all the trial records, gave him his list of potential victims. I told him when there were new ones, names and addresses, I did *all* that. I traced Mercer's car and checked the CCTV footage when he asked me to, but then he asked me to go into the ANPR system . . . into *another* system, and that just seemed like a step too far. Like we'd finally reached the point where he really didn't give a monkey's how much trouble anyone got themselves into for him.' He shook his head. 'I had to draw a line somewhere, you know? I mean . . . don't you reckon?'

Hendricks stared at Holland, watched him sit back and close his eyes and swear under his breath. The jaw muscles were tensing beneath his skin. He looked wretched.

'What have you done, Dave?'

CHAPTER 62

Thorne's first morning back on early shift was relatively uneventful.

The previous night's drunk and disorderlies were released and the burglaries followed up. A supermarket trolley was removed from the front window of a shoe shop. The manager of Boots opened up to discover that every drug on the premises had been stolen in the early hours and a car that had escaped pursuit across half the borough was found burned out behind the leisure centre. A missing girl was located and both her parents arrested. A woman attacked after refusing to make her husband something to eat at midnight was off the critical list, while an RTA that had resulted in serious injury due to the actions of the coked-up teenage girl behind the wheel was now being treated as a manslaughter enquiry as the victim had died overnight.

Not *remotely* uneventful, Thorne thought, for any of those involved.

He spent an hour writing reports, then he and Christine Treasure took a car out.

As was usually the case on a routine patrol, if there

were no incidents that required their attendance they called in at several of the other stations in the borough. Tea at one place or a sandwich mid-shift; five minutes for a fag and a catch-up with colleagues at another.

Catford, Sydenham, Brockley, Deptford.

At each station, Thorne contrived to find a few minutes alone with someone he could chat to about the local drug dealers. He took care to slip it casually into conversation; just wanting to know, while he remembered, which of them they might have had dealings with. He mentioned a name he'd heard in passing, just to see if it rang any bells.

Nobody at any of the stations knew anything about a drug dealer called Dean. Not one of the four different officers he talked to during a longer than normal stop-off at Deptford. A couple offered to ask around for him, but Thorne assured them it wasn't important.

'Might be something, probably bugger all,' he said.

Driving back to Lewisham for lunch, Christine Treasure said, 'How come you've got such a spring in your step today?'

'News to me,' Thorne said.

She grinned. 'Saturday night leg-over was it?'

'A gentleman never tells.'

As it happened, he and Helen had done nothing more energetic the previous evening than answer the door to the pizza delivery man and point the TV remote, and later on Alfie had been the one sweating and wriggling in bed. Thorne still had very fond and vivid memories of the night before that, though, despite the slapstick with his injured hand.

Treasure reached to poke him in the arm. 'Come on then.'

'Just enjoying my job,' Thorne said.

Treasure grinned even more.

Walking out of the rain into the station a few minutes later, Thorne was approached by PC Nina Woodley. She handed Thorne a tatty-looking coloured envelope with his name scribbled on the front.

'I ran into that kid, 2-Tone,' she said. 'The one that took a pop at you a couple of weeks back. He said to give you that.'

Thorne glanced at Treasure and saw that she was clearly every bit as desperate as Woodley to know what the envelope contained. He hadn't said anything about making the bail order disappear and would tell her the same thing he'd told the custody sergeant if she ever asked. He wandered away towards his office, leaving Treasure and Woodley nattering, then opened the envelope and pulled out a scrap of paper torn from a spiral-bound notepad.

Dennison had clearly heard the good news from his solicitor.

this don't make me your bitch

The station canteen had long since ceased to be somewhere officers went to queue up for reheated shepherd's pie and jam roly-poly. These days the shutters at the serving hatch were down more often than not and officers and civilian staff only went in to buy snacks or drinks from the vending machines. At mealtimes, they went in to watch the TV in the corner and eat the food they'd brought in from home or from one of the shops outside.

Thorne bought himself a burger in the shopping precinct, walked back to the station with it and found himself a table in the corner.

It was twenty minutes before the woman he was hoping to see walked in.

He watched her sit down and take a can of Diet Coke and a Tupperware container from a plastic bag. He waited until she'd peeled the lid off and dug a fork in once or twice before he wandered across and asked if he could join her.

She looked up, reddened. Said, 'Yeah, course.'

Jenny Quinlan was a young trainee detective constable with CID. Thorne had spoken to her once or twice, before running into her at a crime scene in Forest Hill a few months earlier. What had appeared to be a domestic murder had become something rather more headline-worthy, when it emerged that the victim had been responsible for abducting and killing two teenage girls.

Something had bothered Thorne about that case at the time. Things that had refused to add up. He had kept his concerns to himself though; still only a week or two back in uniform and wary of rocking the boat.

416

He thought about what he'd spent the last few weeks doing. That early reticence had vanished quickly enough.

He asked Quinlan what she was eating. She showed him what was in her lunchbox and moaned about having to eat salad to keep her weight down. He told her she'd have no need to eat rabbit food if she came back to uniform, that nine hours a day lugging a stone of Met vest and belt kit around was the best diet he could think of. She laughed and said the problem was the 20 per cent discount police officers got from Nando's and Domino's Pizza.

'Can't resist cake or a bargain,' she said. 'That's my trouble.'

They chatted for a few more minutes about nothing in particular. It was enough for Thorne to establish that she was still a trainee. Still eager to please.

'So how are you finding it?' he asked.

'It's good,' she said. She tucked a strand of dark hair behind her ear. In a grey skirt and a white blouse that was perhaps a little small for her, she was doing her best to look confident and on top of her game, but something suggested that she did a fair amount of bluffing.

Thorne puffed out his cheeks. 'Not all the time.'

'No. Not all the time.' She took another forkful of salad. 'Some of the people, the politics.'

'You get past that,' Thorne said. 'It's the other stuff. The stuff that makes you want to do the job in the first place. It's having to give up thinking you can make a difference.'

'Yeah.' She put her fork down, reddening again. 'Stupid, right?'

'Not stupid, but you need to accept that you probably won't.' He shrugged. 'The best you can do is help. Clean up. There's nothing wrong with that, by the way. It's a good enough reason to get up every day.'

'So, how do you deal with it?' Quinlan asked. 'You just become immune?'

'You . . . get used to it, which isn't the same thing. Not completely, though, and you shouldn't.' Thorne looked across at some of the men and women at other tables. Talking, laughing; others that needed time alone for one reason or another. 'The day you stop feeling disgusted or angry or afraid, the day when you stop feeling like you want to hurt somebody, or hold them. That's the day you need to be honest with yourself and admit that you're probably in the wrong job.' He smiled. 'Probably . . .'

Quinlan nodded, thinking about it. She ate another mouthful, pulled a face and took a sip from her can. 'So, how are *you* finding it?' She looked at him. 'You were a DI with the Murder Squad, weren't you?'

Of course, she knew, and Thorne was counting on the fact; counting on the kudos it might give him in the eyes of an ambitious trainee.

'Yes, I *was* . . .' He could see that she was waiting

for him to explain why he was sitting there in uniform. Instead he lowered his voice and leaned closer. Said, 'I was wondering if you might be able to help me with something.'

She looked pleased, though not particularly surprised. He had finished his lunch by the time he'd come over after all, and he'd made it clear enough that he wasn't flirting with her. Not obviously, at any rate.

She said, 'Sure, if I can.'

Thorne told her that he was keen to talk to a particular drug dealer, but that he didn't have enough information. He suggested that she might know someone who could let him have the details he needed. He said that he wanted it done quietly, that he needed to be sure about a few things before he took it higher up and that he'd heard she might be the right person to help.

'Word gets about,' he said.

She tried not to look too thrilled and thought about it while she pushed the contents of her Tupperware container around. Then she nodded. 'I can think of a couple of people I might be able to talk to. There's a lad on Drug Enforcement I'm pretty matey with.'

He thanked her, said, 'No problem if you can't.'

Thorne scribbled down his mobile number on a piece of paper Quinlan dug from her bag and the twinge of guilt at using her so blatantly was shunted aside by the sobering realisation that he was doing much the same as the man he was after.

Mercer had called in favours or demanded them; for somewhere to stay, for help tracing his victims, for a car. Thorne wondered why so many people were doing favours for *him*. He couldn't believe that any of them were afraid of him and he was damned sure it wasn't respect. Was he just a . . . bully?

Thorne surreptitiously checked his watch. He wanted to go, but thought he should probably wait until Quinlan had finished eating. After a few more mouthfuls she pushed the container away.

'I can't eat any more of that,' she said. She looked at the empty Styrofoam box in front of Thorne. 'Might have to dash across to your burger place.'

Thorne patted his Met vest. 'You can borrow this if you like.'

She pulled a face. 'Not with this skirt.'

'I don't think it suits me either,' Thorne said.

CHAPTER 63

Mercer doesn't mind the rain.

If he was to tell anyone that, they'd presume it was because it's been so long since he was out in it. Felt the raindrops on his face, whatever. Same with snow, same with bloody sunshine come to that, but the fact is it's just because it's never really bothered him. Obviously there were things he missed when he was inside, but you can't just come out and start devouring those experiences like a madman. The food, the booze, the women. Some do, of course, a few go well over the top, but they're usually the ones who find themselves back behind bars before they've had a chance to sober up.

You need to ease back into it.

It *is* nice to be out and about though. It would hardly be natural if wide open spaces weren't a bit more attractive to him than poky rooms, or if time on his own wasn't more precious than being jammed up close to other people. No point being stupid, time inside does change a person.

For now, he's happy enough walking and getting wet. He's had things to do of course, which is probably another reason he hasn't gone bonkers as far as all that other stuff goes. Arrangements to make, and there's still a few bits and bobs that need attending to if he's going to be around long enough to enjoy a bit of wine, women and song. Maybe even meet someone one day, who knows.

It had been worth a try, that business with the car and Jeffers. The thief takers are clearly a bit brighter than they were in his day, plus there's all that new technology, *CSI* stuff, which is why he's been so cautious about fingerprints and what have you up to now. Probably no need to be quite as careful any more though. He knows that if they've worked out who was dangling from that banister they'll be looking for him by now.

Course, he knows there's been at least one person on to him for a while.

A Woodentop, too, of all things. One with as much of a point to prove as he does, by the sounds of it. A man with a mission.

In the end, he'd decided against going into that church. Worked out that when it comes to the 'big' questions, worrying about it too much is only going to do your head in, and anyway, there were probably just as many answers in the bottom of a pint pot. He'll find out what comes afterwards when it's time.

For now, he's still got a life to live.

Mercer walks down the hill and stops opposite a nice terraced house near the park. Even from here, he can hear the odd squeal of excitement coming from inside.

He puts his hood up and waits.

He doesn't mind the rain, but it's a pain in the arse trying to keep the camera dry.

CHAPTER 64

Thorne was away from the station just after five thirty and his radio stayed on the passenger seat next to him, spitting its staccato bursts of chatter and hiss as he negotiated rain and rush-hour traffic on his way to Deptford. He switched between the different Borough frequencies every few minutes, listened to voices he had begun to recognise. He had become used to the near-constant burble of these broadcasts from across the city. It had started to feel like a lifeline.

He was listening carefully for those same two words as usual.

Chances were, of course, that if and when they came, they would have nothing to do with what Terry Mercer was doing. There were plenty of ways to die in London and, like Thorne had told Hendricks, Mercer might be long gone by now. Still the possibility remained that as far as the process of tying up loose ends went, getting rid of George Jeffers had only been the beginning.

That morning, Thorne had left a phone message for Frank Anderson.

He told him that Jeffers was dead. Told him that though he had singularly failed to keep his head down in the toilets a few nights earlier, it might be a very good idea to do so now.

'Why don't you get gone and stay that way?' Thorne had said. 'Do everyone a favour.'

If Mercer *had* begun to work his way through a new list, it might well include those who had provided somewhere to stay while he was crossing out the names on the last one. If Frank Anderson was in danger, then the man Thorne was on his way to see was probably not safe either. A good many *ifs*, but it was certainly what Thorne was planning to tell him.

He glanced at the note stuck to the dashboard; a postcode scribbled down from the text Quinlan had sent just before the end of his shift.

A name and an address.

Hope this is what you're looking for. Let me know if you need anything else. JQx

The house was on a quiet road two turnings off Deptford High Street. It was a mid-sized semi; unassuming enough, but ideally situated within easy reach of station, park and primary school, as well as being close to half a dozen top-notch locations for the buying and selling of cocaine and heroin.

Thorne doubted that Dean Leonard had specified those requirements when he'd first spoken to the estate agent.

He parked a few houses along and walked back.

There were no cars parked on the large drive and no sign of life inside, but he rang the bell anyway. He looked up and noticed the security camera above the door, the red light winking.

He jogged back to the BMW to wait.

He turned the radio down a little and listened to the six o'clock news, followed by a comedy programme that was only marginally funnier. He listened to the rain on the roof and to a bluegrass compilation which lifted his mood a little. Then, as it began to get dark, he drove back to the High Street and bought himself chicken and chips, which he ate in the car.

Some time later, he called Helen and told her that he could not say exactly what time he would be getting back. Not for a while, anyway. When she asked why, he told her that he was waiting for a drug dealer to get home and she didn't ask any more.

He hadn't lied, which he told himself was the important thing.

It was nearly five hours since Thorne had arrived when a white Range Rover Evoque with a personalised number plate passed him, slowed and indicated to pull into the drive. There was a woman driving and a child was in the passenger seat. The rear windows were tinted.

He waited ten minutes more, then walked quickly back through the rain to the house. A security light came on as he approached the front door and he had to ring twice before it was answered.

'Is Dean in?' Thorne had his warrant card at the ready.

The woman was in her early thirties and glamorous; the sort Thorne guessed would change and put on full make-up to visit the supermarket. Her eyes dropped for a second to the warrant card. 'No,' she said. 'He isn't.'

'You'd be Mrs Leonard, would you?'

She nodded. She had only opened the door six inches or so and seemed content to glare at him from around it.

Thorne said, 'Well, hopefully you'll be able to help me. Shouldn't take too long.' He smiled, thinking that actually he might have better luck with the wife anyway. 'I was wondering if you'd had any houseguests lately?'

'Any what?'

'People to stay. In your house.'

She shrugged. 'Had my in-laws here a couple of weeks ago.'

Thorne became aware of the child who might have been the one he had seen in the front seat of the car pushing at his mother, desperate to see who she was talking to. 'Nobody else, then? Nobody Dean might have known?'

'I said, didn't I?'

'Might only have been for a night or two.'

'It's my house, so I think I'd know.'

The child's head suddenly appeared, waist high to his mother as he shoved himself into the gap. She tried to push him back.

427

'Does he mean the old man?' the boy said.

Thorne looked straight at the woman. 'Yes, I mean the old man.'

The woman peered over Thorne's shoulder, as though desperate to see her husband turning into the drive or perhaps afraid of exactly that. She said, 'I don't have to talk to you,' and tried to close the door.

Thorne's foot stopped it.

'What's your game?'

'Sorry,' Thorne said. 'Big feet.'

'Really?' She narrowed her eyes as she opened the door further and stood square on to him. She was clearly happy enough to scrap, well used to dealing with the likes of Thorne. 'Well that doesn't mean what a lot of people think it means.'

The boy moved close to her, sensing the conflict.

'If this old man's who I think he is,' Thorne said, 'he's killed seven people since he came out of prison and now he's started getting rid of the people who helped him out while he was doing it. People who did him favours. We found the first one the other night.'

Thorne stood on the doorstep getting wet and watched the woman's face tighten and pale a little beneath the pancake.

'He gave me some sweets,' the boy said.

'Did he?' Thorne said. 'That's nice.'

'I need to call Dean.' The woman looked towards the road again. Her voice was a lot quieter once she'd caught her breath. 'Warn him.'

428

'Makes sense,' Thorne said. 'Now, have you got any idea where he went after he left you?'

'No.'

'He never said anything?'

'I hardly saw him.'

'You never heard him on the phone, anything like that?'

'He stayed in his room.'

'In *my* room,' the boy said.

The woman said, 'All right, darling,' and tried to push her son back into the house. He took a step back and then came forward again.

'I saw him using our phone.'

'*What?*'

'Did you?' Thorne said.

'He used our phone?' The woman was glaring at her son. 'When?'

'Dad was out and you were in the garden,' the boy said. 'I saw him from the top of the stairs.'

Thorne leaned down towards the boy. 'Did you hear what he said?'

The boy shook his head. Said, 'He's got a very quiet voice.' His own voice dropped to a whisper. 'Very quiet . . .'

Thorne stood up again and stared at the boy's mother. She was running a hand through her hair, the other curled tight around the edge of the door, fingernails whitening. 'You know it's easy enough to get your phone records, don't you?' He smiled. 'Yeah, of course you do. Thing is though, it's stupidly time-consuming, filling in all the forms,

429

getting them signed off . . . even getting the money agreed, because the phone companies make us pay for all that stuff now. Takes bloody ages and the simple fact is, the sooner we find this man, the quicker Dean will be really safe.'

The woman thought for ten, fifteen seconds, looked towards the road again. She said, 'I think I've got a phone bill.'

CHAPTER 65

The car still smelled of chips, so Thorne opened the window as soon as he got back in. Soaking, he took out his phone and stared at it, waiting for his heart rate to settle just a little before he made the calls. He knew that Dean Leonard's wife would have been on the phone to her old man before the security light on her drive had gone out and, sitting there, he half expected to hear the squeal of tyres and see the flashy car that Mercer had mentioned to Keith Fryer come tearing around the corner.

A big Lexus maybe, or a Porsche Cayenne. A Hummer if the bloke was a *complete* knob.

DEAN0 100

He pushed the water out of his hair and looked at the two numbers he had copied from the phone bill the Leonards had received only a week before. The two mobile numbers that the wife had not recognised.

He wound the window back up.

Were these the numbers of people Mercer had stayed with later on, or gone to for help in some

431

other way? Were they now taking up space on a new list of potential victims?

He called the first number, his own withheld, listened to it ring.

'Hello . . .'

'I was given this number by Terry Mercer,' Thorne said.

'Terry *who*?'

There was genuine confusion in the voice. Pub sounds in the background. Thorne just said, 'Wrong number,' and hung up.

He dialled the second number.

'Yeah?'

'I was given this number by Terry Mercer.'

A pause, just a small one. 'Never heard of him.'

'Really?'

The line went dead.

Thorne imagined the man who had just hung up on him staring at his handset, alarmed and unsure what to do. Or perhaps he knew exactly what to do and was already stabbing at the keys as he tried to call Terry Mercer himself. Thorne sat with the BMW's windows steaming up, struggling with what his own next move would be. Obvious enough, were this in any way legitimate, but as things stood . . .

The story he had told Dean Leonard's wife about phone records was true up to a point, but when it came to circumnavigating the system, there were always ways and means. If it was important enough, a trace or even a tap on any number could be authorised, but 'sneaky-beaky' stuff meant going higher up. Ordinarily, his first port of call would be Chief Superintendent Trevor Jesmond and that was clearly out of the question. He thought about his old DCI, Russell Brigstocke, which might be possible, but having seen the strain it had put on Dave Holland, he was wary of bringing anyone else into the loop.

There were enough people he didn't trust already.

He told himself he was being stupid even thinking about it, getting over-excited and ahead of himself. Now, it was down to him alone. He went into his phone's settings to ensure that his own number would be displayed when the text was received.

Terry Mercer's tying up a few loose ends. Think you might be one of them.

He pressed SEND.

He did not really expect that the man he had just spoken to would call back, not immediately anyway. But it felt good to have done something. He would keep on thinking and he would find some way to track down the owner of that phone. But whatever happened, he knew that as far as Terry Mercer went, he was closer than he had ever been.

Maybe only one call away.

Thorne started the car, switched his radio on again and began driving back towards Tulse Hill.

He held his breath for a few seconds when he turned into the road and saw Dave Holland's car parked outside the block. Copper or not, it was rarely good news to come home and find a police officer waiting at your front door. The frozen moment of dread was not helped by the somewhat forced smile when Holland climbed out of his car and began running through the rain towards Thorne's. The wave that was just a little too cheery when their eyes met.

Holland yanked open the passenger door and got in, shook away the rain and released a noise somewhere between a moan and a sigh.

'What's up, Dave?'

'Listen.' Holland took a deep breath and stared forward. 'I need to come clean about something.' He took another one. 'I messed up, OK?'

Thorne knew what was coming. Those nagging suspicions had been spot on. He nodded. He had no right to be angry, no right to judge. He had no right to shout or smash Holland's face down into the dashboard.

He said, 'Let's hear it then.'

'When you asked me to put Mercer's car into the ANPR?' Holland turned to look at Thorne and shrugged. 'I didn't do it.'

'I thought not,' Thorne said. He was relieved that Holland's confession had not been the one he was expecting. The relief quickly gave way to guilt that he had expected it at all. 'So many of those cameras around, we'd surely have got a few hits.'

'Yeah, we would, and we might have caught him

by now, and I feel shit about it. I fucked up.' Holland smacked a fist against his leg. 'I chickened out.'

'Dave—'

'So, I've been working on it today.' Holland turned further round in his seat. 'I thought I might be able to get some hits another way. You know, see if we might at least be able to find out where he'd *been*. I ran the registration number through every system we've got. Borough databases, MIT, Traffic, everything . . . CRIMINT, HOLMES, the lot.'

'Dave, it's OK.'

'I got something,' Holland said.

Thorne saw the excitement on Holland's face and the spark passed between them. He lifted his hand to what he thought was a raindrop crawling down past the nape of his neck. He waited.

'PC on a night shift out of your place, a couple of weeks ago. A routine sweep of dogging sites.'

Thorne nodded. He knew what that meant, having done it himself with Christine Treasure when they were bored. Something to do when there was nothing important happening. Half an hour spent putting the wind up a pervert or two.

'There's a car park behind the industrial estate in Addington,' Holland said. 'Well known for it apparently.'

'I know it.'

'So, this PC approaches two men in a red Vauxhall Astra . . . *our* Vauxhall Astra. Nothing to

435

get excited about, so he has a word, sends the pair of them on their way. Does the sensible thing and makes a note of the registration numbers, the Astra *and* the other bloke's car on the other side of the car park.'

'What kind of car?'

Holland told Thorne the colour, make and model.

'My first thought was it must have been Jeffers, right? Meeting up so Mercer could get addresses off him, photos or whatever. Then I remembered that Yvonne had found a Travelcard, when she was looking through the clothes Jeffers left at that flat, so maybe he didn't even have a car.' He looked at Thorne. 'Long story short, I traced it and it's . . . interesting.'

Thorne tried to swallow but it was tricky. 'Interesting' was not the word he would have chosen himself.

'Guess who that car belongs to,' Holland said. 'Who was meeting up with Terry Mercer.'

But Thorne did not need telling. He had recognised the car as soon as Holland had described it.

It was one he had seen several times before.

Now, Thorne knew exactly where Neil Hackett had been getting his information.

CHAPTER 66

Thorne put his shoulder against the door the moment it was opened and the man behind it staggered back, shouting and swearing, into his hallway. Thorne stepped in and slammed the door behind him. He watched Ian Tully clamp his hand to the side of his head where the edge of the door had made contact, then remove it and stare down at the blood on his fingers.

'Fucker,' Thorne said.

Tully's dog appeared behind him and began to bark.

The ex-DCI's hands became fists and his shoulders went back as if he were about to take Thorne on. Then he saw the look on Thorne's face and turned towards the kitchen instead. Thorne stayed close behind him as he lurched away into the kitchen, shouting at the dog to be quiet, then snatching up a tea towel from the worktop before dropping down into a chair.

Thorne stepped to within a few feet of him and Tully moved as far back in the seat as was possible. He kept his head down, the tea towel pressed to the wound on the side of it. Even the dog, who had happily come to Thorne the last time he was in this room, now stayed close to the man in the chair, muzzle against his leg.

Thorne took a breath and jammed his fists into the pockets of his jacket.

'So, here's what I think you did,' he said. 'From the first time I told you what I was doing, you saw me as your way back in. God knows when, but you went to the MIT at Lewisham, because you knew that was the place I'd taken this in the first place. You told them you were on to a nice big murder case, but you didn't tell them everything, because you wanted something to bargain with. Something you could use to wheedle your way back into the Job. You told them just enough, told them that I was putting it together, that I'd connected the murders, but you didn't tell them about Mercer.' He paused, moved a little closer. 'Are you listening?'

Tully raised his head.

'Problem was, you weren't quite as indispensable as you thought, because you'd given Hackett plenty. He knew he could get the rest himself just by sticking close enough so that I'd lead him to the killer. He didn't need you, did he? Didn't need to offer you anything. Told you to piss off, I'm guessing, same way he told me.'

Tully muttered something.

'What?'

'Arrogant arsehole.'

438

'Oh for sure, but he'd got your number, hadn't he?'

'Same as he had yours.'

'This isn't about me.'

'I just wanted to be useful again,' Tully said. 'Don't tell me that doesn't ring a bell.'

'Don't try and make me feel sorry for you.' Thorne spat the words out and moved closer still. 'Don't even think about it.'

Tully sat up a little straighter. He took the tea towel away from his head and tossed it aside. 'You're younger than me and probably a *bit* fitter, so if it's going to make you feel better to give me a pasting then you might as well get on with it.' He held out his arms in invitation. 'See, I couldn't care less how upset you are because I was only doing what I had to. Trust me, the last thing I want is sympathy from the likes of you, but look at this place! I'm skint and I'm bored stupid and yeah, I'm pissed off at being ignored and stepped over and looked down on by kiddie coppers with poncy degrees. I saw a way out, so I took it. I *tried* to take it.' Tully dropped a hand down to his dog's head. He was starting to sound a little more relaxed. 'I went to the proper authorities and told them that a rogue officer was making illicit enquiries. I offered to help. I don't think I'm the one that's done anything wrong. I'm certainly not the one who's done anything he might get arrested for.'

The dog lay down with a contented sigh. The

boiler in the corner of the room was grumbling quietly.

'You think that's why I'm here?' Thorne asked. 'You think that's the reason I'm *this* close to redecorating this shithole with your face?'

Tully looked at him.

'Hackett wasn't the only one you talked to, was he?'

Thorne stepped away and began to walk slowly around the room, into the kitchen area and then back. It was the sort of thing he'd done in interview rooms, that Tully had almost certainly done in his time. It was something coppers did, a tactic designed to intimidate, but Thorne's reasons were purely practical. Standing as close to Tully as he had been, the desire to punch him into the middle of next week had become overwhelming. Thorne certainly had every intention of doing so, but not before he'd said what he'd come to say.

Not before Tully understood why.

'Once Hackett had knocked you back, you found yourself another way to make some money. A lot more money, I'm guessing. Playing both sides against the middle, that's probably the nicest way I can think of putting it.'

'Hang on a minute—'

'The only thing I'm not quite sure of is what Terry Mercer was thinking,' Thorne said. 'Maybe he just thought you were more useful to him alive, though I've got to tell you it's looking like he might well have changed his mind about that.'

440

'What's that mean?'

'Or maybe it was because you were the one person he couldn't threaten. Not the same way he threatened all the others anyway, because the fact is there isn't a single soul that gives a toss about you, is there? Nobody you care about, either. I mean, yeah, you've got your poor old mum tucked up in some care home, but getting rid of her would have been doing you a favour, far as I can tell. So Terry Mercer came to you knowing you could help him or you offered to help in exchange for your life. Either way, he paid you for information.'

'With what?' Tully raised his arms again and stared wildly around the room. 'Where's the money?'

'You found out where his brother was, didn't you? You gave him the address.'

'What brother?'

'The one who helped you put him away in the first place. The one you put into Witness Protection. What was it you said to me, first time we met? "I've still got plenty of contacts. Plenty of favours I can call in." You called one in and gave the information to Mercer.'

Tully could do no more than shake his head.

'OK, forget putting it nicely,' Thorne said. 'Accessory to murder, that's what we're talking about.'

'I can't see you having an easy time proving it.' Tully was trying desperately to muster some last-gasp confidence. 'Hackett told me you weren't a great believer in evidence.'

Thorne walked slowly past him into the kitchen, stopped and stared out of the back door. 'Well, he's right. Aside from the report of the copper who took your registration number down when you met up with Mercer in that car park, I've got sod all.' He began to walk back. 'But who says I want to prove anything? Be a damn sight easier to let nature take its course. Lay off Mercer for a while and give him time to catch up with you. You know Jeffers is dead, right?'

'Jesus . . .'

'So I don't think you'll have very long to spend that money.'

As he passed Tully again, Thorne could see that he was about to cry. Or was doing his very best to make himself cry.

'It just got out of hand,' Tully said. 'I swear.'

'*What?*'

'I thought he was just blowing off steam, you know?'

'You knew him,' Thorne said. 'You knew what he was capable of.'

'Yeah, but . . . I didn't know there'd be that *many*.'

Thorne stopped, took a second, then turned fast and kicked Tully's legs from beneath him as hard as he could, the tip of his DM flattening the meat of one calf and smashing into the back of the shinbone. Tully screamed as the dog jumped to its feet and began barking again.

Thorne heard his mobile chime in his pocket.

He stepped away and watched Tully slip, moaning, to the floor, pulling his legs up to his chest and pushing away the dog that continued to bark while it was scrambling to lick his face. Thorne pointed at the animal and yelled above the noise. '*That* is the only fucking friend you've got . . .'

He reached for his phone.

Thorne opened the message and felt his own legs begin to weaken when he looked at the single image it contained.

A photograph of Helen and Alfie.

There were other children in the background, standing on the path with parents or waiting in the doorway of the childminder's house. Helen was waving to someone, her other hand holding tight to Alfie's as they walked away, heading home.

The photo had been taken from the other side of the road.

Thorne leaned forward, readying himself for one more kick at Tully's face.

Tully groaned and wrapped his arms around his head.

Thorne turned and ran for the door.

CHAPTER 67

The seat he is lying on is sticky, smells of vomit, wet beneath his face.

Face down, back of a car.

A series of bumps and a swerve to the right, then a seemingly endless corner and his head is pressed into the door, the handle sharp against his skull. He struggles to inch away and is sick again.

He turns his face into the rank, sweating cushion, fighting to breathe.

Can't move his hands . . .

He hears voices, distorted . . . two men. Two men in the front of the car, arguing. A voice he knows. One man says he doesn't want to do this, says it's stupid, keeps saying it until the other man tells him to shut up. The backs of their heads are washed orange every few seconds, light sliding across the cabin as the car passes beneath streetlamps, then light and weight shift as someone turns to look at him.

'He's coming round.'

He feels the moan vibrate in his throat, something tight inside his skull and burning where his arms are pulled back and held.

Tongue too thick to spit.

444

'Hit him again.'

A shape looms, rises up from the front seat. An arm comes down and the pain explodes in a cascade which blazes for just a moment behind his eyes before it fades.

A grunt and a warm trickle running into his eye, and a phone starts to ring somewhere as he sinks back into the blackness, the sound warping as he falls fast away from it . . .

Helen's face, and Alfie's. A picture he thinks he should recognise, but he can't quite place it and he doesn't know why Helen is waving.

Hiss and babble, like voices from his radio.

   do your bloody job
playing detective
     listen to yourself
I know what you're doing by the way
   the whole lot's going to unravel . . .

Drifting now through a dream or a memory; a bleached-out film of his mother and father at the beach. Jim Thorne's looking at the paper while Maureen holds the towel in front so the boy can wriggle out of his trunks and back into his underpants and trousers. Sand sticking to his arms and legs and belly. Then his mother moves the towel just for a second, a quick flash of the boy's pale backside which makes his father laugh and the boy shouts at him to be quiet and tells his mother not to be so bloody stupid.

Screaming at them both and there's sand in his mouth.

Her favourite summer dress, white with small blue flowers.

The one she's had since she was in her twenties, that she wears while she dances to Hank and Merle and Willie. That still fits her perfectly, but not for long. Nothing left of her by the end, so the funeral directors have to gather the material up, fasten it behind her back like she's a shop dummy.

His father's huge, smooth hands around the pages of the *Daily Mirror*.

Moving like a conductor's, long fingers delicate through the air as he curses in the bar or at the bingo. Clawed with rage while he stamps around his kitchen, because *no*, he didn't leave the stove on, *Tom*, because he isn't a child and he knows how to work a *fucking* stove.

Faces floating in and out of shadow. His own name on lips that are twisted in fury, tight with despair, slack in confusion.

Hendricks, Holland, Helen, Alfie, Helen . . .

. . . and the face of a child he doesn't recognise, as he tumbles mercifully further down into sludge and silence.

Moments or minutes or hours later, there are flickers of light again and suddenly there's rain on Thorne's face as he's pulled from the car. Hands slide beneath his arms and haul him roughly to his feet. The two men drag him along in the dark, through long, wet grass and across concrete walkways.

446

His arms are still tied behind his back.

'Stupid,' says the man whose voice is familiar.

'Five minutes, then you're done,' says the other one.

Thorne tries to struggle but there is nothing, not an ounce of strength in him.

There is traffic moving close by, lights somewhere above him, and suddenly it gets a lot brighter as he's bundled through an entrance of some kind. A dirty white space with metal doors. They stop, waiting for something, holding him up as his feet paddle against the floor before urging him forward again into a space that's even smaller.

Piss smells and spray paint.

The man in charge says, 'Press it.'

Thorne's guts lurch and heave suddenly and they let him drop to his knees, stepping back while he spits and coughs up what little is left in his stomach. He stays there for perhaps half a minute then is hauled back to his feet and out when the metal doors slide open.

'Over there.'

One man steps forward to open a door in the corner, then comes back and helps the other one to bundle Thorne along a corridor that smells of damp and disinfectant. They crash through a second door, then moments later they're moving up and Thorne's shins smash against metal treads as he's dragged up a short flight of stairs.

Now they're in the open air, it's blowing a gale and, save for the noise of the wind and the rain, it's suddenly very quiet.

447

'There.'

Thorne has a little more strength in his legs suddenly, but not quite enough to raise his head as he's marched across a slippery cement floor and dropped on to his knees in front of a low wall. He takes a deep breath, then another. His eyes slowly begin to focus on the rough patterns of the brick, the shallow puddles of rainwater gathered around him.

'Now you can piss off,' says the man who was driving the car.

Thorne hears footsteps hurrying away, the clatter of them descending the metal staircase. Slowly, he shifts his shoulders, which have begun to cramp and spasm. He breathes through the pain in his arms and skull.

He starts to raise his head, then stops when something is jammed hard into the back of it.

A voice close to him says, 'Know where you are?'

CHAPTER 68

Hendricks sounded as though he had been asleep, but when Helen apologised for calling so late, he said that it was fine. He told her he would probably be up for hours yet, making notes for a lecture he was giving to students first thing the following morning.

'Cellular adaptation to injury, regeneration and healing, and it's not as interesting as it sounds. Trust me, it's taking a lot of coffee to keep me awake.'

Helen grunted something like a laugh as she walked across to the window again, looked down at the street and watched for headlights. 'I was just wondering if you'd heard from Tom,' she said.

'Since when?'

'Tonight, I mean.'

'I haven't talked to him since Friday night.'

'Right.'

'Everything OK?'

'I'm probably just being an idiot,' she said. She walked across to the kitchen table, poured herself another half-glass of wine. She explained that she had last spoken to Thorne some time around eight, when he had told her that he would not be home for a while.

'OK, so that was what . . .?'

'Four hours ago.' It was now nearly midnight. Helen had been checking her watch every few minutes. She heard Hendricks hum, non-committal, clearly unconvinced that there was any problem at all. 'I know, like I said, I'm being stupid . . . I mean he told me he was going to be late, right? Thing is, he tried to call me about half an hour ago and when I picked up there was nobody there. It just went dead. I've been calling him back, but now he's not answering.'

'He's probably not got any signal.'

'No, he's definitely got a signal, because it's ringing. It just rings out until it goes to his answerphone.'

'You left a message?'

'Yeah, I told him to call.' Back to the window. She caught her breath as lights appeared, then released it when the car accelerated past. 'Listen, sorry, Phil.' She walked back to the table. 'I'll let you get back to your . . . what was it again?'

'Did he sound all right when he called?' Hendricks asked.

'He told me he was waiting for some drug dealer.'

'Well there you go then,' Hendricks said. 'They don't tend to keep regular hours.'

'He did sound a bit odd, though.'

'Odd like . . . he was lying?'

'No.' Helen picked up her glass. 'No, I don't

think so.' She used the edge of the old T-shirt she was wearing to mop up the ring of moisture where the glass had been. 'You don't know what that's about, do you?'

'What?'

'This drug dealer business.'

'Not a clue,' Hendricks said. 'Must be something that came up today.'

'But I mean, nothing to do with the suicides thing?'

'Not as far as I know.' The doubt was evident enough in Helen's silence. 'Listen, I'd tell you if it was.'

'Yeah, I know. Sorry.'

'You ask me, he's got his phone on silent and he's stopped off for a kebab. That, or it was his own drug dealer he was waiting for. Maybe he's just off his tits somewhere.'

'I'll call him again,' Helen said.

'Listen, call back if you're still worried.'

Helen was swallowing a mouthful of wine, so did not have a chance to say that she wasn't worried.

'Or if you just want a natter, whatever,' Hendricks said. 'If you're gagging to find out about cellular regeneration . . .'

CHAPTER 69

'Any idea?' Mercer asked. 'Go on, stand up, have a look around.'

With his hands still tied behind his back, Thorne had to lean his shoulder into the wall in front of him, use it to heave himself to his feet. It took half a minute, the pain in his arms, the pain everywhere causing him to cry out with the effort.

Then, looking out and down, he understood that it was not a wall.

The edge of a roof . . .

Through the rain he could see the cars a hundred feet or so below, uneven strings of light moving in a dozen different directions. The Shard rose up, shining in the distance. A little nearer, the beacon on Canary Wharf flashed away to the east and closer still he could see the spidery legs of the O2, squatting in the crook of the river ahead of him. Directly below, he saw the dark sprawl of smaller buildings and T-blocks, the walkways and rat-runs between them. To either side of him, a ten-storey block identical to the one he stood on top of. He could just make out figures in one or two lighted windows, the glow of TV sets and a necklace of coloured lanterns strung from a balcony.

He knew exactly where he was.

'The Kidbourne,' he said.

'Spot on,' Mercer said. 'Don't suppose you've ever seen it from this angle though.'

'No . . .'

'Can't hear you.'

Thorne raised his voice above the noise of the wind and the rain. Said it again.

'Turn round,' Mercer said.

Thorne did as he was told and took half a step away from the edge.

'I grew up here.' Mercer used the gun he was holding to gesture with, waving it around, pointing with it. 'Three floors below where we're standing right now, as a matter of fact.'

He wore jeans and training shoes, a dark windbreaker buttoned up just below his chin. He had cut his white hair back to the scalp, but despite this, Thorne was surprised to see a face that seemed far from hard. The smile, wistful if anything, further softened a face that was fuller and less lined than he had expected and which looked almost pinkish in the bleed from the emergency lights dotted around the rooftop. An old man who would probably not merit a first look, let alone a second.

Then Thorne realised that he'd seen the face before. The old man the female PC had spoken to outside the house in Woolwich. The 'friend' of the man who'd been found hanged.

Mercer saw the recognition on Thorne's face and smiled. 'Well, me and him *were* pretty close at one time,' he said.

Thorne narrowed his eyes against the stinging rain.

'Mid-fifties when this place went up, it was paradise,' Mercer said, looking around. 'We thought we'd died and gone to heaven. Central heating, no damp, playgrounds for the kids, what have you. State of the art this place was back then. Social housing, that's what they called it.' He shook his head and the smile began to slip a little. '*Social* housing. Great big con, that's what it was, and I'll tell you something, it wasn't very long before the cracks started showing and we knew we'd been cheated . . . before everything started rotting or breaking down, but it was all a bit late by then.' He looked left then right, to the towers on either side. 'Slums in the sky, that's what they really were, but that was the whole point, wasn't it? Basically, they were designed for the likes of us, for the "problem families". Makes life that much nicer for everyone else if you round all the scum up and stick them in one place. Makes it easier to keep an eye on them. Who gives a shit if nothing works? Who cares if there's no decent bus service and rats the size of dogs?' He wiped the rain from his scalp with the flat of his free hand. 'Brutalist, that's what they call this style, isn't it? Just chuck a shitload of steel and concrete at everything, no need to tart it up too much. Brutal buildings for brutal people to live in, right?'

454

Thorne said nothing. He tried to loosen whatever had been used to tie his hands, but there was no give in it.

'Even more of a shithole now, isn't it?' He looked at Thorne. 'No-go area for you lot, am I right? Gangs, whatever.'

'Yeah, there are gangs,' Thorne said.

'Well, what do you expect? Vicious circle, isn't it? You treat people like dirt they're only going to behave one way.'

'It's not an excuse,' Thorne said.

'Come again?'

'Any of that. Where you grew up. It's not an excuse for what you've done.'

'Never said it was.' Mercer rolled his shoulders and adjusted the grip of the gun in his hand. 'Just telling you the way things were.'

Thorne's phone began to ring in his pocket. He and Mercer studied one another as it rang out and suddenly the minutes Thorne had lost started to come back to him. The blanks filled themselves in. He remembered running out of Tully's flat and sprinting across the street to his car, reaching for his keys with one hand and trying to dial with the other. Helen's phone had just begun to ring out when he'd become aware of the figure behind him and turned . . .

On the roof, his phone stopped ringing and there were a few seconds' silence afterwards. Then the sound of the alert to signal that a message had been received.

'Someone who's worried about you?' Mercer asked. 'Someone you care about?'

The rainwater was running from Thorne's hair into his eyes and, unable to use his hands, he did his best to shake it away. He said, 'That's not an excuse either.'

'I don't need excuses,' Mercer said. 'I have reasons.'

'I know what those years in prison cost you. I know you didn't have any visitors. Wife, kids . . .'

'You *know*?' The gun moved slightly in Mercer's hand. 'It's easy to say that, but why don't you let me know how you feel when you lose all the people you love?' He smiled. 'I mean obviously you won't be able to, but you get the point.'

'Blaming people changes nothing,' Thorne said. The wind was blowing harder, whipping the rain into Thorne's face, forcing him to raise his voice still further to make himself heard across the six or eight feet that separated him from the man with the gun. 'Won't bring your wife and kids back, will it?'

If Mercer was listening, he chose not to react. 'The interesting thing is, I'm giving you a choice. Kind of choice I never had, but like you say, no point dwelling on ancient history. Now, you obviously saw that picture I sent you, the speed you came tearing out of Mr Tully's.'

'I saw it.'

'Good, so you understand.'

'If you go near them, I'll kill you,' Thorne said.

Mercer smiled. 'I think you've got things

456

arse-about-face, old son. I won't be paying a visit to your nearest and dearest until after *I've* killed *you*. And only if you make me do that by refusing to kill yourself. Simple enough to grasp, I would have thought.'

'Why should I believe you?'

Mercer's chuckle was high and wheezy; nails on a blackboard. 'Yeah, a couple of the others said something like that. Suggested I might be making empty threats, that I wouldn't go through with it.' He shrugged. 'I just gave them a few more details, let them see I'd done my homework. You want to know what I've got in mind for your two?'

'No . . .'

Ignoring him, Mercer calmly recited the address of Helen's flat, the name and address of Alfie's childminder. 'I think I'll do the boy first,' he said. 'Watch his mother's face while she listens to him scream—'

'OK,' Thorne shouted, his voice breaking. 'I believe you.'

'Yeah.' Mercer looked pleased. 'That's more or less what the others said.'

'Please don't hurt them.'

'Quite a cutie, the little lad.'

'*Please* . . .'

A small nod, as though a simple accommodation had been reached between them. 'Well, like I said, it's entirely up to you. You can die having saved the people you love. The people who love you. *Or*, you can die knowing that you were responsible for their deaths.' He scratched briefly at his neck with the barrel of the gun. 'Funny really, because suicide used to be a sin, didn't it? Eternal damnation, all that. But this way, you're choosing to save lives while you take your own, so if there *is* anything waiting for you on the other side . . . well it'll be a nice warm welcome, I expect.' He waited, cocked his head. 'Come on, it's no choice at all really.'

The roar of a jet on its way into City Airport drowned out Mercer's voice right at the end. Simple enough to make out what he'd said though.

'Is it?'

Thorne lowered his head, then was bent over violently by a sudden attack of dry heaves and retching. He coughed and spat. When he lifted his head again, he was shaking it.

'Good,' Mercer said, waving the gun. 'So, up you get.'

Thorne turned and moved slowly forward, until his feet were pressed against the brick. He had to wait for the gap between involuntary gulps of cold, wet air before he could get the word out.

'Can't . . .'

'Yeah, sorry,' Mercer said. 'Stupid.'

Thorne heard Mercer moving towards him. He felt the barrel of the gun against his head again, then the rough tug on his shoulders as whatever was binding his hands behind his back was cut away. He heard Mercer step back. He massaged the cramp in his shoulders and rubbed at the welts on his wrists.

'On you go . . .'

The first step up was hard, but the *second* – the one that actually lifted him on to the ledge and to within inches of what lay beyond it – was more terrifying than anything Thorne had ever experienced. He badly wanted to close his eyes but knew that balance would be impossible if he did. He fought to control the urge to void his bowels and bladder, at the same time knowing such a worry was foolish, pointless.

'Almost there,' Mercer said.

The ledge was no more than a foot wide, smooth and slippery. The toes of his shoes hung over it as he squatted, clinging to the edges of the bricks with his fingers.

'This is the trickiest bit, you ask me. Once you actually step out, it's a piece of cake.'

Thorne let go of the edge and grabbed it again, let go and grabbed . . . then slowly, an inch or so at a time, he began to get to his feet. The wind pushed harder at him the higher he rose. He used his arms, windmilling to steady himself against the force of it, the weight of the rain, heavier against one side of him, and the convulsions that shook his body from head to toe every few seconds. Head swimming as he forced it up a little further into the blackness, further from his feet, further from anything solid. Pausing for long, desperate seconds and struggling for control of his limbs, while the rain stung and the breath sang like a tea-kettle out of him, until finally he was standing.

Then he took a few moments and looked down, and suddenly everything was nice and still and simple.

His face was slick with rain, snot and tears. The ground a little blurry down there, soft even.

It was not that far to fall, not really.

Not when he thought about how far he'd fallen already.

He had lied without thinking. He had believed those closest to him, *all* of them, capable of betrayal. He had become mistrustful and devious and worst of all, he had put lives at risk. He had been willing to take a chance on the safety of others for his own ends. He had become the worst type of copper there was.

A fucking glory-hunter.

He lifted his toes, then stretched them, and the tips of his shoes moved a little further out across the ledge.

Yes, he had been lost and unhappy, exiled from a life he had loved, the job that had got his blood pumping every morning. They were not excuses, though, he didn't have them any more than Terry Mercer.

There could be no excuses.

He rose up on to tiptoes, lifted his arms a foot or so away from his sides.

Most importantly of all, who the hell would miss him?

Now he closed his eyes, and behind them was

the picture of Helen and Alfie. She might as well have been waving goodbye.

This would be the last decent thing he could do for them . . .

'Put the gun down, Terry.'

'Fuck are you?'

'Put it down . . .'

Raised above the rush of the wind and the rain and the babble inside his own head, it took Thorne a few seconds to realise that the voices were real.

'Listen to me, Tom. Just turn round and get off the ledge, nice and easy.'

'No!'

'Do it, Tom . . .'

Thorne moved each foot a few inches at a time, tried to keep his upper body as still as possible, his weight evenly distributed. He turned slowly around until finally he was staring back across the roof, towards the door through which he had been dragged a few minutes, a lifetime before.

The figure was in shadow, but the size of him was unmistakable.

'Down you come, Tom,' Hackett shouted.

Mercer had turned the gun towards the newcomer, but now he wheeled and levelled it at Thorne again. He shook his head. Said, 'Only one way down for you, son.'

Hackett stepped smartly forward into the light. 'There are firearms officers in position on top of both the other towers.' He nodded once towards each block, the wind whipping the bottom of his long coat around his legs. 'You understand? The inspector goes over the edge, they fire. They get so much as a hint that you're going to use that gun on either of us, they fire. A pre-arranged signal from me . . . see how this works, Terry? Now drop the gun, kneel down and put your hands behind your head.'

Mercer shifted his position, stepping carefully back and to his left until he was side on to Thorne and Hackett, with a good view of each. 'Now, let's just think about this for a minute,' he said. 'Shall we?' He slowly moved the gun back and forth between the two of them.

'Come on, Tom. Get down.'

Eyes on the gun as it moved, Thorne took a breath and jumped down on to the roof. Mercer snapped his arm round and trained the gun on him.

'Terry!' Hackett raised his hands when the gun swung quickly back round to him. 'Listen to what I'm saying now. The men on those buildings don't need an excuse, all right?'

Slowly, Thorne eased his hand into the pocket of his jacket and felt for the switches on his radio. He turned it on, then moved his finger to the top of the unit and pushed the 'Oh Shit' button.

'What do you think scares me more?' Mercer shouted. 'Going back inside for the rest of my life, or a bullet between the eyes?'

'I know which one scares *me*,' Hackett said. 'So let's get rid of the gun.' He was coming gradually closer, every bit as focused on the gun as Thorne was. His eyes left Mercer's for just a moment, flashed to Thorne's.

A nod.

'Seriously,' Mercer said. He lowered the gun a few inches. 'That's no more of a choice than I gave your mate.'

'Everyone wants to live,' Hackett said.

'You think?'

'Every one of the people you killed.'

'What about them?'

'Didn't they beg for their lives at the end?'

'Not the same thing.' Mercer thought for a few seconds, slowly shifting his weight from one foot to the other. 'Besides which, it doesn't really matter anyway, because I'm not sure I believe you.'

'Believe what you—'

Mercer raised the gun again, took half a step across the roof and straightened his arm as if preparing to shoot. He paused, lowered the gun, then turned to look left and right, mock-confused. 'Looks like your firearms officers have fallen asleep on the job,' he said. He shook his head and slowly raised his arm again. 'Nice try, though.'

Now, Hackett looked afraid, eyes wide as Thorne inched across the rooftop, trying to close the gap between himself and Mercer without being seen. He watched the DCI's mouth fall open when he realised what was about to happen. Mercer smiled, and an instant before he snapped his arm straight again, as the necessary muscles began to move beneath his windbreaker, Thorne threw himself across the few feet that remained between them and made a grab for the gun.

The impact carried them both several feet as they grappled for control of it. They flailed and grunted, wet hands slipping against flesh and metal, faces pressed together. Hackett rushed to help, but was still seconds away from reaching them when Thorne's shoes lost purchase on the rain-soaked surface and he tumbled backwards, pulling Mercer down on top of him.

The gunshot was deadened by the bodies on either side of it.

Thorne lay on his back and fought for breath. His legs kicked slowly against the sodden asphalt as he watched Mercer get to his feet and saw Hackett begin to run. The old man's arms hung at his sides. His eyes were down, searching the floor for the gun, and when he finally looked up, there was barely a moment for his face to register the surprise before Hackett's head had smashed into it.

A noise like stepping on a snail in the dark.

A grunt of pain and realisation.

Mercer tumbled back against the ledge, and over.

It began to get darker as the blood leaked from somewhere in Thorne's side and the rain poured into his eyes. He was aware of Hackett bending over him, saying something. Before he went under, he thought he could hear Mercer scream as he fell, then realised that he was being stupid, that the old man was dead already.

It was sirens.

CHAPTER 70

Helen leaned against the arms of Thorne's wheelchair and bent down to kiss him. 'I'll be back tonight,' she said. 'Anything else you need?'

'I don't think so.' Parked at the end of his bed, Thorne turned in the chair and looked around his room. He had music on his phone, decent biscuits in the cupboard, a pile of books and magazines on the side-table that he would probably never read. 'Why don't you bring Alfie in?'

'I'll see,' she said. 'Probably easier just to leave him with Jenny.'

'Be nice to see him.'

Helen nodded. 'Well, let's see what kind of mood he's in, shall we? If he's tired he'll just be grizzly and if he's too lively he'll end up pulling one of your tubes out or switching some machine off.'

'That won't be a problem,' Thorne said. 'They've got some great sedatives in here.'

Helen kissed him again and walked to the door. She told him to call if he thought of anything else.

He picked up the TV remote and began flicking through the channels on the small flat-screen

465

mounted high in the corner of the room. Music videos, cartoons and couples looking at holiday homes. Jeremy Kyle was berating some toothless philanderer but Thorne skipped quickly ahead, having more reason than usual to worry about his blood pressure.

Blood that was no longer wholly his own.

Thorne had already lost a good deal of it by the time he had arrived at hospital two nights earlier. He had needed multiple transfusions. The bullet had missed all his vital organs, but the surgery to remove it had not been straightforward and though he was and never had been in any real danger, he would be in hospital for at least another day or two.

Several weeks' recuperation at home after that. Helen was already trying to organise compassionate leave.

'That doesn't mean you can mope around the flat listening to cowboy music all day,' she had said the day before. 'I'm not that compassionate.'

He settled for an episode of *Family Guy*, though it hurt like hell when he laughed and he was happy enough to turn it off when DCI Russell Brigstocke walked in a few minutes later.

'All right for some,' Brigstocke said, looking around.

Thorne was pleased to see him, and scared to death.

They were old friends, but months before it had been Brigstocke who had broken the news of his transfer back to uniform. It had not been a pleasant encounter for either of them, but still, Thorne could not help but suspect that Brigstocke was here now to deliver a rather more devastating blow.

'Nice en-suite too.' Thorne scraped a smile together and nodded towards the door in the corner. 'If I'd known the Met were going to stump up for a private room, I'd've got myself shot ages ago.'

The DCI perched on the edge of the bed and they made appropriate small talk. Bed baths and nurses' uniforms, catheters and morphine highs. The growing impatience on Thorne's face must have been obvious enough though and, after a few minutes, Brigstocke got down to business as if it were something that had merely slipped his mind.

'They arrested Ian Tully,' he said.

'Good,' Thorne said.

'Conspiracy to commit, perverting the course of justice. Kidnap thrown in for good measure, obviously.'

Thorne nodded. Unwillingly or not, it had been Tully who had helped Mercer bundle Thorne into the back of the car that night. Helped drag him up to the rooftop.

'I don't know what he has or hasn't told them,' Brigstocke said. 'But the DPS *have* been asking a few questions about you and the information you may or may not have withheld about Terry Mercer.'

'Only a few?'

'How much you knew, when you knew it. Why

467

you chose not to share that knowledge with the appropriate people.' He shrugged. 'I don't think any of this is coming out of the blue, is it?'

'What about Holland and Kitson?'

'I haven't heard anything,' Brigstocke said. 'They'll be interviewed, almost certainly. I mean, I know they were doing stuff for you on the side . . . and when I say I know, obviously I mean I *don't* know.'

Thorne nodded his understanding and his thanks.

Brigstocke asked if there was anything to eat and Thorne pointed him towards the cupboard by the bed. Brigstocke rummaged inside for a few moments and came away with a couple of Thorne's biscuits.

'Missed breakfast,' he said.

'So where are they going with this?' Thorne asked. 'The DPS.'

'Yeah, well.' Brigstocke swallowed. 'I talked to your mate Neil Hackett first thing this morning.'

'That doesn't sound good.'

Hackett, who had stayed talking to him on that rooftop while the sirens had grown louder, who had been there alongside the paramedics as he was wheeled through the doors of the hospital. Had he still been there hours later when Thorne had come round from the surgery? Looming on the far side of the recovery room? Perhaps Thorne had imagined that. He certainly remembered seeing Helen and Phil . . .

'Actually, he's doing his best to dig you out of a hole.'

'*What?*'

'Not all the way out, but it's certainly not doing you any harm. He's told them that you *did* go to him with your suspicions and that he chose to ignore them. He's also told them that you saved his life up on that roof.'

'He said that?'

'I don't think he's recommending you for a medal, anything like that.'

'I think it's fairer to say he saved mine.'

'You made a pretty decent job of that yourself,' Brigstocke said. 'Pressing your EMER button. If that ambulance had taken very much longer . . .'

Surprised as Thorne was to hear it, what Hackett was now doing on his behalf made sense. At the time, Thorne had had more important things to worry about, but Hackett's appearance on that rooftop had confirmed what he had suspected for a while and explained why the MIT man had not gone to the authorities.

He was every bit the glory-hunter that Thorne was.

From the moment Ian Tully had come to him, drip-feeding information and trying to strike a bargain, Hackett had wanted whatever it was Thorne had stumbled upon for himself. He had been happy to let Thorne do the donkey work. Content to step in at the death to discredit Thorne and claim the credit for Mercer's apprehension.

The death.

It had been unfortunate for Hackett that choosing to follow Thorne and the men who had abducted him on to that roof had almost cost him his own life as well as Thorne's. His actions now were tantamount to an unspoken offer; a suggestion that the pair of them should keep their actions and their motives for them to themselves. An understanding that neither would say anything about what the other had done. That all debts between them were settled.

Most importantly of all, it was an agreement that nothing more would be said about what everyone presumed to have been Terry Mercer's suicide.

'So come on, Russell,' Thorne said. 'Let's have it.'

'Let's have what?'

'Jesus, your bedside manner's bloody awful, you know that?'

'You're not even in bed,' Brigstocke said. The tone was flippant, but he suddenly looked very serious.

Thorne tried not to lose his temper. 'Are we talking about a few pips getting knocked off or worse than that?' He waited, but Brigstocke would not look at him. 'Seriously, if they think I'm going back to wearing a tall hat, they can shove it, and if they want me out altogether I'm happy to chuck it in anyway.'

Brigstocke brushed crumbs off the bed, turned to him. Sighed.

'You want the good news or the bad news?'